Alaska

Alaska

A Novel

JANA HARRIS

Grateful acknowledgment is given to Carol Beery Davis for permission to quote lines from *Songs of the Totem* (Juneau: Empire Printing Co., 1939) and to the University of Washington Press for the use of lines from *Alaskan Eskimo Songs and Stories*.

Koranda, Lorraine D. *Alaskan Eskimo Songs and Stories* © 1972. Reprinted with permission of the University of Washington Press.

Lines of verse on page 22 form John Gay's "If the Heart of a Man"; lines of verse on page 23 are from Leigh Hunt's "The Fish, the Man, and the Spirit" and Percy Bysshe Shelley's "The Cloud."

The poem on page 196 originally appeared in *New Letters*, Winter 1979–80, edited by David Ray and David Ignatow.

Cover design by Kat JK Lee

ISBN: 978-1-5040-1893-7

Distributed in 2015 by Open Road Distribution
345 Hudson Street
New York, NY 10014
www.openroadmedia.com

For M. A. B.

ACKNOWLEDGMENTS

For their devotion and faith in my work: my husband, Mark Bothwell; my dear friends and colleagues, Mary Mackey and Valerie Miner; and my agent, Carol Murray.

For their stories, their bits and pieces: Marie Dern, Carl Dern, Vicki Noble, Robert Cunningham, Mary Kaczenski Brandon, Tennessee Harris, Lonesome Pete, Ron Wolff, Marny, Tony, Renee Lieberman, Margo Laine, and Don Cook.

For their caring editorial and research assistance: Marie Cantlon, Marie Dern, Janan Ali, Sharon Thompson, Margot Winchester, Gunvor Scordelis, Susan Stern, Jane Ellis, Mary-Helen Palmer, Joanne Farness, and Kathy Reigstad.

For their support: Ishmael Reed, Al Young, Kate Ellis, Peti Taylor, Alie Smaalders, Louise Bernikow, Carol Bergé, and *Center* magazine.

And these institutions: the Museum of Natural History at Princeton University, the Firestone Library, the Alameda Public Library, the Berkeley Public Library, the Sheldon Jackson Museum and Sheldon Jackson College, the British Columbia Provincial Museum and Archives, and the New York Affiliate of the National Council on Alcoholism.

Alaska

... the savages
in his heart are coming home,
and they are his children
more savage than ever he dreamed

—Susan Griffin

FAMILY TREE

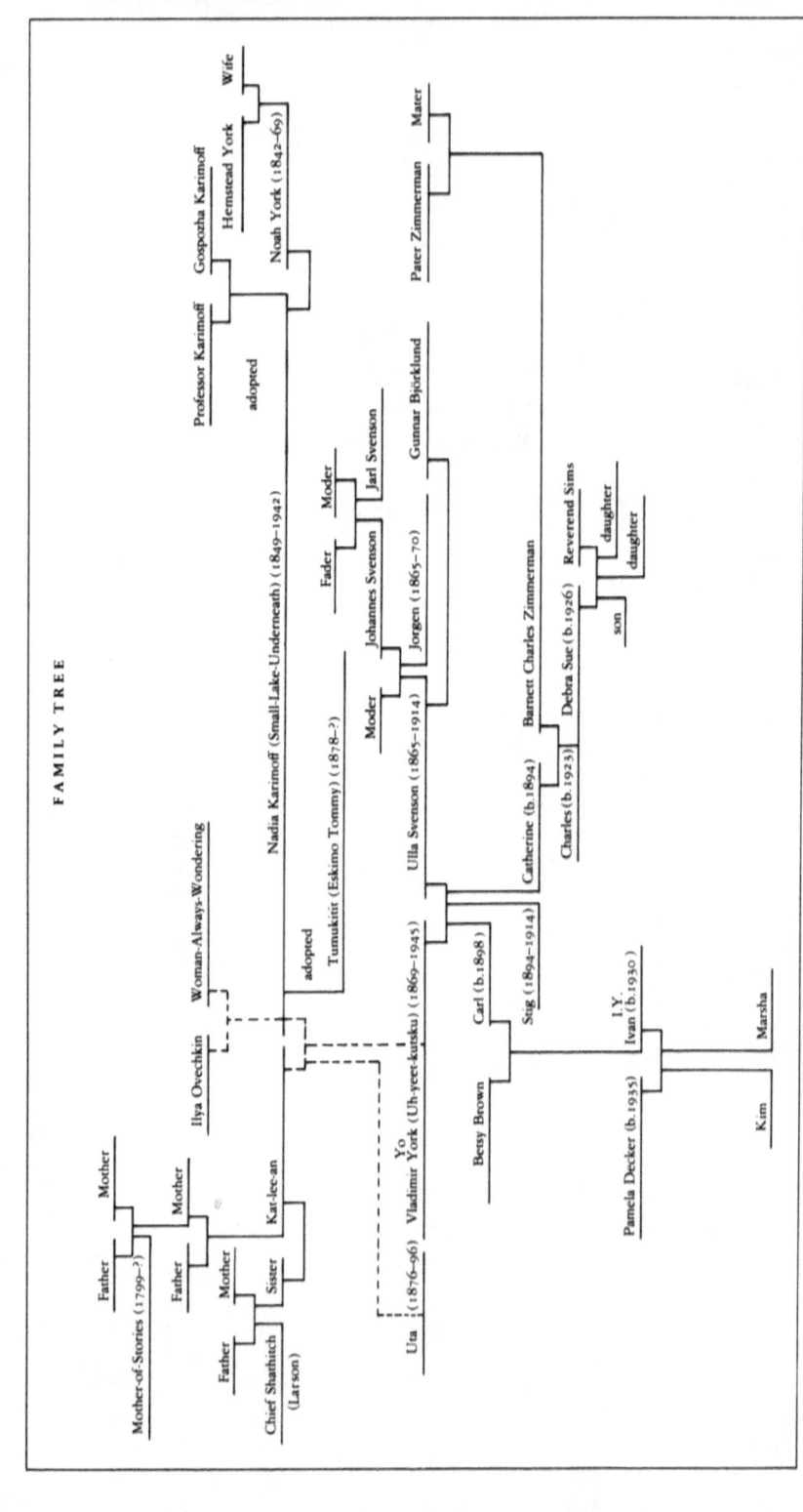

CHRONOLOGY

1741   Vitus Bering lands in Alaska sailing under the flag of Russia

1784   Russia establishes her first permanent settlement in Alaska at Three Saints Bay, Kodiak Island

1799   Russian colony at Sitka Bay founded

1799   Russian-American Company is chartered; Alexander Baranov is installed as the first manager

1802   Russian colony at Sitka Bay is destroyed by Tlingit Indian attack

1804   Russian colony at Sitka Bay is rebuilt by Alexander Baranov

1842   Noah York born

1844   Russian Orthodox Church of Saint Michael is built at Sitka Bay colony

1849   Nadia Karimoff (Small-Lake-Underneath) born

1865   Ulla Svenson born

1867   Treaty for the purchase of Alaska by the United States is signed; formal transfer ceremonies are held October 18

1869   Vladimir York born

1869   Noah York dies

1878   First fish cannery is established in Alaska at Sitka Bay

1878   Eskimo Tommy, Tumukitit, born

1880   Gold is discovered at Camp Juneau

1884	The Organic Act of May 17 establishes the first United States civil government in Alaska
1886	Gold is discovered at Fortymile in the upper Yukon
1894	Catherine York born
1894	Stig York born
1896	Gold is discovered in the Klondike, Yukon Territory
1898	Carl York born
1900	Capital of Alaska is moved from Sitka to Juneau
1913	Alaska becomes a territory
1914	Stig York dies
1914	Ulla York dies
1923	Construction of government-owned Alaska Railroad from Seward to Fairbanks is completed
1923	Charles York Zimmerman born
1926	Debra Sue Zimmerman born
1930	Ivan York born
1940	U.S. naval station is established at Sitka
1942	Nadia Karimoff York dies
1942	Dutch Harbor, Unalaska, is bombed by the Japanese
1942	Kiska and Attu islands are occupied by the Japanese until 1943
1945	Vladimir York dies
1945	Eskimo Tommy is committed to the territorial hospital
1949	Donna Lee Douglas born
1959	Alaska is admitted to the Union as the forty-ninth state
1968	Oil strike at Prudhoe Bay
1969	Alaska governor Walter Hickel is appointed as Secretary of Interior by Richard Nixon
1970	Nuna Pipeline Service Company is established
1970	Walter Hickel is replaced as Secretary of Interior by Rogers Morton
1974	Official work on the Trans-Alaska Pipeline begins

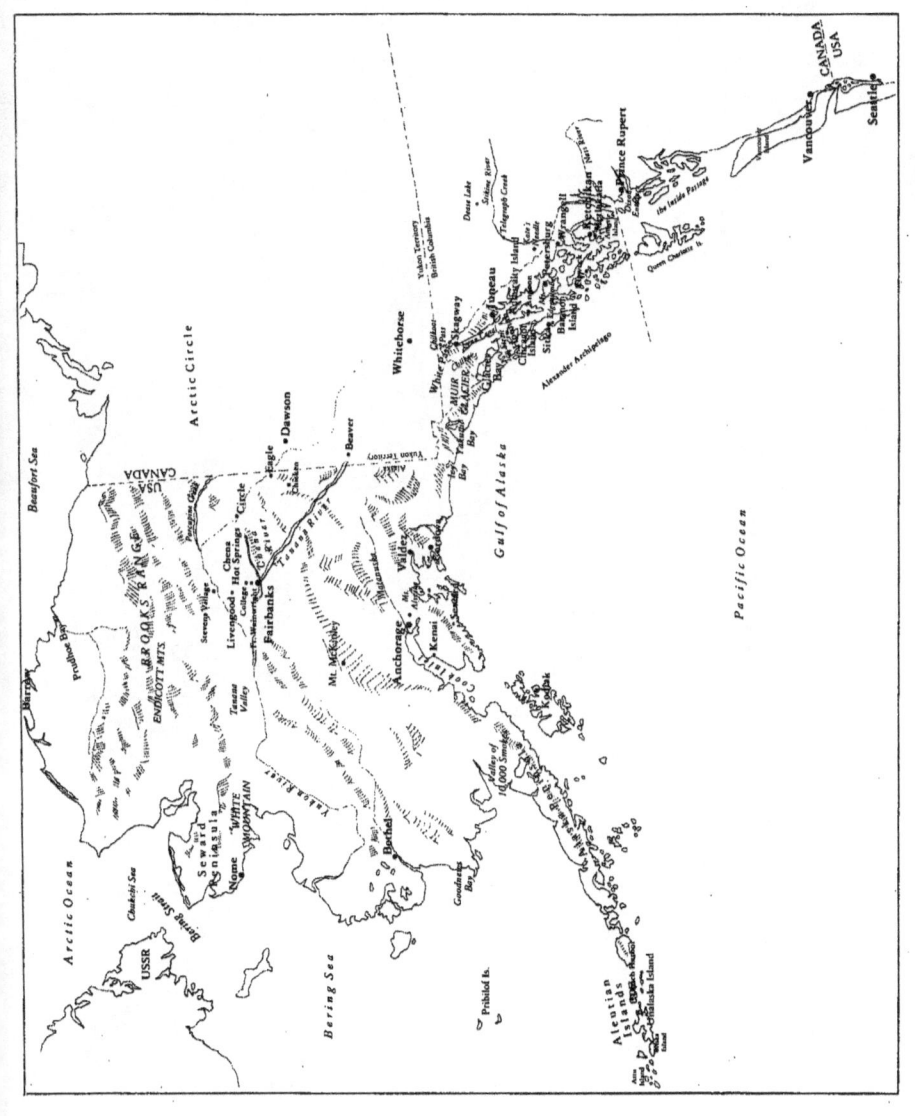

PART I

1867–69

Nadia Karimoff

(Small-Lake-Underneath)

1. NEW ARCHANGEL SETTLEMENT
Russian Alaska
Spring 1867

"How much did you pay for me?" I yelled at Noah York as he paddled the dugout across Sitka Bay. "How much did you pay for me and what do you want me for?" I screamed, feeling the muscles of my stomach go rigid underneath the heavy starched gathers of my black muslin dress.

With silent deliberation, the American pointed the bow of his canoe away from New Archangel's familiar shipyards, and the trappers' sealskin boats grew smaller in the distance.

"What do you want me for?" I yelled again. But he was like a deaf-mute. Behind me I saw the cedar-plank castle of Prince Dimitri Maksoutov begin to disappear, along with the gold onion domes of the Church of Saint Michael.

"You're as bad as the Russian priests!" I screamed at the Yankee, remembering the Mission Fathers who had stolen me from my Indian mother when I was a little girl of ten. But my new American owner never even looked in my direction. *"Bozhe moi,"* oh, my God, I moaned, thinking that by now I should be accustomed to being owned by people. For the last eight years my Russian guardians had treated me like a serf. And as I looked back where New Archangel stockade had vanished into the fog and the steep green mountains of Baranof Island, I wondered if this new servitude could be any worse.

"What do you want me for?" I asked again, my voice cracking as I stifled a sob.

Noah York lifted his paddle from the calm water. "Never end a sentence with a preposition, Little Nadia," he said, and spoke no more.

* * *

The first time I saw this Noah York, he was walking down the gang-plank of the *Calafia*, an ice ship just in from San Francisco via a lumber camp all the Americans call Seattle. I noticed him right away, because of his sunset-red hair and his clothes, which weren't rank-smelling peasant trousers and a baggy shirt like the *promyshlenniki*, the Russian trappers, wore. He was dressed in city clothes like they must wear in Saint Petersburg or Moscow. But I had no time to contemplate the redheaded stranger, because that had been the day after my master, old Professor Karimoff, died; and since I was the smartest pupil in the Russian church's Mission School I had been ordered to give the lessons in my dead master's place.

Later that afternoon this same stranger passed by me on the Governor's Walk, his white teeth grinning down into my face. So it didn't surprise me when he came to Gospozha Karimoff's door the next day and began to bargain with my mistress to purchase me.

At first he offered only a few rubles, saying that I was undersized and probably weak. "Couldn't weigh more than a hundred pounds wet and with her pockets full of silver dollars."

My mistress frowned, her broad forehead wrinkled in lines that ran into her thick black-graying hair. "My husband die," she said, crossing herself with two fingers. Six armed and black-booted Cossacks marched by, one of them smashing a vodka bottle on the graveled pathway. "I not so good feelingk," Gospozha mumbled as she eyed the soldiers, then gave the American a cold stare. "Nadia, she tiny little thingk, but she is strongk like vwild boar. Listen, I tell you how to get much vwork out of her. Always, once, twice a day, vwack her mouth, is only vway. *Da.* Nadia, she little, but vwack her hard. Get much vwork out of her." Gospozha shook her finger in the American's long thin face.

Mr. York reached out his arm to touch my red-black hair. "A half-breed," he said, stroking my head and looking at me as if he were measuring my height and breadth with some invisible ruler. "Can't be more than five feet tall. She doesn't look like the other Indians I've seen around here, not with that dark auburn hair." His vowels came out like sharp noises, not at all the way Professor Karimoff had taught me to speak English, and I almost had to bite my tongue to keep from correcting him.

"Nadia is Haida Indian." My mistress rested one hand on her skirt-layered hip as she shifted her weight nervously from one foot to the other. Then, for once, she began to recite good things about me. "She best student in Russian Fathers' colonist school. She experiment of Professor Karimoff. *Da*, is true." It had been her dead husband's dream, she said, to educate the Indian savages, but since the tall, war-loving Tlingits refused to learn European ways, Professor Karimoff had given up on them and concentrated on just teaching me. "Nadia, she speak three languages," Gospozha told Mr. York, as if she were proud of me for once. "English, French, and Roossian, she speak."

I wanted to tell the stranger that my mother had also taught me the Indian tongues before I was taller than a deer's leg, but Gospozha forbade any mention of Indian cultures in her house, or even under the hand-hewn lintel of her doorway. And since she was grieving for her husband, I remained silent to spare her the added trouble of having to slap my mouth.

"*Da*, Meester York," said Gospozha, as the American stared at the black bodice of my dress, making me feel as if he were unbuttoning it with the dark pupils of his gray eyes. "Professor Karimoff used to tell me that vwhen fur business got better, he take us back to Roossia, show Nadia to university in Saint Petersburg—savage servant girl readingk three languages."

I stood beside her, remembering the day Professor Karimoff had told me that if I were good and did all my lessons, perhaps the chamberlain of Prince Maksoutov, Governor of all the Alaskas, would ask for my hand in marriage. How excited I felt when the professor described my wedding at the Church of Saint Michael and my chambers up in the Castle, with their grand rooms, ceilings carved in angel's faces and walls painted red and gold. Yes, I would live in the Castle, where huge chandeliers hung in a giant mirrored ballroom and rows of Cossacks in silver-buttoned uniforms danced with Russian noblewomen dressed in purple Chinese silks to the music of clavichords and balalaikas. Late at night, when I wasn't doing chores or language lessons, I would sit at my tiny upstairs window, dreaming of my noble husband and watching the brilliant seal-oil light that burned in the Castle's cupola to guide the Russian-American Company's fur ships back from Canton. With all its rum- and cognac-drinking celebrations, the Castle was so grand a place that Professor Karimoff called it the Paris of the Pacific. I never asked my Russian master if this noble husband of mine would come with us when he took me back to the old country to show me off. But now the professor was dead, Gospozha was going to sell me to a Yankee American, and I would have to forget all my hopes of living in Maksoutov's castle, studying at Russian universities, and finding my mother, whom I hadn't seen since the Russian priests stole me from her eight years ago.

"Does she speak the Tlingit language?" asked Noah York.

"*Da,*" said Gospozha, blushing. "Awful heathen vwords."

The American smiled as if she had just told him that I could make shrimps whistle. "What's your Indian name?" he asked, addressing me for the first time.

"Small-Lake-Underneath," I said in English so that he could understand. The last time I had spoken of Indian ways in Gospozha's presence she had washed my mouth out with soap every morning for a week, saying that it was the only way to get rid of the Indian pigment and the devil inside my mouth.

My mistress scowled but didn't strike me. "How much you give me for servant girl?" she asked the American in a voice surprisingly loud for a widow in mourning.

I cringed, remembering the awful rumors I'd heard about Americans. In camp Seattle, the *promyshlenniki* said, lumbermen hired Indians to drag felled trees from the hills down to the harbor, where boats towed logs to San Francisco. When the Indians finished a week's work and demanded their wages, the lumbermen herded them into the bay, drowning hundreds.

"And her parents?" Noah York was concerned whether there were other claims on my head.

"*Nyet, nyet.* Father die long time ago. Vwoman-Always-Vwonderingk is Nadia's mother. Vwoman put hex on father; she was vwitch, always makingk the evil eye. Priests always vwanted to burn her from vwitch tree." Her voice was shrill as she pointed a narrow finger up the graveled walkway, past the wooded Russian tea gardens, to an old hemlock where the mission priests hung and then burned Indian shamans who refused to be converted.

"Vwoman-Always-Vwonderingk, one day she disappear." Gospozha spoke with a note of disappointment, as if she might have enjoyed seeing my mother sacrificed to the golden Madonna of Kazan at the altar of the Church of Saint Michael. "One day after priests take Nadia to be servant of my house and servant of the Lord, Vwoman-Always-Vwonderingk go off vwith *promyshlennik.*"

Gospozha clutched her handkerchief to the high collar of her black mourning dress. I flinched at her lies about my mother but said nothing.

"Nyet, nyet," Gospozha continued, reassuring the stranger. "Nadia, she not bootiful, eyes too small, too slanted, but is nothingk she vwill not do."

No, Gospozha didn't tell the Yankee American the bad things. She didn't say that my father, a Russian convict I'd never met, had bought my mother for ten rubles from a Spanish clipper captain who'd stolen her from her Haida tribe in the British islands north of the Oregon Territories. My mother, the Russians said, was ungrateful to the white men for saving her from the heathen world. She wanted no part of my father, Ilya Ovechkin, wouldn't even marry him, and when I was born she took me to live in the Tlingit Village of the Raven, the nearest Indian village to the New Archangel stockade. I can still remember the Russian Fathers stroking their pointed black beards as they told my mother that she should be punished for not marrying Ovechkin and that she should punish me as well by leaving me alone in the woods with no food, the same way so many other half-breed children had died.

"Nyet." Gospozha was beginning to haggle with Mr. York over my price. As I listened to them argue—would payment be in rubles or in pieces of silver?—I shuddered at the thought of being sold like the squat, docile, half-starved Aleuts whom Prince Maksoutov brought in boatloads from the old Alaska capital at Three Saints Settlement, or Kodiak, as the Indians called it. I looked squarely at the American. He even had hair the color of Gospozha's orange dahlias on his large-knuckled hands. Perhaps he had this same hair all over his arms and chest. Was he alone, this Noah York, or did he have a wife? I felt ill as I imagined his naked figure, with long red hairs growing even out of his backside, coming toward me, moving his lips and wagging his tongue. Gospozha had only tolerated me in her house because I had been her husband's experiment. I hated chopping wood for her and cooking *pirozhki* and cabbage in her tiny kitchen, but the thought of being sold to this man whose face reminded me of schoolbook pictures of Ivan the Terrible brought a dizziness to my head and a nausea throughout my body.

"You do this awful thingk to vwidow? Take her servant girl for pennies?" Gospozha continued to bargain. I took a deep breath, embracing myself with my own arms to try to calm my shaking body. Once I knew the number of rubles I was sold for, then I'd know how many blue-fox pelts I'd have to tan to buy my freedom so that I could go in search of my mother and her Haida tribe. But just as the two were about to agree on an amount in silver, my mistress sent me into the kitchen to stoke the dinner fire.

Later, when Gospozha helped me pack my few belongings into a trunk, she told me that Noah York was from a place called Massachusetts. She had found me a good master, she said, a rich one. Mr. York's grandfather had made a fortune selling railroad land, and his father had made another fortune selling munitions during the civil war they'd just had in America. But Mr. York was both an abolitionist and something called a Unitarian, who didn't believe in going to war.

The constant southeast Alaska fog dripped on the roof above us. There's more to this Noah York than meets the eye, I told myself. If he's an abolitionist, why has he just bought a slave girl? Perhaps he thinks he's saving me from a fate worse than slavery—that of being turned out by my mistress into the woods to starve and die. Perhaps in his eyes he is doing me a favor by purchasing me and giving me a home to work in and a man to serve, since no one in New Archangel has offered me a proposal of marriage. Whatever his reason, I thought, taking a breath of damp cedar-scented air, certainly an abolitionist who journeys five thousand miles from his homeland to buy a slave girl is a very queer sort indeed.

Mr. York's father was a world traveler, continued Gospozha smugly;

Paris, London, Athens—he went wherever he could buy gunpowder for the lowest price. But Mr. York's poor mother had been bedridden with arthritis and a diseased hip since his birth. The American, Gospozha Karimoff said in a haughty voice, had gone to some school called Harvard, where an American czar's children, if there were such people, would attend classes. All during his studies, she said—crossing herself with two fingers and making a half bow to the icon in the corner of the room—Mr. York had been a good son, living at home to see that his mother got proper care. When his mother died, he had become so grief-stricken, like herself, that he had decided to leave home. So he had booked passage for New Archangel on Baranof Island, Alaska, to live in a cabin among the Indians and Eskimos, or as Gospozha always called them, the people with the tails of dogs.

As my mistress's broad hand closed the lid of the trunk, I eyed her with distaste. At last I was free from the Russian colonists. Free from the stench of their cabbage-smelling kitchens, free from the relentless criticism and dour faces of the Russian priests.

How much did you pay for me? I wanted to scream it loudly enough for the Sea Spirits to hear me, but I knew by now that the American wouldn't answer. As he paddled the canoe, Noah York looked across the island-dotted water of Sitka Bay toward a rock-strewn shore where some Tlingits clad in deerskin were gathering seaweed from tide pools, standing on the same large flat rocks that my mother and I used to sit on before the Russian Fathers took me to live with the Karimoffs. Woman-Always-Wondering and I would come to this bay every day during the spring and summer, awaiting a "message." I remember how we sat for hours on the largest rock—the Wishing Stone, the Russians called it, because of us—watching the tide move in and out. Then my mother, wearing her necklace of salmon vertebrae and wolf-fang amulets, her long black-red Haida hair tied in a topknot and a jade labret in her lower lip, would point to a sea gull on a floating log. "Good omen," she'd say. "Sea bird riding log that floats against tide. Thoughts of Haida people are with us, Small-Lake."

My mother's grandmother was the head of her tribe, and she'd prepared my mother to succeed her. My mother knew that her Haida people would come for her in a canoe someday. I wanted to tell the American that my mother's people had found her; she hadn't run off with *promyshlennik,* as Gospozha had told him. I wanted to tell him that if I waited long enough my mother's people would one day come for me.

I turned to look across the water at the sea gulls floating on the tide. Mr. York pointed his canoe toward Indian River, near where the Raven tribe of the Tlingits lived. Dark hemlocks and spruce lined the shore, but the sun burning through the Alaska fog shone so brightly on the snowcapped crater of Mount Saint Lazaria and the white tips of Three Sisters Peaks that my eyes squinted in the glaring light. Perhaps the old ones in the Village of the Raven will have news of my mother, I thought, avoiding Mr. York's intense gray eyes. Even though the Tlingits were usually at war with the Haidas before the Russian colonists came, they had welcomed us into their village, knowing that my mother was a shaman. They gave us food and baskets and asked Woman-Always-Wondering to tell them what she knew of the salmon runs in her islands to the south. For days my mother told them about lives of her ancestors. Each one had a story, and each year of my mother's life she had learned about another ancestor until she had seen sixteen salmon runs and learned sixteen stories. I remembered hearing her tell each one several times with not a word altered. When my mother had seen sixteen salmon runs and learned sixteen stories, she said, she was stolen from her people by a man with yellow hair and gold teeth.

I sat erect in the canoe, suddenly filled with the memory of my mother. I was being stolen just as she had been. She had also felt this fear of a strange, chalk-faced wordless man, this fear that made my small red, work-swollen hands lie numb in my lap.

All at once I knew that the thoughts of Woman-Always-Wondering were with me, and I stood up in the canoe, rocking it dangerously from side to side. "You bastard," I screamed, "tell me how much you paid for me and what the hell you want me to do or I'll dump us both overboard!"

Noah York's paddle arm stopped in mid-stroke and his eyes filled with a new light as they leaped back and forth from my waist to the top of my head. "A bag of silver," he said, sitting perfectly still in the rocking canoe.

2.

My new master maneuvered between the rocks of Indian River, past low-hanging alder branches and vines. At a sandbar below a salmon-berry bush heavy with moss, he beached the canoe and wordlessly carried my trunk into a cabin built back among the trees. Noah York's house was an old, decaying log building, probably abandoned by a *promyshlennik* who had gone to Fort Wrangell in search of better trapping, as so many others had done now that the fur animals were getting scarce.

My new home was only about twelve by twelve feet, the roof covered with new sealskins and the north wall built of stone with a hole for a fire. Inside, the cabin was dark; a skin covered the one window. As I looked around, I noticed that there were maps in frames on the walls, all badly in need of dusting. In the center of the room was a plank table where I could roll pastry dough and chop vegetables. A frying pan and the cooking kettle I needed for boiling water hung on pegs near the fire hole. The wall opposite was crowded with shelves full of food supplies. And in one corner was a cot heaped with red and green Hudson's Bay blankets, a carved wooden chest at its foot. Not much of a house to clean, I thought, as Mr. York put my trunk down next to the shelf wall and walked back outside to the boat.

I sat erect in one of the two chairs at the table, nervously awaiting my first instructions. Would he want me to dust the shelves or make up his bed? I wasn't at all acquainted with the domestic habits of Americans. Slowly my muscles began to relax and I slumped down in the chair. It was a dingy cabin. Only yesterday I had been dreaming of being a fine lady married to a Russian Cossack officer who would take me on his ship to find my mother and her Haida tribe on the islands to the south, where, she said, the winters were warmer and it seldom snowed. Now, here I was with this strange fire-headed American who would not tell me what he wanted from me. I sat in the damp room for an hour, awaiting instructions, then got up and went to search outside for my new owner, but he was gone and so was the canoe.

I looked up into the spruce trees near the cabin and there four bald-headed eagles sat watching me. They were as tall as an eight-year-old child, and their wings spread wider than my five-foot height. The one white-headed male eagle tilted his beak and eyed me benevolently. The others, two black females and an immature bird, sat unmoving, as if they were sentries sent to guard my safety. Yes, the spirit of my mother is with me, I thought, remembering that the eagle was the crest of her Haida tribe.

Near the cabin were large rocks the same craggy granite color as the giant *kekoor* rock where Alexander Baranov had built his castle, overlooking Sitka Bay. Unlike the rocks near Mr. York's cabin, the *kekoor* site was sacred to the Tlingits: Home-of-Spirits, they called it. The Indians had been furious when Baranov violated the Sea Spirits' home and retaliated by massacring all but two of the first Sitka Bay Russian settlers—cutting off their heads and eating some of them, the Mission Fathers said. But more Russians came, mainly priests and convict workers like my father. The newcomers made the *kekoor* rock so angry that all the hair seals and fur otters finally disappeared from Sitka Bay just as they had done in Kodiak. Perhaps, I hoped, the Sea Spirits in the *kekoor* rock will become angry with Mr. York and make him disappear as well.

Exhausted even though I'd done no work, I went inside, lay down on the cot, and fell asleep for a while. After several hours I awoke, opened my trunk, and put my few belongings—my three black muslin dresses, my comb and brush, my winter shawl, and my fox hat—on one of the kitchen shelves. Then I built a fire and sorted through the American's dry foodstuffs, thinking to prepare some sustenance for my new owner. Keep his hands busy eating, I told myself.

There were boxes of tea and spices and chocolate, canisters of dried meat, and sacks of onions. What kind of a man was this Noah York? I wondered. He had a larder better than Gospozha Karimoff's, maybe as grand as the Castle's itself. Perhaps this American simply wanted me to cook these fine foods for him. Yet I doubted he'd come all the way to Alaska just to while away the long winters doing nothing but grieving for his mother and eating the pounds of plump dried figs he kept in the largest canister. Other than wild game and fish, food was rare in Alaska, and this American had a fortune in edibles alone. Perhaps Noah York was a chamberlain of the American President, sent to the Russian colonies on some secret mission. Perhaps, I hoped, he had bought me to be his secretary.

I boiled water for tea, or *chai,* as Gospozha would have called it. And then, since the drizzling spring rain persisted outside, I lay on the cot, listening to the sounds of the woods, the sounds of the giant yellow and red cedars and of the ravens. I had not lived in the forest since the Russian priests had taken me away from my mother, and I had forgotten the voices of the animals. So I listened closely to each of them, remembering my mother's stories. "Small-Lake, never kill a squirrel or an otter. If you do this, the soul of the creature will enter the body of a woman, who will kill you the same way you killed it." I remembered my mother's stories and listened for the sounds of a squirrel in the trees above the cabin.

Then I thought of Mr. York. His was a small house, and I had no room of my own here, as I'd had at the Karimoffs. There was only this one cot, no other separate bed for me to sleep on. My muscles froze when I thought of becoming Noah York's concubine, and I imagined the terror that must have overtaken my mother each time the convict Ilya Ovechkin forced himself upon her. But surely, I told myself, a woman as religious as Gospozha Karimoff would not have sold me for such purposes—Gospozha, who had locked me in my room for a week because the son of a Russian sentry touched my breast by accident as he brushed by me on the Governor's Walk; Gospozha, who always told me that such touchings would soil me and that I should abstain from them if I ever hoped to marry. What if he gave me a child, this Noah York? Would the Mission Fathers steal it from me as they had stolen me from my mother?

It was late when the American returned, without even a lantern on the bow of his canoe. I had boiled some dried fish with the parsnips and potatoes that I found in barrels under the table, deciding that since he had given me no instructions, I would act as if he had bought me to cook for him and be his chore girl, just as I had done for the Karimoffs.

Mr. York entered the cabin, took off his black-tarred rain cape, and ate what I had cooked for him without a word or even an acknowledgment of my presence. After an hour had passed he asked, "Nadia, when do the berries get ripe?"

"What?" I was shocked at finally hearing his voice again.

"You're part Indian, aren't you? When do the berries get ripe?"

I didn't know what to say—this wasn't what I'd been brought up by the Karimoffs to discuss with my betters—but I answered obediently. "At the end of the summer, when the night comes back. First the salmonberries, the yellow ones, then the elderberries and the huckleberries, and higher up, near the glacier on Mount Saint Lazaria, the blueberries."

"And this drizzling rain," he said. "It's enough to drive a man into a fit of gloom. There hasn't been a dry day since I arrived. When does it stop?"

"The rain?" I asked. "The rain is always with us. In the winter it turns to snow for a month or two, and in the summer perhaps for a week there will be no dampness falling from the sky." I began to wonder what it would be like to live in a place which did not always have rain. Hadn't Mr. York noticed that once a day the ravens parted the clouds and brought in the sun? The Indians had countless words to describe the rain—falling-like-pine-needles, with-the-force-of-war-arrows, lake-that-falls-from-the-sky. If it weren't for the rain, I wanted to tell him, the cranberries and huckleberries wouldn't grow so thickly in the woods and bogs. The small animal people would have nothing to eat, and the fish would have no rivers to swim in.

"Ah, well," he muttered, as if resigning himself to a seasonless climate, "it's magnificent country, so densely green—even in winter, I'm told."

Then he took a leather-bound notebook from the chest at the foot of the cot and wrote down everything that I had just said, as if he were one of the small children at the Mission School where I had taught the day after Professor Karimoff's death. I was amazed. Why would anyone write down such things about berries and rain? Couldn't he remember them?

"When they get ripe I want a red elderberry pie," he said. "Remember that."

"The red ones are poison, they'll make you sick," I said, eager to show off my Indian knowledge.

"I want a red elderberry pie," he said again, as if I had not spoken.

A strange feeling ran down my spine. Did Mr. York not believe that the berries were poison, because I was a simple servant girl whose knowledge was always to be tested and verified? Or was it that he truly wanted to make himself ill—and not by his own hand, but mine? For a moment I stood as motionless as a deer frightened by a hunter. But no, I told myself, surely Mr. York wasn't a lunatic. He was just eccentric in his ways, a foreigner who wanted to test these new Alaskan elements.

He cleared off the table, took the Hudson's Bay blankets from the cot, and arranged them on the cabin floor. "We sleep here," he said. He took off his boots and all his clothes except for the long woolen underwear and lay down under the blankets next to the fire hole. I stood in the corner and watched him, my body shaking. All the blankets were on the floor and none left for me to sleep under . . . unless I slept with him.

"We sleep here," he said again and turned his head away from me.

So, I thought hopelessly, he did buy me to be his concubine. Slowly I removed part of my clothes, my black muslin overdress and shoes, and quietly crept under the blankets, lying as far away from him as I could and still be under the covers.

"Take more off," he said. "Not everything, you'll catch cold."

I took off two of my slips, but not my long underwear. As he put his hand over my breast, my muscles tightened to his touch, but he never looked at me. Then the American unbuttoned the lower part of his long underwear and put his hand inside, moving it back and forth, up and down.

"Touch yourself," he commanded, taking his hand off my breast. "Touch yourself," he said again.

But I could not. The Mission Fathers had told us about touching in religious class. They said that being a toucher was sinful and that we should never touch ourselves in those places, especially if we were girls. If we were girls we would ruin ourselves for our husbands. We would become tools of the devil, they said; the devil possessed our fingers when we did this, and we would grow to love it, and to want nothing else all during our lives. In extreme cases we would be able to do nothing else all day. Witches did this touching, they said. Whenever they talked about touchers, the priests would look at me for a long time, probably because they thought my mother was a witch. Perhaps I was the child of a union with the devil, they said, and that would explain why I was the most clever student in the Mission Fathers' school.

Slowly I began unbuttoning the lower buttons of my underwear, thinking that the Russian priests god would strike me dead before each button. Mr. York's hand was moving up and down, faster and faster now, and he was breathing hard.

"Touch yourself," he commanded.

3.

I cried for hours, not just about becoming a toucher but about Professor Karimoff dying and leaving me alone in New Archangel Settlement without my mother, and about Gospozha selling me to this strange foreigner whose body was covered with red hair. I hadn't grieved the day the professor died in the drafty Russian hospital-morgue at the back end of the Baranov fur company warehouse, where, in winter, the priests kept dead bodies until spring, when the ground thawed enough for a Christian burial. I hadn't even grieved as the bishop of the Church of Saint Michael the Archangel lowered the professor's cedar coffin into his grave at the cemetery up on the hill near the eight-sided blockhouses. As the bishop read the final eulogy, Gospozha had whimpered under her heavy black veil and I had watched the blockhouse sentries aim their long-barreled rifles toward the Tlingit Village of the Raven, prepared against a surprise Indian attack.

Now Professor Karimoff had been in his grave five days and I lay on the cold floor of an old *promyshlennik* cabin trying to cry in whispers so that my new master wouldn't awaken and begin to touch himself again. Finally I couldn't be quiet and the American awoke, but he neither spoke a word of annoyance nor reached out his hand to console me.

"Professor, Professor," I sobbed. My Russian master had wronged me by dying, and he had lied in telling me about all the fine things that would happen to me if I did well in my lessons, if I mastered my calculus and declined all my irregular Latin verbs. How would I ever buy my freedom from this foreigner? I had no money, no jewelry or furs, and I couldn't buy freedom with well-done lessons. How would I find my mother and my Haida people? Surely now none of those young Russian nobles in New Archangel would ever ask for my hand in marriage as Professor Karimoff had promised. I was a mere servant girl, living in a dingy cabin, and even though I was still a virgin, I was soiled with touching. The Russian priests had taught me that it was a sin not to forgive the dead, but still I felt that Professor Karimoff had truly wronged me and that I would never be able to forgive him.

As I cried over the loss of my Russian master, I began to contemplate this foreigner who lay under the blankets next to me. Did he have a wife somewhere, I wondered, a woman that he was saving himself for? He had only made me commit the sin of touching and had not pried my legs apart, forcing himself into me as Ilya Ovechkin had done to my mother. But if this Noah York had a wife, why had he purchased me? Perhaps I was to help him with his work. But what was this American's work? He was much too high-bred to be a *promyshlennik;* what did he plan to do here in the Russian colonies? And—I shuddered—what was it, other than touching, that he would want from me?

Finally, my nose was so stopped up and my lungs gasping so hard that I knew I would have to stop crying or choke. As I grew quiet I began to hear the noises of the forest. A wolf howled, maybe only a quarter of a mile away. They were big, those wolves, two hundred pounds with a five-inch spread to their paws. The *promyshlenniki* were terrified of them, because shooting a wolf only made her go mad enough to rip a hunter apart before she had time to bleed to death from her wound. I listened to the wolf howl again, making the same noise that my crying had made. In one of my mother's stories, she had told me that wolves don't bother adult Indians, that even though I was part European I had come from the body of an Indian, and the wolves could smell this and wouldn't harm me. "The wolf is very smart," my mother once told me. "The wolf knows which people are her enemy.

They hunt the same land, the wolf and the Indian, but they do not hunt each other." I turned my face toward Mr. York, who had fallen asleep again and was snoring loudly. Perhaps, I thought, this foreigner would meet the she wolf of this forest and then I would have my freedom.

One early summer day when the sun was high above Mount Saint Lazaria and wouldn't set until after midnight, I was washing blankets in a big cast-iron pot over a fire I'd built down by the river. Up-creek, Mr. York suddenly began screaming loud enough to chase the ravens away. At first I thought he'd been stung by the hornets who had recently built a nest in the ground near our cabin. But when I walked over to find out what was the matter, he just pointed to the silver fish in the white water of the river rapids. So, the salmon have started to run, I thought to myself. But doesn't this American know that the salmon run every summer? Doesn't everyone know such things?

He was beside himself as he ran into the cabin for his feather quill pen and leather-bound notebook. "Get that laundry done and out to dry on the rocks," he yelled. "We've got work to do!" Obediently I began spreading the wet blankets across the warm, flat rocks along the riverbank, contemplating these first few months I'd spent in his service.

Other than questions about the elements, Mr. York seldom spoke to me and never mentioned the touching of that first night or commanded me to do it again. About a week later he'd gone into New Archangel—or Sitka, "in this place," as the Tlingits called the settlement and the bay it was built on—bringing back another cot and more blankets. From then on he slept on one side of the fire hole and I slept on the other. Often I could hear him touching himself across the room, his breath coming harder and harder.

How will I get away from this strange man? I would think each time his moanings filled the one-room cabin. Sometimes I would reach down into my long underwear and touch myself but then remember the Russian bishop. Since I didn't believe that any man would take me as his bride, I no longer cared about ruining myself for my husband. But I was afraid that the priests would be able to look me in the eye and see that I was a toucher. I was afraid that someday they would call me a witch, just as they had called my mother a witch, and the touching that they saw in my eyes would be part of their proof.

"How do we catch the salmon?" Mr. York asked in a high, excited voice as he ran toward me, stepping all over the wash.

"With a club, of course," I answered, sighing at his dirty footprints on the blankets. Could it be that Mr. York had never had to do daily labor? That he had no regard or reverence for the labor of others, because he had never done any? Possibly he had never had to hunt his own food to stay alive either. Perhaps his journey to Russian Alaska was to him a great adventure, a lark, and I, Nadia Karimoff—Small-Lake-Underneath—would have to show him how to hunt and gather food for the winter. It was I who was responsible for keeping us both alive. Suddenly I began to feel the weight of my new servitude, and my shoulders drooped like tree limbs heavy with ice.

Mr. York followed me into the woods, where I wearily chopped each of us a club. I told him that we would have to walk upriver, to where it branched out into a shallow creek, then club the fish as they leaped over the rocks. I handed him a pair of flour sacks in which to carry the fish back to the cabin, and he followed me for half an hour as I walked upriver through the high ferns and low-hanging moss.

The humpback salmon plunged up an Indian River tributary, climbing toward their spawning grounds in the mountains behind the Tlingit Village of the Raven. My arms ached from washing the heavy woolen blankets. "We should start catching fish tomorrow," I said in a tired voice, "after we've built alder-wood fires for the smoke-curing." But it was as if I had not spoken. Mr. York was already wading knee-deep into the water trying to catch a fish with his hands.

I shook my head despairingly. Daily labor and the gathering of food was just a game to this man. What a useless person he seemed to be! Perhaps that's why he left his home in Massachusetts. He was probably just as useless to his family as he was trying to help me gather food.

Red thimbleberries and huckleberries were ripening on bushes near the bank and I ate handfuls of them, knowing that Noah York wouldn't stop for us to eat once we'd started to catch the salmon. He was so odd, this man. Indeed, he was capable of hard work—

splitting logs for four hours straight—but he had not yet learned to stop for sustenance and rest until he was too exhausted to care for himself.

I walked into the glacier-cold water and began to club the salmon on the head, being careful not to damage what was left of the meat on their bodies. My new master never hesitated; he went on clubbing fish as the sun traveled across the sky. When we had filled the flour sacks with salmon, we harnessed them to our backs and around our waists and started back to our cabin. I led the way down the trail toward Indian River, my head bent to keep the wet hemlock limbs from lashing at my face. Then, in front of me, instead of a tree stump or a fallen branch, were the two legs of an Indian.

At first I shuddered from the surprise, but Mr. York never flinched, just studied the Indian's skin and his woven cedar-bark clothes decorated with white-tipped eagle feathers. I could tell by the black tar markings painted on his red face and his exceptional height that he was from the Tlingit Village of the Raven. The Indian stood directly in front of me, but he didn't grip my shoulders in friendship, and from the stern expression on his high young forehead I knew he had been watching us for most of the day.

As the Indian spoke, the Tlingit language sounded strange to me, because the Russian Fathers had for eight years forbidden me to speak the language of heathens. But slowly I found the words and spoke to the tall man, telling him that my mother was a Haida and that I had once lived in his village with her. I asked after the old ones of his tribe and knew from his relaxed posture that he would not harm me.

"Fish of my people," he said, eyeing the salmon-filled sacks. I began to undo my harnessings to return his fish. "No," he said in a deep, throaty voice, "take fish, make Sea Spirit happy." Then he asked why I had come to live on his river and had not come to visit his people. I told him that the Russians who had taken me from my mother had sold me to this Boston man—the Indian term for Americans because of the Boston whalers who fished in Tlingit waters at Yakutat Bay— and that although he was not my husband I must do his bidding. The Boston man, I told the Indian, had not given me permission to go to the Village of the Raven.

The Indian smiled. "Big wolf hunt Indian River," he said, his white teeth, which had been filed into points, smiling down at me as he gestured to Mr. York. I bowed my head so that the Tlingit wouldn't see into my eyes. It was as if he knew just by looking at me that from the first night of my servitude I had hoped Noah York would be eaten by the wolves. "I go," said the Indian and gently touched the top of my head.

As he passed me on the trail, I knew that we had an understanding, this tall Tlingit man and I: The people of his tribe would let me pass over their land unharmed. I must, I decided, go to their village to speak with the old ones, even if Mr. York denied me permission. Perhaps they would have news of my mother.

"What's your name?" I suddenly remembered to ask the Tlingit, calling over my shoulder in a loud voice that echoed across the narrow canyon of the creek below.

"Kat-lee-an," he said, the words of his name coming down upon me like a sudden Alaskan summer rain.

"Kat-lee-an," I whispered to myself. The young chief of the Tlingit Village of the Raven, the warrior who had led the last attack against New Archangel Settlement, massacring a group of unsuspecting mourners at a funeral in the Russian cemetery. It had been Kat-lee-an, disguised as a giant raven, brandishing a *promyshlennik* rifle and swinging a blacksmith's hammer, who'd led a band of Indian warriors to another victory over the New Archangel settlers. "Kat-lee-an," I whispered again, rolling the power of his name across my tongue.

Mr. York acted as if meeting the Tlingit were of little consequence, though he did make me tell him exactly what the Indian had said so he could enter it in his leather book when we returned to the cabin. He was like a schoolboy, this man, and seemed to be pleased with me for talking with the Indian.

"Good, little Nadia," he said. "Very good." While Mr. York wrote in his notebook, I began to cut and gut the salmon, saving the pink-orange roe in a large canister to be eaten with the unleavened bread I'd baked over the fire hole the day before.

After he'd put his notebook safely inside the hand-carved chest at the foot of his cot, the American built a lean-to outside the cabin and strung the fish in rows under it. Then he built a fire among stones gathered from the riverbank.

"These fish are the size of small children," said Mr. York as I swung the heavy ax over my head, splitting more logs for the fire.

"This is a good year," I replied, thinking that, as usual, he'd have nothing more to say to me. "We caught them close enough to the bay water so that their bodies aren't beaten by the river rocks."

"I didn't like clubbing those fish," he said. "No, I didn't like it at all. It was almost like clubbing a child, like killing a human being—my own little son, if I had one. . . ." His voice trailed away.

I put down my ax in amazement. I had been with this man for three months, and this was one of the few times he had spoken more than a passing sentence. "In Massachusetts, do they believe that the souls of the dead go to live in the sea?" I asked, wondering why it made him so unhappy to club the fish.

"What?" he asked. "Why would they think that?"

"There are people in the ice fields to the north," I said, "Eskimos—people with the tails of dogs, the Russians call them. When they die, their souls go to live in the sea. One of these people was brought here once by a Russian-American Company clipper. This Eskimo said that he was sad to be away from his people, that they were unlike the Indians here. Their skin was yellow, like his, and they didn't eat what grew on the land, only animals from the ocean. But this man said that he was happy, because on the boat from the Bering Sea he had seen many fish. The face of his grandmother, he said, was on those fish."

It took days of stoking the fires before the fish were smoke-cured. When we'd stored them in the log cache built up on stilts to keep our winter food supplies safe from bears, Mr. York said that we'd be going into New Archangel the next day. I hadn't been back to the Russian settlement since Gospozha had sold me, and I couldn't get to sleep until the middle of the night because of my excitement. Maybe I'd see some of the girls with whom I'd gone to school: plump, rosy-cheeked Anya Rezanov, daughter of the Czar's chamberlain, or Natalia Primak-off, Anya's freckle-faced, wavy-haired best friend. Most of the Mission School students ignored me, saying that I smelled like an Indian. But

I had lived in the house of the head schoolmaster, Professor Karimoff, and was the smartest pupil. So often the two prettiest and most popular girls, Anya and Natalia, would greet me on the Governor's Walk with a few words of French, the language spoken in the Czar's court and Maksoutov's castle.

Together Mr. York and I paddled our canoe across the quiet waters of Sitka Bay. I looked out toward the Pacific at all the tiny spruce-covered islands and then at the largest, most densely wooded one of all—Japonski Island. The Russians had named it for a Nippon junk that had come unmoored in Tokyo and was carried by a storm and the warm oriental current all the way to the rocks of Sitka Bay.

I looked down into the green-gold seaweed, watching the thousands of small herring, the same silver color as the coins I'd need in order to buy my freedom from this American. Just how many pieces of silver had been in that bag that Noah York had given to Gospozha Karimoff? Perhaps today, if I lingered near the doorway of the fur depot, the *promyshlenniki* would discuss the cost of half-breed women servants. But what good would that do? Even if I did know exactly how much Noah York had paid for me, how would I get hold of a bag of silver?

We tied up the boat at the end of the pier and walked across the beach slopes where the sentries paraded their weapons each day, marching in formation during the early morning hours. Passing through the huge spiked wooden gates of New Archangel stockade, Aleut slaves dressed in coarse black *muzhik* clothes were hauling bales of blue-fox pelts down to a clipper bound for Canton. As we approached the Russian-American Company depot, I was amazed to see how many unfamiliar faces stood in the doorway. Americans, I thought. Why have so many Americans come here?

Silently I followed Mr. York to the windowless log countinghouse, where my master said he might have a letter brought in on the last ice ship. I wondered if Gospozha still lived in her steep-roofed cottage or if she'd really gone back to Russia. While Mr. York stood in line, waiting for his letter, I strolled up the Governor's Walk, hardly recognizing anyone except Yuri Dysokar, the harelipped son of a Russian fur agent and a former student of Professor Karimoff's. Where were Anya and

Natalia? I wondered, as Yuri pretended not to recognize me. Had my schoolgirl classmates married visiting ambassadors sent by Czar Alexander II and returned to Russia with them?

Along the paths between the bare-board village houses, chalk-skinned Americans were speaking a strange language, not always English words but nonsensical Russian words interjected at the beginnings and endings of their sentences. Every so often I heard them speak a word of Chinook, the language that the British Hudson's Bay Company had invented to speak with the Indians. I wondered if these newcomers, or *cheechakoes*, as the Indians called foreigners, knew that Chinook was forbidden in Russian Alaska because the mother country had been at war with the British in Crimea.

As the noise of New Archangel's lumber-mill saw and blacksmith anvils echoed against the walls of the stockade, I stood in front of the house where I had lived for eight years, hardly recognizing it. Someone had taken Gospozha's white lace curtains out of the front windows and smashed the flower boxes. Americans, I thought, more Americans.

I walked back down the path toward the stockade gate and the fur depot warehouse where Mr. York was buying his monthly supplies. The Governor's Walk was crowded with the crewmen of a newly arrived California ice ship awaiting a load of ice to be cut from Swan Lake in the steep hills behind New Archangel. Americans with canvas packs of surveying equipment talked among themselves. It was good just listening to people talk, no matter what languages they spoke or the fact that what they were saying had nothing to do with me—I hadn't heard the sounds of other humans for months. As I lingered outside the door of the log fur depot, the American surveyors were speaking broken Russian to the *promyshlenniki*, telling the ruddy-faced fur trappers a wild tale of building something called a telegraph line all the way across the great ocean from the northern Alaska ice fields to Moscow. The trappers rolled their vodka-glazed eyes in wonder but then sobered as they told the surveyors that the number of seals in Alaska's rookeries had dwindled to almost nothing. As soon as their sealskin *bidarka* boats were stocked with supplies, the Russians said, they were moving on to better trapping near Fort Wrangell.

Then the American surveyors began to talk about Camp Seattle, telling the *promyshlenniki* that if a man didn't mind muddy streets, canvas houses, and Indian women, there was a crying need for coopers, tanners—any able-bodied man with a craft. "Future New York of the West," one narrow-faced surveyor called the lumber camp. "Gateway to the Orient," another added smugly.

Inside the depot I was amazed to find Mr. York buying spools of patterned silk material and canisters of dry foodstuffs imported from Canton. The one-armed, potbellied fur agent was trying to sell him ermine pelts, but my owner waved them away. Why was he buying all that merchandise? We couldn't possibly use it up even in two winters—our food cache was filled with dried fish and our cabin was so small I couldn't guess where he intended to put it all. These Americans, I thought, such strange and foolish plans they have.

"Nadia," said Mr. York in a gruff voice, "do you know how to tan skins?"

"Yes, of course," I replied. Didn't every servant girl know such things?

"I bought some hunting supplies. We should begin collecting pelts rather than buying new blankets," he said earnestly.

"Yes," I agreed, conceiving a plan. I could hoard some of these pelts until I had enough to trade to the fur agent for a bag of silver. For a moment I forgot about Noah York and his spools of brightly patterned silk. Where would I hide my pelts, I wondered, in a fallen log or the hollow tree near our cabin?

My owner began strutting nervously back and forth across the plank floor of the warehouse, examining his purchases. The one-armed fur agent followed Mr. York, his eyes smiling, probably at the thought of all the pieces of silver he would make. My owner must be going to take up some sort of business, and these were its beginnings here on the fur-depot counter. After all, Mr. York didn't have a profession, not like Professor Karimoff, who'd been a schoolmaster, or Prince Maksoutov, who governed the Alaska colonies and who no doubt would come to tea when he came to inspect my master's new business establishment.

That night after we'd returned to our cabin, Mr. York strung the paisley-patterned silk across the walls to make it look as if the cabin had been wallpapered. After he finished, I gazed around the room. Here and there I could see mud from the moss-chinked logs showing through. Not half as grand as the wallpaper in the Castle, I thought. Prince Maksoutov would find Noah York's quarters uncomfortable.

"I received a letter today," my owner said as he sat down at the table. "She's coming next week. Now, I don't have time to build another room onto the cabin, so we'll just have to—"

"She?" I asked in surprise. "She? You've bought another servant?" I said, dreading that I would have to share my already small quarters with another girl, who might not take to me, who might be like my Russian classmates, jeering and pointing at me, whispering that I smelled like a savage.

"Of course not. Your services have been adequate, perfectly adequate." I waited for at least a word of praise for my household accomplishments, but none came. "She," he said with great reverence, "is Miss Emily Gore of Stamford, Connecticut, my fiancee."

"I see," I said with a sudden feeling of jealousy and fear—not because I'd have to share Mr. York's attentions, but because I had become accustomed to having a free rein in running his house. His fiancée might find my services inadequate and have me sold to one of those new American surveyors bound for the ice fields to the north or to a craftsman en route to Camp Seattle, where they drowned Indians who demanded their wages.

"We were to have been married last year, but Ma-*ma* died, jolting my whole outlook on life." Taking no notice of my sullenness, he went on. "I decided at Ma-*ma*'s funeral that before I married "I wanted to do something exciting with my life. I wanted"—he cleared his throat, moving his Adam's apple up and down—"to become a pioneer, not to tame the wilderness but to live in the wilds. I wanted to do something on my own, not go to law school and be my father's lackey, no, sir. I wanted to do something artistic but constructive. Something that, when I finished, I could stand back, look at, and say, 'I did that, all alone, without using my family's influence.' I wanted to do something, Nadia, that other men could look at with me and say, 'Marvelous— *encore, encore!*'"

ALASKA

I stared at his pale complexion and his fire-red hair. A pioneer, I thought, like the Russian colonists and trappers? But the *promyshlenniki* hunted fur animals and exchanged them at the depot for rubles or supplies, while Mr. York seemed to get his silver without working, through the mail at the countinghouse. It was as if Noah York had been put on a perpetual vacation—*zapusk,* as the*promyshlenniki* would say.

"You're part of my life's plan too, little Nadia," he said, his teeth smiling down at me white as the ice caps on Three Sisters Peaks. "Yes, you're to help my bride and me. We'll be married almost as soon as she arrives. She's not a pioneer, and she's rather fragile. That's why she'll need your help, Nadia. She'll be enchanted to have a little Creole doing chores for her."

"A Creole?" I asked. So, I thought to myself, Mr. York did have a wife he was saving himself for—a frail and probably sickly woman like his mother.

"Yes," he said. "You know, part European and part native, very exotic."

I wrinkled up my nose at the word as I recalled my looking-glass image: a small head, two tiny black eyes, and coarse red-black hair that always looked uncombed no matter how often I brushed it. Was that what these Americans think of as exotic? "But I'm an Indian," I said, not understanding this word *Creole.* Then I began to wonder where I would sleep once Mr. York's wife-to-be came. They'd probably put me up in the drafty food cache built in back of the cabin. "I'm an Indian. My name is Small-Lake-Underneath." I was angry at the thought of being moved out into the cold.

"Ah," he said with a serious expression, "don't tell Miss Emily about your Indian name at first. Let's let you grow on her. Let her become attached to you like her little white pet terrier, Abraham Lincoln."

Mr. York read Miss Emily's letter over and over far into the night, then finally laid the white leaves of paper aside and opened a small, thin book. From my bed I watched him silently mouthing the words, nodding his head back and forth as if he were singing. What could he be doing now? I wondered.

I shut my eyes but was awakened by something that in my groggy state I first thought was an Indian chant:

35

"'Roses and lilies her cheeks disclose, / But her ripe lips are more sweet than those. . . .' Do you like poetry?" he asked, smiling and gleeful as a small child on his birthday.

"I've never heard it read aloud," I answered, remembering the dry volumes of verse from which Professor Karimoff had taught: "Define epic simile," the professor had commanded. "Compose an invocation to the Muse." I remembered asking if I could not do my trigonometry lesson instead. But Mr. York's poetry was much different; it was almost like a song.

"You should study verse," instructed my master. "In a poem one can transcend oneself into anything . . . even a fish:

"Dreary-mouth'd, gaping wretches of the sea,
Gulping salt-water everlastingly . . ."

His hands were animated, and I could see his eyes sparkle even from across the room. "Or a cloud," he continued:

"I am the daughter of earth and water,
    And the nursling of the sky;
I pass through the pores of the ocean and shores;
    I change, but I cannot die."

I closed my eyes again, thinking that a man who dreams of being a fish or a cloud must be a good man. Until now I'd thought that only the Indians regarded the elements with such kindness. I nestled my head into my pillow. Mr. York wasn't well skilled in the ways of survival and the woods, but he certainly had a lot of university knowledge which he could teach me, knowledge which Professor Karimoff had probably never heard of.

He left in the canoe the day before Miss Emily's ship was due to drop anchor in Sitka Bay. I sat in the empty cabin trying to picture her face: a girl perhaps my own age with long blond ringlets, blue eyes, a book in one hand and a parasol in the other, followed by a small dog with a pink ribbon around its neck. Perhaps she would like me, and then I would finally have someone to talk to, to keep me company during the long winter nights. In a year's time, maybe, if she wasn't too frail, she'd have a pink-cheeked baby that I would care for. We would be a family, all of us, and I would be happy with my new owners, so happy that I shouldn't mind if I never earned enough money to buy my freedom or find my mother and her Haida tribe.

Then I remembered that the wild strawberries on the wet mossy slopes beside Indian River had begun to ripen. I decided to welcome my new mistress with a fresh batch of strawberry conserve to go with the fancy Russian silver tea set that Mr. York had just bought—a house-warming present for Miss Emily, he'd called it. The American had asked me if I'd ever served a Russian tea, with *zakuska* and tea made in a samovar. He'd said that Miss Emily would like that sort of thing, that she would prefer the Russian colonies to the American West, because the Russians had a keen sense of tradition and good taste.

It took me most of the morning to pick enough berries. When I'd gathered half a pailful, I sat down on a rock in the tall horsetail grass growing near the riverbank. There was a rustle in the dense white-trunked alder forest in back of me. A rabbit, I thought, or maybe a deer.

I watched the grass bend in the late summer breeze. What would life be like with Miss Emily? I looked up at the high mountain peaks around me, tracing their outline with my finger in the air, my arm dropping sharply as they plunged four thousand feet into the waters of Sitka Bay. Again I heard the forest move and saw, out of the corner of my eye, that Kat-lee-an was watching me. I'll pretend not to know he's there, I told myself. It would hurt his pride to know that a strange girl, an intruder on his people's land, knew enough about the forest to discover him hiding.

I broke off a piece of horsetail grass and began sucking on it, thinking about Noah York. Were all Americans as odd as he? Some days he never got out of bed, and then others he'd be up at dawn wielding an ax as fast as any cossack in New Archangel. One Sunday, when I'd been in his service for about two months, Mr. York went out into the spring rain, built and fenced a kitchen garden, and planted a small pear and apple orchard before dark. Then he'd sat up half the night writing in his leather book and drawing queer little houses and plans for gardens.

Indeed, Mr. York had in a short time learned to do hard labor well and at a furious pace. But there was a certain desperation in the way he worked. Sometimes when I walked up behind him, bringing him a bowl of bear-paw stew for his midday meal, I'd catch him hysterically wielding his ax on a mutilated tree stump and ranting in a loud voice to his invisible father:

"How am I to make a fortune as you and Grandpapa did?" he'd yelled once. "There's no new commerce to be had, no wars to profit from." The ax split the stump, and wood chips ricocheted into the forest. "And why should I, for Christ's sake? Papa, you stingy bastard, you're as addicted to collecting money as any dope fiend is to opium!"

Sad, I thought to myself as I sucked the horsetail grass and cautiously eyed Kat-lee-an hiding behind a giant red cedar. I'd always wondered about my father, Ilya Ovechkin, but after hearing Mr. York's rantings, I was glad that I didn't have a father to drive me to such unleashed anger. And sad, too, that Mr. York had traveled five thousand miles to a foreign land but still wasn't out of earshot of the voices of his elders.

Even from a distance I could see that Miss Emily was a real lady, dressed in a brown tweed traveling suit with a huge, black ostrich-feathered hat. But instead of a pink ribbon around its neck, her white terrier, Abraham Lincoln, had a heavy chain and leash which Miss Emily appeared to be clinging to as tightly as she clung to the side of the canoe. Abraham Lincoln barked in shrill yelps as Mr. York poled the canoe upstream toward the cabin. I walked down to the river beach, waving and watching them approach. There were trunks and hatboxes of all sizes and shapes in the canoe, so many that Mr. York had to sit on them instead of safely down in the hull of the boat.

I could not imagine why Miss Emily thought she would need so many hats here in Alaska. I wondered if my master had deceived his bride-to-be about this wild country. Had he told her that instead of hunting bear and gathering berries, she'd be whiling away her days with long strolls up the Governor's Walk and going to fashionable teas in the Russian gardens?

As the canoe neared the cabin beach, I was disappointed to see that Miss Emily didn't look at all like I'd imagined her. She had thin, colorless lips and there was no light in her face. She wasn't my age or Mr. York's either. He was twenty-five, and Miss Emily looked about five years older.

Little Abraham Lincoln pulled tightly against his leash, barking wildly as another boat carrying a giant trunk appeared at the river bend. I recognized Yuri Dysokar as he poled his boat against the current and upriver toward our cabin. Where were all Miss Emily's belongings going to go? My master had talked about building another room, but that last trunk wouldn't even fit through the cabin doorway.

"Nadia," said Mr. York nervously as he pulled the canoe up out of the water, "I'm going to take Miss Gore up to the cabin. You wait for the boatman and help carry the trunk." Mr. York hardly looked at me when he spoke, and his hands shook as he pulled the canoe onto the bank.

When he helped her out of the boat, Miss Emily stood as tall as Mr. York and was perhaps even a little more broad than he. What could be so fragile about this woman? I wondered; she was almost twice my size. Under her hat I could see that her hair was brown and her eyes smaller than mine. She didn't look at me, or even at Mr. York, for that matter. She just stood staring open-mouthed at the cabin while Abraham Lincoln tried feverishly to get out of his collar and chase a squirrel that had scurried from the cabin roof.

As Mr. York guided his bride-to-be up the pathway to the cabin, the ravens in the spruce trees began to squawk wildly. One even swooped down toward the pair, diving at Miss Emily's feathered hat. Abraham Lincoln was beside himself, standing on his tiny hind legs and barking at the large, yellow-eyed black birds. When the couple entered the cabin, the noise of the ravens grew even louder as more birds joined their numbers.

"Nadia!" commanded Mr. York from inside the house, his voice so tense that it cracked. "Make those birds stop that racket. They've upset Miss Gore terribly." He came to the door, wearing a serious but frantic expression. For the first time since I had known him I felt truly sorry for my master. Did he really suppose that because I was part Indian I could talk to the ravens and make them stop squawking? And the pleading way in which he had looked out of the cabin door at me. It was almost as if he were a small child asking his all-powerful father for a favor, instead of his servant girl.

Yuri, with his split upper lip and large ears, poled the boat upriver to the cabin. As I helped him beach the craft, he didn't appear to remember me, though I recalled his coming often to Professor Kari-moff's house and mouthing his lessons horribly.

"Such a strongk vwench," he said in his curious fashion as we tipped Miss Emily's black-and-brass trunk over the side of the boat and dragged it up the riverbank. Suddenly, before I'd put down the trunk's carrying handle, Yuri grabbed my waist, knocked me over, and pushed his saliva-covered face into mine as I lay on the ground. I screamed louder than if a bear had clawed me, and Mr. York and Miss Emily came rushing from the cabin, with Abraham Lincoln unleashed and barking at their heels.

"Stop," I managed to shriek before Yuri plunged his tongue into my mouth.

"Noah." It was Miss Emily, speaking for the first time since her arrival and making her vowels in the same sharp tones as Mr. York. "Noah, leave well enough alone. She probably provoked him. Why, it's plain as the nose on my face that she's nothing but a shameless strumpet."

"Get off me!" I screamed again as Yuri's heavy, sweat-sour body pushed my hips into the sand and the trees spun above me.

4.

Mr. York picked up the ax near the chopping block and, cursing, wielded the blunt end of the head at Yuri. "Get out of here, you son-of-a-bitch," he yelled.

I lay beneath the devil-faced boatman, shrieking when the ax came close enough to graze my ankle. For a minute I was afraid that Noah York would do me more harm than my attacker.

My master sent Yuri off in his boat without pay and helped me into the cabin. "Tea, Nadia," he said, as if nothing had happened. "I think Miss Gore would like her afternoon tea." Miss Emily stood in the doorway, looking annoyed.

"Yes sir," I stammered, still stunned by Yuri's attack—Yuri, who had always pretended not to know me when I walked by him on the Governor's Walk, who had always been respectful and polite to Gospozha when he came to Professor Karimoff's house for lessons.

"Noah," said Miss Emily as I reached for my water bucket, "does your father know you've engaged such a shameless wench? I'm not at all sure he'd approve of her." Mr. York's bride-to-be talked about me the same way that Gospozha used to talk about me, in the third person and as if I weren't in the same room. I wondered if Miss Emily would lock me in the food cache for a week like Gospozha had, because I had allowed Yuri to touch me. I wanted to tell her I'd done nothing to provoke him and it wasn't my fault he'd attacked me, but like a good servant I said nothing.

As I walked down to the river to fill the bucket for tea, the black cast-iron pail banged against my leg, bruised when Yuri had knocked me to the ground. Perhaps it wasn't that Miss Emily didn't like me, I thought. Perhaps she's angry because she was told the same lies that I was told. Perhaps she had also done well in her lessons and was even asked by a rich man for her hand in marriage, but instead of living in a home like Prince Maksoutov's Castle, Mr. York had brought her here to a small abandoned *promyshlennik* cabin.

I'd left the cabin door ajar, and Abraham Lincoln had dashed outside and into the woods to look for his squirrel. A minute later Mr. York ran after him, with Miss Emily, her long tweed skirts gathered in her hand, following right behind her husband-to-be.

"Noah, don't let him get away! He'll get lost in these trees. I'll die if I never see my little vanilla boy again, I'll just die!" Miss Emily bellowed like a moose cow who'd just lost her mate. Then she turned her flushed, sour face toward me. "I'll have you discharged for this, you incompetent little know-nothing."

Discharged? Didn't Miss Emily know that I was Mr. York's property? Discharged? Did that mean that my master would sell me to the highest bidder, a ruddy-faced *promyshlennik* bound for Fort Wrangell? As I quaked at the thought of the rat-faced fur trapper who would buy me next, I realized that I had grown almost fond of my master.

I had just dipped my pail into the water when Abraham Lincoln came yelping out of the woods, chased by a black furry creature with a black-and-white plumed tail raised high in the air like a spinnaker.

"A skunk!" I shrieked so that Miss Emily would run to the safety of the cabin. It was too late. As she knelt to rescue her little white terrier, the angry skunk—undoubtedly awakened from his day's sleep in a hollow log—turned, lifted his thick striped tail even higher into the air, and sprayed both Miss Emily and her dog.

Rushing from the woods, Mr. York chased the skunk off with the same ax that he'd used to drive Yuri away and then ran to help Miss Emily, who had lost her wide-brimmed hat and was choking from having inhaled the skunk fumes. She's the one who's a know-nothing, I thought, feeling resentful. How could she not know that a skunk isn't afraid of anything, that the skunk people have no enemies other than the *promyshlenniki?* Even bears ran from their terrible trail-spewing scent.

Abraham Lincoln was squealing louder than the ravens squawking in the trees, and Miss Emily was tearing at her clothing. I turned toward the river just in time to see my bucket begin to float downstream, so I waded out into the water after it.

"Be brave now, darling," said Mr. York, attempting to help his bride-to-be to her feet. "Remember, you wanted to be a pioneer. Be brave. Nadia'll have you into a fresh day dress in no time."

"Noah," Miss Emily yelled angrily to her fiancé, "until today I thought that my stay in Seattle was the nightmare of my life, but the obscenities of drunken loggers are tame compared to *this*. Do you hear me, Mr. York? Tame!" She held her nose with her thumb and forefinger, making her voice sound high-pitched and nasal. "At least Seattle has a college—not even a cobbled street, but a college—and there certainly weren't any of those foul-smelling black and white rodents there. Why,"—she looked in my direction—"I wouldn't be at all surprised if a Russian peasant hadn't brought those animals here on the boat from Europe."

I began to move back to shore but soon saw that I was safer in the water. Abraham Lincoln had unearthed a hornet's nest, and the angry insects were swelling up from their hole in the ground near the cabin and savagely attacking the three onshore.

Such wailing I never heard, almost as loud as the Russian settlement during Kat-lee-an's massacre of the funeral mourners. The ravens had become suddenly quiet while Miss Emily and her dog writhed on the ground. Mr. York, who hadn't been stung as badly, was trying to drag them to the safety of the river where the black swarm wouldn't follow, but it seemed that a hornet had gotten inside Miss Emily's blouse and she was ripping frantically at her buttons and laces.

"Nadia," called my master. "Nadia, *do* something."

I walked up on shore, my black muslin dress wet and heavy from the water. But as I approached the now half-naked Miss Emily and the dispersing hornets, Mr. York's bride-to-be began to shriek even more wildly.

"No, get her away from me, Noah, get her away. It's bad enough for you to see me naked, let alone a half-wit Indian girl."

Mr. York looked up at me in despair. "Go," he stammered, "go to the garden, Nadia, and pick some spinach greens for dinner . . . and," he added, "don't come back until I call you."

"Yes, sir," I said, almost whispering, as I watched the pale white of Miss Emily's flesh roll from her large hornet-stung breasts to the folds of her stomach. Such white skin she had, so white I could see the blue veins in her nipples.

As I averted my eyes from her chest, I studied, for a brief moment, the expression on my master's face. His lips were trembling not only with the desire to please his distraught bride-to-be but with an air of helplessness I could not quite fathom. Suddenly I was overcome with pity for him. But, I realized, mine was not the compassion one human feels for another but the pity a hunter feels for a gun-grazed and confused animal before it falls to the ground dead.

Turning away, I walked obediently to the garden, which Mr. York had planted on a piece of low-lying ground south of the cabin where it would get the most sunlight. After I'd picked an armload of spinach leaves from the sandy silt loam, I sat among the rows of blue-flowering borage and green chard. The mosquitoes danced on my arm but didn't bite. "When the mosquito people bite, eat the kernel of the wild oat grass," my mother would tell me. "Then the mosquitoes will not like the smell of your skin."

I could hear the river moving over the rocks down into Sitka Bay and, in the distance, the echo of the bells of Saint Michael the Archangel. I wondered if Mr. York and Miss Emily would convert to the Russian Orthodox faith and be married there. Then I began to think of how much I hated the Russian priests with their pointed black beards and their stale-smelling incense. The Karimoffs had made me go to church with them each Sunday. Gospozha and I would stand together on the left side of the altar in front of the gold Madonna of Kazan with the other women. Professor Karimoff would stand on the right side of the altar with the men. There were no chairs in the church, so we had to stand or kneel all during the two-hour service. After the mass, the men would file into the inner sanctuary. Women weren't allowed inside—unless they were nuns or over eighty—so I had to stay with Gospozha, who was always poking at me with her narrow pencil-point fingers and whispering that I should keep my head bowed and my mind on the prayers. I'd always wanted to be in the church choir, but the priests only allowed boys to sing the old Slovakian hymns.

As twilight approached and a light drizzle began to fall from the gray sky, I wondered why Mr. York hadn't come to fetch me. Would he just abandon me here because of Miss Emily's threats to discharge me? Surely he wouldn't leave me outside all night, I thought. I knew that Mr. York was anxious to please his bride-to-be, so I consoled myself by listening to the ravens talking. Maybe now that I lived in the woods again, I would learn to understand their language as my mother had.

It grew dark. My dress was damp from fetching the pail out of the river and damper still from the rain. I shivered and my skin turned to gooseflesh. Clutching the spinach greens, I walked slowly back toward the cabin. If I did not soon warm myself, I might catch pneumonia and die as Professor Karimoff had.

I kept trying to imagine what Miss Emily would look like when I walked through the cabin door. Would she be all face-swollen and sick from the hornet stings, or would Mr. York have covered her naked body with river-bottom mud, a poultice to ease the pain?

As I approached the cabin, I saw that not a lantern had been lit. Indeed, the cabin door was wide open and all of Miss Emily's trunks had been flung ajar and their contents scattered across the beach rocks like laundry. As I walked toward the dark house, I smelled the sharp skunk scent, then heard my cast-iron pots and frying pans clanging together as if they'd been knocked off their wall pegs.

Mr. York and Miss Emily were nowhere to be seen. I paused to look at the cluttered beach. The raccoon people, I thought angrily, and hurried toward my kitchen to frighten them away from Mr. York's supply of rare dried fruits. The couple must have walked upriver to bathe Miss Emily in mud, and now raccoons with their black and white masklike faces were eating up the food supplies.

A hundred feet from the door I heard a morose grunt and stopped motionless, dropping my armload of spinach so that I could stifle the scream that was about to come out of my mouth.

5.

Almost without thinking, I climbed up the pole ladder to the top of the cabin roof, howled like a seal who'd just lost her pup, and danced every Indian dance I knew. "Small-Lake," my mother once told me, "if you are alone in the great trees and come upon a bear"—a *hootz,* she always called them—"act like the crazy one. A *hootz* is afraid of the crazy one and will not harm you."

I beat my arms wildly against my sides, imitating the four eagles who nested in the hemlocks on the ridge in back of the cabin, and squealed like Yuri Dysokar's idiot brother. I tried not to think about the grotesque way that the *hootz* had probably eaten my master and Miss Emily, consuming the warm liver and the stomach parts first. "*Oi, oi, oi,*" I screamed into the night, thrashing my arms and beating my feet to the steps of the loon dance. "*Hoo-hooh, hoo-hooh, yelth,*" I shouted, pretending I was a shaman woman like my mother, Woman-Always-Wondering, dressed in a caribou skirt, shaking my caribou hoof bangles, with my hair in a topknot and a labret in my lower lip.

Had the *hootz* killed my master because I had wished him dead on the first night of my servitude? Tears began to form in my eyes. My soul shrank from the thought of possessing such powers. I'm free! I thought, as my feet moved frantically up and down on the cabin roof and my voice howled into the night. The remains of Noah York and Miss Emily probably lay across the blood-soaked Hudson's Bay blankets as the *hootz* picked through the canisters of dried fruits and tossed the empty containers on the floor. Had I murdered my master with my thoughts? My freedom had cost me a terrible enveloping guilt. I vowed that never again would I be so savage with my thought powers. But how had these powers come to live inside me?

A six-foot brown bear emerged from the cabin door. Standing on his hind legs, he cast an annoyed glance toward the roof. His head was larger than the heads of five men, and his eyes glowed amber in the dark. As he glanced up at me a second time, a partially eaten dried fig fell from the side of his long, jagged-toothed snout. He's eaten all the winter supplies, I thought. I began to yell like a raven whose nest has just been robbed and moved my legs like a Cossack dancer. If he doesn't eat me, what shall I eat for the winter?

The *hootz* growled, turned his eyes away from me, and lumbered into the forest. When I saw his huge backside disappear into the trees, I sat down on the slightly pitched cabin roof, my heart pounding louder than the noise of the river. I looked out over the beach and saw all Miss Emily's dresses strewn in the salmonberry bushes. Then I noticed that the canoe was gone.

After half an hour, the *hootz* had not returned. I climbed down the pole ladder and walked slowly toward the door. Had Mr. York and Miss Emily gone off in the canoe before the *hootz* had come, or had the canoe just come unmoored and floated away downriver? Slowly I looked through the cabin door and into the one-room house. The silk wallpaper hung in tatters, and pieces of every shelf, barrel, and canister lay strewn like kindling across the floor. I kicked at the rubble. No bodies.

But there was no food left from Mr. York's well-filled larder either. As I began to sift through the debris, I wondered if Mr. York and Miss

Emily would return or if they had abandoned their cabin and me to go back to America. Surely Mr. York wouldn't leave all his belongings behind him, I told myself. But I remembered that I wasn't at all acquainted with the customs of Americans, and perhaps it was just their way to desert their possessions without a word of good-bye.

It took me two days to straighten up the remains of Mr. York's belongings. At night I built a large fire in the fire hole and an even larger fire outside on the river rocks so that the *hootz* would not return. After a fortnight, Mr. York had still not reappeared. I was sure that he had abandoned me, and by Russian law I was a free person. Freedom. I turned the word over and over in my mouth, feeling the strength of the river current flow through my hands. But my heart darkened when I wondered what I would eat all during the long winter. The *hootz* had consumed almost everything, except for the dried salmon in the food cache.

After I gathered Miss Emily's garments together and packed them into the trunks, I decided to make my first visit to the Tlingit Village of the Raven. Perhaps, if Mr. York didn't return, they would allow me to live with them for the winter.

As I walked through the dew-covered ferns along the banks of Indian River, I was conscious of Kat-lee-an following me. After walking upriver for a mile, I sat down near a red huckleberry bush that grew in the stump of a cedar tree and waited for him to come out into the open.

"Do you follow me wherever I go?" I asked, when he'd finally crept out from behind the veil-like branches of a hemlock tree. "Do you?" I said using all the Tlingit inflection that I could muster.

"No," he said, as if I had insulted him. "Many fish to get for winter." He gestured toward the few silver humpback salmon still trudging upriver. "Must go soon to Yakutat Bay for hair seals. Long journey, almost to land of Aleut people. Hair seals leave our waters. Sea Spirit angry." When he narrowed his slanted eyes, the tar streaks of his face paint looked like the whiskers of an angry she-wolf. "Come to Raven Village?" he asked, extending his hand in the direction of his tribal home.

"Yes," I said, watching his black lidless eyes—almost as black as his long, braided hair. "Yes," I said again, realizing that my heart warmed to this tall, strong-fisted warrior.

He went ahead along the trail, leading me into a clearing in the center of which was a twenty-foot raven totem pole marking the entrance to his village. The huge black-and-aquamarine-painted raven face looked down at me with piercing red eyes, the totem bird's large blunt beak like a caricature of Kat-lee-an's nose.

The Village of the Raven looked very much as I had remembered it: clusters of small log and bark huts with cedar-shake roofs and small animal totems atop ten-foot poles in front of the huts of the tribal elders and the houses of the dead. Everywhere I looked, men and women dressed in bark and deerskin clothing were preparing their narrow ax-hewed canoes for the journey north to Yakutat Bay. Nobody paid much attention to us as Kat-lee-an led me to the house of the most revered of the tribal elders, his mother's sister, Mother-of-Stories.

Small, gray-haired, and more gaunt than I remembered her, she sat on the floor of her house, holding the warp of an unfinished basket between her teeth. It was a large basket, probably to hold seal oil, and the bindings were tight and close together.

"For three months I make basket," she said, her voice as powerful as the tales of Kat-lee-an's Russian massacres. "People of Village say you live near us. I wait long time for you, Small-Lake." Her large dark eyes looked me up and down. "You grow like fawn," she added, her almost toothless smile shining into my face.

"Thank you," I said, sitting down beside her on a sealskin. Kat-lee-an left the hut without even giving me a good-bye with his eyes.

"Small-Lake not with Russian schoolmaster?" Mother-of-Stories asked.

"No," I said and told her how Gospozha Karimoff had sold me to an American, Noah York. I didn't tell her that perhaps I had gained my freedom and needed supplies for the winter.

"Many Boston men here," she said. For a few moments, deep in meditation, she said nothing more. "What passes, Small-Lake?" she asked at last.

I told her that I'd learned to read and write three of the white man's languages but that I wasn't able to practice them, living with a master who never spoke.

"Days not good here," she said, her voice turning raspy and moving like wind through her few cracked teeth. "White man bring sickness. Smallpox, influenza, typhoid they name it. No cure. Before white man, no sickness. Since last salmon run, ten die, even Kat-lee-an's mate. The sick, they go to sweat out the white-devil illness in hot springs of our people near river to the south. But when they return to our village, they die." I remembered the hot sulfur-smelling mud which bubbled from out of the ground sixteen Russian *versts* to the south of New Archangel.

"Kat-lee-an follows me in the woods and watches me," I said.

"He lonely, he not married long. Why Small-Lake not have mate?" she asked.

I avoided her stare, knowing she wouldn't understand the white man's beliefs about touching and soiling and how no man would ask for me. "I must find my mother before I marry," I said. If Mr. York did not return, I could stow away on next spring's first southbound California ice ship in search of Woman-Always-Wondering's island. "Besides," I added, "whoever wants to marry me will have to buy me from Noah York. And money's scarce among the colonists, just as scarce as the fur animals." Then I remembered the pale-haired American surveyors and their wild tale of stringing wires from the ice fields of the north to Moscow. "Of course," I said, "there are the Boston men with many bags of silver."

Mother-of-Stories narrowed her black leaf-shaped eyes and rocked back on her haunches. "I have no word of Woman-Always-Wondering," she said as if she could read my thoughts. But then, seeing the sadness that passed over my face, she added, "Tlingit from Village of Raven jouney soon to Yakutat Bay. Many seals there. Many Indian nations. Kat-lee-an will listen for stories of Small-Lake's mother. I will ask it of him."

"Oh, thank you, thank you, Old Mother."

"Come to me again," she said, as if she didn't want me to leave, "before days of moon return. Bring yellow moss to me. Moss good dye for basket design. I old, not walk far. Amber moss grow on river near Small-Lake's house. You come soon?" she asked insistently.

"Yes," I said. Even if my master returned to his cabin, I vowed to visit the Village of the Raven with or without his permission. If he did not return, I would ask Mother-of-Stories to allow me to live among the Tlingits. I breathed a sigh of relief at my plan, glad that I would neither have to live alone in Mr. York's cabin on short winter rations nor work as a servant girl in New Archangel.

"Kat-lee-an," said Mother-of-Stories, touching my arm, "he not harm Small-Lake." She rose slowly to her feet and walked toward a stack of blankets in the corner of her hut. Reaching underneath the bottom hand-woven goat's-wool blanket, she gave me a small beaded basket no larger than my palm. It was covered with aquamarine glass trading beads that the Russians had used to buy land from the Tlingits. "Is basket of northern lights," she said. "Northern lights above white mountains."

I took the basket and secured it under my waistband. "Thank you," I said, feeling warm inside. No one had ever given me anything so nice. It must have taken her months to make such a basket. "Thank you, Mother-of-Stories. I'll come to you again before the dark night skies return."

I had walked out of her hut and past the totem pole with the raven crest at the top of it when she called me back. "Take care, Small-Lake. Shaman of Raven Village say that before salmon run upriver again many in Sitka will die," she said, calling New Archangel by its Indian name, *In This Place*. "Young warriors talk. Say Sea Spirit in *kekoor* rock angry; few fish, no seals, no deer people, no otter people." She drew me close. "Stay out of Sitka when sky is dark, Small-Lake," she whispered. Then she clasped me with her bony hands and looked at me up and down. "Woman-Always-Wondering brave woman. Russian shamans told her not feed Small-Lake; punish Small-Lake, they say. Child of devil, they say. Russian shamans come to Woman-Always-Wondering, four-five together. She not yield. Small-Lake now is brave like mother," said the old woman. "Remember, Indians are Small-Lake's people."

As I walked back downriver toward Noah York's cabin, nibbling sweet-sour huckleberries that I plucked from the tall bushes, my spirits were as bright as the sun on the ice crater of Mount Saint Lazaria. Why, I asked myself, had I waited so many months to go to the Village of the Raven? The Tlingits were my people. They were the only ones who had ever been kind to me, who were concerned for my life. I was so elated that I didn't care if Mr. York did come back to his cabin or if Miss Emily yelled at me. If Mr. York hasn't returned within another fortnight, I told myself, I'll harvest the kitchen garden and take the dried fish from the food cache and go live among the Tlingits.

While I walked along the riverbank, I tried skimming stones along the water, sometimes pausing to watch the salmon rest in a deep pool, hiding in the shadow of a fallen log. As I rounded the bend in the river near the cabin, my head jerked up. Noise. Someone was stacking lumber.

My heart sank as I saw that Mr. York had not only returned but brought with him a load of wooden planks from the sawmill in New Archangel. My freedom's gone, I thought, the disappointment running in a sharp pain from my shoulder blades down my back. Wood for Miss Emily's new room, I supposed. But Miss Emily was nowhere in sight.

I stood quietly, like a deer in the forest when she knows a hunter is near. Perhaps Mr. York hasn't seen me and thinks I've run off for good. By Russian colonial law, the punishment for a servant's deserting his master was a week's flogging without food and water, but still I thought of slipping away, back to the Indian village.

"Nadia," called Mr. York, spotting me on the trail. At the sound of my name, my stomach felt as if I'd been socked by one of my Russian classmates at the Mission Fathers' school. "Nadia," he called again, as I slowly approached the cabin, "prepare some food."

"For how many?" I wondered if Miss Emily had returned with another servant more to her liking.

"You have eyes, girl," he said, an angry tone in his voice. "How many do you count?"

I looked among the piles of wood, but I didn't see Mr. York's bride-to-be or a new servant girl anywhere. "A bear ate most of your supplies," I said. He did not respond. "What about Miss Emily?"

"Miss Gore and I have severed our engagement." He pulled a plank down from one of the stacks of wood, then looked up, not at my face but at the bodice of my dress.

Lifting my arm, I shielded my breasts from his Russian-priest-like stare. "Small-Lake," my mother once told me, "when a warrior comes upon his enemy, he puts the blue flame of a winter fire around him like the thick hair of a *hootz*, holds his cedar war shield over his stomach, and looks into the enemy's eyes before they look into his. If the warrior does this," my mother said, "no one can steal his spirit out of his body."

"Stop looking at me," I demanded, feeling the power of the river current surge into my hands. Mr. York's face flushed. And although I knew that in the Russian colonies the penalty for striking one's master was flogging or disfigurement—the loss of an ear or a nose—I also knew that if this man touched me the Indian warrior within my spirit would overwhelm my sense of servitude.

Mr. York took a step toward me. Feeling the strange magic that grew inside of me swell into an imaginary cedar shield, I looked my master straight in the eye, knowing that if he touched me, I would strike him with the power of a giant spruce tree felled by an avalanche.

6.

Mr. York took a step backward, shifting his eyes to one side, then focusing them on my bodice again.

"If you hurt me," I said, like a warrior aiming his spear, "I'll wish you dead and the bear will eat you."

My master's cheeks flushed as red as his hair. "Go into the cabin, Nadia," he said, in a voice that pretended nothing had happened, "and fix me some nourishment."

As I walked past him toward the log house it was as if the white water of Indian River ran down my spine. It was true what the Russian priests had said about my mother. She was a witch . . . and so was I. And it would be this witch-shaman magic growing within me that would keep me safe from Mr. York—for a while, anyway.

Inside the cabin I skinned the rabbit he'd shot that morning and began to roll out dough for a pie. Speaking to one's master in such a way was punishable by flogging, but somehow I didn't believe that Mr. York would beat me as Gospozha Karimoff had. No, I thought, pondering my recent encounter with Noah York, my master wouldn't beat me. What he wanted wasn't a battle but merely the thought of a hunt. Indeed, my new master was a man of thoughts, not of actions. I spread the piecrust dough across the table, then raised the rolling pin above my head, pretending to be a Tlingit warrior. Yes, I, Small-Lake-Underneath, had spoken bravely. I owned no property except my body, and I had defended it against the eyes and thoughts of my master.

When the meal was prepared, Mr. York sat down at the table, hunched over his bowl of rabbit pot pie as if he had no strength in his body. I busied myself darning our woolen clothing in preparation for the coming winter, watching him between each stitch. My master's eyes were downcast, and for the first time since his return I noticed that they were red around the lids from crying. I began to feel sorry for him, almost regretting that I'd threatened him with my magic.

"We've severed our engagement," Mr. York repeated. "Miss Gore is no longer interested in my plans or being a part of them with me. . . ." The last part of his sentence trailed away as he dropped his spoon with a clank into the empty bowl.

"What's the new lumber for?" I asked, afraid to ask why Miss Emily had fled Mr. York and Alaska. Perhaps, I imagined, he had tried his touchings out on her just as he had commanded me to touch myself. Clasping my hand over my mouth, I stifled a laugh as I pictured Miss Emily's eyes blaze like the eternal fires of hell into which she knew that she would fall if she committed such a deed. Miss Emily's a toucher, Miss Emily's a toucher. I giggled to myself, remembering the sing-songs of my schoolgirl days.

"I like this country," Mr. York said in a tired voice. "I'm going to build a bigger house farther up on the riverbank. Of course," he said with a faraway look in his eyes, "the whole project will take several years to complete, but I want to get the frame up before winter sets in." He paused, then helped himself to another bowl of rabbit pie.

"Are the elderberries ripe yet?" he asked in a childlike voice.

"Yes," I said, putting down my darning, "they're almost past their prime."

"I told you I wanted a red elderberry pie," he said, "and you forgot."

"Red elderberries will make you sick," I said in my teacher's voice. "The birds won't eat them, and the Indians only use them in their medicines."

"A pie," he commanded, the strength of a grown man returning to his voice. He got up from the table and went outside, and I could hear his ax splitting wood as he raved at the imagined image of his father:

"Papa, when will you admit . . . you've always hated me?" The ringing of the ax echoed across the rocks of Indian River. "Always abroad collecting bits of money. Ma-*ma*'s days were filled with waiting for you. . . . She hardly noticed that I was there. And her dying breath: 'Hemstead, Hemstead York.'" He was sobbing now. "You weren't even there to hear it."

My body went rigid as I tried to blot out the noise of his monologue. The red elderberry pie, I thought. Does he want this pie because he wants to defy the harsh northern elements as he wants to defy his father? Perhaps that's why this strange man has come to Alaska, not only to disobey his father's wishes for him to become a lawyer and a collector of money, but to escape a world where he thought himself doomed to failure. But, I sighed, taking a deep breath of the damp moldy-smelling air, when Noah York doesn't encounter failure, he commands it as he has commanded me to make him a poison elderberry pie.

It took me almost an entire morning to pick a basket of those little red berries. And picking the stems off took even longer. In the end it was a pie fine enough to take to the Russian All Souls' Day feast. I'd never eaten any of those berries. Everyone knew that they were poison. Anyway, I thought, if Mr. York eats this pie, he'll be too ill to think of forcing himself on me for at least a week. And even if he ate the whole dessert in one sitting, it wouldn't prove fatal, because I'd mixed red huckleberries in with the poison ones.

A vision of Kat-lee-an seal-hunting at Yakutat Bay flashed in front of me as Mr. York eyed the red elderberry pie admiringly and cut himself a large slice.

"Tomorrow," he said, "we'll go up the mountain together, Nadia, and pick gallons of berries. I want to make a store of that Indian liquor everyone talks about—hooch, I think they call it."

But the next day Mr. York was horribly sick. His face was even paler than usual, and his stomach and bowels were in a terrible confusion. Late in the afternoon I had to move him, staggering like a drunkard, outside with his blankets and cot so that I could clean up the stench inside the cabin. He moaned and looked at me with sad, seal-pup eyes.

It took my master more than a week to recover his strength. In the meantime the river shrank as it always did in late summer, leaving salmon aground and dying on the dry rocks. The ravens and the sea gulls were everywhere, pecking out fish eyes even before the salmon were dead. Then the whole river canyon began to smell and the water wasn't fit to drink. I had to walk with buckets upstream to the tributary where I'd first encountered Kat-lee-an to get water for the cabin. It took me half the day, and my master was in no shape to help me. Maybe now Noah York will heed my warnings, I thought, but somehow I doubted it.

While my master was still recuperating and unable to keep track of my comings and goings, I walked upriver to the Village of the Raven. I had gathered a flour sack full of amber moss to give to Mother-of-Stories, the moss she needed to make her basket dye. As I walked along the shrunken riverbank, I imagined her soaking the shafts of dry grass in a wooden bowl of moss and water until the grass turned bright yellow and could be woven into patterns like the many-sided figures I once drew in my geometry lessons.

Except for the totem faces atop the tall poles in front of the bark and log houses of the tribal elders, the Village of the Raven was almost empty. I walked past the sealskin doors of the huts until I found Mother-of-Stories sitting near a fire pit, stirring red and green dyes for recoloring the totem poles. A wrinkled old man, the village woodcarver, sat near her, carving the head of an animal into the trunk of a felled cedar tree with a beaver-tooth chisel.

"Small-Lake," Old Mother said with delight, her slanted eyes smiling up at me. "It makes the Sea Spirit happy that you have come." I sat down on the thatched rug beside her and watched the old woodcarver whittle the eyes of a bird into the tree trunk.

"Totem pole of Kat-lee-an," she said. My heart flinched at the mention of the young chief's name. "Not yet return from land-of-ice-in-the-sea," she said, as if she could speak the language of my body. I kept my eyes fixed on the cedar log, afraid of what Mother-of-Stories would read in them. Each totem pole told the story of a family history, and each animal, one on top of the other, told how the family of one crest had come into contact with the family of another.

"Story of my grandmothers," she said, gesturing toward the wood-carver and naming the family totems that would appear on Kat-lee-an's pole: the raven, the frog, the killer whale, and at the bottom the fog symbol—a mother with two children, one the spring growth and the other the salmon fish. Mother-of-Stories was the matrilineal elder of her tribe, and after Kat-lee-an it would always be her grandchildren or her sister's grandchildren who would lead the Village of the Raven.

"How go Small-Lake's days?" she asked, showing me her newly woven seal-oil basket.

"They're long and filled with work, Old Mother," I said, admiring the tight weave of the gallon-sized half sphere. "The water in the river isn't fit to drink and I have to carry it in buckets from the mountain creeks."

"Ah," she said, "now there is terrible sickness from river water." She rose from beside the fire pit, hobbled into her hut, and returned with her medicine basket. "Take this," she said, handing me a swan's-foot pouch. "If you get sickness-of-the-river, eat what is in this."

"But what is it?" I asked, looking at the red powder inside the webbed-foot pouch.

"Many things—fish eyes, beaver blood, wet-of-beaver-mouth, skunk urine. I make it in spring," she said, "mixed in cedar bowl and dried in sun near black-hole-in-the-earth where tar comes from."

I held a pinch of the powdery medicine between my fingers. "Old Mother," I said suddenly, "I have magic like my mother, Woman-Always-Wondering. Sometimes I feel the power of the river during a spring flood inside my hands. And when I wish things," I said, my voice rising with excitement, "sometimes these wishes happen, almost."

Mother-of-Stories put down her seal-oil basket and held my shoulders. "Small-Lake," she said, "do not speak of this magic to Boston men. Do not speak of it to anyone."

"I don't have it all the time," I continued. "Just sometimes."

"It grows," she said. "Use magic wisely. Never harm that which will not harm Small-Lake. Magic will grow as Small-Lake grows."

For a long time she sat looking at me. I wanted to ask her about Kat-lee-an, to tell her that often during the day his sharp-featured, dark-skinned face would flash in front of me. But I knew that she could read my thoughts, so I said nothing.

"Much noise at house of Small-Lake," she said after a long silence.

"Yes, my American master is building a great house."

"Ah," she said, "many *cheechakoes* come to land of Tlingit. Old ones' stories say Indian not first people to come to Sitka. People with yellow skin in land-of-ice-in-the-sea, they not first people either. Tlingits, Eskimos, Aleuts, Russians, Boston men—many tribes come and go like birds." She looked into my eyes and began to stroke my arm. "Beware, Small-Lake. I listen to noise-in-the-ground. I hear many wars. New tribes will come bringing new wars." She took a deep breath, her eyes following the woodcarver's knotted hand as he whittled the giant face of a raven into the bark-stripped cedar log. "Kat-lee-an will carve war canoes, *kladushu etlan,* all winter long," she said. "Many foreign hunters on Tlingit land now. *Cheechakoes* with traps. White hunters catch men in traps, make terrible noise in forest. I listen to noise-in-the-ground. Noise of winter storm below Great Land."

As the sun began to set behind the tall mountain peaks, I walked slowly back to the cabin. Before I left, Mother-of-Stories said that when the seal hunters returned from Yakutat Bay there would be a great potlatch and that I was invited. "Before first frost," she said. "Come when you hear sound of elk-skin drum."

As Noah York's cabin came into view, I wondered how many more days it would be before he recovered from his poison pie and would again look at me with lust in his eyes. Perhaps I should just consent to be his concubine, I mused. But what if he gave me a child? I would have to buy my child's freedom as well. The face of Kat-lee-an flashed in front of me, his raven nose silhouetted against the cone-shaped mountains. He would return soon from seal-hunting, perhaps bringing news of my mother. I closed my eyes and wished that Kat-lee-an with his large cedar war canoe would take me from

Mr. York to the islands of the British colonies in search of Woman-Always-Wondering.

The next day my master was able to help me carry the rotting salmon from the riverbed up to the garden for use as fertilizer. Most of the fish were half eaten by either sea gulls or bears. We buried the fish along the furrows and rows, digging shallow graves with our hands, crawling along the ground. As we did so, I noticed which patches of garden had flourished more than others. These were the places where I had bled my monthly blood into the ground, the way I'd once seen my mother bleed into the earth. I wanted to point to the tallest onions in the garden and proudly tell Mr. York about nourishing the ground with womanblood. He might want to write about it in his leather-bound notebook, I thought, but I remained silent for fear of arousing his lustful eyes. I remembered how I had once bled on Gospozha's dahlia bulbs and how she had discovered me, becoming hysterical and flogging me about the head and chest before she locked me in my room for a week.

I looked down at the onions I'd planted a month after Mr. York had brought me to his cabin. Their bulbous roots pushed through the top of the soil and were ready to harvest. Mr. York pulled them up and shook the dirt from the roots while I began braiding the stems into chains so that the onions could be dried hanging from the walls of the food cache.

"Why were you taken from your mother?" my master asked, speaking for the first time since his sickness.

"It's a long story," I said, thinking that it would bore him.

"I want to hear it." He handed me more onions to braid. "I like stories," he said in his schoolboy voice.

"Well," I said, "the Mission Fathers once built a church just for the Tlingits. The Russian priests were always trying to convert the Indians, but they wouldn't let the Tlingits go to church with the Russian settlers. The settlers were too afraid of getting jumped and knifed to death by the Indians during mass. So the Fathers built the Tlingits their own special church near the cemetery in back of the stockade."

"I never saw this church," said Mr. York. "Where is it, near the blockhouses?"

"It was," I said. "The Indians have a terrible grudge against the Russians for building the Castle on top of the Home-of-Spirits, and they saw a chance for revenge when the Fathers allowed them to come and go freely to their little church, built near where the white people lived. One night about eight years ago, a band of young warriors camped inside the church and attacked the villagers at dawn when the sentries opened the stockade gates." Mr. York raised his eyebrows, and for a minute I thought he was going to run to the cabin for his leather-bound notebook.

"Ha," he said, "guerrilla warfare, beat at their own game. It was the Russians, you know, who invented that sort of fighting when Napoleon's army stormed across Europe to Moscow. . . . And the people in New Archangel never suspected a thing?" he asked.

"Nothing," I said, putting down my onion chain and beginning another. "Everyone was horrified when they saw the Tlingits in their black tar warpaint and war masks. The noise of the Indian war drum alone caused some of the more fragile noblewomen to faint, I'm told. But I lived with my mother in the Tlingit village then, not in New Archangel. The priests said that somehow the Indians got hold of their cannon and turned it on the colonists. The Indians even cannonballed the gold statue of Saint Michael the Archangel in the inner sanctuary of the Russian church."

"How many were killed?" asked my master, always interested in numbers and measurements.

"Many, but I don't know how many. And in the end the Indians burned down their little church."

"So why were you taken from your mother?" he asked again, sounding as if he was bored with my story because I couldn't tell him the exact numbers of the warriors and the dead.

"The Russian Fathers had a meeting," I said, braiding another strong-smelling onion stem into my chain. "They decided that retaliatory action had to be taken. The Tlingits had to be shown that they couldn't get away with killing Christians and burning churches. At first the priests condemned all Tlingits to hell, but the Indians don't put much stake in the white man's hell. They can't imagine what's so terrible about fire. Fires keep them warm. So the priests decided that for every Russian killed they would take a Tlingit child in return."

"And they came and took you?" Mr. York shook the dirt from a large onion.

"No, not at first. The problem was that none of the Russians wanted to go into the Tlingit village and take away their children for fear of more acts of retribution. I was the only part-white child living with the Tlingits at the time, and the priests said that because my father had been Russian I was the property of their church. But my mother wouldn't give me up. So the church fathers waited until most of the Tlingit hunters had gone north seal-hunting and then came and stole me from my mother's hut."

I felt my throat tighten and couldn't go on with my story. As the aroma of fresh onions filled the air, I wanted to tell Mr. York about the weeks after I'd been taken away from my mother. How the priests kept me inside the House of Bishops, the large log building where the Russian Fathers lived, to cleanse me. I wouldn't utter a sound, and to make me speak to them, the fathers put candles under my fingertips until I cried out. In the end Professor Karimoff took me home to be his servant girl and his great experiment.

"Your mother," Mr. York said, "I've forgotten her name—she was a Haida, was she not?"

"Woman-Always-Wondering," I answered. "Yes, a Haida from the islands to the south of here near the Oregon Territories."

He repeated my mother's name several times. "How I love the sound of it! Have you ever been to her island?"

"No, but I'm sure I'll find my mother and her tribe someday." I closed my mouth, regretting what I had just said. I certainly didn't want my master to know that I was planning to run away.

"Perhaps we could go there . . . together," he said, laying down his onion and beginning to stroke my arm. "When things get settled here," he added, glancing at my thighs.

"Could we?" I was so surprised at his suggestion that I hardly minded his touching me. Was this man trying to tell me that if I became his concubine he'd help me find my mother's island?

Silently I stared up at the narrow two-hundred-foot hemlock trees, contemplating Mr. York's proposition. I was his slave girl. He could take advantage of me if he wanted to, but for some reason he had not. Was it for a religious reason? No, I mused, Mr. York didn't even own a Bible. Was he afraid of failing, as he had with Miss Emily? Probably not, I told myself; failure seemed to be what Mr. York thrived upon. So what is it that this man wants from me?

Suddenly I felt a terrible dizziness. Too much smell of the onions and the thought of Noah York touching me again, I guessed. But as I walked back to the cabin my head began to ache and my body felt as if I'd been crushed in an avalanche. And as I climbed up into the food cache to hang the onion chains from the rafters, I was again overcome by the dizziness and almost lost my balance.

All night long I retched and in the morning felt no better.

"I've got to go to New Archangel to fetch some men to help me raise the poles of my new house," said Mr. York, shaking my cot to awaken me.

"I'm ill," I said. "Please don't leave me alone. I think I have the sickness-of-the-river."

"You're a strong girl, little Nadia," he said. "I'll be back by nightfall." I heard his canoe scrape over the river rocks and then fell asleep.

When I awoke the dizziness was worse and I felt cold to my bones even though the sun was shining. I'd never felt so sick. Then I remembered the swan's-foot pouch of medicine powder that Mother-of-Stories had given me. For some reason it took me a long time to find it. I couldn't make my way around the cabin, and it hurt my eyes to focus them.

Mr. York didn't come back that night as he had promised. My body ached terribly and I coughed for hours without stopping. Somehow, though, my sickness and my master's absence didn't concern me and everything became very gay and cheery. I looked out the small cabin window into the sun and laughed because the glowing ball looked so ridiculous sitting in the sky with nothing holding it up.

But even though I was lightheaded and laughing, I knew that the sickness-of-the-river was dangerous, that I'd die if I didn't eat and drink some water. I got up with all the blankets around me, knowing that I had to eat, but I couldn't find the supplies. And this too was humorous, because I knew that the cabin was filled with food and that the food was alive and hiding from me.

I could die from this sickness if no one comes to care for me, I thought. Maybe I should walk down to the river and wait for a boat. But even if a *promyshlennik* did pass by in a sealskin *bidarka*, I wouldn't have the energy to explain my predicament.

Looking out the window at the dark evergreen of Three Sisters Peaks, I collapsed on the floor. When I awoke, Mr. York had returned with another man, an American whom I'd never seen before. They both stood in the cabin doorway staring down at me. I got up, saying that I'd prepare a rabbit pie for them.

"She must be all right," said Mr. York to the tall yellow-haired man standing next to him, "she wants to cook." But I knew that I was contagiously ill, because Mr. York wouldn't come near me and the yellow-haired American made some excuse to leave immediately.

Suddenly the cabin floor leaped up into my face. Then Kat-lee-an appeared in front of me, dressed in a bearskin garment and a boar-horned chief's crown. He beat on a plate-shaped shaman drum with two moons and a killer whale painted on the outside of the tightly stretched elk skin and one moon painted in black tar on the inside. The Tlingits believe that the drum represents the entire world. Looking into the drum, I saw the face of my mother, her long red Haida hair undone from her shaman topknot and her breasts adorned with her necklace of salmon vertebrae and wolf-fang amulets. In her palms she held out water for me. "Drink," she said, her large dark slanted eyes imploring me to obey her.

When I awoke the dizziness and the terrible oppression inside my head had gone, but there was a chill in the damp air and I knew that it was well past summer. Mr. York stood above me, holding onto something which, when my eyes finally focused, I realized was my own hand. Looking down at myself, I hardly recognized the thing that lay under the blankets. I was so thin I didn't know my own body.

"You almost died of typhoid, Nadia," my master said.

"What day is it?" I asked, my voice sounding lifeless and strange to my ears.

"The eve of the eighteenth of October," he answered.

"October! *Ohhh,*" I moaned, not from my illness, as Mr. York thought, but because I had long missed the hunters returning from Yakutat Bay and the potlatch to which Mother-of-Stories had invited me. I tried to rise up on one elbow, but didn't have the strength.

"You're all dressed up," I said, noticing that my master was wearing the same clothes he had worn the first day I had laid eyes on him as he got off the *Calafia.* "You've been into New Archangel?" I asked, not expecting an answer.

"*Sitka,*" he said definitively. "They've renamed New Archangel *Sitka.*"

"What?" I asked in amazement. "The Russians have given their settlement its Indian name?"

"No, no," he said. "You're still very ill, you don't know what's happened. I've just come from the Transfer Ceremonies." He cleared his throat. "Your Czar sold Alaska to the Americans for seven million dollars. Of course, the colonists are outraged at their ruler for selling Russian soil to foreigners."

"You mean I've been sold again?" I asked, finding it difficult to understand what he was saying.

"Of course not. America is a democracy. We don't buy people. You're a 'citizen by purchase,'" he said. I gave him a confused look. "In America," he explained, "there are no slaves, not even savages. You're free to go on your way."

I sank back into my pillow. Free, I thought. The beginnings of an autumn gale were cold on my arm, and I didn't even have the strength to lift my head up on my elbow. Free. I put my hand across my eyes to make sure I wasn't dreaming. My fingers stretched across my face, temple to temple, then felt my scalp.

7.

"My hair," I wailed, looking into the ivory hand mirror that Miss Emily had left behind. I hardly recognized the frightful person whose face looked up at me from the glass. Her hair was only an inch long and growing like pine needles out from her head.

"You were delirious for nearly a month," said Mr. York, latching the cabin door against the howling southeast *saanah* rain-wind. "I had to go into Sitka and bring a doctor out here." His pale face flushed, either with concern or annoyance, I could not tell which.

"But what happened to my hair?" I sneaked a second glance into the mirror and immediately turned it upside down on my cot. I looked like a shorn dog, like the paintings that hung in the House of Bishops, pictures of early Russian colonists who were taken as slaves by the Tlingits and tortured.

Mr. York sat down at the table and began to sharpen an adz with a bluestone. "Doc Spencer, our new American physician at the settlement, said there wasn't much he could do for you. 'Keep a wet rag dripping into her mouth and another on her forehead,' he told me. Then he shaved your head so all that hair wouldn't keep the heat in. Fevers damage the brain, Nadia." Mr. York ran his finger across the sharp blade of the wooden-handled adz and then glanced at me but didn't look me full in the face.

He suspects I've turned into a half-wit because of the fever, I thought, remembering how I always watched Yuri's harelip out of the side of my vision, because Gospozha had said that it wasn't polite to stare at God's mistakes. Mr. York oiled his bluestone and pressed the blade against it, moving the tool in a circular motion. He was looking at me the way one looks at a freak.

Then I remembered that I had my freedom. Free. But where could I go and what could I do? Without provisions, I was a liability, even to the Tlingits. And who would hire a freak, a hairless girl who could barely sit up in bed? I began to wonder about the Americans. Would they be as strange as the Russians had been? My mother and the Indian people had had difficulty becoming aquainted with the Europeans' customs. In the Indian world, freaks were also people with special powers, usually shamans.

"And," said Mr. York, laying his axlike tool on the table, "when the fever didn't kill you some damned Indian almost did."

"What?" I asked in disbelief. "Why would an Indian try to kill me?"

"Yes," he said, resting his chin in his hand and finally looking me square in the face. "I saved your life. When I returned from giving

Doc Spencer a boat ride back into Sitka, there was an Indian in here. He was standing over you mumbling something, I don't know what, I couldn't hear. And when he saw me, he started shrieking worse than a madwoman—something that sounded like 'who got you, who got you,' over and over." Mr. York's words spilled out faster than a snowball rolling down Mount Saint Lazaria, and he gasped for air as he continued his story. "A tall, horribly ugly man who looked as if he was going to choke me with his bare hands, and there I was at the cabin door with my rifle back in the boat. Then for some reason the young savage ran past me and into the woods. Horribly ugly," said Mr. York again. "Black paint on his face and horns tied to his head. He would have killed you, Nadia, if I hadn't come back in time. I saved your life." He glared at me with cold gray eyes.

"Kat-lee-an," I said. "It was Kat-lee-an. The Indian we met on the trail. You remember. He's my friend. He meant me no harm." So Kat-lee-an really had come to see me, to my American master's house. Perhaps the young chief did care for me, I thought, feeling a new energy grow in my fever-drained limbs.

"He was about to murder you in your sickbed," said Mr. York in a positive tone. "He was screaming like a crazy woman." But seeing that I was unmoved by his story and purported heroism, Mr. York's mouth curled down and he began to pout like a spoiled child.

"'White man's witchery,' that's what Kat-lee-an was saying," I told Mr. York, ignoring his mood. So he wants me to think him a hero, this American does. Well, I thought stubbornly, I'll have nothing of his invented bravery. This behavior is well enough for the children at the Russian Fathers' school, but not for an adult creature of the woods. "'White man's witchery.' Kat-lee-an meant me no harm," I said with a stiff lip. "He probably thought you were punishing me by cutting off my hair."

"You must at least thank me for nursing you," Mr. York commanded. "I could have turned you out into this terrible autumn wind and rain."

"The Indians call it the *saanah*." I pretended not to hear his threat. If Mr. York could make believe that things didn't happen, so could I.

"I'll give you a few weeks to recover your strength." He got up from his chair and took hold of the adz. "Then you owe me a lot of work."

Turning his back to me, he put on his black-tarred rain cape and walked out into the weather to work on his new house.

I touched my emaciated legs and arms. If Mr. York turns me out before I'm strong again, no bear would ever bother eating my meatless body, I thought, trying to console myself. Then I lay down and covered my head with a blanket. Kat-lee-an, I'm free, I whispered. And as I drifted into sleep, I dreamed that the young Tlingit took me to live with his tribe.

I don't remember that Sitka had ever had such a cold winter. But maybe it was because I was living a few feet from Indian River, with its chilly mist rising up into the rain each morning. There wasn't much work to do inside Mr. York's cabin. A good thing, too, because when I finally got up from my sickbed I could only take a few steps before I'd tire and want to lay my head down. I didn't dare go outside, even though my heart yearned to go to the Village of the Raven to show Kat-lee-an and Mother-of-Stories that I wasn't dead or bedeviled by the white man's doctors.

During the next few months, each time I swept the cabin with my pine-limb broom I would have to remind myself that I had my freedom, the freedom I had long dreamed of. But I didn't feel free, I thought with disappointment. I felt like the same servant girl that Mr. York had bought from Gospozha Karimoff for a bag of silver. Then I would think of Kat-lee-an, and when I daydreamed that I, Small-Lake-Underneath, had a suitor, my heart filled with excitement.

No one ever came for Miss Emily's trunks. They sat outside in the winter rain, next to the south wall of the cabin. Mr. York told me that I could have their contents, articles of such finery that they were almost worthless to someone living in a log hut. But down at the bottom of the largest trunk there was a book of American cookery and novels like the ones Gospozha had forbidden me to read, saying that ladylike girls didn't do such things with their learning. I read the novels, *Ruth* and *Jane Eyre,* stories about servant girls like myself. With every leap of their hearts, it was as if I, not these characters on the book pages, was in love with a strange and powerful man. Kat-lee-an—my days were filled with the memory of his tar-streaked high-cheekboned face.

After the icicles had grown about two feet from the eaves of the cabin, and a light snow lay on the evergreen slopes of Mount Saint Lazaria, my hair was long enough so that it lay down flat and could be parted on one side. I looked at my face in Miss Emily's hand mirror. I still looked like a freak, like the pictures of beggars in Moscow. Good thing, though, because Mr. York didn't like freaks. Since my illness he hadn't once looked at me with lust in his eyes.

Propping the mirror up on the kitchen shelf, I tied one of Miss Emily's fancy silk scarves around my head to keep it warm, all the time pretending that those long silk ties were really my hair hanging down my back. I looked at my still yellowish complexion in the mirror. Grow, hair, grow, I whispered, imagining each individual hair elongating under the scarf. Then I remembered my magic and wondered if the sickness-of-the-river had taken it away. If I still have my magic, I thought, maybe it will make my hair grow down to my waist again before a year is out.

I'd never seen so much snow fall at Sitka Bay, four or five feet instead of just one or two. The Sea Spirit must be angry at the Americans. Outside the tiny cabin window it began to look like the stories of the land-of-ice-in-the-sea, hundreds of miles to the north. Mr. York was starting to feel the elements, too, and spent most of the daytime reading nature books and writing in his leather-bound journal. As I swept the cabin, now and then I'd look up from my pine-branch broom, staring at the fire-headed American whom I'd never again have to call "master." But who shall I work for and what shall I do? I wondered, looking out the small cabin window into the dead of winter.

"What's it like now that the Americans have taken over New Archangel?" I asked Mr. York while I stoked the fire. With a shudder I remembered the Seattle chamberlain of the American President, who, when a band of young Indians attacked a sentry, burned down his own offices and all the homes around it, just to incinerate five Indians. Would this same man be sent to New Archangel to keep the peace?

"The United States Navy is quartered in the Baranov Castle now," said Mr. York, looking up from his book, *Wild Edible Plants of North America*. "The officers are bunked up in the Castle chambers, and the troops are busy keeping the new curfew inside the stockade. Seems like there's trouble concerning the Russians' relinquishing their rights to the town, and"—he eyed me scornfully—"those haughty Russian women don't seem to take to our boys in uniform."

What Mr. York means, I told myself, is that *this* haughty Russian-Indian hasn't taken to him. Well, if he wants my sympathies, he'll have to come up with a better wound than that.

"Does the Navy have celebrations in the grand ballroom?" I asked, putting a cast-iron caldron of soup over the fire hole. "What do the uniforms of the American navy generals look like? Do they have gold and silver buttons on their jackets like the Cossacks?"

"Brass," he said in a flat tone. "We call the military 'brass' back home." He closed one book and opened another, a book on birds by John Audubon. "Rumor has it that the troops are using the ballroom as a rollerskating rink. They're all pretty homesick. Not even allowed to tip the bottle and ease their pain—Washington outlawed the sale of alcohol, you know. Yes, it seems that liquor trading with the local Indians has turned the Tlingits into bloodsuckers."

"Washington?"

"Where we Americans make our laws—analogous to the Russians' Moscow. But of course Congress forgot to outlaw the importation of molasses, and about ten taverns have opened along the Governor's Walk. I hear they're more crowded than a church on Sunday."

"Tavern?" I asked. These Americans had many new words that Professor Karimoff had not taught me.

"Where they sell liquor in a drinking glass," he answered. "A sort of public gathering place. Ah." He took a deep breath. "The boom is on. There's a hundred new Americans in Sitka, and the taste of adventure is in the air. One fellow from the States, Barney O'Ragan, has a tavern and newspaper office set up in a tent. Calls it *The Sitka Times* and hand-writes it himself once a week—mainly just advertisements for contraband liquor."

"But why are there so many navy men?" I asked, stirring the fish soup with a wooden ladle. "Surely there can't be that many Russians left to govern in New Arch—I mean, Sitka."

"General Davis told me that there's trouble with the Indians," Mr. York replied, as he wrote notes in his leather journal. "Seems the Tlingits have themselves a young stud chief who's all fired up and blood-thirsty as hell. The troops are building a stronger stockade and waiting for a fresh shipment of rifles."

The rain-wind blew through the trees' limbs and battered the cabin door.

"A bloodthirsty chief?" I stammered. Kat-lee-an, the Indian we met on the trail, I started to say, and then closed my mouth as if I had suddenly told a terrible secret. Was Kat-lee-an planning to massacre the new American rulers? Mother-of-Stories had told me that he'd spend all winter carving *kladushu etlan,* war canoes six fathoms long. Kat-lee-an. The name went around inside my head, and suddenly I felt a terrible division inside my body. I couldn't tell a word of what I knew of the Tlingits to this man, this American book reader, Mr. York. I couldn't be unfaithful to my people. But would the Tlingits still consider me one of them? Or was I an enemy, bedeviled by the Americans' medicine, my hair cut off and the strength of my body gone? A cold chill ran down my back. Things had changed so much in the three months since I'd seen them. Suddenly it seemed that the Tlingits' very lives depended upon my silence. I vowed not to speak another word of the Tlingits to Mr. York or anyone in Sitka.

As the weeks of long nights wore on, I had a terrible craving to see Kat-lee-an, to tell him about the soldiers and the new load of guns that Mr. York had said was due any day. But, I told myself, Kat-lee-an was one of the strongest people I knew, Indian or white, and taller than most. Why did I have such a fierce notion to protect him? I had never felt this way about anyone else.

Although the snow was heavy on the ground, I took short walks each day to get my strength back, walking farther and farther each time—now into the spruce forest and then to the meadow where the dead squirreltail grass shone with ice and hoarfrost. Mr. York and I both wore four-dollar Hudson's Bay blankets made into coats, and he had even talked of buying ermine skins for me to line the blankets with. When he wasn't working on his grand two-story log house, Mr. York left early in the morning, taking the canoe. To go into Sitka for ermine skins, I thought at first, but each night he'd return without supplies. When I asked him where he'd been, he never answered me.

Perhaps he has a new sweetheart, I thought, and goes off to court her every day.

Each night I lay awake, listening to the *saanah* wind rattle the branches in the spruce forest and thinking of Kat-lee-an. Always I could hear Mr. York on the other side of the fire hole touching himself, his breath coming hard and fast. Then I would fall asleep and dream, night after night, that Kat-lee-an and I were adrift in a canoe, the boat rising and falling over the crest of each wave. Sometimes in my dream it would be night and the only light was the phosphorescent white of the water breaking on the beach and the white of Kat-lee-an's eyes. He would chant, *cultus coly*, aimless journey, *cultus coly*, over and over. And, although the shore of Sitka Bay and Baranof Island was but a few yards away and there was a paddle on the floor of the canoe, we sat adrift forever watching the waves.

When I was feeling stronger I went for longer walks, almost to the Village of the Raven, hoping that Kat-lee-an would follow me as he had done so often last summer. He's waiting for me behind the next tree, I would tell myself, but I never saw him watching me in the frozen woods. Perhaps he was busy with the gathering of Tlingit tribes, planning their strategy against the new American rulers.

One January night I attempted a cobbler made of dried imported pears, Mr. York's favorite. He'd planted a small orchard of pear and apple trees last spring, saying that they'd bear fruit in a few years' time. Fresh fruit was hard to come by in Alaska; even shriveled fruit imported from California or China was rare.

"Nadia," said Mr. York, eating the cobbler as he sipped the hooch we'd made from wild salmonberries. "I told you three months ago that you're not my property any more. I estimate that I've gotten a bag of silver's work from you, probably more. So you'd best be thinking about being on your way."

I was almost shocked to speechlessness. It was the dead of winter, the worst winter I'd ever seen. Where did this man expect me to go? I hadn't a gold or silver piece to my name, not now or ever.

"But where shall I go?" I asked, hoping that he would remember he had once talked of taking me in search of my mother's island. "I can't work in Sitka," I said in a small voice. "I'm not at all acquainted with the American *cheechakoes* and their ways."

"There's a good number of Russians still living there," he said bluntly. "Not many of them had the money for boat passage back, and the rest—well, most of them never learned the difference between a nickel and a ten-dollar gold piece. Most sold all their possessions for just a dollar or two, hoping to raise enough for boat fare."

"Like the Russians trading with the Aleuts, swindling them out of food and furs in return for glass beads and buttons," I said, thinking out loud. Perhaps these Americans were more devious than the Russians had been.

"You stole away to that Indian camp this summer," Mr. York said accusingly. "Why don't you go live there like you used to?"

He's been spying on me, I thought with a shudder. He isn't content to lead his own life, he must follow the lives of others. And when he's bored with the lives of the people he reads about in books, he watches me! But why has he been so secretive? It's almost as if he were observing the habits of one of the birds in his illustrated Audubon book.

"Would you allow me to take winter provisions with me?" I asked, knowing that in this cold winter my life was at stake and I had to be calculating. Besides, hadn't I cured and gathered most of the salmon stored in the food cache?

"Good God, girl," he said, slamming his enamelware hooch cup down on the table. "It's bad enough that your Czar sold this land out from under you. Changing the laws meant I lost title to you. Of course," he went on, with a far-off look in his eyes, "it was debatable if I ever owned you. In Russia they outlawed serfdom in 'sixty-one, but it was never clear if the same laws extended to savages in Russian colonies. . . ." His gray eyes began flashing from under his fire-red hair and eyebrows. "It's bad enough that I lose title to you, but to lose some of my provisions to boot is bad business, as my father would say. No, girl, your freedom's gift enough. I can't throw away all my wealth."

"But what am I to do?" I asked, amazed at his stinginess. Since last spring I had listened to him rave about how he loathed his father's conservative dispersement of money, but now Noah York was treating me just as his father had treated him. Why? And if he was truly an abolitionist as Gospozha had said, why would he be so annoyed by the acquisition of my freedom? It was as if the voice of Hemstead York had overtaken Noah. "Bad business," he'd just said. But what were a few rations of food to my master? After the bear had ravaged his supplies, Mr. York had gone to the fur company depot and bought enough provisions for two winters.

"It would be a hardship for the Tlingits to take me in without provisions," I said. "They can barely gather enough for themselves these days, with the hair seal gone to live all the way north where the Ottermonster hides and the Boston men killing their blackfin whales."

"Ottermonster?" asked Mr. York as if he'd suddenly forgotten the subject at hand.

"*Koosta-kah,* the Indians call him," I answered obediently. "They say he steals people in their sleep and abandons them up in the glaciers. . . . Things aren't peaceful between the Americans and the Indians," I said, seeing that Mr. York wasn't really interested in my story. "I'm not at all sure the Tlingits will want me now." I could feel the tears forming in my eyes. Kat-lee-an, I thought. Why had he come to see me and not taken me away with him?

Mr. York poured himself another cup of hooch as I began to cry, a thousand pictures flashing through my head. There was a deserted *promyshlennik* shack on the edge of Sitka Bay about a mile south of the Tlingits' village. Perhaps I could go there, I thought. I had no food and no money, but I could dig clams for sustenance and perhaps prevail upon Mr. York to give me a cast-iron water pot and some blankets.

"It's not as if you didn't have choices," Mr. York said, putting down his enamelware hooch cup and folding his hands on the table as if he were about to say grace. "Look at me, Nadia," he said, and although I must have been an ugly sight, with my hair like a porcupine and my face all red and terrible from crying, I obeyed. "It's not as if I'm turning you out into the cold. I'm willing to marry you," he said calmly.

"Marry me!" I gasped, feeling as if I'd just been socked in the stomach. Surely this man was having a good joke on me.

"Of course," he said. "You're a hard worker, a pioneer. You're what I need. When you get your health back, we'll discuss having a little son. I've been dreaming about a little son lately, someone I could teach carpentry and woodlore to, someone to keep me company...."

I scarely remembered what else he said. Mr. York wanted to marry me? I had never had a romantic inclination toward this man. Ever since the first night I'd spent in his cabin, I'd kept my distance from his person and wanted nothing to do with him. It was as if his body was unnatural, even repulsive to me.

"I—I don't know," I stammered, biding my time against the cold winter outside the cabin door. "I just don't know."

"Well, you don't have to give me your answer immediately," he said, picking up his book on birds. "Women like to play these little games. You consider the question for a few days"—he leafed through the pages—"and give me your answer at the end of the week."

"Yes, sir," I said, as if I were still his slave servant girl. "Thank you, sir." I cleared away the cobbler dishes and Mr. York's blue-enameled hooch cup. Kat-lee-an would save me from Mr. York's marriage proposal. His wife had died last year and it was time he took another. Tomorrow, I thought as Mr. York began to draw pictures of wild birds in his leather-bound notebook, I'll go to the Village of the Raven, no matter how hard the southeast *saanah* gale blows—no matter if the wind is so strong I have to crawl.

8.

The next morning, however, Mr. York had other plans for me. As I boiled water for breakfast tea, he told me that I should accompany him to Sitka village, where he had to discuss land claims and real estate with General Davis. The new American land laws were all too difficult for me to understand, he said, but now that I was an American citizen by purchase, I should become acquainted with something he called the Great American Way.

I stoked the fire below the black cast-iron water caldron, wondering why everyone but the Indians treated me as if I had no power of reason. Whenever I recited my lessons exceptionally well at the Mission Fathers' school, the priests said it was because I was the daughter of a witch. Whenever Mr. York listened to me with both ears, it was as if he were sitting in judgment rather than having a conversation.

I waited for the water to boil, thinking that it had never been like that with the Tlingits. With the Indian people, if anyone spoke, man or woman, it was for good reason and everyone listened. But with the Americans and the Russians, it seemed that all the important people were men. If it wasn't a man, personally, then it was his work that was revered. Scrubbing floors and boiling water for tea wasn't considered important work—unless, of course, it didn't get done. With the Tlingits and the Haidas, everyone was too busy gathering food to preach about himself or herself being the better. An Indian never even considered his or her father's parents as relatives. It was your mother's people who were your tribe, and that's why my mother told me not to worry too much about who my father was.

As I ladled hot water from the caldron into one of the china teapots which Mr. York had bought for Miss Emily, I wondered what the American rulers would be like. Glancing over at Mr. York, his red head buried in his notebook, I knew that I'd be forever proving to these newcomers that a half-breed Indian girl could think as well as they could—just as I had had to do in the Russian Fathers' school. I sighed as I poured Mr. York his morning tea. At least Professor Karimoff and the Russian priests had answered me when I spoke to them. Could it be that Mr. York rarely spoke because he feared I would think him stupid and worthless as his father thought him? Or was it merely because he had nothing to say?

After a breakfast of tea and dried bear meat, Mr. York and I paddled through the low-hanging winter fog across Sitka bay. The boat harbor was busy with new American shipbuilders, but inside the stockade the village was in terrible confusion. Gazing at the Governor's Walk, past the Russian church, and up to where the long street ended in the wooded tea gardens, it looked as if the population of New Archangel, or Sitka as the Americans now called it, had doubled. Tent houses and new, slapdash pole and canvas shacks lined the main street. The footpaths to the Russian houses were clogged with tents occupied by Boomers—chalk-faced, pale-haired Americans who'd come from the States to seek their fortune as trappers or fox farmers, raising scores of small fur animals on the little islands in Sitka Bay. Everywhere there were American soldiers in drab blue uniforms. As Mr. York and I walked to the fur depot, now owned by an American whom everyone called Cornelius, I could see that men outnumbered women ten to one. Was that true everywhere in America?

General Davis, a stout man with a huge paunch and a full brown beard, had posted signs in front of the fur depot declaring a prohibition on liquor. But as Mr. York and I walked up the Governor's Walk toward the countinghouse—or the bank, as these newcomers called it—I saw five or six tents each with a homemade still behind it. Inside, ruddy-faced men sold blue enamelware cups of some awful-smelling hooch that they'd made from molasses, dried fruit, berries, potatoes, flour—anything that would ferment and could be had in Alaska. Drunken Boomers stood in front of the tent taverns, all of them hooting and calling out to six fancily dressed ladies parading in red silk dresses inside the front porch windows of the old Russian sailors' boardinghouse.

I hardly saw a Cossack face anywhere, none of the girls I'd gone to school with, and after I'd walked up the Governor's Walk, or Lincoln Street as these Americans now called the avenue, I knew why. I'd never heard such insults, not even from the Russian priests. Even with Mr. York walking beside me, men were calling out after me and pinching at the sleeves of my winter coat.

A tall, scar-faced man named Seattle Charley stopped Mr. York in front of the Church of Saint Michael, talking to my former master in a hushed drawl about the contraband liquor trade. I stood silently at Mr. York's side while Seattle Charley's small, marble-shaped eyes stared at my breasts. Russian priests draped in black robes and ermine skins ran back and forth from the church to the House of Bishops, talking about American converts and alluding to the large numbers of American churchmen who'd come to build new sanctuaries. I listened intently to Mr. York and scar-faced Seattle Charley as they talked of real estate claims and the laws of the Oregon Territory—something about Congress not ruling Occupied Alaska with the same territorial laws and everyone being in a state of confusion.

"A fine piece of country this is," said Seattle Charley, gazing up at the crater of Mount Saint Lazaria. "Even the Injun women is better lookin' here than the ones in Washington." He eyed Mr. York with a knowing glance that made me shudder inside my black muslin dress. "When I first went to work haulin' logs down Skid Road," he continued, "the closest white woman was in San Francisco. 'Course then the president of that new college that they got in the Seattle hills started importin' women from the East, and tensions eased up a bit."

After the gaunt, scar-faced man took his leave and went strutting down toward the wharf, we were approached by a stubby-legged American religious man whom Mr. York addressed as Reverend Hitch.

"Good day to you, Mr. Y," he said, pronouncing his vowels the same way as Mr. York. "And this must be the missus." He addressed me in the third person as if I weren't standing there in front of him.

When the stumpy, bald-headed minister discovered that I wasn't Mr. York's wife, he began to admonish him. Shaking his finger in front of Mr. York's face, the minister told us that he and his church, temporarily quartered in a tent down on the old Cossack parade grounds in front of the wharf, were available day and night for marriage ceremonies. "And I'll be most happy to help you up at the Registry," he told Mr. York, referring to the new American law office which General Davis had installed in Prince Maksoutov's old quarters up in the Castle.

The bald-headed minister said good-bye and hastened after a "lost soul" Aleut dock worker. As Mr. York and I turned and walked down the Governor's Walk to the general's quarters in the barnlike Castle, I could see that what I'd been told about the Russian capitol building was true. Soldiers in tens and twenties, some of them so drunk they were vomiting out of the third-story windows, appeared to be roller-skating around and around the ballroom floor. From where I stood I could even see that some of them had carved large initials into the red and gold *fleur-de-lis* wallpaper.

While Mr. York went into the Castle, I sat on the *kekoor* rock, looking down at the shipyards, watching a group of soldiers and Aleut workers unload a cargo clipper that had somehow found its way through the southeast Alaska gales to Sitka Bay. A shipment of guns and munitions, I told myself, following the Aleut workers with my eyes as they carried the heavy wooden crates to their storage place in the old Russian hospital-morgue. Tomorrow I'll go to the Village of the Raven and tell Kat-lee-an about the warehouse full of guns.

It seemed like hours that I sat on the rock, waiting for Mr. York. I felt depressed and downcast as I studied first the town and then the frost-covered islands wintering in the bay. It was almost as if the Russian village of New Archangel, or *Novo-archangelsk* as Gospozha would have called it, never existed. Only the gold dome on the church, the hand-hewn Russian cottages near the tea garden, and the cemetery on the hill beside the blockhouses looked unchanged. The Americans had rearranged the village almost overnight: munitions stored in the hospital where Professor Karimoff died, taverns set up along the Governor's Walk, where fur agents used to conduct business. After his last visit to Sitka, Mr. York had told me that soldiers were frequenting the darkly wooded paths of the Russian tea gardens accompanied by newly converted Christian Indian women, telling them that it was all a part of the white man's church initiation. "Lover's Lane, that's what everyone calls the tea gardens now," Mr. York had joked.

These new Americans speak with such an odd drawl, using strange words and incorrect grammar, I thought, as I huddled inside my Hudson's Bay blanket coat and looked away from the confusion of the town on Baranof Island and out toward the tiny islands in the Pacific. I hadn't much hope of finding a position in any of the homes in Sitka. The only families in need of a servant girl were the Russians, and from their narrow, serious faces I could tell they were in need of money and supplies as well as help. The American Boomers hadn't brought their families. Oh, what awful men they were. My arms were bruised from their pinching. I wouldn't want to keep house for one of them—assuming, that is, that they had houses to keep. The few American women in Sitka were the wives of those new religious men, and they were so somnolent-looking that I knew their religion wasn't any better than the Russian Fathers' had been. While I sat on the *kekoor* rock waiting for Mr. York to finish his business with the General, three minister's wives approached me, saying that I should come on Sunday to their church tent and hear the Good News. I didn't know what that was, but from their faces I decided they couldn't have anything that would be good news for me.

* * *

It was dark as we paddled back to Indian River and then poled the canoe up-creek through the heavy winter fog. All the way home Mr. York stared at my body with a strange curve to his narrow lips. But since I'd just spent the day with American men poking and pinching me and American women nagging me to come to their church on Sunday, I hardly minded his staring any more. I wanted to ask Mr. York about his business with General Davis and why all those Boomers had come to Sitka, leaving their homes and families behind.

"How does one make a real-estate claim?" I asked Mr. York as he stood at the stern of the canoe. "Professor Karimoff taught me calculus. I can understand land parceling."

Mr. York averted his eyes from my body and waved my question away as if it were a summer mosquito. "It's all too complex for you, little Nadia," he said. And as we approached the cabin, the fog became so thick that I could hardly make out his shape at the other end of the canoe.

"It's all too complex for you, little Nadia." I mocked Mr. York's voice over and over to myself. Then I remembered the men in Barney O'Ragan's saloon tent gambling with cards and playing a game they called poker. I'll lay you odds, I thought, recalling the rough voices of the Boomers, that Mr. York doesn't understand the new real-estate-claim rules in Alaska either. In fact, considering the confusion in Sitka, I'll bet these Americans haven't even made up any Alaska land-claiming laws!

Tomorrow, I told myself, I'll visit the Village of the Raven and Kat-lee-an.

The next day the snow turned to slush and the long limbs of the fir trees began to lift up instead of sagging under the weight of this terrible winter ice. I walked to the Indian Village without even becoming short of breath. I've completely recovered my strength, I thought happily. But before I'd walked half a mile up Indian River, I could hear the Tlingits' large, flat elk-hide drums pounding. What could be the matter? The warriors wouldn't attack the Americans now, not while winter is still in the air.

As I approached the bark and cedar-roofed huts, everything was in a state of disorder. Some American trappers had traded the Tlingits a barrel of homemade rum for a bale of blue-fox pelts, and the older Indians were drunk with delight. The woodcarver and some of the older women had decorated their faces with war designs, using tar and fish-oil-based red and aqua mineral paint.

The old ones were so drunk that they hardly took notice of me as I walked toward Chief Kat-lee-an's hut. I stopped in front of the newly painted façade adorning the front of his house. It was the huge face of a raven with a beak hanging over the door, and the door itself was the round hole of an animal mouth. I peered inside and saw Kat-lee-an smoking *kinnikinnick* with two Chilcat Indians. One was a huge man wearing a ridiculously small pair of gold spectacles which had probably been stolen from a Russian emissary, spectacles which magnified his eyes so that they were the size of the large dark stones at the bottom of Sitka Bay. The other was a woman wearing a *hootz* robe with the bear head still attached. A few years older than the others, she sat silently listening to the men talk as they squatted on finely woven goat's-wool rugs. The three were deep in a *hyou wawa*, talking intensely, and not one of them looked up to see me standing in the animal-mouth doorway.

I turned away from Kat-lee-an's house and walked toward Mother-of-Stories' hut. The drunken Indians were dancing the dance of the loon, dressed in bird masks, brandishing spears and cedar war shields. The old woodcarver was shaking a loon rattle with his left hand and waving a cedar wand with his right. "*Oi, oi, oi, yelth*," shouted an old woman as she moved the beak of her raven mask open and shut.

When I appeared at her door, Mother-of-Stories looked up at me with her dark questioning eyes and put down her blanket loom. "Small-Lake," she said, "is it you and not creature out of hooch barrel I see before me?"

"Yes," I said, "yes." She reached her thin, aged arm up to touch the silk scarf wrapped around my head where my hair should have been.

"Small-Lake not bedeviled?" she asked.

"No," I said, "I contracted the sickness-of-the-river. Mr. York brought an American doctor to attend me, and he shaved my head to save me from the fever."

"Witchery," she said. "Weak and sick ones are their prey."

"Did Kat-lee-an tell you?"

"Yes," she said. "Small-Lake not come to great potlatch. Much seal grease this year, good grease, *hyas klosh*. Small-Lake not come. Kat-lee-an, he go for you."

"For me?" I said with joy. "For me?"

"He say white man's devil take you. He say you look like sapling tree too weak to bear cold winter. He say white witch take spirit of Small-Lake. No words would open your eyes to see him."

"I was very ill," I said, "but now I'm well." She touched my head scarf again. I unwound it and showed her my few inches of new growth, thicker and redder than before. She smiled and we both laughed. Then she stored the blanket she was weaving and looked down at the seal-skin-covered floor.

"Kat-lee-an moaned much for Small-Lake," she said.

"But now I'm well," I said again.

"Now," she said, "much changed. . . ."

"Old Mother," I said, remembering her promise that Kat-lee-an would ask about my mother while he was seal hunting in Yakutat Bay, "was there any news of Woman-Always-Wondering in the land of the Ottermonster, *Koosta-kah?* Was there any story, anything at all?"

A look of relief passed over her face. "Ah," she said, "there were many tribes, Hootz-noo, Chilcats, and even Hanega from Islands of South Wind. There is story," she said, "that one Hanega brave told Kat-lee-an. Two winters ago this one Hanega heard story of one Tongass who came and shared seal grease with him. Woman, Haida shaman-woman who wears the necklace of salmon neck bones and wolf-fang amulets, roams southern islands stealing children of white settlers, he say. Her child was taken from her, and stealing is her revenge. Name of woman he could not say, only that she goes from island to island living in woods, in houses of hollow trees, following white settlers—swimming between the islands as the deer people do."

"My mother?" I asked, taken aback by the story. "Do you think it's her, Old Mother?" My voice was more excited than the drunken loon dancers outside her hut.

"It is story," she said. "One Hanega will tell one Tongass of daughter who lives between Village of the Raven and village of the white men, daughter who looks for mother who wears the necklace. Then two stories. Ah"—she sighed—"not even my sister the shaman-woman knows if two stories will be one."

I felt a strength grow through my body as if my tap root had struck good water underneath the earth. "And Kat-lee-an?" I asked.

"He is *ankow*, chief, of all Tlingit tribes now," she said with unusual solemnity in her voice. "On way from Yakutat Bay he battled black-fin killer whale. Save lives of many Chilcat Indians. For this Chief Shathitch, *ankow* of all Chilcats, made him friend. *Shathitch* mean Hard-to-Kill. He now among us for marriage of first-born sister. . . . Small-Lake," she said, grasping my hand, "is much trouble. Noises beneath ground get louder. Shathitch, he most powerful of Indian people. He tell Kat-lee-an how trade furs with white men. Shathitch, he good fur trader, bring much wealth to tribes. Shathitch live far to north where few white men threaten him. I no like Chief Shathitch," she whispered.

"I saw this chief in the great house with Kat-lee-an," I said, "and a woman in a bear robe as grand as a Russian princess."

"Kat-lee-an's new mate," she said, looking again at the sealskin-covered floor.

"His wife?" I felt as if a great rock had fallen from Mount Saint Lazaria on top of me.

"Yes, sister of Shathitch."

"But she's old, much older than Kat-lee-an." I could not believe what Mother-of-Stories had just told me.

"Yes," she said in a mournful voice. "Kat-lee-an wanted you for wife. At great potlatch he come for you, but devil took you first. White witches are close upon Indian, Small-Lake. Much blood shed. New white priests come every day to teach Indian white witchery. They tell white story, only story in world, they say. . . ." Her voice trailed off into the winter air. "Kat-lee-an, sometimes hooch make him crazy like bear. He hungry for blood like *hootz* hungry in spring.

One full moon, Kat-lee-an hung three Indians who go to Boston man's church. Small-Lake," she said, with tears in her narrow slanted eyes, "I frightened."

I sat still, hardly able to assimilate what Mother-of-Stories was telling me. Kat-lee-an was married. The Tlingits were free to take more than one wife, but I wanted him to myself. Perhaps, I thought with dismay, I have been bedeviled by the white man's ways. My arms felt lifeless and my stomach shrank from the two roads left open to me, keeping house for a newly arrived American Boomer or marrying Noah York.

"It has been a hard winter," I said, taking hold of Old Mother's withered arm and drawing her close to me.

"Yes," she said, "*Koosta-kah* who haunts northern ice has found his way to Village of the Raven. Taken many of our people. Others have lost ends of noses to ice and black rot."

"Do you know what the Americans and Russians say?" I asked, trying to console her with one of the white people's strange stories. "They say that the Tlingits lose their noses not to the cold but because they have been unfaithful and their spouse has bitten it off!"

"Ha!" She laughed, sitting up, the strength returning to her voice, "let them believe this."

We both laughed loudly.

"Small-Lake," she asked, "how white man say it? Small-Lake in love with Kat-lee-an?"

"Yes," I said without the reservation one would have to use when addressing white people on such matters. "All during my sickness I thought of nothing but him."

"Speak with him before you go."

"I don't know."

"Your face deep water," she said. "Go to him, speak, see that he has much changed. Since Kat-lee-an befriended Shathitch, he think of nothing but revenge and trading guns. He talk of taking new slaves as Shathitch does." She took a deep breath and returned to her blanket loom.

"I must leave before the early night comes," I said, feeling sad and tired.

"Come back soon, Small-Lake, there is good reason." She looked deep into my eyes. "I tell you many stories, all stories I know. Not much time I have on land under sky arch. I go live with noise-in-the-ground soon, yes. I feel winter always. In my arm bones it is always winter. Many of those who know stories, stories of this tribe, they the too young to pass them on. But you, Small-Lake, you must know my stories. You, I know, will keep them. You will prevail."

Despite the terrible disappointment I felt over Kat-lee-an, what Old Mother had just told me raised my spirits immensely. It was a great honor to be the keeper of the tribal history, as great an honor as it was to be chief. Tribal stories were considered private property among the Tlingits, something owned by them, stories no other tribe was allowed to tell.

"But," she warned me, "beware *hootz*. He will come out of winter sleep soon. He hungry."

I said good-bye and walked aimlessly toward the edge of the village, the noise of the drunken dancers ringing in my ears. When I was beyond the houses a voice called out from behind me, "Small-Lake." I turned. it was Kat-lee-an.

He came toward me, his large hands grasping my shoulders in friendship. "Small-Lake," he said, over and over. I stared into his raven-beaked face, his head at least a foot taller than mine. As I looked at his high forehead and into his dark eyes, my heart sank into my stomach. He took one broad hand from my shoulder and pulled the silk scarf from my head. Looking with caution at my new hair, he began to pet it as if it were a dog that would bite him.

Mother-of-Stories was right, there was a new light in his eyes. Even his jaw hung differently. I turned from his grasp and walked down the trail, leaving him holding my red scarf in his hand, then called out to him, "The white men have many guns for war, Kat-lee-an." But he didn't flinch. I took a deep breath and turned to look him straight in the eye. "You will be a great chief, my friend, perhaps the greatest of them all." I walked away from his motionless figure, not knowing that the prophecy of my words would echo louder than ever I dreamed.

9. SITKA, ALASKA
U.S. Possession
1868

On March 9 Mr. York and I stood side by side amid the tattered wallpaper and shabby furnishings of the Registry in the once-grand Baranov Castle as Reverend Hitch pronounced us man and wife. From then on the stumpy, bald-headed minister proceeded to address me as "Mrs. York," a name I could never find it in my heart to adopt. I had had so many names. If my mother ever returned to Sitka Bay, how would she find me? To her I was Small-Lake-Underneath, a girl with a waist-length braid of dark-red Haida hair. Now the two things dearest to me, my name and my hair, were gone. My hair, I knew, would grow back, and my name, I vowed, I'd somehow get back as well.

As my new husband and I walked down the Castle steps hand in hand, I pretended that it was Kat-lee-an in his raven mask who walked beside me. I wore one of my black muslin dresses, as I had no others, and my short hair was done in curls, the latest American fashion, Mr. York said. After the brief ceremony, my husband had a daguerreotype made of me and then took me to meet the proprietor of the fur depot, now called the Alaska Commercial Company. Proudly Mr. York, dressed in his fancy city clothes and top hat, introduced me to the man behind the long split-rail trading post counter, a man I recognized immediately as Yuri's father, Sasha Dysokar, one of the Russian fur agents who'd stayed on in Sitka to work for the Americans. But where, I wondered, was the owner of the fur depot, Mr. Cornelius? Some people said that he ran the business from a law office in Seattle, others said he was a senator in California. Such strange ways these Americans had, I thought to myself, living so far away from their property as if they were all czars themselves.

Dysokar, who'd never even greeted me as we passed on the Governor's Walk, now beamed happily down into my face. "Meestris York, Meestris York," he said in such a jolly voice that it was hard to believe he had never condescended to speak to me before. "Vwoould you vwant to see some silks? In store, vwe have bootiful silks. She vwant, she shall buy it?" And he turned his smiling face toward Mr. York.

I was introduced to each of Noah York's acquaintances: Barney O'Ragan, busy at work tending his tavern and editing his newspaper; scar-faced Seattle Charley; even General Davis himself: It was as if I had suddenly attained respectability. But I knew that men whose opinions sway so easily were not to be trusted, not ever. Underneath my new name and American curls, I was still a servant girl with no more freedom than a half-breed Creole who made her way in life by chopping wood.

At home in our cabin, things changed as well. I was his wife now, Mr. York said, I had to be his partner, his little helpmate. I was supposed to help him raise the scaffolding against the walls of his new house, scaffolding fashioned from logs of back-breaking weight and uncontrollable length—unmanageable for a team of men, let alone just him and me.

Once, in the early spring before the small trees in the pear orchard began to flower, Mr. York and I were moving the scaffolding from wall to wall as we moss-chinked the logs of his house. My body buckled under the stress of balancing the tall scaffolding, and it fell to the ground around us, a pole striking Mr. York on the leg. We might have been killed, but luckily we got away with only bruises.

"Clumsy woman," Mr. York screamed, all red and angry in the face.

"I haven't the strength of two people, let alone four," I called back to him.

"It's not strength, Nadia," he yelled, rising to his feet and brushing the mud from his canvas work trousers. "It's that you know nothing of leverage, balance, and base."

I pulled myself out from under the wood rubble, not knowing what to say. What could leverage tell me that common sense could not?

"You've failed me, Nadia," he said in a stern voice, readjusting the scaffolding. "Perhaps I've made the wrong choice in a wife."

His voice cut into me like a knife. "Perhaps you have," I said, trying to control my anger. "Perhaps you should have married an ox or a mule—or Miss Emily," I added, knowing that I'd played my trump card.

His expression immediately changed to one of despair, and for the first time in my life I felt guilty for having defended myself with my wit and my words. Picking up an ax, he swung it violently into the log wall of his new house.

"Damnation," he cursed, his face growing redder than the cedar bark. "Why have I been predestined to failure?" Then he sat down upon the chopping block and began to sob. I'd never seen a white man cry before, and cautiously approached his slumped figure to try to soothe him. Perhaps *I* was a failure and a misfit too. Perhaps it was true what the white men said about the Indians—that the Tlingits were too savage to learn the European ways. Surely, even though I'd studied calculus, I never understood the sense of the scaffolding and never trusted my life and limb on it. Slowly I reached out my hand, wanting to tell Mr. York that I too was a misfit and that he was not alone in the world. But when I touched him gently on the shoulder, he flung me to the ground as if I were a discarded apple core.

Rising to my feet, I took a long, sad look at my husband. It was as if he was obsessed with failure. Then, as if I were a hunted animal just grazed by a human's bullet, a frightening thought rang through my head. Had Mr. York knowingly set up the scaffolding so that it would fall—so that he would fail with it? This man must be watched like a sailor watches the weather at sea, I told myself, and tried to put the scaffolding incident out of my mind for the moment.

That evening I attempted a meal I'd studied in Miss Emily's cookbook—a good Yankee meal, Mr. York called it. I added a spoonful of seal grease to each dish, the taste of which I'd grown fond of as a child—the Tlingits ate seal grease with everything, even wild berries. But Mr. York was unaccustomed to its odor and swore at me, saying that only a savage could palate such rancid-tasting fat.

In bed under our *hootz* rugs, we lay side by side. At first, as usual, I heard my husband touching himself. Then he took hold of my hand and showed me how he wanted to be touched, telling me to make my hand into a vestibule. He became hard, coming wet and sticky into my hand almost immediately. Then he threw himself upon me.

"I'm an eagle plummeting into the water," I heard him whisper to himself as he began biting at my breasts and in between my thighs until I screamed out in pain. But it was my screaming that he thrived on, again becoming hard and jabbing himself into me, never quite penetrating my interior walls before he had saturated my thighs with semen.

When my hands and legs were not the right vestibule, it was my mouth he wanted. He became so elongated that I almost choked, and to his great disgust I vomited between his legs. Although he was adamant about the conservative use of my teeth on his sensitive skin, he took no heed of the pain that his biting caused me.

This biting and touching went on for a month after our marriage. Mr. York always had difficulty penetrating me deeply, getting past the first folds of my opening without ejaculating across my stomach or into the *hootz* rug. He cursed time after time, then mounted me again or pushed my mouth around his elongation. Finally, he began to complain about the stench that came from between my thighs, and we attempted sex less often.

"It has more to do with my dislike of your monthly blood than your Indian blood," my husband said one night as we lay beneath the *hootz* skins. "I can smell your monthly blood before it starts. You have to wash yourself, Nadia. Wash yourself in the river before, during, and after." And because he had such an aversion to my smell, he would take my hand and move it up and down with his, then thrust himself in the direction of my mouth. Afterward, when he'd fallen asleep, snoring and blowing air through his lips, I lay next to him with my face turned toward the fire hole. My body ached from the digging of his teeth, and between my legs I felt a terrible craving.

How weary I'd become of being Mr. York's scapegoat! So often when he failed, as he had in his conjugal duties, he would turn the situation upside down so that it was me and my womanblood that was at fault and not him. And then, despite my weariness, I began again to feel pity for him, the same pity I felt for a beached salmon who could not swim.

"Teach me a poem," I would say, hoping to raise his spirits. Often he ignored me, but on one occasion his tightly pursed lips parted into a broad smile, the way two dark winter clouds sometimes part to let down a ray of false spring sun.

"'Ode on the Death of a Favorite Cat Drowned in a Bowl of Gold Fishes,'" he laughed, reading from one of his favorite verses, as I listened, marveling at the new life that Mr. York injected into what I had always thought of as dry and boring words.

"Teach me another," I begged, suddenly missing the lessons that Professor Karimoff had given me. But my husband had grown despondent again and closed his book of verse with a definitive thud.

When the fog mother and her two children, the salmon fish and the spring leaves, came to Sitka Bay, I felt a tremendous restoration. It was as if the fog mother had brought me new life as well as the orchard leaves and the red squirreltail grass. When the glacier melt and the floods ran downriver from the green cone-shaped mountains, Mr. York and I were forced to move from our small cabin into the new house before it was completely built. I was delighted. It was a grand log house, even larger than Professor Karimoff's, with several upstairs sleeping lofts and partitioned rooms.

The morning of our sudden decision to move, I awoke to the noise of Mr. York, clench-fisted and cursing at the river from our front door. The glacier melt was but a foot or two from the walls of the old cabin, the water level having risen almost ten feet in the night. From my bed I watched his ridiculous figure, raving against the flood of the river, and I laughed. How could this man not know that the river might flood? Could he not see with his own eyes the high-water marks left on the inside of our cabin from years past? Did he not see how the riverbed had changed, how it moved from one bend to another? I laughed again. For the first time in our marriage, Mr. York had endeared himself to me.

From that day on he placed more belief in what I had to say, and because of that I decided to try with all my energy to make myself love this man. But I soon realized it would be of little gain to me. To Mr. York, I was just his helpmate, his little work ox, someone to do his bidding mindlessly. Perhaps, I thought with despair, those stories of passion that men had for women were just another hoax perpetuated by the Russian Fathers and the American churchmen. All Noah York and the American Boomers talked of was business: claiming land, getting a top price for a fox pelt, and killing Indians as if aboriginals were animals to be hunted.

Above the noise of the river flood echoed the sound of the bruin and the fox caught in the traps of the American hunters, and my heart was heavy with the pain of the animal people. The Tlingits said that the *hootz* had become more vicious, that even the Indian warriors did not hunt them now. A fifteen-hundred-pound bear could crush the head of a man with a swipe of his paw, and the only time that the Tlingits declared war on a killer bear was when he'd gone mad, *quonsum sollex*, in the spring. Then the Indian warriors would hunt the *hootz* in large war parties and only by boat as the huge animal came to fish the salmon out of the tide.

I thought of Mr. York's anger at the river and wondered how someone who had studied at a university in America could not know about the ways of the *glate*, the ice, melting in spring. I tried to tell myself that I was just angry with this man for his constant criticism of me and therefore found fault with what he did. I tried to joke with him as I saw him joke with his friends in Sitka, Seattle Charley and the Reverend Hitch; but somehow Mr. York always misunderstood my humor, taking it as criticism or ignoring me altogether as if I were speaking a foreign tongue. Was I wrong in thinking that he would be a danger to me? Or had my anger for his constant criticism overpowered my sense of reason?

As the month of June approached, I knew that if I did not go to the Village of the Raven I would become sick from loneliness. Mr. York and I paddled our canoe into Sitka once a week, but on each visit I stood silently at my husband's side, afraid to speak for fear the Americans would ask me about the Tlingits. Kat-lee-an was a subject much discussed since he had begun avenging himself against those Indians of his tribe who had forsaken the Tlingit shaman for the white ministers' Good News—those Indians who had gone to live in what the Americans called Indian Town, a small cluster of plank shanties built along Sitka's boardwalk near the parade grounds. In the past month the Tlingit warriors had ambushed claim stakers and trappers as well, dismembering their parts and hanging them from trees as a warning to other newcomers.

On the second day of June as I returned from weeding the chard in the kitchen garden, two Russian men, the sawmill owner and

Sasha Dysokar, were talking to Mr. York. Neither of them saw me, and I crouched down Tlingit fashion among the new ferns to listen to their words. The sawmill owner stood silent while Yuri's father addressed Mr. York.

"Your vwife, Meester York," he said in broken English, "vwas vward of Professor Karimoff. She speak Roossian and English, no?" he asked.

"Yes, she's very well schooled," Mr. York said proudly, the first time I'd ever heard him praise me in the presence of others.

"Vwee need teacher in Mission School," he said. "American czar, he give us no schools, no teachers. Roossian priests very busy." Mr. Dysokar crossed himself with two fingers. "Your vwife, Meester York, she be Mission School teacher, no?"

I was suddenly elated. Why had I not known that there was such a position available? I would have much preferred teaching in the Mission School, even though I hated the Russian priests, to marrying Noah York. . . . But, I thought, would it have mattered if I had known? Would I have believed that the town people would hire me, an Indian half-breed woman?

"I'm sorry," I heard Mr. York tell the two Russian men, "but Mrs. York is with child and entering into her first confinement soon."

I felt as if my soul had departed from my body. Was my husband drunk from the hooch? I was no more with child than a bull seal. Why would Mr. York tell such a terrible lie? Indeed, what was I supposed to tell Sasha Dysokar when I went to buy supplies at the fur depot without a swollen belly?

I heard Mr. York walk into his new log house and slam the heavy door. Dysokar and the sawmill owner departed, and I sat in the ferns beneath the hemlock trees for nearly half a day, feeling as if I were a fish stunned by a hunter's club and unable to swim out with the tide. I was Noah York's wife and according to the American laws, I, like the servant girl I had been just a few months ago, had to do his bidding. Would I have to hide in the new house and pretend to be with child? Would I have to stuff my black muslin dress with a feather pillow whenever I went into Sitka village?

I walked into the house and confronted Mr. York, who sat in his rocking chair in front of the large stone fireplace, writing in his journal.

"The two Russian men," I said, "what did they want?"

"Business, Nadia, business," he said, motioning me away and into the kitchen to prepare a saddle of venison for dinner.

"I'm your wife now," I said sternly. "I want to know your business."

He looked up from his notebook, his gray eyes gleaming under his curly red hair. "I just bought the sawmill in town," he said, waving a bill of sale at me.

Taken aback, I examined the document. It was, indeed, a bill of sale. A clever liar he is, I thought to myself, and spoke no more on the subject. It was useless to talk to my husband. I would go more often to the Village of the Raven. Perhaps Old Mother or her sister, the Tlingit shaman, had had news from the Tongass tribe to the south, news about the woman who stole white settlers' babies. I knew that hearing the stories that Old Mother had promised to teach me would be the only thing in my new life that would soothe my spirit.

As the June days grew longer, Mr. York completed the interior of our new dwelling, larger now than any house in Sitka. But after he drove the last peg into the stairway, he began to disappear for days at a time, sometimes taking the canoe and never offering me any warning or explanation for his absences. Once, when I ventured to ask why, he just mumbled something about hunting the "wee beasties," but he never ever came home with a kill. Then, knowing that I'd caught him in another lie, he began to go on about taking the next California ice ship south to help me search for my mother in the islands of the British colonies.

On the third Sunday in June, Mr. York left early without a word and I knew that he would not return until late twilight. After I'd eaten some cooked cornmeal, I began walking to the Village of the Raven. Today Mother-of-Stories had told me that she would begin calling the salmon up the white water and into Indian River.

I walked through the meadow near the Village, through the blue summer lupine flowers and the red and yellow columbine shining beneath the dew of a soft summer drizzle. As I entered the woods surrounding the village, I spotted a Tlingit sitting on a fallen fir log. He was so deep in thought that he had not heard me, unusual for a warrior. I looked closely at him, hardly believing my eyes. It was Kat-lee-an.

"I wait for Small-Lake," he said and motioned for me to sit down beside him. His face wasn't painted, and I could see worry lines upon his brow. He wore elk-hide pants and a trapper's shirt decorated with shell buttons and small round mirrors sewn onto the shirt bib in the figure of a dancer. Wordlessly I sat down beside him.

"Small-Lake take Boston man for husband?" he asked.

"Yes," I said, but his face remained as unchanging as a face on a totem pole.

"You know ways of Americans?" he asked.

"Yes," I said again, feeling that I was answering questions in the Russian Fathers' school rather than talking to the man I had once thought of as my sweetheart.

But then his face muscles relaxed and he began to talk with me in a manner which was very much unlike him, the words flowing like water from his mouth. He told me how strange the Boston men were, even stranger than the Russians had been. And their numbers, he said. There seemed to be no end to the Americans arriving on every clipper and whaling ship. He talked of their brutal ways, saying that although they were unlike the animal people and were unable to understand the language of the sun and moon, they somehow prevailed. One of these Boston men, he said, had laid claim to two square miles of Tlingit hunting and fishing land, and his wife's brother, Shathitch, had vowed to help avenge the Village of the Raven.

I listened intently to Kat-lee-an, watching the sharp features of his nose and cheekbones, remembering how his face had loomed above me during the high fever of my typhoid sickness. I began to feel stirrings inside myself and remembered the novels, *Ruth* and *Jane Eyre,* and the characters' love for men that were forbidden to them. Then I discovered the source of Kat-lee-an's new personality; a carved wooden flask of hooch lay amid the ferns and fungus flowers.

"The brew," I said, thinking out loud. He grinned into my face and then pressed his teeth, powerful as the white water of the river rapids, against my cheek.

I didn't resist. Married or not, it was his warmth I craved. We lay side by side in the ferns on the wet decay of fallen fir branches. He began to draw imaginary designs on my face, as if he were painting my cheeks for an attack on the man who had claimed his land. His finger traced an image on my neck, and I began to remove my clothing like a child being taught a new game. I took off my skirt and underslips and lay down upon them. When he had drawn the design of the eagle over one breast and the design of the raven over the other, he lay upon me and I felt a terrible longing between my thighs. He pointed to the bruises and teeth marks on my breasts and thighs. I told him that they were from Mr. York and showed my teeth to make the Indian understand how the white man liked sex.

Kat-lee-an began to stroke my belly with his tongue, licking the salt from my skin. Then he licked between my legs into my innermost folds, drinking my monthly blood. I don't remember how he first entered me, but we lay there for hours entwined amid the new spring grass, our bellies heaving and the colors of blood and semen drying on our skin.

The trees above us rustled with the wings of hummingbirds as he entered me again and again. Each time it was like the force of the river falling over rocks being pushed between my thighs. Each time there would be the craving, and each time it would suddenly subside like water plummeting into a pool of quiet salmon.

When the sun began to fade into the late-night light, we lay still on my rumpled black muslin dress. The trees behind us rustled, almost too late for hummingbirds to be winging about, but perhaps their hearts were as light and unconscious of the time as mine. Upriver I could hear Mother-of-Stories and the other villagers chanting and beating on their broad shallow drums. How strange it was, I thought, as the branches of a salmon-berry bush near us rattled together, though no bird lit upon it, for Old Mother to be teaching me her stories, the history of Kat-lee-an's tribe, when I did not even know the story of the man, my husband, with whom I had lived for more than a year.

As I lay on Kat-lee-an's arm, I began to piece together the words of the Tlingit villagers' fish-spawning chant:

Remember the creek of the grandmother fish
Fish that change the moon face
Fish that make the *saanah* wind-woman song,

Rise up the white water
Rise up the rain
Rise up.

Throughout the summer Mr. York was gone frequently on his secret business, and I would often come upon Kat-lee-an in the fir forest. He did not understand the strange way that the Boston man had taught me to have sex and never asked me to touch him while I lay unattended.

Mr. York hardly attempted sex at all any more, and when he did it was usually just to command me to touch myself. My husband would become aroused at the sight of me fondling myself, and then he would touch himself while we lay side by side. I didn't mind the touching any more. I just lay under my *hootz* skin and thought of Kat-lee-an. Sometimes Mr. York would attempt to enter me, but usually without success.

"My father was right, I am a failure," he moaned. Always I would try to console him, stroking his thick, curly red hair or playing with his newly grown beard, but my sympathy was only fuel for the fire and he'd cry even louder. It was as if he considered me an artesian well of good water from which he could always drink. But, I thought angrily, unlike the Indian people, Mr. York never sang to the spirit of the good water well, and never gave thanks to it . . . or me.

When the salmon fish had been running up Indian River for about a month, I began to feel a tenderness and swelling in my breasts and the feeling of water gathering within me. As Mr. York and I were smoke-curing a supply of fish and moose meat, I told him that I thought I might be with child. Carefully, I pieced the words together and watched his expression out of the corner of my eye. I was terrified that he would go into a rage and stone me or tie me to a rock at low tide, as the Russians would have done to an adulteress. But instead, he was overjoyed and never questioned the child's origins. Surely this man cannot think that this baby is his own, I pondered.

But it was as if he was blind to my sin against the Christian faith, for all during the late summer months, my husband would talk of nothing but *his* little son, about how he would teach the child to hunt and fish. He told me how pleased his father, Hemstead York, would be, how at last he'd satisfied the old man. He rambled on about the child's college education—he would study at Harvard and then go on to the Sorbonne.

"What if it's a daughter?" I asked, surprised that he had never considered the possibility.

"That wouldn't please my father at all, not at all. A son, an heir," he said firmly. "Concentrate on bearing a son, Nadia." And he would discuss the subject no further.

Will I ever understand these foreigners, I wondered? The Russians and the Americans, why do they value male babies more than female babies? As Kat-lee-an had said, these Boston men did not understand the language and the ways of the animal people.

When the *saanah* wind began to howl up Indian River canyon, my belly broadened like a creek overflowing its banks. Mr. York measured my growth daily with a cloth tape, but other than that he wouldn't touch me or even ask me to touch him when we lay under our *hootz* rugs in the sleeping loft.

On October 18, the celebration day commemorating Alaska's first year under American occupancy, General Davis invited Mr. York and me to tea up at his quarters in the Castle on the *kekoor* rock. I was the only woman sitting at the long table in the formal dining hall that day as General Jeff Davis, with his full beard and huge paunch, sat at the far end of the room toasting mugs of tea filled with contraband liquor. The General and all his men treated me with kindness and respect, as if I were a china figure that might be blown over in the southeast Alaska wind. But none of them once looked at my face. They either averted their eyes or looked quickly at my belly as if I were a freak or one of God's mistakes. The General asked my opinion on which way a new street should be laid and if the troops should plant cherry trees along it. Would cherry trees survive in Alaska? he asked. What was it, I wondered, that these men saw in me? Why had they suddenly welcomed me as an American when I'd never even been considered a member of the white race by the Russians? I had to admit that I was flattered and taken in by their cordial words. But their kindness, I knew, was as changeable as the tide. With each kind word I smiled, thinking, these men cannot for one minute be trusted.

From the far end of the table General Davis proposed a toast. "Hip, hip," the men all cheered. "To Mr. and Mrs. Noah York and their unborn son, perhaps the first American to be born in Occupied Alaska."

10. SITKA, ALASKA
U.S. Possession
1869

My husband named him Vladimir, and while I lay exhausted and blooddrained from birthing, he wrote to his father that he'd eloped with a Russian princess who'd just borne him a royal son. For some unfathomable reason, Noah York never confronted me with the possibility that this child was not his own. Dark-eyed and olive-complexioned, *Uh-yeet-kutsku,* my dear little son, was like a tiny mirror of my own face.

My labor pains had begun the week that the fog mother and the spring leaves returned to Sitka Bay and just before Kat-lee-an massacred a dozen drunken American trappers who were attempting to trade him a barrel of wood alcohol for a bale of fox pelts. At first Mr. York was delighted with the baby, nicknaming him "Yorkie" and calling him his "treasure." But during Yorkie's second week of life, when I was finally strong enough to get up from my childbed and see to my husband's meals, the baby began to squawk like a surf duck, *qua, qua, qua,* all during the night. I began to see more of the light of the candlefish and the seal-oil lamp than the light of day. Mr. York was annoyed and wanted to punish the baby for being so unruly, saying that I was spoiling him for his later life by staying up nights with him. Nevertheless, night after night I sat up near the warmth of the cookstove, rocking my newborn son in his wooden cradle as my husband slept alone. With each one of Yorkie's screams, I gazed helplessly into his tiny squirrel-like face, knowing that there was no power, no magic within me, that could make me ignore my little one's cries.

That spring the baby wailed all night, and at dawn my husband would disappear for most of the day. One April morning I thought of following him, but I knew that with little Yorkie it would be impossible. I would have to strap the baby to my back in a basket as the Tlingit women carried their children, or leave him in the house unattended. If I took the baby with me, he might catch a chill from the damp of the constant spring rain, and I dared not leave him alone because an angry she-wolf was wandering this part of Indian River looking for her two stolen pups.

I sat alone in the large log house, rocking my *Uh-yeet-kutsku* week after week, longing for someone to talk to, longing to listen to Old Mother's stories. But I dared not go to the Village of the Raven for fear the Americans would discover my knowledge of the Tlingits and try to force me to help the new government in their fight against the Indians.

Seattle Charley, with his awful jagged-scar forehead, and stump-legged Reverend Hitch visited our home on Indian River more than once a week, asking for Mr. York's advice and assistance concerning Kat-lee-an's savage murdering and dismemberment of the local trappers. I always remained silent as I methodically served the men tea out of a samovar. Mr. York's friends must have thought that I had little schooling and was ignorant of the American language, because they spoke to me as if I were a foreigner—in pidgin English and usually only to ask for another cup of tea or to admire Yorkie.

"You," said Seattle Charley, pointing in my direction, "pour me more tea." He gestured in sign language and I had to stifle a pretend cough to keep from laughing.

Each time I filled his cup, I wondered what Seattle Charley and Reverend Hitch would say if they knew that the son of Kat-lee-an was right there under the same roof with them. And I swore I'd never tell anyone of Yorkie's parentage, not even Vladimir himself.

Just before the salmon fish started to run up Indian River, Mr. York said that we should replace some of the faulty shakes on the roof. He told me I should do it, because I was light in weight and would cause less damage. He held the pole and log ladder for me, and I climbed onto the roof with a basket of cedar shakes strapped to my back. I must have been up there for an hour, working my way from the eaves up to the peak of the roof, when I heard a gunshot ring out from across the river followed by a strange, elongated scream—not the voice of an animal, but a man.

"Mr. York," I shouted, "some trapper's shot himself!" But as usual my husband didn't answer. I looked to see if he was running for the boat to aid the injured hunter and saw that the canoe was beached on the wrong side of the river, a stone's throw downstream. My hands began to shake. Had Mr. York gone off while I was up on the roof instead of minding the baby inside the house as he had promised he would do?

I scrambled to the eave above the kitchen, but the pole ladder lay on the ground two stories below me. How would I get off the roof? I panicked. Baby Yorkie screamed from the noise of my clatter above him as I began to rip off the shakes beneath my knees. I wore no gloves, and splinters stuck under my fingernails. Maybe the pole lathing underneath the shakes would be wide enough for me to slip through. It had to be; there was no other way down. I tore at the rain-swollen shakes and at the same time gripped the side of the roof with my knees as if riding the ox that drew the sawmill cart.

Finally there was a hole large enough for me to slip between. I was broader than the span between the pole lathing, and the branch stubs in the wood tore at my clothes, skinning my ribs and hips as I lowered myself through the roof into the sleeping loft. When I got to the baby, my dress torn and my hands bleeding, little Yorkie was howling and gasping for air. I picked him up and strapped him to a basket on my back.

Rushing outside and toward the river, I remembered that the canoe was moored on the other side. There was a cedar log on shore, one Mr. York had cut into bolts to make cedar shakes from. I rolled the largest bolt into the water, using it to float myself across. The water in Indian River came straight out of the *glate,* the glacier, and it stung like fire, causing my feet to cramp. The swift spring current pushed me downstream toward the rocks and rapids, but I kicked furiously toward the opposite shore where the canoe was beached. Baby Yorkie screamed wildly from the cold of the water and thrashed in his basket, pulling at my hair.

I ran up the riverbank and down a deer trail to where I thought the shot had rung out. I didn't know the lay of the land on this side of the canyon; there was no cause for me ever to come here except to climb up toward the *glate* when the blueberries were ripe. The deer trail entered the woods, and I ran with my wet skirts clinging to my legs.

My running put little Yorkie's stomach into confusion. He began to vomit into my hair, and I had to pause so that he wouldn't choke. Then I ran on through the thickly wooded incline up toward the snow, the glare of the ice crater of Mount Saint Lazaria causing my eyes to squint. The Tlingits believed that the souls of the dead lived in the glaciers, and it was said that the living must never journey there.

I came to a clearing on a ledge above the river and spied a strange bark and pole shelter just into the woods on my right. Surely the dead souls of the Indians do not build houses, I thought, as I approached the small hovel. My feet slowed beneath me as I perceived the gruesome creature lying on the ground in front of the shelter. A man, a white man, lay breathing heavily on the ground. He was barely dressed, only wearing a clumsily constructed elk-skin loin covering, his legs encased in bark. A rifle lay a few feet from him.

As I moved closer I could see that half his jaw and the side of his head were gone. Blood ran from the pores of his forehead as well as from the head wound. Bits of flesh and bone lay around him, and the smell of blood, like the smell of my birthing, permeated my nostrils.

I stood just four or five feet from him, unable to move or avert my eyes from the terrible mutilation of his head. If he could still register visual objects in his half brain, he must have recognized me before I would let myself recognize him. Mr. York lay in a horror on the ground.

I approached slowly, watching his chest heave and twitch. He was like a dog crushed under the sawmill lumber cart. Nothing could be done for him. Had my husband moaned or writhed in pain, I might have shot him, but he did not. He only breathed heavily, his chest moving up and down.

The bullet had ripped open a cavern along his head and neck, and I turned away from his glassy eyes, feeling as if I were about to vomit. I took off one of my underslips, wrung it dry, and placed it over Mr. York's head. As I fell to the ground beside him, putting little Yorkie on his stomach, I realized that I was sobbing and shaking like the old ones mourning the dead.

Looking up into the trees, I saw the four eagles watching us, each perched in a wind-topped spruce. They are not carrion eaters, these birds, and I wondered why they were up near the *glate* during the day and not in the eagle trees closer to the bay, diving for fish. I stared at their enormous bodies, their wingspread almost as tall as a man. It was rumored among the Russian colonists that the bald eagles often carried small children away with them. But the four birds only watched me, sitting unmoving. The spirit of my mother is with me, I thought, remembering that the eagle was the totem of her tribe.

After my body stopped shaking, I picked myself up and went into the hut. There were strange garments made of filthy blankets along with oddly carved figures on the dirt floor. Amid the pile of Mr. York's unusual clothes was his leather-bound journal and a feather quill pen.

The late-summer-night twilight came and Mr. York still lay breathing on the ground while baby Yorkie slept on his stomach. I lay down next to my husband and arranged the strange garments from the hut over us for warmth. The animals, wolves and wild dogs, can smell blood two miles away, but somehow I wasn't concerned for my safety. I fell asleep next to Mr. York with the baby wedged between us. In the morning he was dead.

Afraid that the carrion eaters would get to him before I returned from the cabin with a shovel, I covered my husband's remains with spruce branches and small logs. Looking up, I saw that the four eagles had not moved from their watch in the trees above me, and I knew that they would at least keep the small beasts and ravens away from the body.

In the old days, the Tlingits buried their dead in mortuary poles, hollowed cedar trees with one totem, the crest of their tribe, atop the log and the ashes and belongings of the dead secured inside. But since the white men had come with their grave markers and church preaching, the Indians now buried their dead beneath small death houses alongside a totem atop a tall pole to mark the exit of the spirit. And so I buried Mr. York, beneath the dirt floor of his hut together with his strange carvings and his elk and buckskin clothes. The leather-bound journal I put inside my waistband and walked with little Yorkie, feeling heavy in his basket, toward the river and the canoe.

The next day, although the sun shone bright on the ice-topped mountains, it was as if I were navigating through a heavy winter fog. I paddled across Sitka Bay toward the *kekoor* rock and the two-barred cross atop the Church of Saint Michael to report Mr. York's death to General Jeff Davis. As my paddle cut into the glass-smooth water, I pondered Mr. York's strange encampment. Then I remembered the first time he and I had paddled across this bay together, that day he bought me from Gospozha Karimoff and took me to his abandoned shack.

How much did you pay for me and what do you want me for? The memory of my words rang back at me like the eerie call of a loon echoing off the bay rocks.

Such a strange man he is, I thought, not yet able to think of Mr. York in the past tense. Perhaps his death was just a bad dream or a terrible hoax that Seattle Charley and Mr. York himself had constructed as a joke on me. Perhaps my husband, body intact, would appear at General Davis's quarters, telling me that it had all been just a bit of good old Yankee fun. . . .

I reported that Mr. York had had a hunting accident and that I had buried him near his log house on Indian River. General Davis looked stunned. Sitting behind his cluttered, dust-covered desk, the General pulled at his full beard, saying that Sitka had lost an important citizen. He ordered the flag flown at half mast, declaring it a day of mourning among the populace. At first I thought the stout general a little too patronizing, but I didn't have the energy to give it further thought.

"What about you and young Master York?" asked the General, motioning to Yorkie, who slept in his basket. "I can't possibly ensure your safety unless you move inside the stockade."

I stared at the picture of President Andrew Johnson on the wall where once a painting of Czar Alexander II had hung. "But why should I do that?" I asked, imagining Andrew Johnson with half his head blown away like Mr. York had done to himself.

"Because the chief of the Tlingit tribes has sworn your death," roared the General, his blue brass-buttoned uniform stretching across his broad chest.

"Kat-lee-an?" I asked in disbelief, beginning to emerge from my fog.

"Your husband claimed two square miles of forested land outside the stockade, and those savages vowed to kill him on sight! Unfortunate accident, of course, but if those savages had gotten hold of Noah York, it might have been even worse." The General raised an eyebrow as if he enjoyed tales of bloodshed and cannibalism. "Now it's you and Noah's heir that this raven-masked heathen will be hunting for."

The General sat back in his leather chair, telling me that my husband had bought the town sawmill and owned an interest in the Alaska Commercial Company, the old fur depot, as well. But the thought of Kat-lee-an, my own child's father, beating the death drum for me weighed so heavily on my spirit that I couldn't comprehend General Davis's list of my husband's property.

As I poled the canoe up Indian River, I felt as if the blood of my body was going into the glacier water instead of through my veins. I walked into the log house, clutching Yorkie tightly in my arms and moaning a Tlingit death song that Mother-of-Stories had taught me:

"Yak-kak khi-nin tuwati tu-tuwn she-ya-ti-yelth
attakh tliyen Kakh tustinch."
In the middle of the ocean the Wolfs soul is dropped.
Raven, you will see the soul no more.

Would Kat-lee-an kill me and my baby as if we meant nothing to him?

I sat down in my husband's rocking chair beside the cold, unlit fireplace. No matter what General Davis says, I thought, I'll live in this house until I die—whether it's after Yorkie's grown into a man or killed by Kat-lee-an's own hand tomorrow. Then I began to rock, holding the baby in my arms. I rocked, moaning my Tlingit song, Uh-yeet-kutsku sucking at my breasts. I rocked until the late summer twilight had come and gone four times and the milk in my breasts went dry.

After four days the fog in my brain began to lift and I rose, preparing a pot of soup in the fireplace caldron. As I waited for the parsnip and salmon broth to boil, I picked up Mr. York's leather-bound journal and thumbed through the pages. There were notes of his travels on the ice ship from San Francisco to New Archangel and notes on the ways of the woods that I had related to him. Then, to my surprise, in the back of the journal there were bits of code or a made-up language. Sounds and words that made the noises of Indians talking, but nothing making sense. I studied the lists of vocabulary, the word he'd invented for *tree* and the word he'd invented for *frog*. Had he followed me to the Village of the Raven? Had he spied on me, listening to the Indians talking and trying to write their language?

Then I came upon a list of words arranged like a poem. As I read the odd sounds over and over to myself, I realized that it was Mother-of-Stories' fish-spawning chant. My heart sank as I realized that Mr. York might have been there with the hummingbirds rustling in the trees when Kat-lee-an and I met in the woods. But did my husband see us? I wondered. Did he know all along?

As I leafed through the pages of Mr. York's notebook, I noticed that the journal entries continued until the day of his death, but somehow I wasn't ready to know what they said. Methodically I picked up Yorkie, put the journal in his basket, and walked down to the orchard in the kitchen garden. I sat down among the sticklike pear trees now bearing their first fruit, the tiny, stone-hard pears lying on the ground as hornets swarmed to each piece of rotting fruit. I haven't the energy to collect and prepare them for winter storage, I said to myself, feeling as if I hadn't even the energy to live out the coming winter, to chop wood for the fire, to change and wash Yorkie's bedding each day. And if I did live out the coming cold, how would I keep the two of us alive for all the winters to come? Inhaling the incense of pears, I had a vision of myself clubbing salmon fish as they made their way up Indian River in the summer and selling the dried meat to the trappers. Perhaps if it was a bad year for salmon, I could use Mother-of-Stories' recipe for hooch and sell the brew to Boomers. Then I remembered that Mr. York had purchased the sawmill. But the trees in the forest belong to Kat-lee-an, I thought. I can't use the Tlingits' trees for houses of Americans, Americans who would kill the Indians without provocation.

Reaching into the baby's basket, I picked up Mr. York's notebook and studied the fish chant over and over. Then, taking a deep breath, I turned to some of the journal entries:

July 14.   The hemlock trees in Sitka Sound glitter in the rain. Betweentimes, the sky is bright. Towering clouds. Four bald eagles nest in the spruce snags, the fiery sunset shining on their heads.

July 17.   On this day I saw clearly that it is not the challenge of living in the wilderness that is my opiate, but raw fear itself. I am convinced beyond a doubt that this is what I will have in common with the aboriginals of Alaska, this hunger for the chase, which, philosophically speaking, is the hunger for fear. To be mortally afraid, to not know if I shall reach the other side of this fear and still be of this world; this is my opiate. This is why I have come into this country.

July 21.   At first the purchase of the Indian servant girl, Small-Lake-Underneath, distressed me. But only in purchasing an aboriginal was I reasonably assured of not being deserted in my purpose. And in my purpose she has swelled my heart with joy. She goes about her daily life as the beaver in the stream, unaware that I crouch in the bushes to study her every habit. Today I followed her to the Indian encampment and from the bushes watched an old wench sew bark-leg casings, using a bird beak as a needle. Casings probably for warriors' armor.

July 30.   Fear has become my sustenance, as real a physical need as bread and water. Each day, as I master the terrain of this rugged mountainous country, I find that I must go farther into the forest to meet a challenge. Yesterday it was a black she-bear whom I shot at the last possible instant before her lumbering weight sprang down upon me like a felled tree.

Aug. 9.   Small-Lake-Underneath conveyed to me that the
             aboriginals in the encampment to the north have an
             ancient remedy for quinsy: fermented wild rose hips,
             which here are the size of crab apples, taken alternately
             with bay water. This is combined with a journey to the
             Indian hot springs some miles south, where the red
             men sweat out their illness.

Aug. 15.   On this day I first saw the northern lights: luminous
             beams, as if it were the glow of a giant supernatural bird
             pulsing light across the darkened sky as it watched me.

Aug. 20.   Today again Small-Lake-Underneath proved her-
             self more faithful to my purpose than in my wildest
             dreams. I watched her in another clandestine meeting
             with crow-nosed aboriginal. During union, her peri-
             odic blood was ingested before fornication. The male
             was horribly ugly. To know that her desire to please
             me, to present me with a son, could lead her to commit
             an act of such revulsion, filled my heart with an elas-
             tic buoyancy. Surely this small girl loves me more than
             anyone in my life. Surely she has guided me through a
             savage country as my father never guided me through
             the world of the merely genteel.

Sept. 1.   Last night, perhaps it was the night before, I dreamed
             that the only way to fulfill my hunger for fear was to
             become one with the aboriginals, to take up their life.
             Leaving home most of the day, I began construction of
             my secret encampment.

Sept. 5.   There was a hard frost and a lunar halo around the full
             moon through the night fog. All day I watched waves,
             crash on the rocks of Sitka Sound. The water is the
             visual consistency of glass. Winters appear to compare
             favorably to the north of England.

Sept. 9.   This night Small-Lake-Underneath related to me an Indian myth as she built a fire to warm my feet: When the eagle, the crest animal of her Haida mother's tribe, beats his wings, it causes the thunder. When he blinks his white, bald-headed eye, lightning cracks over the earth.

Sept. 21.   Fear is my opiate. I want nothing else but the test, the gamble, daily now—myself against the elements of this raw land. If I win, my reward is not money as my father would have rewarded me for doing well in school or commerce, but rather—as it was this day—the towering white clouds, these Godlike green mountains that jut out from the quiet bay, and of course my wife. But always the question is with me; what lies beyond fear? What lies "on the other side" of this mortal life?

I put Mr. York's journal down and slowly with one hand began gathering the decaying pears from beneath the fruit tree, and with the other rocking little Yorkie in his basket. What sort of a wife would my tiny son have? I wondered. A great sigh overtook me, and I began to feel a terrible loss grow within my chest, a loss that would be remembered many years to come when I would again come upon the leather-bound notebook with my husband's name engraved across the front cover: Noah York.

PART II

1893–98

Ulla Björklund

11. U.S.S. RESOLUTE
The Inside Passage
1893

Ja, sure, inside my low-waisted corset my stomach has been pitching and turning with this steamer boat ever since I left San Francisco for Alaska. And since I was afraid to tell my folk about this adventure, there was no one on the wharf to wave me a good-bye like the good-byes and good lucks I remember when I left Sweden with *Mor* and *Far* as a little girl.

Again and again I put my hand inside my satchel to feel for the gun. I've lost track of the days on board *Resolute,* but it must be close upon the Feast of the Green Leaf, and me I spent all last night wondering if it is the right thing I am doing, selling out my house and the cabbage field across the San Francisco Bay on Alameda Island and going to Alaska to find the men who done my Gunnar in.

Outside my porthole the fish are celebrating this first clear day by leaping like little goats, just like I'd be doing if I were home with my people dancing the swing *polska* and eating *lax* and *knäckebröd* from the *smörgåsbord.* But on board *Resolute* there is no celebration, only blue-eyed, white-haired Joaquin Johnny outside my window on the promenade deck talking in his Scotsman's tongue to the men all going sluicing for gold like my Gunnar done.

Oh, Jonah, it makes me cry, the constant green mist along the hilly shoreline and me all the time thinking of my Gunnar in some damp Alaska grave. Last night there was fog so thick that *Resolute* had to drop anchor and wait it out for fear of running aground or into one of these unfriendly islands where I know the wood-woman and the *skogsfolk* must be breeding stumpy children and trolls in every dark green nook.

The mist from this island-dotted ocean makes me cold inside my flannel traveling suit; I huddle under my cloak, wondering if my folk have discovered me gone yet. No one to water the cabbages and the new owner saying he's going to rip them out and build Queen Anne cottages for the railroad men.

For a whole year after Gunnar died I wanted to tell *Mor* about my secret plan, but no—*Mor* never likes my plans. She never even much liked Gunnar. "Ulla," she'd say, "I tell you to marry a Swede or a real Amerikaner, not a Wegie like that Gunnar man." And *Mor* all the time talks of Sweden, Sweden, since I was a little girl, since I was five and we left for San Francisco in America.

Alaska, Gunnar told me, would be looking just like the fjords of Norway and the waterways of Bohuslän. New Scandia, I tell *Mor;* Gunnar and I are going to New Scandia. I tell her that Gunnar and I are not good with cabbages. There is no other work, and rascals from Oakland cross over the salt marsh and steal our cabbages at night. But what is to be done? I ask *Mor.* The poor rascals have no food. The only money Gunnar and I make is from the cabbages, so first Gunnar goes to Alaska and then I go. There is free land there, Gunnar said, and plenty of water—many lakes like Sweden. If Gunnar doesn't find gold at Camp Juneau, I tell *Mor,* there's fishing for herring like his grandfather in Oslo done.

But *Mor* always is unhappy with me. "Ulla," she said, "I tell you, Ulla, now, if you and Gunnar leave you are quitters, *ja.*" She comes some days with *Far,* when he's through working on the ferry that goes across the San Francisco Bay; she comes to me and Gunnar in the cabbages and says we are quitters to leave our folk because of hard times. Somehow I never make *Mor* happy.

I was twins, and often I think she'd rather have me dead instead of Jorgen. I remember her screaming *vakna, vakna,* wake up! when she found him dead in our trundle bed the morning after Santa Lucia's Day. She washed him with *brännvin* and put him in a white box with pine branches around his head. Ångel, she called him Ångel. I remember trying to make her stop wailing as the sled pulled the small box up to the snow-covered graveyard. But I was no comfort to her. Jorgen, Jorgen, *vakna,* she wailed. Somehow she was never my mother again, even though I was her only *lilla barn*. The next spring we came to California, and the snow falling on Jorgen's grave was the last winter I ever saw.

When I got the letter from Reverend Hitch telling me about Gunnar and the foul play, I could only think about *Mor* washing Jorgen's body. *Mor* had a body to wash, to dress in a white nightgown with a lace cap and pine needles around his pretty dead face. But I had no proof, nothing to know that my Gunnar had really passed over, only the letter still here in my satchel next to Gunnar's pearl-handled revolver—Barbro, he named it, the one he'd left for me to fend off the cabbage-stealing rascals.

For a year I thought of going after him with no one to know I was gone until I was halfway to New Scandia. Was I doing the right thing, going now to find Gunnar's grave? The days go by so slowly since he died, and all I think of is murdering those two men—sourdoughs, Gunnar called them in his letters—his partners, Seattle Charley and Joe Sprout.

When I wrote to the Reverend to ask where is my Gunnar's claim and where are the bits of gold he had been saving, Reverend Hitch replied that no such valuables were among Gunnar's few belongings and his partners were nowhere to be found. The Reverend wrote that in the streets of Wrangell there was talk of foul play, with my Gunnar being found dead in a bruin trap, but that it was a lawless country and I should be praying for salvation rather than revenge. And all the time I am thinking, Oh, Jonah, they no more like Swedes and Wegies in the northland of Alaska than they do in San Francisco.

Outside now the men on deck are packed closer than herrings in a barrel to hear what Alaska story old blue-eyed Joaquin Johnny is telling this time. And him addressing the others as if he were Lord of the Goths and the Vandals:

"Let me tell ye lads about ma poor wee dog, Yukon, and how I once almost lost the beastie inside a northern cavern of ice. Oh, but it was like a heavenly vision, that ice cave, showin' the stained-glass window colors of heliotrope and aquamarine down there in the dim light. And without a thought for ma own life, I entered into the cavern calling for Yukon.

"Further and further down the steep icy stairway I walked before I realized that I'd lost ma way. Oh, lads, I tell ye, ma heart was in ma mouth. But in the end it was the barking of bonny Prince Yukon himself that led me out of that palace of ice. And indeed, the echo of ma own dog's bark caused God's ice temple to close its doors in a thunderous avalanche, not a moment after I'd found ma way out of its hungry mouth."

Then all the men troop after Johnny while he's tickling and cajoling the only *flicka* to come out of her cabin this first clear day. Such a frail thing she is, with a tiny *barn* in her arms. In Alaska, they tell me, there are ten men to every woman. All those men. How will I find my two claim swipers among all those men? Oh, I moan, thinking of my poor dead Gunnar. I wonder if this Johnny has a wife who pines after him while he's run off to explore the dangerous northern ice, just as I waited for letters from my Gunnar gone off to the goldfields.

There is nothing to do but sit in my cabin watching the shoreline and thinking of my murder plans. All the time I have with me my lucky ten-*öre* piece that Uncle Jarl gave me when I left Sweden as a little girl. I turn the coin over and over in my palm. I can no more think of what will happen when my money runs out, when I haven't a *krona* to my name. No more husband, I say to myself, so I will do washing and ironing for others, not much different from being married to Gunnar or living in *Mor's* house.

Outside now, white-bearded Johnny's trying to get a peep at the baby. And I am all the time thinking of the babies inside me dying before they were born. Like a pot at potato-boiling time, my belly, as soon as the kicks and quivers come, spills over a *barn* too early to be born. Then I feel so depleted all the next day, weeding cabbages and hauling fodder for the *mjölk*-cow and thinking of the night before. *Mor* says it must be that the Nis in my house steals each *barn* away, just like the Nis stole baby Jorgen. But my girl friends say it is because there is too hard work in the house and the fields. *Ja*, sure, Kerstin and Inga, always good friends to me.

At night when I undress I sometimes look at my poor empty belly, the skin in folds hanging like a grandfather's face. And my face: There is such sagging around the eyes. Twenty-eight years I am, and it makes me sad—no babies and no more to be young, no more to be the pretty *ung flicka* I never was.

Through Queen Charlotte Sound and past Prince Rupert village. It is like a fairyland sometimes, these green and tiny islands of the Alexander Archipelago. So far north we've sailed, and always the air is cool on my arms, but even so, when the sun peeks through the clouds this new land reminds me of Uncle Jarl's paintings of the Leeward Islands and the blue-green Caribbean Sea.

"Metlakatla," black-whiskered Captain O'Sullivan calls. Metlakatla, a missionary island, our first Alaska port-of-call. We pull into the rustic harbor. No one to go ashore, the captain says. *Nej,*nothing here for the men, not a tavern to be found. A Christian Indian reservation, I hear Joaquin Johnny say, as a man in a cleric collar escorts a single passenger, a *liten* dark auburn-haired woman, on board *Resolute*. Johnny is calling hellos to the man. "Father Duncan, Father Duncan," he says, waving his big bony fingers. Johnny has made this trip many times, I think. What does he do? I wonder. Why is he so famous with all the folk aboard and in the town? He seems to know the tiny dark woman as well. He is jumping and clapping his hands. "Old friends, old friends," he shouts to*Resolute*'s new passenger.

Maybe fifty Indians stand on the log wharf to wave, some to pray on their knees. They look not very much like the picture-book Indians—animal men in bear rugs with painted faces. *Nej,* in Metlakatla all the Indians are dressed in black with vacant smiling faces.

As we wait for *Resolute* to load food supplies before pulling out of the harbor, I look down into the water, watching seaweed tails thrash at the rocks and silver fish dart like shooting stars into the boat shadow. I half believe that maids and mermen in their greeny skin live down beneath the rocks with all the dead drowned souls whose bodies were never found. My girl friend, Kerstin, always tells her *barn* at bedtime about a mermaid and her herd of snow-white cattle that come out of the sea to graze on the hills of Gothenburg. I think of Kerstin, and my eyes focus on what has caused my mind so much to wander. Like eyes in the earth, the bay water mirrors white jagged mountains. Mountains behind Metlakatla, and on the peaks the first snow I've seen since

I was five, since I went with *Mor* every day to scrape the snow from Jorgen's headstone.

By Jimminy and by *Gud*, here they got mountains bigger than any I remember in California, twice as high and green as Yosemite, where *Far* took us to camp in the piney woods one summer. Sure, these mountains got snow-topped crags coming out of the sea so suddenly one might think they were the mermaid driving her herd of white cattle. An omen, I think, first to see the giant mountains of Alaska down in the water.

O'Sullivan pulls up the gangplank and we are on our way. Blue-eyed Johnny rushes to the rail to wave good-bye to Father Duncan. The tiny dark woman does not wave; she looks angry. Such beautiful hair she has, all wound in a braid about her small face, and her head shining like a copper pot in the sun. Our new passenger pushes her way through the men toward the purser. But Johnny chases after her, as she clutches her only satchel close to her breast to fend him off.

"Leave your wife behind again?" I hear her say.

Johnny's Scotsman's tongue thickens and he wails that he'd rather the amid the ice of Alaska than perish picking his rich father-in-law's cherry crop while some Chinese fruit picker accidentally dumps a box of deadly phosphorus pest killer on his head. "Give me the white death in the glaciers any day, lads," he says. "Civilization is for the caged spirit, not mine." All the men cheer and go to tipping their flasks of whiskey. "Ketchikan before dawn tomorrow and Wrangell in two days' running," yells Joaquin Johnny, as he begins to weave another tale of adventure about him and his dog Yukon exploring the ice caverns in the land to the north. The men pant after Johnny as if they were dogs themselves, and me, I'm left alone on the bow thinking scornful thoughts: Why did Johnny marry if he wants to run wild and free as a forest beast? I'll bet it's his wife's money, too, that pays his passage on this ship. Oh, that Johnny's a devil in the potato patch, but who'd be asking me?

Later, when the sky is like the midnight sun in Sweden, there is a bold and manly knock at my door. It is the captain and the tiny dark woman who's just come aboard. "Mrs. Björklund," black-whiskered O'Sullivan says to me, "I've a favor to be askin' of ye. You bein' a woman travelin' alone, you're sure to be lonesome. You'd be doin' both of us a kindness by sharin' yer cabin with Mrs. York here. We got none empty, and I can't go puttin' her down in the hold with Johnny and the boys. I'd be forever in your debt if ye could see your way clear to obligin' me, Ma'am." A woman alone, the captain says, as if it were a sinful thing. Feeling like a naughty child, I look up at O'Sullivan, who, even though he is Irish, has *Far*'s stern and wind-chapped scowl.

"*Ja*, sure," I say, smiling into Mrs. York's friendly face. She does not much look like a woman who is unhappy to be traveling by herself. I think she is about forty years, but with the face of a *flicka*, high cheekbones like the Indians at Metlakatla and a European nose—Creoles they call them here. She sits quiet as a redheaded flicker bird while the midshipmen bring in her satchel and a cot.

"I'm getting off tomorrow," she says, smiling, her eyes dark as charcoals. Why does she stare at me like this? But before an hour is up we are sitting next to each other, with me telling her all of my woes and sorrows, just leaving out the part about murder—except to say that my Uncle Jarl once chased a fisherman into the Norwegian Sea for stealing his sweetheart away.

"You know this man Joaquin Johnny?" I ask.

"Yes," she says. "The Indians call him Ankow Glate, the Great Ice Chief." She speaks with an edge to her voice. "He says he studies world making and the *glate*."

"What is this word *glate*?" I ask.

"Glaciers," she says. "People say he's famous down in the States. They say he writes books for senators in Washington. Another white chief," she says. "The one white man among the Indians. Just like Father Duncan back in Metlakatla, who's convinced the Indians to forsake the stories of their ancestors for the Bible and the Good News. Men like this Johnny, they hear that the Indians up here pray to bears and ravens, and they think, aha, perhaps these dark skins will pray to me as well. They all want to be gods, I think, white gods among the savages.

The little dark woman takes a deep breath. "But at least the Indians in Alaska have fared better than those in Seattle," she says, with a look of sadness on her lips. "By the time Great Northern built a railroad west to Puget Sound, all the cheap Indian labor had been massacred or died of starvation. So the Seattle city council had to bring in Chinamen to lay the iron road. . . ." For a moment Mrs. York's voice trails off like the echo of a far-away bird.

"Father Duncan in Metlakatla?" she continues. "He's the only white man among a hundred Tsimshian Indians. He converted the whole tribe, and now they can't even cook dinner without asking his advice. I went to visit his cannery to observe the salmon run. My son and I have a cannery in Sitka. He doesn't like me much, Father Duncan, because I tell stories to his Indian converts. I grew up with the Tlingits near Sitka, and on my visits to Metlakatla I tell his people the stories that the old ones told me. The Tsimshians like to hear my stories. It makes old Duncan mad as a *hootz* in spring. And something in me is happy when I make this man angry."

The bell rings for dinner: tinned beef, mashed potatoes, and turnips again. But Mrs. York and I, all the same we eat it. There is no more to do on board than eat, eat and watch scenery which is beautiful but by now becomes boring. Yesterday I counted ten brown moose, all with reindeer horns and big as horses, grazing along the shore among these giant trees. Virgin timber, O'Sullivan calls them. And in and amongst the trees are beautiful pink and lavender rhododendron flowers, looking more like they should be growing on some tropical island and not at the foot of these steep northern mountains. Always the landscape is like a painted picture. And to think that all I knew about Alaska when I left San Francisco was that it's where one gets gold and whale baleen for corset stays.

At the end of the galley dining table, Johnny and the men have begun to tip the bottle, reminding me of my folk and the Feast of the Green Leaf that's probably now already past. Kerstin, Inga, and Olaf chain dancing and tipping the *öl* and *akvavit*. And for me it would have been my first *polska* after a year of mourning.

"Nadia," Johnny calls across the table, "you've been without a husband all these years, why not come dancing in ma cabin with me and the wee beasties?"

The men roar with laughter, but Mrs. York sits calm as a witch on Easter Eve. "Johnny," she says, "the beard on your face is as inviting as the barnacles on a rock. No wonder your wife prefers her father's California cherry orchards." Johnny gets red as a cherry himself and begins sputtering. Mrs. York grabs my wrist and we go back to our cabin, me with some toast stolen off the dinner platter wrapped up in a napkin. As soon as she bolts the door we near pass over with laughter. Then I unfold the toast and begin making *skorpor*, sweet toast, with the spice I've hidden in my satchel.

This Mrs. York, I think to myself, such a brave outspoken little woman she is to talk to Joaquin Johnny so. Perhaps she's like me, with a husband who left his folk to look for gold just as my Gunnar did.

"Cinnamon," says Mrs. York, smelling my spices. "The Russian fur ships used to bring boxes of this from Canton." We eat *skorpor* and she begins to stroke my hair, which has come undone from its knot. "It's like the gold silk cloth from China," she says. "I've never seen hair like yours."

"I'm Swedish," I say. "At school they called me towhead. They pointed and laughed. Big towhead Swede, they said."

"You look like the pictures of Russian noblewomen in the books the Mission Fathers used to show me," she says, "when the Russians were in Alaska. You're pretty, like the pictures of girls with long ring-lets in the Czar's court."

No stranger has ever spoken words like this to me, *nej*, except maybe the men on the ferry dock before I married my Gunnar. No one has ever called me pretty. She is a stranger, this Mrs. York, why should she lie to me? I secure my loose hair back in a knot. "In Sweden," I say, "married women don't let their hair show out of their caps. *Mor*, even now in America, does the same. And when she came to visit Gunnar and me and found me on my porch bare-headed, she chided me like the parish priest calling out the devil."

"An old woman once told me," says Mrs. York, "that to the east beyond these mountains, beyond the home of the Athabascans, there lives a tribe of white Indians. Blue eyes, the old woman told me, with white hair on their faces and golden hair on their heads. No white man has ever seen this tribe," she says, "but like Joaquin Johnny they're always trying. The Indian stories say that Raven made all the aborigi-nals in Alaska, but Raven didn't make the white Indians. The white

Indians live inland in the high valleys and mountains where the dark Indians have never ventured, because the bear with the moose foot and evil spirit lives in those valleys as well. Perhaps it is you, Mrs. Björklund, that these Indians resemble."

I pull the porthole curtains shut and lie face down on my pillow. The bear with the moose foot, I think to myself. Hadn't *Mor* once told me a tale about *elvefolk* and bears with one reindeer foot? Mrs. York unknots my hair and combs it with her fingers. "Like gold silk," she says. "Like the moon when the late-night skies come back."

Mrs. York lies down on her cot, rearranging her long black dress and shawl for warmth. But as she moves her arm up, I notice under her woolen blouse that she wears such a strange necklace—ivory bonelike beads and white fangs like icicles strung together with a rawhide string. So beautiful a necklace, though with a frightening look, reminding me *of Mor's* tales about the magic of the wood-woman and *skogsfolk*. Where did Mrs. York get such a necklace? I wonder.

I dream of Gunnar on our wedding night. Dream of him chasing me around the bedroom yelling and laughing. "Ten thousand Swedes ran through the weeds chased by one Norwegian." Dream of his body on mine rocking me like a boat.

So late I awake, and Mrs. York is not with me in the cabin. I see that her satchel is gone and quickly I tie my hair back and run to the black-whiskered captain on wheel watch atop the steamer's bridge. "Mrs. York?" he says. "Got off at Ketchikan before dawn. She's good company, ain't she now? Hope it didn't inconvenience ye none. Thought I'd be doin' both of ye a favor, two widows alone in the world. Could be dangerous, ye know, Mrs. Björklund, a woman traveling alone like you're doin." He looks down at me with *Far's* stern and disapproving face, then lifts his binoculars, surveying the flat gray sea.

I go back to my cabin and pull the curtains. My legs, like iron pipes, fall across my berth. Ulla, I say to myself, you are Ulla now alone in the world. I reach inside my satchel and pull out Barbro. I aim her at the door lock and practice spinning the cylinder and cocking the hammer. Ah, Barbro, I say, today I am too tired for murder. Carefully I put her back in the satchel. I lie face down on my pillow and comb my hair with my fingers, feeling as if I've just lost the only real *moder* I ever had.

12. WRANGELL
District of Alaska
1893

"Ah, my regal miss, your tits'r as big as the U.S.S. *Res-o-lute*," says Montana to one of the three queens in his hand while he curls his black mustache. *Ja,* and *Mor* would have drowned herself at the bottom of the lake if she could see me now sitting with two old tarts in the Stikine Saloon.

At the table next to Montana's card game, some old herrings boast of their Dease Lake diggings ten years gone. And all the time I am eavesdropping like an elf-maid to hear the name Seattle Charley or Joe Sprout. Most of the population of Wrangell must be either in this saloon or next door at the Arctic Brotherhood Fraternal Order and Tavern.

Why did my Gunnar come to Wrangell? I keep wondering. The town is half deserted, with the plank walkway of the main and only street all broken into pieces and mud everywhere washed down from the steep, bare hills in back of the false-front dry-goods stores and bars. These hills where they've cut down every tree look as bald and weathered as the skull of a *mjölk*-cow two years dead. Everywhere unpainted plank houses like wooden boxes are boarded up, with a hotel in a beached steamer the only place for me to stay. And the only people to be warm and hospitable are these two henna-haired tarts, Aggie and Marvis, who tell me that the Cassiar goldfields are all run out and those that didn't strike it rich or the from the elements hung around to pickle themselves here in the Stikine Saloon.

"Hey, Marvis," I hear one old herring say, "did ya know that Yo and Eskimo Tommy blew in last night?" He laughs, showing his toothy stubs, and pounds his three-fingered hand on the bare board table. Marvis is busy looking over Montana's shoulder while he's playing a game of cold-deck draw poker with an Indian who just got paid for unloading a lumber schooner.

"Marvis's too old to hold her piss," says Montana. Marvis dumps her whiskey shot on Montana's head.

Oh, Jonah, the men are crazy up here. I slump down in my chair and decide to act as if I am used to this vile talk.

"Marvis, ya ain't good for shit," Montana goes on. "Every time we do the conjugal act, ya dang near piss all over me."

Marvis goes to the bar and Fat Bartender Arny gives her another shot. "Aggie, we oughta take our show south to See-attle," she retorts. And me, I am wondering if my Gunnar, before he died, sat in this same saloon and talked like these old billy goats.

"Wolf scat," I hear Bob Harper, the white-haired U.S. Customs agent, say, "you all'r gonna get Marvis in such a fix that her facial hairs'll fall out."

"Hey, Marvis," says an old herring sitting in back of me. "You ever done it with Yo?"

"Hey, Agg," Bob Harper chimes in, "what's Eskimo Tommy's dinger like? What's it like, bein' dinged by a half-wit Eskimo? Hell, if I give ya six bits and a yardstick, will ya measure his dinger for me tonight? Me and Montana's got this bet goin'."

Aggie goes to fanning herself with an ostrich feather fan to hide the smile on her toothless face and the wink that's intended for me.

"Shit," I hear another one say, "you ever heard the story of Yo's daddy? Died a long time ago, but I heard this story straight from ol' General Davis 'fore they sent the Navy back. Seems that Yo's daddy did it with animals. You know, like rabbits and sea otters, maybe porc-u-pines even, for all I know. Whatever he could catch. Had a special hankerin' for big game. Davis swore they went out huntin' together once just for a bear in heat. He shot it dead, see, and then commenced to tie its legs apart. If ya wanted to make that guy happy, the General said, ya just had to shoot him a bear in heat. Hell, ol' Yo's daddy practi-cally got himself a her-ni-ation every year when the salmon started to run. Ever twanged a live fish, Amy? Well, I guess that's what this guy done. Picked up the fish on the bank, ya know, the ones the gulls have pecked the eyes out of but they're still alive. Picked 'em up and pro-ceeded to twang 'em to death through the mouth. Never hear of a guy like him near or far, 'cept maybe back in Connecticut where my pappy used to raise sheep. Hell, Pap could tell by runnin' his fingers through the fleece just which shepherd had twanged which sheep. . . . So, anyway, ol' Yo's daddy finally did himself in one day when he couldn't catch himself nothin' and he went to twanging his shotgun and killed himself by accident."

Å Gud, I say to myself, covering my ears. *Mor* will see the sin in my face if I listen to many more stories like these.

"This con-ver-sation is unfit for ladies to hear," says Marvis, grasping my hand, and the whole barroom near collapses with laughter.

"You ain't no lady," shouts Montana. "In fact, if ya don't learn to hold your piss ya ain't even a one-dollar lay."

"Ple-e-e-ase, gents," says Aggie, "you all are forgettin' about Ulla here."

All the men turn to look at me, sitting with my union suit hanging out the arms of my canvas digger's clothes and my hair all hidden under a black scarf. "Ulla," says one old herring, "uh-la-la," and grabs hold of his crotch.

For the love of Jonah, why does Aggie point me out like this? "A lady miner, she is," says Marvis. "Been bunkin' with us over at the Steamship Ho-tel, seein' that there's no other place suitable for her in this has-been town."

Montana and Fat Arny are now staring at my breasts instead of my face. White-haired Bob Harper deals another hand, giving me a sneak peek at some of the cards. "What brings you to these parts, little lady?" he says.

"To be striking it rich," I say, hoping that he can't smell a dead fish.

The whole barroom roars with laughter again, and Montana throws his cards on the table. "A lady miner," says one old herring. "Well, don't that beat all."

"Would you like to feel of my muscle?" I say, and think, *nej, nej,* that was the wrong thing for me to have done.

Bob Harper and some of the others near fall off their chairs. "Now you ol' sourdoughs stay clear of Ulla," says Aggie. "We're mighty taken with her, Marvis and me, and we're gonna be watchin' out for her around here."

"Who's gonna watch her when you're twangin' the half-wit Eskimo tonight?" chimes Fat Arny in my ear.

Aggie stands up, lifting her dress, and bends over without any bloomers on underneath. "Kiss it, Arn, your iron hasn't worked in years."

"Just sit down, Agg," he says. "Ya don't start showin' it off till the piano player gets here, and that ain't till eight o'clock."

"Goose shit," says an old herring standing at my elbow. "I hear tell of a lady in Sitka who did it with that Eskimo, and all she got for her trouble was a silver dollar and a terrible sore where her pee-pee comes out. Now she's got scabs all over her face and no one'll come near her, let alone give her any business. Well, she's been sellin' it so long that she's got this fer-o-cious appetite, so ol' Doc Spencer's plannin' some technical operation to keep her from hankerin' after the men and infectin' them with her terrible disease."

Five days I've been in Wrangell listening to the sinful stories of the streets, and not a word about my two claim swipers. And from the looks of this almost ghost town, not a claim to be swiped except up the white rapids of the cold and fast-flowing Stikine River at Glenora or up the narrows at Juneau. Aggie and Marvis, they're good friends to me, and neither one of them ever heard of these two men or even of my Gunnar. Reverend Hitch, they tell me, is inland converting the souls of Indians and won't be back for weeks. So, I think to myself, maybe just a few more days in Wrangell and then I head north again. Tonight the lumber schooner men will come for the show, Aggie says, so there will be more new names and faces. Marvis says that this man Yo owns most of the lumber and fishing schooners, and a sawmill and farmstead in Sitka as well. Maybe he knows this Seattle Charley, I think to myself.

Ja, and at eight o'clock, when there's still enough light for me to be reading a week-old copy of the *Sitka Times* without a lamp, the one-legged piano player starts rolling his fingers across the keyboard. The afternoon drinkers snoozing on the floor lift themselves up and go back to their tables or over to Montana's card game, where the Indian has just a few dollars left.

I hear a ruckus at the door and in walk seven, maybe eight, broad-shouldered men from the lumber ship, all singing a chorus of "Daisy Bell," with one old herring warbling a profane variation that I am trying not to hear. Aggie and Marvis, bedecked in red taffeta dresses and holding a rusted bicycle built for two, go to tapping their feet up on the rickety platform at the far corner of the room. And me, the only woman in the audience, I sit back in a little nook.

"Where do all the womenfolk go?" I had asked Marvis.

"Women?" she said. "There's not many of 'em, 'cept me and Agg, and you, since you arrived. The others is ministers' wives and converted Indian squaws, and they're all busy readin' their Bibles or listenin' for the Good News."

So I sit trying not to be noticed by all these sourdoughs while Aggie and Marvis are up on the platform mounting the bicycle seats. They rotate their torsos around and around, and I see that the old herrings are panting like dogs.

"Don't waste it on no bicycle," yells Bob Harper.

"Don't pee on it," yells Montana.

All the time I am wondering, no women here; why do these old sourdoughs stay on instead of returning to their folk? Sad to think that there might be wives somewhere waiting for these men as I waited to hear from my Gunnar. But by *Gud* and by golly, I say to myself, looking at one of them, surely his wife is better off alone than having to care for such a drunk.

Up on stage the girls dismount and the bicycle falls off the platform. Somebody calls out that the next round's on him, and all the old herrings run to the bar to get their shot glasses filled. Always I am listening for two names, Seattle Charley and Joe Sprout, but all these men talk of is the strike at Forty Mile Creek or doing what they call "sticking it" to various parts of Aggie and Marvis.

Someone brings out a scuffed-up roulette wheel and the girls dance the can-can around it while the men make bets, spinning the wheel and reaching their arms between Aggie's legs. *Da, da, da, da,* goes the piano while the girls lift up their skirts to show their bare rumps with only their garters holding up their stockings. Oh, Jonah, I say to myself, what kind of a *Gud* is it that would lead these two good-hearted *flickas* into a life such as this?

My thoughts are broken by the cheers of the men from the lumber ship. One sourdough is throwing buckshot pellets at Aggie's behind.

Someone brings me a shot glass of whiskey and I pretend to drink it in little sips. Everyone is drinking whiskey, lots of whiskey. Everybody laughs. But me, I don't have so much to laugh about. "What d'ya say, little lady?" someone yells to me. I make sure that the scarf is tied tight on my head. I ignore the man who has yelled at me and keep watching the door for new faces. The air begins to have a terrible stink.

Then I see two dark men walk in, one tall with thick black hair and the other about a foot shorter, with yellow skin, rounded shoulders, and glasses. "Yo, Yo!" everybody screams.

Aggie jumps off the platform, knocking down the sourdough who was supposed to catch her. "Yo," she says, "come sit your little fanny down and meet my new friend and Wrangell's newest citizen. Ulla," she says to me, "Yo. Yo, Ulla."

He is tall, taller than my Gunnar, and with a face that couldn't be more than twenty-three or twenty-four years. "Hel-lo," he says, his brown eyes looking at me like a cautious *mjölk*-cow. Never once does he stare me full in the face. The short man behind him must be the half-wit Eskimo that everybody talks about. "This here's Tommy," Yo says to me. Tommy turns his slant-eyed, pie-shaped face to the floor and mumbles.

They sit at my table, and Bartender Arny brings Yo a drink. Some sourdough shouts out, "She's a big un, Yo. Ya know what they say about big women." Everybody laughs, and I am wondering how long it will be before everyone calls me Big Swede, Big Towhead Swede. Some of the men are falling over each other. They must be awfully drunk. Marvis and Aggie start to dance around the roulette wheel while the piano player is playing the Daisy song again. I look at this man Yo. He doesn't look like someone whose father carried on so with beasts and wood folk.

Yo sends Tommy to get me another glass of whiskey. The little Eskimo sets the drink down in front of me and begins to stare at my body like I was a painted picture. Like a curious baby, he starts with my hand on the shot glass and goes slowly over all my parts with his eyes. He must not have more than fifteen or sixteen years, but with a grandfather face. Big ears like the iceman's mule and glasses with lenses as thick as jelly jars.

A troll, I think to myself, a hillman from one of *Mor*'s Swedish fairy tales. Then I remember that the ringing of bells drives trolls away. But, *nej*, I am not wanting to drive this little fellow away. *Mor* says it is Sunday children that see the trolls and *skogsfolk*. Jorgen and I were born on Sunday: my *söndagsbarn, Mor* used to call us. This Eskimo Tommy is a troll, I think to myself. And if the stories that I was told as a child are true, then this troll Tommy can tell the future for me as well as the whereabouts of my two claim-swiping murderers.

Yo makes polite conversation. From where do I come? What do I do here? A lady miner, I say. He doesn't laugh. Tommy doesn't take his eyes from me, but when I try to talk to him he looks at the plank board wall. "Are you Yo's partner?" I ask the *liten* one.

"Someone," he says, referring to himself, "someone doesn't know." He speaks with a heavy speech impediment, and all the time I am thinking, Oh, Jonah, I have found myself a troll.

I look away from Tommy to see sourdoughs falling in every direction and the piano player standing up on his one leg to pound violently on the tiny keys. Montana wins the last dollar from the Indian and jumps up, pulling his manhood out of his pants. By *Gud*, I think I will burn in hell if I don't close my eyes to the sight of him, but for my own safety I keep them open. Montana strums himself violently to the rhythm of the piano. Marvis and Aggie are doing their pink-ostrich-feather fan dance. All the old herrings pull out their manhoods and point them at Marvis. I think that there must be something about the cool wet air in Alaska that makes men go mad. Bob Harper's pants fall completely to the floor, and someone pees across the room. "Here's to ya, Marvis!" Montana shouts. Suddenly all the men are shooting semen or peeing across the room. The old sourdoughs next to me seem to be engaged in some kind of a contest. "A little to the left, Montana," screams Bob Harper, "you're gettin' me all wet." All the men are trying to pee on Marvis and Aggie.

Yo, Tommy, and I dive under our table to get away from the line of fire when the men at the next table point in our direction. Never have I heard or seen such things as these! Even as a schoolgirl when Inga and Kerstin and I would eavesdrop on the men at the ferry dock there was no mention of anything so vile.

I knock my head on the table and my scarf falls off, with my hair coming undone in my face. Tommy lets out a little shriek. "Angel," he says, "an angel." He touches my hair as if it were fire that could burn him. Then he begins to stroke it and stick the ends in his mouth. "Angel, angel," he says. Oh, Jonah, if this little man is a troll, then this is a good omen for me.

"Don't mind Tommy none," says Yo. "Reverend Hitch's been show-ing him too many religious picture books." But I see that Yo himself is looking with awe at my hair. "It *is* pretty," he says in a gentle voice. "Don't be angry with Tommy. Not many women as blond and pretty as you live up in these parts. I reckon you're the first one he's seen."

"Reverend Hitch," I say. "Do you know this man?"

"Sure," says Yo, "everybody knows Hitch. One of the first American churchmen to come to Alaska, or so the old-timers say."

I tie my hair up again, and we go back to our chairs. Most of the men have used up all of their liquids and are at the bar filling their glasses while their manhoods hang limply in front of them.

Tommy moves his chair closer to me. Now he is maybe two inches away and staring at my scarf with the blond ends sticking out. "Angel," he says. "Baby Jesus."

"Jumpin' Jehoshaphat," says Yo, "you're embarrassin' the lady. And get that fool Hitch's preachin' outa your head." Tommy's seaweed-pod eyes roll beneath his thick-lensed glasses and his ears wiggle.

Over at the other end of the bar, Marvis is shrieking with delight. Someone has brought in a whole crate of fish, salmon two and three feet long. The Indian is supposed to roast them up out back, says Bar-tender Arny. "Feast," yells Montana and—oh, Jonah, tell me it isn't so—he holds a fish with both hands over his newly erected man-hood, trying to fit the fish's mouth over his shaft. The men who don't fall off their chairs from laughter go to grabbing a fish and imitating Montana. Why, I wonder, is Reverend Hitch so busy saving the souls of Indians when there are so many damned ones here in the Stikine Saloon? When there's not a fish left in the box, Bartender Arny starts throwing his voice like a ventriloquist in a carnival, using his man-hood as if it were a dummy doll saying all kinds of profane words. I fold my hands and begin to pray. I bow my head but keep one eye open and try to remember the soothing words of the pastor at the Ebenezer Lutheran Church back home. I say the Lord's Prayer as fast as I can.

"My name's Cockerell," says Arny's shaft, "and I want Marvis." Out of my one eye I see him wiggle his manhood at Marvis, who shrieks and runs out the door without a customer. Tommy is all the time looking at me, and Yo laughs at the men.

Two old herrings next to me are playing with their manhoods as if they were puppets. "My name's Chief Big Bear," says one. "My name's Chief Beaver Eater," says the other. The men are all playing with themselves or with fish.

"Our Father who art in heaven," I say, loudly enough to drive the profane words out of my heart.

Tommy looks around at the noise of the men, sees them with the fish, and jumps out of his chair, yelling, "Grandmother, grandmother," through his broken teeth. His face is beet red as he starts for Montana. Yo and I jump from our chairs and pull him back, but this little man has the strength of a horse.

"Let's get him outside away from the damn fish," says Yo. I do as I'm told, wondering why it is only the fish that upsets the little man so.

In front of the Stikine Saloon, Tommy is like a hurt calf in my arms. He has three fingers in his mouth and he is making ear-piercing noises. There is nothing else for me to do but rock him like a colicky baby. "Grandmother," he wails.

Arny pokes his head out of the bar. "Marvis out here?" he drawls.

"She and Agg are off diddlin' each other," I hear someone inside shout.

My legs buckle under Tommy's weight and I sit in a squat position on the plank walkway in front of the bar. "*Aanaga*, grandmother, grandmother," he wails. Yo is mopping Tommy's brow. Tommy begins to shriek, piercing noises like no others I have ever heard: "*Koma ka ka suuma nay, koma ka ka suuma nay, nuka sa ku ka, nuka sa ku ka, a a a ahh.*"

"Is he dying?" I ask.

"He's praying that the souls of the fish be returned to the sea," says Yo. "He'll be shipshape in a minute or two."

I am beginning to wonder if this man Yo is crazy like a herdsman alone too long with his sheep. "Why does Tommy do this?" I finally ask.

"He's an Eskimo," says Yo. "He believes that when people the their souls go to live in the sea. Whenever an Eskimo kills an animal for food, they pray for the soul of the animal to be returned to the sea. The fish in there probably remind him of his dead grandmother. Maybe he thinks her soul lived in one of those fish. It always sets him off, seein' sea animals bein' done like that."

Tommy pulls my scarf off and begins sucking the ends of my hair.

"Where ya bound?" asks Yo.

"What?" I say.

"Where ya bound? There's no more gold in these parts."

"Oh," I say, remembering my masquerade. "I'm looking for two men, friends of *Far*'s, Seattle Charley and Joe Sprout."

"Those old chiselers," says Yo.

"You know them?" I say. "You know these men?"

"Sure," he says. "Charley lives in Sitka; haven't seen him in about a year, though. But the last time I was in Juneau, ol' Joe Sprout was braggin' about some gold that'd just come his way."

"Juneau," I say, almost dropping Tommy's head on the walkway. "Then it's Juneau that I'm bound for on the next ship out."

"Me'n Tommy have to take a sloop up that way tomorrow," he says. "It'll take us three or four days runnin', but I could get ya there before the next steamer ever could."

I stare Yo square in the face. Such an unusual look he has. Where have I seen this look before? He looks familiar, like a Finn or a Russian maybe. Does this man know the ways of the sea, he and his Eskimo friend who is still sucking on the ends of my hair? This isn't a wise idea, I say to myself. If I go with them I'll probably end up drowned and living with the mermen. "How much is the passage?" I ask.

"Nothin'," he says, "nothin'. Like I said, I've got business there before I head back to Sitka."

First to Juneau for Joe Sprout and then to Sitka for Charley, I say to myself. I think of my dwindling money hidden under my berth at the Steamship Hotel. What would it be like without a *krona* to my name in this wild Alaska? Working with Aggie and Marvis or eating nail soup, that's what I'd be doing. Not much prospect of taking in wash and ironing in Wrangell. But, I sigh, at least no one here is passing judgment on me for being a woman on her own without a husband or looking for one.

The Eskimo begins to wail again and I rock him in my arms. "He's not getting better," I say. "What can we do?"

"Tell him you'll come to Juneau with us," says Yo. "That'll pull him outa it. He likes you, he thinks you're an angel." The troll begins again to suck the ends of my hair like a newborn calf. "His grandmother always gave him gold kelp to eat," says Yo. "Sometimes he just up and goes back to his cradle ways."

"*Ja*, all right, all right," I say, "I'll go with you." *Å Gud*, I think to myself, is this the right thing that I do, to go with these two men?

The *liten* one's eyes begin to focus on me and his muscles relax. He stands up and shakes himself and spins himself around. Yo grabs him by the hand, and we start to walk through the deserted main street of Wrangell to my room at the beached steamship. "Maybe a storm," says Yo, looking out into the Narrows.

"Then we don't go," I say with relief, thinking that I am still not sure that these men know the ways of the sea.

"Tommy'll pray to the weather," Yo says. "That usually works."

From the deck of the Steamship Hotel we hear the echoes of gunshots in the mountains behind town.

"Rabbit huntin'," says Yo.

"Seals," yowls Tommy, pointing to a salmon schooner moored farther around the bay. Some men are standing on its deck shooting into the water at the puppy-faced seals that fishermen say tear their nets. Tommy begins to cover his ears and moan. Yo grabs him by the elbow and pulls him along the deck toward the gangplank. They say good-bye and that they'll come for me and my satchels at high tide tomorrow. I am left alone on deck wondering what fool thing I've just done. These two, maybe they're in cahoots with the *elvefolk* and wood-woman. Perhaps they want me for breeding their stumpy children. *Nej*, Ulla, I tell myself. To believe in elves always is to be as old-fashion superstitious as *Mor* and my other folk from the old country.

In the end I decide that it is probably better for me to go with these two men than to bear witness to the sins in the Stikine Saloon. I take a deep sigh and look down along the disintegrating promenade deck of the Steamship Hotel, the smell of rot and creosote so strong I almost faint. Like a beached dead whale this ship lists to one side on the sandy shore, her hull decaying and her ribs starting to show.

All around me the echoing of guns against the tall tree-stump-covered mountains in back of Wrangell reminds me of Barbro. I haven't target-practiced since I sold the cabbage field, I remind myself, going below to my cabin and taking the gun out of my satchel. I go back on deck with lead pellets sagging in my pockets. No people, only rocks that look like *elvemills* on the beach. For a moment I listen again to the echo of gunshots from the hills and fishing boats. That pile of seaweed across the beach is Joe Sprout asleep in his bed, I say to myself, and pull the trigger.

13. THE WRANGELL NARROWS
1893

For three days now we have been aboard the sloop, *Noah II*, with Tommy at the tiller and Yo hoisting the one sail up and down the mast. Three or four days Yo had said it would take to get to Juneau, but either there has been rain or no wind to fill the sails, and we're only halfway there. They aren't in a desperate hurry, these men. Most of the day they spend watching fish down in the murky blue. Yo makes notes as Tommy calls out names of fish: porpoise, halibut, cod.

"What is it you do?" I ask.

"Notes for the canneries," Yo says, brushing his black hair from his dark eyes.

Before I left Wrangell, Marvis and Aggie told me that this Yo went to a college in Seattle. He studied commerce, they said. Marvis kissed me good-bye and told me that Yo was smitten with me sure as a moose has horns. Maybe she's right, I think to myself. Surely she knows more about men than I do.

Yo points the bow of the *Noah II* through the riverlike *saltvat-ten* waterways of the Wrangell Narrows. Here the tree-covered islands come so steeply out of the turquoise water that there is no beach at all, just rocky cliffs lined with black cormorant birds, their wings spread as if they were on crucifixes drying in the wind, and ravens in the red-bark cedar trees making a noise that could call out the dead, *ja*, sure.

Ever since we set sail, Tommy follows me everywhere with his eyes. Last night he begged to let him comb my hair. Yo caught and cooked a fish for our dinner and Tommy combed my hair. They are sweet-tempered, these two, not like those old sourdoughs in Wrangell who were always gambling, using profanities, and who no doubt wanted advantages from me. But, oh, Jonah, I'm too old for a schoolgirl crush, and besides, my heart has been blackened with thoughts of murder.

The *Noah II* pitches back and forth. By now I am used to the rocking of boats and the constant water, which to me is like a desert, flat and barren. "What did you learn at the university?" I ask Yo.

He looks up from his notes. "Nothin' much," he says.

"How can this be?" I ask.

"Ah, it was a lotta hooey about London and New York, stock exchanges 'n business. I only stayed there a year. Don't do me much good, all that book learnin', up here with the fish."

"It was no good to you, reading books?" I ask doubtfully. But what do I know about schooling? After the eighth grade I had to leave school to help *Mor* take in laundry.

"It helps sometimes," he says with a cat smile. "It impresses the tar outa people. They think I know things. They listen to me. They think I'm honest."

For a moment I shut my eyes, remembering the Port of Seattle when I docked there on board *Resolute*. "GATEWAY TO ALASKA," read the banner that flew above the harbor. And it looked so much like San Francisco, this hilly city that had also grown up along a bay. "Started as a lumber camp supplyin' the California gold rush," Captain O'Sullivan had told me as I gazed all along the miles of docks built to outfit ships bound for Alaska and her gold.

"Why did you leave the university after only a year?" I ask Yo.

"Seattle had a terrible fire," he says. "Damn near burned the city to the ground. Somebody printin' Bibles let a glue pot get too close to a blast furnace, or so the story goes. Rebuilt the whole city in brick, just to be on the safe side. But when my Ma heard about the fire, she wrote me to come directly home. 'Course, she wanted me to have an education and all, but Seattle don't exactly sit well with her. It wasn't long ago they was burnin' Indians there, and when Ma heard about the fire, well. . . ."

Yo puts down his notes and takes long looks at me. Tommy watches him, and I pretend to be preoccupied with the large white birds feeding in the shallow water near the shore.

"Know how the crane got blue eyes?" asks Tommy.

"What?" I say.

"Crane on the beach eating berries," he says. His words through his crooked teeth still sound odd to me but, all the same, understandable. "Crane take out his eyes, put 'em on a log. 'Tell me when someone comes,' crane say to the eyes. Crane eats berries: salmonberries, cranberries. 'Someone comes, someone comes,' say the eyes. Crane just ignores. Eats blueberries, eats thimbleberries. Crane goes to the log to get eyes and they're gone. 'Someone stole my eyes,' says crane. Crane tries on cranberries where his eyes supposed to be, but the world's too red. Crane tries on blackberries, but everything's too dark. Crane tries on blueberries. 'This I like,' crane says. Ever since, crane has blue eyes." Tommy sits cross-legged on deck and stares at me with a serious look on his yellow pie-shaped face.

"But why would the crane take his eyes out and put them on a log?" I ask.

"Someone doesn't know," he says, averting his gaze from my face.

Where does this troll get such tales? I wonder. Why does he call himself "someone"?

Suddenly there is no sun and I hear the rumble of thunder. Tommy stands up. "Sky noising too much. Sky noising too much," he shouts. We all climb into the cabin before the downpour. Tommy in his sealskin parka goes back out to pull down the sail and Yo drops anchor.

I have never seen such rain. It is like the stories of the monsoons that Uncle Jarl and his sea-captain friends used to tell me as a child. The rain is so loud I expect the giants of the sea to thunder up through the bottom of the boat. "An unseasonal southeast gale," says. Yo. "It don't rain like this all year round. Usually just drizzles." The three of us huddle around a seal-oil lamp which stinks like rancid fat. "Sila, Sila," says Tommy. What is the little Eskimo saying? Even though I hear the words I don't understand him. "Sila, Sila," says Tommy.

"The Sila," says Yo, "the Weather Spirit."

"What?" I ask.

"What-what," mimics Tommy. "Ulla's a what-what bird," he says. "What-what bird with yellow feathers. What-what bird flies around and around. What-what bird flies up-crick and down."

"That's just his way of sayin' he likes ya," says Yo. "Sing to the weather, Tommy." Tommy rolls his lidless eyes beneath his rain-wet glasses. "Christ, Tommy," says Yo, "we've been out here almost four days. Sing to the damn weather and get us outa here."

"Ptarmigan flies around and around," sings Tommy, "ptarmigan flies up-crick and down. Ptarmigan mad at the weather. Ptarmigan hungry, so hungry; ptarmigan thirsty, so thirsty."

Have these men gone off like a bad tin of sardines? I wonder. *Mor's* face appears in front of me. "Ulla, I tell you now, never trust a man," she says. But I blink twice and her image is gone.

Now Yo is pulling on Tommy's arm. "Go up on deck and do it right," he says in a serious voice.

"Do what?" I ask.

"What-what bird," mimics Tommy.

"Sing the Weather Song right," says Yo. How can a man who has been to the university really believe in such tales? Tommy pulls his seal-gut parka hood over his head, secures his glasses, and goes up on deck into the terrible rain.

"He'll catch pneumonia. Make him come back inside," I tell Yo.

"It may be wet out there, but it's still a warm day," Yo replies. "Besides, Tommy likes the rain. He does this all the time."

"Someone does this all the time," mimics Tommy with a shout from up on deck, and I see that these two are just playing like schoolboys.

"Yo, how did you get this name?" I ask, wanting to join in their game and suddenly feeling more lighthearted than I have since my Gunnar died, as lighthearted as if I were dancing a swing *polska* at the Feast of the Green Leaf.

"Tommy gave it to me," answers Yo.

133

The *Noah II* pitches in the storm, I fall down onto the floor of the ship's hull, then Yo falls on top of me. Ropes and fishing lures are jabbing into my back. I try to rise up but knock my head as the boat pitches forward again. *Å, Gud,* I mumble to myself. Yo rises up, pulling me to my knees, then, still holding my hand, rubs my forehead. "Are you all right?" he asks. "Just a few more days of this and you'll have the sea legs of an old-timer."

I moan because I don't know what else to do with this young and handsome man still rubbing my forehead and holding onto my hand. Does he mean to take advantage of me, I wonder? "I'm all right," I say, pulling away from him, but he doesn't let go of my arm easily. Instead he reaches to pull me back for a kiss. What is wrong with this man? I am four or five years older than he is. How can he have these thoughts for me, an almost middle-aged matron? Marvis back in Wrangell said that the few farmstead daughters in Alaska were all smitten with this Yo. Again he reaches to kiss me, playfully, like my Gunnar would have done. Except, I remember sadly, Gunnar would have the heavy smell of *akvavit* on his breath.

Up on deck we hear Tommy suddenly start to make strange noises, a harsh nasal song that resonates over the water:

"*Sila si la si la
Uugituŋa
Niġivik naluvlugu
Sila sila sila ai?*"

"What's he doing?" I ask.

"The Weather Song, little what-what bird," Yo says, stroking my hair.

The noise of the rain on the deck above pounds into my ears. "*Sila sila sila uugituŋa. . . .*" The rain pounds like a drum beating time. "*Sila sila sila.*"

"Is Eskimo Tommy your partner?" I ask.

"Not exactly," says Yo. "My ma adopted him 'bout five years back. Hitch found him with some other starvin' Eskimos up near Bethel. Didn't have no parents and his grandmother'd been raisin' him—

maybe his great-grandmother, for all I know. Anyway, she died of the tuberculosis they're all catchin' from the trappers up there, an' little Tommy was fendin' for himself."

"None of his folk would take him in?" I asked.

"It was hard times," says Yo, beginning to rewind the jute fishing ropes into neat coils. "All them *cheechakoes* came in huntin', trappin', muckin' for gold—anything they could sell, they ain't particular. Well, come winter, their supplies and ammo had run out and they was all starvin'. No one to help 'em out but the Eskimos. Lucky for the *cheechakoes* that Eskimos is right friendly. They gave out all they had, with nothin' left for themselves. Not that they had much to begin with, mind ya—the hair seal and the otter'r practically all used up by the fur trappers, and them whales is smart enough to move to deeper waters. Anyway, Hitch hears God callin' and goes up there to give the starvin' their last rites." The beam ribs of the *Noah II* creak inside the hull as Yo and I sit ourselves down on a steamer trunk.

"So Tommy," says Yo, "maybe, Ulla, ya noticed he's a little different upstairs than most? Well, he'd been apprenticed to a medicine man in some village near Bethel. Spent most of the day in a trance tryin' to levitate rocks that washed up on the beach. Anyway, Hitch decides he's gotta put an end to this fool witch-doctor talk of goin' to the moon and walkin' around under the sea when it's been iced over. So he brings Tommy back to Sitka, see, to show some visitin' congressmen just why they should appropriate money for a home for people like Tommy. 'How's he gonna make the heathens into right Christians,' Hitch says, 'instead of cannibal, bloodthirsty drunks, if Congress don't send him money for a school for half-wit natives?' Well, my ma, she's got a lotta say in Sitka—she came with the Purchase, she did—she took Tommy in and wouldn't let Hitch or the government men near him." My stomach moves up and down as the boat pitches in the southeast Alaska storm.

"Reverend Hitch," continues Yo, toying with a shiny silver fishing lure, "he's a real fast talker, but he didn't get hold of Tommy, no sir. He did get some church to build him a trainin' school for the natives. And got the government to appoint him Director of Education up here. Course, there ain't no schools in Alaska, 'cept church schools. Then—I think he did this just to make my ma mad—he passed himself a law sayin' that once a native went into his school, he couldn't get out till he was finished bein' trained. Trained, that means converted. Anyway—" Yo takes a deep breath—"Tommy never got 'trained.' My ma saw to it that he learned his rightful Eskimo religion."

"By Jimminy, she is good like anything, your *moder*," I say. "But is it true that these Indians want to suck blood?"

"Naw," he says. "Not so much any more. But not too long ago up at Stikine Village some Hooch-nas massacred every one of Hitch's Indian converts, plus a few prospectors and fur farmers who was in the village at the time and just happened to get in the way."

"I hope they aren't wanting me for their spears," I say.

"Then don't go leavin' your eyes on a log," Yo says, and we both laugh like schoolchildren. "Stick with me an' Tommy, Ulla," he says, puttin' his hand on my shoulder. "My ma taught me some Indian dialects. She's part squaw, ya know. Besides, all the bloods in these parts think Tommy's got some medicine-man magic up his sleeve, and they're all scared he's gonna put the evil eye on 'em.

"So don't be afraid of the Indians," he continues. "They're just mad that the white folks stole their fishin' and huntin' grounds. I don't blame 'em, neither. Hell, all those 'come to Alaska' magazines published down in Seattle advertise free land up here. But there ain't no law yet that tells a body, Indian or white, how to get legal title to any land in Alaska unless it's a mineral claim. The Indians say that all these islands and mountains belong to them, and the government says that the Indians ain't American citizens. So you can understand why the natives don't take kindly to gold muckers muddyin' up their fish-spawnin' creeks and wavin' mineral-rights claims in their faces. No, Ulla, the only *legal* rights anyone's got to a piece of property up here is squatter's rights and a gun."

Eskimo Tommy comes down below. Yo and I rub him dry with rags, and Yo goes through the provisions in the steamer trunk for something to make our supper. "Dried fruit," I say, looking into the sacks and tins with him. "Fruit soup, I'll make *fruktsoppa*." They look at me like pet pigeons, these two, as if I am going to throw them a bit of food.

I use the spices in the side pockets of my satchel and heat the fruity broth on the seal-oil stove-lamp. We pass the bowl around, all of us huddled together like wood-folk in a fairy cave. Up on deck the rain has stopped, and Tommy pulls the tarp away from the door hole. Stars. The twilight of Alaska's summer night. "We'll dock in Juneau harbor tomorrow," says Tommy, in a voice as excited as a child on his birthday eve. At last, I think to myself, Juneau and Joe Sprout.

Each of us rolls into a blanket and tries to sleep. All night I hear strange animals howling on the shore. And on board there is the sound of Tommy making sucking noises. Many times I awake in the night. Tommy is crawling around on his stomach. He is moaning and trying to get under Yo's blanket. Yo is asleep. I sit up, careful not to bump my head on the boat beams. Tommy crawls over to me, making pathetic moaning sounds. He reaches his hand up to my face like a hungry *barn*. Pulling off my scarf, he puts the end of my braid into his mouth. Oh, Jonah, I think to myself. For most of the night I listen to the *liten* one sucking in my ear.

Yo gets up before anyone else and raises the sail. I look out through the tarpaulin. Steam is rising from the water like the vapors of tea. "Juneau in two hours," says Yo.

"Flee with light sails, little *Noah* boat," I say, and Yo smiles down into my face.

In every way so different a place this Alaska is than San Francisco. Instead of a horse cart or trolley car, boats are what one travels in. No bridges between these islands in the Narrows of the Alexander Archipelago, and certainly no roads that could climb over the steep white mountains, where sometimes I think I see the black dots of wild sheep grazing on the lower slopes. At home in California, one could walk or take a horse cart around the San Francisco Bay, but *nej*, not here in this watery Alaska. In this *saltvatten* lake of green islands—some no bigger than an elf hill—the small fishing villages and gold towns are like rafts, and without a boat one could not get from place to place.

The three of us sit on the bow, watching loons duck underwater and reappear a quarter mile away. Always I am listening to their lonesome cries echoing across the channel. All along the shore are the biggest trees I've ever seen, taller and more sorrel-colored than any California redwood. And in and amongst them I am beginning to see totem poles like the ones I saw on *Resolute* near Ketchikan. They are like sprites in the woods, I think to myself, as Yo tells me about the heads of the beasts, all painted tar-black, red, and metal green. Blackfin whale," he says. "Raven. Humpback salmon."

"And that one over there?" I ask, pointing to the head of a bearded man holding two children.

"The Bogeyman," says Yo. "The white bogeyman."

Downwind a little farther I see another bogeyman totem. "What is this?" I ask. "These poles aren't like the others, they're not animal carvings."

"It's the story of the white man who steals Indian children," he says.

I cast a sad look at Tommy, who is ducking back and forth under the boom. My poor stolen one, I think to myself. "And that figure atop a tall pole?" I ask, pointing to a carving of a woman among the trees. Her breasts are the heads of wolves and her feet have claws.

"A woman witch doctor," says Yo, "the Indians' religious leader." Oh, Jonah, I think, here they pray to animals and listen to women preach? What a fairy-tale land this is.

Yo undoes my scarf and begins to run his fingers like a comb through my hair as the jib sheet blows in the wind. "Are Tommy's folk still starving?" I ask, wondering why Yo is touching me again.

"Not exactly," he says. "Some dang churchman got a notion into his head that the Eskimos needed a business, what with all their seals dyin' out up there and so many hungry *cheechako* fur trappers to feed. So this churchman, Sheldon Jackson—a friend of Hitch's—gets Congress to start importin' reindeer from Siberia. Thinks the Eskimos can be reindeer farmers, seein' as how the caribou ain't domesticated and have all gone off to wilder regions anyway. Well, the reindeer took pretty well to their new home, seein' as how some government man went along with the first load to show the Eskimos how to herd and feed 'em. But, damn it, the Eskimos are fishermen and hunters, not herdsmen. They don't like trampin' over the tundra day after day followin' some fool animal with too many horns to be believed. Might have been a different story if an Eskimo could slaughter one of them critters any time he got hungry. But, no, he needs a special government permit every time he wants to eat one. All he can do is try to milk 'em. Now there ain't no Eskimo even likes the taste of milk—it don't agree with their stomachs. And nothin' out on the tundra for an Eskimo to eat, with it always bein' a few days' walk back home to his fish supply. So there's the Eskimo out there, still hungry and followin' some fool imported deer around the turf to boot."

"Juneau, Juneau!" shouts Tommy, pointing from the bow. And there at the end of a cove in the shadow of a snowy mountain is a village looking like the pictures Uncle Jarl used to paint of towns on inland lakes back in Sweden. "Frenchie Pete's mine, sometimes called the Glory Hole," says Yo, pointing to a tent camp amid tall trees across the water. A mine camp, I think to myself. Maybe that's where I'll find this Joe Sprout. I look down into the sea and notice that the narrows have changed color from emerald green to muddy brown, with tin-can garbage from the mine camp floating all around. Tommy begins singing and stamping his foot like a drum: "Why is the raven hollerin' in a tree? Why is the raven hollerin' in a tree?"

The main street of Juneau looks like Wrangell, but tidier, with the false-front buildings all whitewashed and wooden step paths up the steep graveled side streets that wind into the wooded mountains. Womenfolk here. One running a laundry—free mending, it says on her sign. Another with a fortune-telling business. We walk along the broad main street and go into Juneau's largest building, the Glory Hole Hotel, with the lintels above its second-story windows all studded in blue enamel fleurs-de-lis. Yo says he has business in one of the back rooms, and Tommy and I sit at a table inside the crowded bare-wood dance-hall saloon. "Business with Shathitch," says Tommy with a wizened look on his face.

"Do you know what Joe Sprout looks like?" I ask him.

"Someone doesn't know," he says, averting his eyes to the wall. What goes on inside Tommy's head? "Someone," he always says, "someone."

A woman about my age in canvas digger's clothes and bobbed brown hair comes over to the table with a smile on her dimpled face. "Dutch Kate," she says to me, putting out her hand. I take it in mine and right away feel welcome and at home in this strange, rainy Alaska. "Yo just told me he was haulin' a lady miner with him. I've been muckin' up here for a year now," she says, taking a split-rail chair. "Where do ya aim to look for diggin's?"

Ja, I say to myself as she sits down, at last someone who might know the whereabouts of my two claim swipers.

"Maybe in the mine on Douglas Island just across the water. Frenchie Pete, does he claim it all?" I ask.

"Naw," she says in her big husky voice, "he sold it out from under himself for nothin' to some guy named Treadwell. And there ain't nothin' a single body can claim over there now. They got a machine diggin' trenches, black holes in the earth. Naw, there's nothin worth claimin' up in these parts. If ya wanna find any gold glitter, honey, ya gotta go to the River up yonder."

"The River?" I ask.

"The Yukon," she says. "Gonna be headin' up that way myself in a week's time. Up over Chilkoot Pass, if'n the Injins don't get me and ol' Ben Moore'll let me cross his homestead."

"Tell me, Katie, do you know a man named Joe Sprout?" I ask.

"Sprout?" she says, nodding her head and squinching her large nose. "Sure, everybody knows Sprout. Last I heard, the li'l weasel was headed for Sitka."

Two old herrings each pull up a chair, one with his upper lip missing.

"Ulla," says Kate, "this here's Red Ellis and Cat Waterberry."

"Nice to be makin' your acquaintance, ma'am," they both say together, like twins.

"She's a pretty one, ain't she?" says Red, tugging at the scraggly hairs of his auburn beard.

"When's you and Yo gonna tie up the knot?" asks Cat through his scarred mouth. By Jimminy, I think to myself, in Alaska gossip travels faster than a runaway sled on ice.

"Don't embarrass her none," scolds Kate with a smile. "She's here on serious business. Gonna set down a claim up on the River soon as she gets outfitted up."

"Hip, hip to lady miners," cheers Red, ordering a round of drinks.

The Glory Hole is cleaner than the Stikine Saloon, with everybody sitting sober at the tables and no dancing girls, or at least none in sight. "Where ya goin' to be jumpin' off at?" asks Red.

"What?" I say.

Tommy jerks up his head. "What-what bird flies around and around. What-what bird flies up-crick and down." Everybody laughs.

"Ya goin' over Chilkoot Pass or up the Yukon on a steamer?" Cat asks.

Oh, Jonah, this lady miner's lie will get the best of me yet, I think to myself.

"Let's get her acquainted with the liquor in these parts first," says Kate. "Then we can get down to less important matters."

"Well," says Red, "if she goes over Chilkoot Pass, ol' Ben Moore's daughter'll have her rifle ready. That little lady's had her eye on Yo for years."

The bartender brings a round of drinks, and I am thinking that maybe it's a good place, this green and soggy Alaska—no one calls me dumb Swede and everybody likes me.

"Well, sister," says Cat, "now for your first Alasky lesson. This here's *Squirrel Whiskey*," he says as I taste the horrible brew. "Some call it hooch. Now, there's various labels of this concoction, ya see—"

"Aw, cut the talk," says Kate. "It's all poisonous as hell. Myself, I prefer the Au-rora Bore-alis. And Red here, if'n I remember correctly, is hooked on Snake Juice. And Cat, Cat'll drink anything short of wood alcohol. But, honey, there's just one thing to remember. No matter what's your cup o' tea, don't never give or sell it to an Injun or you'll really be up a stump. That's dang near the only capital offense in these parts—sellin' alky to the Injuns. Injuns an' Chain Lightnin' just don't mix."

"*Ja*," I say, feeling as gay as I would if I'd had several glasses of *akvavit*. "I will remember."

The two herrings excuse themselves and go into one of the card rooms in back of the bar. Juneau is almost civilized compared to Wrangell, I think to myself. And this Katie here, what a stout and sturdy woman. Carrying on and drinking whiskey as if she were one of the boys. Except she's much smarter. Some of these sourdoughs are dumber than a hedgehog.

"Well," says Kate, getting up, "mighty nice to make your acquaintance, Ulla. Maybe I'll be seein' ya up on the River or at Porc-u-pine Crick."

"*Lycka till!* Good luck!" I say. She pats Tommy on the head and walks out the door. I hear some sourdoughs ask her if she's outfitted up yet. And she says that she's about ready except for some mosquito netting and a trip to Mrs. Rizzio's to get her fortune told.

Tommy is staring in a trance at the wall. Why is it, I think to myself, that my Gunnar was in Wrangell looking for gold if there's no gold left except down below in the Treadwell mine or up north in the Yukon? Who led him astray like that? Every week before he left he'd bring home a copy of the *Alaska Herald*, published in Seattle, and we'd read about the strikes that were goin' on. He had it all mapped out before he sailed, first to Wrangell for gold, then a little farther north to farmstead the free land, and maybe to fish for herring in the winter.

I am looking at all the initials and dates carved into the table—J.B. '89, Homer '91, A.K. from Hey Springs—when Yo walks up to the table with an old man, an Indian with white man's clothes and a floor-length ermine coat. On his large nose he wears a pair of gold-rimmed spectacles, two sizes too small, and the lenses so thick that his black eyes look like huge blackberries poking out of his head. Tommy says something that I can't understand. Yo smiles at me. "This is Chief Sha-thitch—that's Tlingit for Hard-to-Kill," he says.

"Chief Larson," the Indian corrects him in perfect English.

Yo smiles and lets out the beginnings of a laugh. "Chief Larson," he says. "Chief of the Chilkats and the Chilkoots."

"Hello," I say to the tall, bony man. Such a wrinked face he has, I think to myself. And such a beautiful robe, like nothing I've ever seen. The chief doesn't sit down with us. His expression is without a smile and very serious. "Remember to tell your mother to visit the Hootz-noos at Angoon village soon," he says to Yo. The chief puts his hand on Tommy's shoulder and then walks out of the hotel.

"Well, Ulla," says Yo, "ya gonna get outfitted up here?"

"*Nej,*" I say. "Dutch Katie just told me that old Joe Sprout is in Sitka, and I was wondering if I could book passage with you there?" I think that after I've done my dirty deeds I'll certainly come back to this town with all the newly painted stores and take in laundry to earn my passage back to San Francisco.

"Glad to oblige," says Yo, with a wide smile on his face.

He pulls Tommy by the arm and we walk out of the hotel. As I follow the two men, one old herring at a table near the door winks at me. "Yo's got hisself a pretty one," he says, laughing his craggy laugh. "Think ol' Yo paid Dutch Kate to tell her that Sprout's been hangin his hat in Sitka?" The rest is drowned in laughter.

Could this be true? I follow Yo with caution. Such a wild place this is, where nobody has last names and always the stories of gold are changing like the weather. We walk back to the dock past rows of whitewashed buildings, white as the snowy peaks in back of Juneau. Somewhere in the distance I hear the noise of barking dogs, and all the time I am wondering if it is true what the man said in the bar. Did this Yo really pay Katie to tell me a falsehood? Such a nice woman. Would she do that to me?

At the wharf I pause for a moment, looking over the schooner masts and across the channel to Douglas Island, thick with tall evergreen trees. Here and there in the forest is the white canvas of a tent that must house the poor unhealthy men who dig all day down in the dark tunnels of the Treadwell mine. As I look across the water, at first I think the tide is coming in but on a second glance discover it is a family of seals bouncing in the water which has churned the waves, making them splash against the sides of the log wharf. And all the time what I thought were so many barking dogs, I now find are these happy seals, like pups romping across the green of the *saltvatten* channel. Ulla, I say to myself, I tell you now, so what if this Yo paid Dutch Katie to tell you a falsehood? He and his Tommy have made you feel like a young *flicka* again and treat you no different than one of their boy playmates out on a mischievous lark. *Ja*, Ulla, these kindhearted fellows have made you feel like the seals in the tide.

We go aboard the *Noah II* to make ready our supplies for the journey to Sitka. "You'll like it there," Yo says. "Biggest town in Alaska. The capital, ya know, even though there's always been talk of movin' it. A while back some folks wanted to move the capital to Wrangell."

"Wrangell?" I say. By *Gud*, what a city Sitka must be if they're thinking of moving the capital to Wrangell!

"But now," he says, "there's talk of movin' the government offices here to Juneau—what government there is," he says, with a frown on his face. "We got a governor who never even heard of Alaska till the President appointed him, no land laws, no schools 'cept the church schools, and no taxpayers, since no one can legally own anythin' to pay taxes on. Hell, the only way my ma's been able to hold on to the land my pa claimed was 'cause the local Indians don't bother her and she's real handy with a gun."

Tommy secures the sail and Yo helps me down into the hold, where we check our food supplies. Enough for *fruktsoppa* all the way to Sitka, I think to myself as I check my satchel, slipping my fingers inside to make sure that Barbro is safe in her hiding place. Then I check for my money bag. My fingers grope into the corners and through the folds of clothing. Oh, Jonah, where is it? It can't be gone. I throw the contents of the satchel on the floor. "It's gone!" I shout. "Someone's stolen it. Every last *krona*." But it couldn't be Tommy or Yo that's taken my money, I think to myself. They were with me most of the time. "Oh, why did I leave it behind me on the boat?"

On my hands and knees I search through the heap of clothing.

"Gone, gone!" I scream.

"Shysters," says Yo. "I shoulda locked the cabin."

"What'll I do?" I cry. "What'll become of me?" I forget about my two claim-swiping rascals and see images of myself dancing bare-rumped like Marvis and Aggie with old sourdoughs throwing buckshot at my privates. "What'll I do?"

14.

Yo puts a gentle hand on my shoulder and kisses my head. The *Noah II* rocks in the tide. "Everythin's all right," he says. "I have lots of money. I'll take care of you, me an' Tommy." Tommy has begun to moan on the boat bottom among my things, making piercing noises in sympathy. Gone, five hundred dollars, all my money from selling the house and the cabbage field. Other than Barbro, it was the last thing of Gunnar's that I had in this world. "I'll take care of ya," Yo says. "You can be my wife." But his words are no comfort to me. What shall I do in this wild Alaska without a *krona*?And I haven't even found my Gunnar's grave yet.

I look at Yo. Such a kind young face he has. Too young for me, I think. There is no love for him in my heart, only revenge for my Gunnar. "Shouldn't we report this to the *polisstation*?" I ask through my gasping tears.

"The marshal?" says Yo. "We don't have one."

We set our sails for Sitka, through Hawk Inlet and past the dense, unfriendly forest of Admiralty Island. Yo and Tommy make jokes to try to cheer me up. Tommy does imitations of a fox walking up and down the deck. "Know how the fox got red?" he says. "Fox was sittin' on a river-bank, watchin' a goose change feathers. Fox knows when a goose changes feathers, it can't fly. Fox tries to swallow the goose whole, can't get it down. Feathers fly. Goose screams. Fox chokes, almost chokes himself to death. Turns red, ha ha. Red ever since. Yeah." We sail on.

It is like a labyrinth, these waterways, narrow with overhanging trees—sweepers, Yo calls them. "Do these straits have names?" I ask, trying not to think of the lost money and my future.

"Sure," says Yo, "they got lots of names. The Russians called this one Olga Strait, and the Tlingits they call it Auke. And the Spanish, I forget what they call it—named everything after whatever saint's birthday they discovered it on, they did. Don't matter what name ya use anyway. Men from Washington D.C. keep comin' up here to make maps and change the names again. They're real good at namin' things, but they ain't never come up with a map ya can sail by without runnin' aground."

"Ohh," I moan. So much confusion, I think. Men from Washington. As I look up into one of the vast white frozen rivers that Yo calls glaciers, I remember white-haired, blue-eyed Joaquin Johnny, who was sent here by American senators to study these beds of ice. What was the yarn I heard him spinning on my last day aboard ship? That he was going to name the next glacier after his dog? And then he rambled on about how these sometimes silver frozen rivers look so silent and still but are really all the time moving and taking in their wake huge boulders and giant trees. Then—oh, what stories these Alaska men can spin—when these glacier rivers reach the sea at Icy Bay, they break off into the ocean. This is called "calving," Joaquin Johnny said, as if he thought the frozen rivers were alive and making the noises of a *mjölk-cow.*

What am I to do? I think, remembering my predicament. Perhaps Yo would lend me passage back to California, if I did a favor for him. But then I see a vision of *Mor* standing in front of me with a long face on and shaking her finger at my sinful plan. Oh, Jonah, even if Yo did lend me the money to get back to San Francisco, how would I ever repay him? None of my folk have an *öre* to spare, and they'd be chastising me for my foolishness for the rest of my life. *Mor* always did say that I could be the only dark cloud in her blue sky. *Nej,* there doesn't seem to be anything else for me to do but to let Yo have his way with me, because certainly I cannot marry this man. He's too young for a matron as old as I. And it is Gunnar who is still in my heart.

Yo goes down into the hold to fix us some supper. I follow. "Shathitch told me he thought you was a right fine-lookin' woman," says Yo, trying to raise my spirits.

"Is it Shathitch or Larson?" I ask. "And who is he, anyway? Dutch Kate told me that it was a sin and a crime to give liquor to the Indians, and there he was in that bar as if he owned the place."

"Probably does," says Yo, putting his arms around my waist. "My ma knows him from way back. The wealthiest Indian in Alaska maybe, she says. Been tradin' all his life with the inland Athabascans and then sellin' their furs for ferocious prices to the Hudson's Bay Company and anybody else who'll buy 'em. Shrewd a man as ever you'll find. Uses the American name Larson just to appease old Reverend Hitch. Guess he's tryin' to make believe he's a convert. Probably thinks it's good for business."

"Larson," I say. "It is Swedish, this name." Maybe there is good in this Alaska place after all. People taking Swedish names instead of changing them because of prejudice like they do in the States.

Yo pushes his lips into my face and reaches his hand inside my bodice. "Nice," he says, "nice." He pushes me to the floor. I close my eyes tight so that I will not have to bear witness to my own sin while he undoes my clothes and I feel his manhood poke at my thighs and enter me. He is all the time kissing my face and breasts. I try to pretend that it isn't happening, but his body moving into mine makes my breath come hard, makes my muscles contract and release. These are the feelings of a fallen woman, I think to myself as he rolls off me, and I try to hide the tears in my eyes.

Pretending it didn't happen, I continue our conversation about the rich Indian, Chief Shathitch Hard-to-Kill Larson, as if I were still an unviolated woman. "I don't mean to sound un-Christianlike," I say, buttoning my clothes, "but what does this Indian chief with the funny glasses have to do with your *moder?*"

"They knew each other way back," Yo tells me as he buttons his pants. "Seems he did my ma a favor or somethin' when she was sick about fifteen years ago. I don't know, I was too little to remember." He is stroking my forehead. "My ma's right friendly with the Indians in these parts and—well, I don't know what happened, she don't talk about it much. There was some big Indian massacre when I was about eight or nine, and then my ma got sick and had to go away for a while to rest up in Angoon, an Indian village a day's sail from Sitka. Ever so often she goes back there for a visit or to recruit cannery workers."

Inside the damp hull of the *Noah II*, I shut my eyes and try to imagine Yo's mother. Tears are falling down my face. Would she be like Dutch Kate, I wonder?

Yo puts his hands over my eyes. "It's all right," he says. "I'll take care of you, me an' Tommy."

He takes my hand and we go back up on deck. But my thoughts wander always to my terrible predicament. My spirit has sunk so low that, with all the sinful words I know, I am blessing every raven who makes his unworldly noise in my ears. Gunnar, Gunnar, I think to myself, why did you have to come to this wild place and leave me all alone in the world?

"Sitka, Sitka!" Tommy yells from the bow.

I look up from my troubled thoughts to see a town far different from Juneau or Wrangell. Sitka is like a medieval village that grew into the saddle of these tall evergreen Alaska hills, under a single giant white peak that looks like a picture I once saw of Mount Fujiyama.

"Mount Edgecumbe, the Americans named it," says Yo, following my eyes. "But the Russians in these parts still call it Mount Saint Lazaria."

As the boat approaches, I see a deserted, barnlike building with a broken-windowed cupola at the top, built high on a cliff rock overhanging the bay. Then—oh, Jonah, a church like I haven't seen since I left San Francisco, with an onion dome and a two-barred cross. The trees all around have been thinned, so instead of an unfriendly woods, the shoreline looks like a park with lavender rhododendrons growing in every mossy nook.

Yo points to a log lean-to on one of the bay islands as our boat tacks back and forth between the rocks toward the Sitka wharf. "Fox farms, see?" he says. "They raise foxes out here. That way they don't have to cage 'em. Only way they can get away is to swim." I stare at an island beach, realizing that what at first I thought were brown stones are really fuzzy-faced foxes, all bathing in the sun of this one clear hour before the clouds will again close in and dampen the ground.

"Beautiful," I say, "beautiful." Looking toward the settlement, I see that, like Juneau, the buildings, though much older, are whitewashed and the streets are gravel that is evenly raked from one side to the other. As the village opens up onto the beach and the sea, there is a vast and grassy lawn like only the queen of Sweden could own. In the center of the green, an American flag flies from a tall pole where the main street begins to wind its way past the onion-domed church to the parklike forest at the foot of mountains that look much like Uncle Jarl's paintings of the Alps.

"Used to be a fort," says Yo, pointing to the town, "but the stockade fell down years ago. Ya can still see the blockhouses, though. And them log buildin's down by the wharf are the old Russian-American Company warehouses; near a hundred years old, they are. New Archangel, the Russian fur traders used to call this place."

"Set the sail north toward the cannery," Yo calls to Tommy.

"Yo-yo's wife, Yo-yo's wife," chants Tommy, moving the tiller to the starboard side.

The cannery is a long narrow warehouse built on poles over the water, surrounded by its own dock, and moored to it are five or six scows piled high with fish. Already I am feeling faint from the smell of fish rot mixed with creosote. "Planed all them boards myself up at the Sitka mill," says Yo, pointing proudly to the fish cannery. "Fifty thousand board feet of lumber there," he says.

The *Noah II* glides up to the dock as Yo and Tommy wave and call from the deck to the cannery workers, all Indians. Everyone waves and cheers. Tommy throws an Indian worker a rope, and all the time I am wondering what to do: hide in the hold or sit on deck? What could they be thinking? That I'm the new strumpet come to replace the diseased one everybody talked of in Wrangell? The Indian workers are all dressed in baggy black clothes. They stare at me.

"Ma, ma!" yells Tommy. And there amid the piers and pilings I see the *liten* copper-haired woman who shared my cabin aboard *Resolute*.

15. SITKA
Summer
1894

It has been almost a year since I married Yo, I think to myself as I read over the first sad letters that *Mor* sent to me in this wild place:

Where you find this jänkefäller? You mova to Alaska, you make me suffra. You make Pappa suffra. I tell you Ulla it was wrong to leave your folk. But nej, nej, maybe not. Kerstin and Olaf's crop have failed again this year. No rain. All winter, no rain. Olaf and Carl have gone in railroad boxcars to Washington D. C to ask President Cleveland for jobs. Ulla, when I found you gone I was mad like I don't know what. I could killa you. But tell me Ulla now, are you happy? If you are happy, I am happy. . . .

Mor's voice is always inside my head. And it has been so long since I have heard anyone speak a word of Skånska. Mor has even sent me a news clipping from the San Francisco Scandinavian newspaper, Vestkusten, all written up in Swedish about how I married an Alaskan businessman, Vladimir York.

Every week I wait for the steamer to bring me a letter from my folk. Nadia, sometimes she goes down to the beach near the green parade grounds with me and we sit on a rock, watching for the steamer ship—Nadia waiting for news of cannery business and me waiting for a letter from *Mor*. While we wait, Nadia is always telling me stories of her girlhood, how she and her Indian mother used to sit together on this same beach rock waiting for a message from her mother's Haida folk. The Wishing Stone, the Russians called it, because of Nadia and her mother, and me I wish for a letter from Kerstin and Inga, too.

As we wait for the steamer Nadia also tells me strange Indian stories about the salmon fish. When they swim from the sea upstream to spawn, they carry a tiny pebble between their teeth. This, she says, keeps the fish from becoming hungry, for they do not eat all along their last and final journey. Stories of fish, they are everywhere. But ah, I think to myself, so good it is to have this kindhearted woman to tell me stories—to be entertained like a *lilla barn* again. As Nadia talks I look out into Sitka Bay, always having to remind myself that it is not a lake but part of the Pacific Ocean. Everywhere under the cloudy sky are green islands and white sails, boats instead of horse carts running from fox farm to fox farm.

Not much else for me to do here in Sitka but work hard at the cannery and listen to the talk of fish or fishermen's holidays spent in bars and burlesque shows along Seattle's Fifth Avenue. No need for my lady miner's clothes or even my corset and Common Sense oxford shoes. Tarred waterproof boots and overdresses is what we wear, Nadia and I, as we and the Indian women, all with black scarves on our heads, stand at a long table inside the cannery warehouse gutting the red-meat salmon fish.

Cannerymen with weather-beaten faces come from up and down the coast to meet with Nadia and Yo, to contract for Indians to work at the Glory of Seas cannery in Ketchikan. Like old gossips, these men are always talking about what calamity has just befallen their competitors. Last week a terrible gale tore the roof off the northwest cannery of the Old English Fish Company, killing ten Indians. Soon, Nadia tells me, we will go in the new schooner to Angoon village to contract more Indians to work in her cannery: Alaska Fish, she calls it. They are her friends, the Hootz-noos in Angoon and, like the Tlingits in Sitka's Indian Town, probably have hungry faces and look as if they are in need of work. So many times when I walk along the boardwalk to the Russian bakery on Lincoln Street, I look up at the Indian village above Nadia's cannery—whole families in a one-room house with strange paintings of giant red frogs and black ravens together with Christian crosses on the outside walls.

All day, even though I have a new *barn* in my belly, I work at the cannery sorting fish—Dogs, Humpies, Chinook. At the long split-rail tables I stand with the Indian women, who only smile kindly at me and never call me dumb towhead Swede. The smell of fish-gut rot all day does not make me much hungry for the fish that is so coveted in San Francisco. And the constant sea-gull nag outside the warehouse would give even the strongest *flicka* a headache. But just standing at the fish-chopping tables is easy work compared to what I did in the cabbage fields—all day in the sun weeding and hoeing and carrying heavy buckets of water.

The Seattle fish buyers are fickle as any woman could ever be. These men, they don't like the light-colored meat. Red meat, they say, we want red. So our schooners go farther and farther north to get the king and silver salmon for the red meat that the buyers, like spoiled children, want this week. And a senator from Washington even wrote Nadia to say that Alaska Fish and the other West Coast canneries were marketing their product under false labels. Pacific salmon aren't *real* salmon, he said. A real salmon is an East Coast salmon. A real salmon doesn't go upstream to spawn and die. It goes up and returns to the sea again. Not real salmon. Inferior, he says. Fraud. And the price of fish goes down and, *Gud*, all hell breaks loose with Alaska's commerce. To make matters worse, the men in Washington, D.C., seem to consider Seattle and not Sitka the capital of Alaska. This more than anything makes Nadia angry. "I remember," she once told me," when that lumber camp didn't even have a turner, and they had to send their millsaws all the way to Sitka to be sharpened."

In the Sitka saloons there is some talk of the gold mine a few miles north of town, but mainly it is talk of which fisherman's clan has contracted for which cannery. All along the wharf are hundreds of boats. Big schooners, boats that belong to Alaska Fish, private boats, Indian canoes—all with lines and shiny metal lures waiting for good weather so they can troll for fish. Some of the boats are whalers or seal and walrus schooners stopping over for supplies. The stories are still flying through all three of Sitka's bars about the war last week between Old English Fish and Glory of Seas over some poor Indian's fish trap. The Tlingits, with no big boats like the white fishermen, fish from their log canoes. And the white men think it fair game to steal what few fish the Indians catch in their seal-gut fishnet traps.

Yo goes out on the boats for three or four days, always with a shotgun and sometimes with Tommy. Nadia and I wake up at five and work ten, maybe twelve hours at the cannery: sorting, cleaning, making sure that the fires of the blast furnace have enough wood to heat and solder metal lids onto the tins when they are filled with fish. There are almost a hundred Indians working for us. We stand at the long tables together, breathing the fish-gut air and packing the little pink bits of fish tightly into cans.

In July, when the fish began to run, Sitka swelled to twice her winter-month size almost overnight. "They'll all be gone again in a month's time," said Nadia, talking about the narrow-faced transient men who come and go on the steamer ships and seem to have no homes.

Now in the *Sitka Times* there is only news of fish: articles on ice packaging, freezing, brine pickling, canning. The market buyers are always changing their minds. In the newspaper, between advertisements for Squirrel Whiskey and Snake Juice, there are sketches of Indians hauling ice down from the mountains on their backs.

When Yo isn't out with the boats, he's at his sawmill in back of town, checking the wood for fish boxes and for orders to build new houses in Juneau and at the Treadwell Mine Camp. Up at the lumber mill there is the terrible noise of the monster-toothed saw. Noise, so much noise. The *barn* in my belly flinches at the hammer sound of the Indians building fish boxes at the mill. In summer, the noise of the stamp press machine at the gold mine two miles away never ends. Drunken fishermen and cannery workers hoot in the narrow, tidy streets of Sitka. All winter this was a quiet village, the only noise the bell of the Church of Saint Michael and the wind. Now old Barney O'Ragan has hung a sign on the outside of the Mooseloose Saloon:

WELCOME TO SITKA
Pardon our noise
It's the sound of M-O-N-E-Y

At night Nadia and I walk from the cannery up Indian River to Eagle Tree, the name she gave the house Mr. York built. This fall, Yo says that he will build us our own house closer to the mill and Lovers' Lane, the woodsy nook at the end of Lincoln Street where Nadia says a Russian princess who used to live in the Castle on the kekoor rock took her afternoon tea. But, nej, nej, I tell him, Nadia is such a good friend to me. And my garden down by Nadia's pear orchard, oh, I would miss my garden, and my eight-foot-high sweetpea and dahlia flowers, if we moved into a new house way across the village. In California I was not so good growing the cabbages, but here, with Alaska's late-night sun, I grow cabbages that weigh as much as a stone and cantaloupes as sweet as any I ate in San Francisco.

Nadia is a good friend to me, and Eskimo Tommy is too. At night the troll combs my hair while Nadia and Yo talk of fish. "Where are the salmon running now?" she asks, "north or south?" She feels this land as if it were a part of her body. Last week as we were sitting on the Wishing Stone waiting for the steamer boat, Nadia showed me how to look out into the bay and spot the fish. "Where the gulls are gathering," she said, "so are the salmon gathering to swim upstream where they hatched out as fry." Always there is talk of fish. Does the buyer want embalmed fish or brined fish? Buyers from the Alaska Commercial Company, which isn't even in Alaska, but Seattle: buyers and fish.

Last night some cannerymen from Glory of Seas cannery came to Eagle Tree for a friendly visit. "These buyers have a color fetish," said Nadia, laughing. "They want red meat, not pink. The pink tastes better, everyone knows that. Maybe in Seattle they taste with their eyes," she said, while all the men nodded their heads. Then they all bent over the sea maps, charting their sailing course and deciding which wooded island the schooners would be bound for tomorrow, looking for the silver hordes.

In the winter the cannerymen fish for cod and herring. But Nadia says these fish are hardly worth the business. Last winter I made Swedish pickled herring. Most of my crocks went bad, because of the damp weather, but the one good batch pleased Yo. He is always showing it to the cannerymen and the fish buyers. "Take a little taste," he says. "A whole new market, pickled herring instead of herring for fertilizer and fish bait." He takes a bite himself, smiles at the other fishermen, and rubs his stomach with his calloused hand. "My Ulla's the best fish cook in Alaska," he says, with a broad smile across his dark face. He gives me a gentle pat on the head when he sees my face blush pink as an Alaska summer sunset from the praise he is always giving me. And although at night sometimes I pine for my Gunnar and his farfetched stories and dreams of gold, I think to myself, Ulla, this man Yo York will be a good *fader* to your unborn *barn*. He gives you more thank-yous and good words than Gunnar ever did, or even your own folk.

This morning I walk as usual with Nadia to the cannery. "We go to Angoon tomorrow," she says. "You'll like the Indians there. They'll have a feast for us, a potlatch they call it." She smiles like a sprite.

"The Indians in Sitka, they don't do so well," I say, thinking of shabby Indian Town. When I walk on the muddy path through this village on my way to pick blackberries, all the Tlingits seem to stand idle and hungry looking, and almost everyone coughs from the tuberculosis.

"No," Nadia says with a downcast face, "the Indians are dying out like the hair seal and the sea otter."

"You are good like anything to them," I tell her. She has suddenly such a sad face on, even though I have tried to make her happy. "You give them fish and work," I tell her. "And always last winter you were trudging through the cold rain to visit and take them blankets."

"The white people came and stole their land," she says. "And now the cannerymen steal what little fish they can catch from a canoe or in their fish traps. My husband stole the land where my house and the cannery is," she says. "That has caused me great sadness. But I would have starved, Yo and I, if I hadn't built up the fish and lumber business. I thought it would help the Indians, to have a foothold in the white man's world, but no white man will have any business dealings with an Indian, except to sell him liquor, to keep him humble, or rob him of his fish or wages at a game of cards." She takes a deep breath, and I see there are tears in her eyes, almost like someone who has seen their life's work fall in front of them. "The Tlingits were good to me," she says. "They took my mother and me into their village in winter when we had nothing to eat. Most of the Indians I knew as a young girl are dead now."

"And your *moder?*" I ask.

"Oh"—she sighs—"after the Russian priests took me away from her she disappeared. I used to look for her. . . ."

"When we met on *Resolute?*" I ask.

"No," she says, "that was just cannery business. No, this was years ago when Yo was only a little cub."

"Did you find her, your *moder?*" I ask.

"Yes," she says in a small voice, "yes."

Deeply I breathe of the wet, cedar-smelling air. Speak no more of Nadia's *moder*, Ulla, I tell myself, remembering that day almost a year ago when I took a walk alone in the old Russian tea gardens at the end of Lincoln Street—the Governor's Walk, the Russian folk here call it.

Slowly I wandered along the wooded and tanbark pathways of Lovers' Lane, looking out into Sitka Sound and watching Yuri Dysokar, the village blacksmith, who Nadia does not like, ferry his anvil across the quiet water to Japonski Island. Beside the hemlock paths the townsfolk have put up Indian totem poles. Like wood sprites their animal faces smiled down on me, and as I walked I thought of what Nadia had told me about them. They are stories, she said, these poles that are one animal caricature resting on top of another: story histories of the Tlingit and Haida Indians carved in logs instead of written down in books. But the tall narrow poles with one wooden raven or eagle bird at the top are different, Nadia told me. They are mortuary poles, where the Indians have put the ashes and belongings of a dead one.

The day was calm and the air almost as warm as in California. Out in the bay, salmon fishes splashed in the blue-green water, and in the wooded park red-bellied hummingbirds sucked the flowers of the honeysuckle vines. Behind me I heard a hushed whimpering. And glancing into the green thicket, I saw the strangest totem pole of all, a mortuary pole with not an animal at the top, but the carved statue of a bare-breasted Indian woman. Her wooden hair was pulled back in a bun and her lower lip had a real stone in it, just like the adventure-book pictures I have seen of African princesses. For a moment I stared at the statue's narrow eyes, then again heard the whimpering and looked down to the mossy ground. Nadia herself was sitting there, her head buried in her hands and her black shawl cast aside. Around her neck was the necklace she wore on board *Resolute*—ivory bone-like beads and white fangs like icicles strung together with a raw-hide string. I remembered that Tommy once said the necklace had belonged to her *moder*.

Somehow I felt that I should not approach her, so like a little mouse I stood quietly watching. Nadia fingered the necklace, stroking the long teeth with her index finger. Next to her a shiny object caught my eye: a chisel and, beside it, an iron mallet. Oh, Jonah, I thought to myself as Nadia continued to whimper, she has carved this death pole and put it in these woods herself! It is her *moder's* grave, I told myself, suddenly seeing Nadia with new eyes—seeing her as an Indian who once ran wild through the woods like a nimble wolf-woman. Then Nadia began to chant, some words in English and some words in Indian:

"*Nana ne akaxkuxte cha-a thlinedi yatxi azte tane yatxi utu yu taate.*
When I die, will I come alive again . . .?"

Nej, I think to myself as Nadia and I walk to the cannery, do not ask again about her *moder*.

All day we scoop fish from the floating scow at the dock and sort them according to color. In the cannery I stand in my tarred boots to keep my feet dry with the roundness of my new *barn* showing under my apron. I cut and clean, cut and clean. A hundred Indians, all of them smile their wide-mouthed grins at me but seem too shy to talk. "We need more help," says Nadia. We cut and clean.

The vats of innards and roe are dumped into the tide. Gulls and cormorants scream wildly with each new tub dumped in. Everywhere on the dock there are dogs with mouths full of fish heads. Cut and clean. Blood splatters into my face, and there is the powerful smell of fish everywhere. All day I am cutting off the heads of fish, some still alive. At first it bothered me to murder them. Practice, I say to myself, practice for Joe Sprout and Seattle Charley. For a year now I have heard their names tossed about in conversation but have not yet laid eyes on them. Soon, I say to myself, soon.

Ja, it is still Gunnar that I think of. And there is guilt in my heart for not loving my new and benevolent husband, who takes more joy in me than my Gunnar ever did. With such fondness Yo treats me. But all I have in my heart is shame. Sad, I think, here is a man who is young and handsome, who loves me, an almost middle-aged widow woman, who saved me from the fallen life of a tart. And, *nej,* there is no love in my heart for him. I lay my knife into the neck of the fish. *Å, Gud,* what a sinner I am.

At night Nadia and I, in our tarred boots, trudge back to the house exhausted. Our clothes are damp from fish blood and the constant southeast foggy drizzle. "Angoon tomorrow at high tide," says Yo, who is already home from the mill and roasting a saddle of venison. In the little room that he and I have to ourselves, Yo and Tommy both put their ears to my belly trying to hear the tiny heartbeat. "Like the sea," says Tommy, feeling my stomach. "Sea pod," he says, rolling his eyes, "sea pod. Raven made a sea pod, and man popped out. Raven flies around and pulls up his beak. 'Where you come from?' Raven says to man. Sea pod. Raven made a sea pod. Yeah."

In bed Yo mounts me. He is quick: not to hurt the baby, he says. Gunnar mounted me two or three times a night. With Yo it is hard to lie still. He makes a good feeling down there. A sin, I think, a sin to like it, to think of it all day while I am cutting off the heads of live fish. All day I wait for Yo to mount me, to watch his manhood rise like Mount Edgecumbe through the fog and tall trees. With my blond Gunnar I was a holy wife. I lay still. I didn't like *it.* I never asked him to mount me. Oh, Jonah, I have so much to repent.

In the middle of the night little Tommy wakes us up trying to get under the covers. It is cold in his bed up in the loft, he says. He crawls in like an animal burrowing. It bothers me no more that he sucks my hair. I am too tired for the noise to keep me awake. Besides, he helps to keep me warm from the damp, which after California is so hard for me to get used to.

At high tide, aboard the white-sailed schooner *Fylgia,* the four of us and a crew of short Aleut Indians sail for Angoon, north up the canal-like narrows. All Indians and Eskimos, when I first came to Alaska, I thought were the same. But now I am able to tell them apart and how different each tribe looks. The Tlingits near Sitka are tall with raven noses, unlike our small, broad Aleut crewmen with yellowish-red skin. And Tommy and the Eskimos look something like the Chinamen I saw in San Francisco.

The *Fylgia* is Alaska Fish's newest boat; like a silver salmon she shines among the others. The *Ulla I,* Yo wanted to call her. But *nej,* I said. *Fylgia* is a name from one of my grandmother's stories of a Viking woman who protected hunters in wild lands. It was to be the name of my first *flicka,* mine and Gunnar's. I give a great sigh, thinking of all my *barn* born too early to be alive, and pat my belly. Will it be different with this one? I wonder, feeling already the jumps and little kicks.

In every spruce-lined inlet there are dugout canoes trolling for salmon, and the smell of fish is everywhere. My clothes: No matter how long I boil them, the stink is never gone. Fish slime in my hair at night, fish slime and fish blood; I am sick for the smell of it.

Fylgia puts down anchor at the small village of Angoon. So different an Indian town from the one the Tlingits live in at Sitka. Not houses like the shanties of poor white folk, but log houses, with bear totem poles in front and the painting of a strange, open-mouthed, hungry-looking animal on the side wall of the largest, which Yo tells me is called the community house. Onshore I see that the Indians do not wear what churchmen call "civilized clothing": drab black trousers and dresses, the women always humbled before God with black scarves on their heads. *Nej,* in Angoon the Indians are wearing deer-hide clothing and strange animal masks. Some are calling out and beating drums, making the noise of trolley cars colliding. "Drunk on hooch," Nadia whispers to me. Yo rows us ashore in the skiff. A wrinkled Indian with his hair in a long black braid approaches our boat, trying to pull it up on shore. Moosehide, chief of the Hootz-noos, Nadia says his name is.

"*Gusu-wa-eh?*" he calls out to us.

"I need more cannery workers," Nadia answers him.

But Moosehide is too drunk to pull the boat ashore, and his bony limbs fall into the tide.

"What goes on here?" I ask. "They tell me that giving an Indian liquor is a capital offense."

"They make it themselves," says Nadia, pointing to a strange contraption on the beach which looks like it is made of kerosene tins strung together with dried seaweed worms. "Fermented berries and molasses," she says. "Or if there's no molasses, then just fermented berries and pine sprouts."

A tall, bespectacled Indian that I recognize as Chief Shathitch Hard-to-Kill Larson, the man I met in Juneau last year, comes lumbering down the beach. This old billy goat is everywhere, I think to myself. But the chief and Nadia embrace and I can feel the friendship between them, like brother and sister.

Yo hauls the skiff onshore and we go into the Hootz-noos' community house. Huge, maybe forty feet long, with what I recognize now as their bear totem painted on the front wall and a bear snout hanging above the door hole. Inside it is large enough for the whole tribe, most of whom are still dancing on the beach in front of their still, waving rattles and spears. Nadia and Chief Shathitch talk about the cannery, which natives she will hire and how much they will be paid. It is Shathitch who seems to run this tribe and not Moosehide, I think to myself. What a great man among the Indians this bespectacled man is.

Smiling with delight, Yo says there is to be a feast for us. We gather around the graveled fire hole in the middle of the large room. I study the creatures carved into the totem poles that support each corner of the community house as many of the Indians join us, along with three rough-looking white men who seem to be trying to buy fox pelts and gold nuggets from the drunken natives. But when they see us, the three, led by a tall man with a disfigured face, leave the building and go out onto the beach.

Tommy is making funny gestures at me from across the room while a tall young Hootz-noo man piles wood onto the fire. Blue Hudson's Bay enamelware tubs of food are brought to us, filled with dried salmon, small potatoes, berries, and strips of dried deer meat, all of it covered with some sort of fish fat which makes the food smell rancid. Yo cannot take his eyes from the feast. The young Hootz-noo man has put an entire washtub of food in front of me. "You'll hurt their feelings if you don't eat it," my husband says. Everyone is putting food into their mouths in fistfuls. My stomach feels queasy as Yo makes a soft cushion out of blankets, then helps me to sit down in front of the mound of food.

I look around and see that Nadia is gone. Probably off talking business with the chief, I think to myself. "Nadia," I ask Yo, "won't she come and help me eat this?"

"Naw, she always eats with Shathitch," he says. "The old chief of the Tlingits in Sitka, Kat-lee-an—he got killed way back when—him and Shathitch and my ma were all old friends. Kat-lee-an had an idiot daughter, and the Hootz-noos take care of her. Ma comes to see her from time to time, when she's hiring cannery workers. Yeah, my ma and Shathitch were all friends way back during the Alaska purchase, when ol' Kat killed himself a righteous number of *cheechakoes* before Seattle Charley and Reverend Hitch convinced a town vigilante group to hang him and his wife, Shathitch's sister, from the witch tree above Lovers' Lane. The old-timers in Sitka always said there was something going on between Kat-lee-an and my ma, but I never paid their gossip no mind. Naw, Ulla," he says in between mouthfuls of dried fish. "Ya better eat up. Ma's probably busy talkin' old times with Shathitch." I look across at Tommy, who is still waving and gesturing at me. Seattle Charley, I think to myself; again and again I hear his name. "Yeah," says Yo, "the day they hung ol' Kat, I was maybe only nine or ten. They tortured him first, ya know, didn't even call in a judge to pass sentence, didn't have to, since Indians ain't even citizens. And so Ma wouldn't have to hear Kat wailin' from being poked with a blacksmith's iron, she had at least ten virgin cedar trees felled that day. What with Kat wailin' and them trees fallin'—well, it made such a terrible noise, I never will forget it, not to my dyin' day." He wipes the fish grease from his face and gives me a gentle kiss upon the forehead.

"Don't worry, Ulla," he says, when he sees that my face is saddened by his story. "Alaska ain't like that no more. Besides, ain't no man in these parts who'll lay a hand on you as long as they know you're my wife. Anyway," he says, continuing with his tale, "later Ma had the saw-mill men cut down the witch tree, and she carved it herself into some kind of Indian pole."

Oh, Jonah, I think to myself, that must be the statue of her *moder* which is now in Lovers' Lane.

Tommy motions for me to come sit beside him, and I go over to his eating tub as Yo begins to talk about the salmon run with the young Hootz-noo men. The natives are all chattering in dialect like ducklings. I see that they like Tommy; a young girl is feeding him blueberries one at a time. "Tall scar-faced white man," says Tommy, pointing in the direction of the beach. "Seattle Charley," he says.

16.

The terrible smell of fish grease smothers my breath as I look at the man who murdered my Gunnar. My gun, Barbro, Barbro, I think to myself. *Å Gud*, I've left her at home. "I go to find Nadia," I say to Yo, making an excuse to go and look for a rifle.

Quickly I walk out of the community house. Seattle Charley, Seattle Charley, I chant. Most of the Indians who are not inside eating are sleeping drunk beside their still. The little bark and log houses of Angoon are empty. No rifles inside the first three that I poke my head into. I walk along the rows of houses toward a hut with a large carving of a raven holding up the roof. Voices. From the entryway I see Nadia and Chief Shathitch, along with Moosehide and some young Indian women. Nadia motions for me to come inside. They are gathered in a circle, and in the middle is Kat-lee-an's fat idiot child. She does not walk but crawls on the floor. Shathitch is saying that some Hootz-noos want to kill her because they think she is a witch who stopped the salmon from running up the creek on their tribal land this year.

Nadia is combing the strange creature's hair. She is large and round like a walrus and maybe fifteen years old. Her hair is so matted that

I don't understand why Nadia is combing it. Such a kind heart Nadia has, I think to myself, to always have so much love for lost creatures.

The young women are trying to feed the idiot potatoes. They mash them between their hands and then push them into her mouth. The idiot's round, dish face is covered with potato drool. I say nothing. I cannot believe that such a creature could have been born from a human form. She makes noises like the crows. Crawling in frenzied circles, the idiot flips onto her back, trying to put her feet into her mouth and making violent sucking noises. Nadia is all the time petting her as if she were a lost puppy dog.

I look at Nadia. There are tears in her eyes. She is mashing potatoes now and trying to get the wretched creature to eat them. Uta, Uta, she calls her. By the looks of Uta's mammoth body, she is always being fed potatoes.

I put my hand on my swollen stomach and wonder if such a creature could be growing inside of me. There is something about Uta's face. . . . Nadia is weeping now, and Shathitch is comforting her. Uta is making noises of a pig about to be slaughtered. Nadia pulls Uta's face up into hers. There is something between them, a look. Daughter, I think to myself, Nadia's daughter! I grab my belly. Poor woman, I think. Could it be that she has never even told her own son about this, about herself and this bloodsucking Indian they call Kat-lee-an? Nadia looks up at me. She sees that I know and her eyes look down. I go to touch Nadia's face, to dry her tears. Did she see me flinch at the ugly child, I wonder? Did she see me grab my belly? As I lean down to comfort her, my eye spots the long barrel of a new shotgun in the corner by the door. It probably belongs to this rich Chief Shathitch Hard-to-Kill Larson, I think to myself.

They do not notice me leave the hut with the shotgun, because Uta has caused a great commotion by trying to dig a hole under the far wall. From fifty feet I see the three white men talking loudly on the beach. The night before I married Yo I told him about Gunnar, about my real reason for coming to Alaska. Not a lady miner, I told him, only to find my husband's grave. Yo had only kindness in his eyes. "Too bad," he said, "all the prospectors' and fur farmers' graves up the Stikine usually get washed downriver every spring when the *glate* melts."

And the men in the Sitka bars say that all the judges sent to Alaska are drunks, unfit to sit on the bench anywhere but this wild rainy place, and only preside over municipal affairs. They say that murderers are sent all the way to San Francisco for their trials. *Nej*, I think to myself, if my two claim-swiping murderers are found and sent to California, they would no doubt get away.

All during my wedding day I could think only that I had nothing left of my Gunnar, not the money from our house, not even his grave, only a gun. I never told Yo the real reason I wanted to find Joe Sprout and Seattle Charley. Friends of *Far's*, ha. And now, at last, I have found one of them.

I wait amid the empty houses for what seems like hours, thinking of Uta and watching Charley and the two men quarrel on the beach behind the Indian's still. The noise of the feast grows louder, and finally the two other men get into a canoe. Charley picks up a rucksack and walks into the woods. I follow.

I check the gun to make sure it's loaded. Should I give him a fair chance? I think to myself. Should I ask him about my Gunnar and his claim? *Nej*, a scoundrel such as Seattle Charley would never tell the truth. And me with a *barn* heavy in my belly, he could quickly turn my own gun on me, if he's the sly fox everyone says he is. I follow him for about a mile into the woods, the gun under my arm. I think of Nadia and the idiot girl. To have her son's wife a murderess as well. The kind woman does not deserve this, I think to myself. I step quietly. Charley walks down an incline into a creek. I put the gun to my shoulder. There is a blast and Charley falls to the ground. He moans and crawls into the water, then falls face down into it. There is an enormous red hole in his back. Blood pours into the creek water and disappears. Slowly I creep down the path. I wait for him to drown.

Bury him, bury him, I think to myself. As quickly as I can, I hurry back to the village and leave the gun in the nearest hut. If they have heard it, no one seems to be concerned by the gunshot. A shovel. There must be a shovel somewhere. I hear voices inside Uta's hut. Uta is screaming like a San Francisco seal at mating season. The community house vibrates with drunken laughter. A small shovel that the Indians use for digging clams is the only tool I can find.

I go back into the woods and down the incline into the creek. Blood is still running from the hole in his back and into the water. His skin is bluish. Hurriedly I begin to dig in the sandy bank. With each small shovelful, I think, now for Joe Sprout, now for the other claim-stealing murderer. So easy to kill a man. He is alive and walking down a trail, then by a quick motion of my index finger, he is drowned in a creek with a red hole in his back. Cautiously I look down at the body, seeing that there is a burn on his jacket where the shot went through.

I am out of breath and my side aches. There comes a terrible pain in my back and I stumble to the ground. Footsteps. Footsteps behind me. *Å Gud*, to be found out. A vigilante group will hang me from a tree for this murderous deed just as they did Kat-lee-an. *Mor*'s long face appears before me. The pain in my side is like a knife. Run, I think, run. But I cannot rise.

Nadia and Tommy appear at the top of the incline. They run toward me. Nadia wipes my brow with her skirt and holds my head. Her sad face is gone. "Give me that shovel," she says. Tommy is wiping my brow now too. "Give me the shovel, Ulla," she says sternly. "No sense losing your baby over a scoundrel like this."

17. SKAGWAY
Summer 1898

Always I am wondering why other women do not go blind from the sight of my three beauties. But the hundreds of men and women stampeders in the muddy street below are thinking only of the gold nuggets to be found on the other side of these steep Skagway mountains. Together Tommy and I sit in the finest suite that Skagway's Golden North Hotel has to offer; me with baby Carl sucking at my breast in the sunlit window, and Tommy playing an Eskimo string game with my chubby four-year-old twins, Catherine and Stig.

It was when the twins were sucking, one at each breast, that Yo came home with the news of Klondike Creek. "Gold," he said, "a new strike just over the border in the Canadian Territory. Dutch Kate," he said, "she and the others with twenty deer-hide pokes full of gold apiece."

Oh, Jonah, it is like the Second Coming. So many ships, so many men, and terrible stories of last winter with hundreds of them freezing to death in steamships on the Yukon or dying of the scurvy and famine inland near Dawson.

Tommy has not yet finished his string-game story, like the game Cat's Cradle that Kerstin and I played as schoolgirls. Tommy is telling about a fox chasing a rabbit, the string between his fingers making the shape of rabbit ears and a rabbit face. When the story is finished, Catherine will grab the string in her golden fingers and tease Stig with it. The baby sucks at my left breast. Even in sleep his lips are the pink shape of an Alaska wild rose.

I look out the window into the Skagway dock, out at the schooner, the *Ulla I*, then down Main Street to Sylvester Hall where Nadia and Yo have been all day haggling over the price of lumber for a new town hall. Skagway—when the twins were still in my belly, it was just Ben Moore's cow field at the foot of the Coastal Mountains and the Chilkoot Pass.

Gold-crazed men are everywhere, some even sleeping on the plank walkway of the street in front of our hotel. Sweet, cherub-faced Ben Moore told Yo that he looked out of his log house one day and there was Soapy Smith, marking his cow pasture off into lots, and some Seattle real-estate man selling them. "One gun and a daughter was all I had against 'em," he said. "What could I do? They told me that the Chilkoot Pass through the mountains in back of my homestead was the quickest way to the Yukon. And ain't no woman or no gun that's gonna stand in the way of a gold-crazed man," said Ben.

Ja, and before a year was out the U.S.S. *Portland* docked in Seattle, carrying more than a ton of Alaska gold. Sad, that all the wealth of this vast northern land should go to line the streets of an almost foreign city.

Built overnight, these gold-mining towns, I think to myself again, looking down into the shabby mud-covered streets of Skagway. Our mill at Sitka works endlessly to cut new lumber for the shotgun houses. A new mill is being built at Juneau. From everywhere, all corners of the earth, men have come with tents and pitched them on Squaw Hill in back of town. They have cut down all the trees, and mud slides over the new log and canvas houses. These men are like hungry dogs, I think. No thought of what lies ahead. Gold, they think. Gold will feed them when the heavy snows hit. Gold will keep them warm.

There is so much talk about the Beach at Nome and Anvil City. Everyone in Skagway is afraid that business will all go to the Beach instead of coming here to Skagway and the Chilkoot Pass. Railroad, these men are already talking railroad—over mountains that even a wild Alaskan goat wouldn't climb in winter.

I move baby Carl to my other breast. All over the creosote-painted dock there is luggage and miners' gear, some of it falling into the water and some of it being pushed by a stout bald man, Soapy Smith's right-hand scoundrel. Everywhere there are stampeders. And there goes slick-haired, handsome Soapy himself, strutting out of Shoemaker Brown's storefront. This Mr. Smith is kind to me and always gives my twins hard candy. But Yo tells me to stay up here in my room, away from the ill-gotten gains that Soapy's reaping in the streets. "Oh, there is war in heaven," I moan, homesick for Sitka and my garden, where Nadia's pear trees will soon be bearing their sweet yellow fruit. . . .

Footsteps in the hall outside. Tommy goes to the door. Nadia and Yo walk in. Nadia, her face is so drawn around the eyes, how tired she looks. "Goose shit, Ma," says Yo, kissing me on the back of the neck as I am bending over baby Carl. "Somebody's gotta tan that sow bug's hide."

Nadia just shakes her head.

"Soapy says he's got a Skagway recruitin' outlet for that Cuban War," says Yo, "but that's not what I call it. And it's the same shenanigans that's goin' on at his Information and Welcome to Alaska Agency. Ol' Soap's out there robbin' gold-crazed men as they get off the boat with the expensive price of his fal-lacious information; then he gets 'em again as they leave town with their Yukon gold nuggets by takin' 'em in over at his Cuban War recruitin' office.

"Ma, I wanna tell ya about this so-called recruitin'. He gets men in the office there and steals the money from their pants pockets while they're stark naked waiting for the doctor—if that's what the man is—

to give 'em a physical. Soap's got his eyes on the stampeder's wallet, and I ain't sayin' in front of you all what Doc Spencer's got his eyes on. Hell, Soapy's got Shoemaker Brown and Waterfront Eddy both paying 'insurance' out the nose—health insurance, inventory insurance, employ-ee insurance, and ain't neither one of 'em got an employ-ee."

Nadia just shakes her head and bounces Stig on her knee. Catherine has stolen the string from Tommy's fingers, and Tommy is pretending to whimper. Her eyes are like the Eskimo troll's, like shiny dark stones underwater. Stealing the string from Tommy is her favorite game.

There is a knock on the open door and smiling Ben Moore pulls up a chair, extending a friendly hand to Nadia. Quickly I button up my flannelette blouse so that this man does not see my breasts. "Well, how are y'all?" he says. "Ya know that by the grace of Soapy Smith and the devil y'all are sittin on the former sight of the best red-oat hay pasture this side of See-attle?"

Nadia laughs and clutches plump-faced Stig to her body.

"Well, what's passed with you folks since they cut up my homestead into the future capital of Alasky?" he drawls to Yo.

"Got another youngun," Yo says, smiling with praise at me. "Got two or three new fish contracts and two new schooners in the makin.'"

"Feedin' the hungry hordes," says Ben, laughing. "Well, someone's gotta, that's for sure. Didja hear about our new telegraph office right here in Skagway?" Ben says to Nadia.

"Do you think that because my mother was an Indian, I'm fool-headed enough to believe a wild story like that?" she asks. "Mind you, I'm not implying that Indians are dim-witted," she says, with the light returning to her eyes and Stig all the time trying to play with her graying hair braid.

"Hell no, woman," says Ben. "Ya know damn well I've always admired your spunk. But I'll be confounded," he says with a look in his eye, "if we don't have a telegraph office down on Tent Street. Yeah, no wires or nothin', but all these stampeders don't seem to notice. Hell, for five bucks ya can send a message anywhere in the con-tee-nental United States, and I hear tell that they got a file of make-believe replies that would burn your ears."

"One of Soapy's operations, no doubt," says Yo, lighting a cigar. "I was just tellin' Ma and Ulla here that someone oughta do somethin' right quick about that fool."

Nadia sends Tommy out for a fifth of squirrel whiskey. Fat sturdy-legged Catherine is pushing baby Carl out of my lap. "*Nej*," I tell her with a pat.

"And a pie from Ma Pullen's Grub Tent," Nadia calls after Tommy. "Blueberry, if the mountain bushes are bearing." Ben slumps down into his chair and Yo pets Catherine's dark-brown head.

"Five hundred men landed here in Skagway just last month," says Ben. "I hear Wrangell's boomin', advertised in all the Frisco papers. Mainly they's advertisin' all the death and mutilation on the Chilkoot trail, hopin' everyone'll consider Wrangell as the most dee-sirable jumpin'-off point for gettin' inland. And hell, there's all this business competition with Cordova and Copper River, to boot. But ain't no one in his right mind who'd go there. They ain't even got all their last winter's dead buried yet. The Beach, I tell ya that's where I shoulda home-steaded. Long as my life's work in clearin' out pasture had to be spirited away, the least I coulda done was to do it up yonder where I coulda picked up gold nuggets outa the sandy shores of the Bering Sea in my spare time. Well, I still got myself a fair stake in the real estate in these parts. I mean Skagway's biggest business may be Soapy Smith and his outfit, but at least we're fairin' a might better than Wrangell and that shanty town near the Yukon River that everyone's callin' Fairbanks."

"Word has it in Sitka," says Yo, "that the head of Fairbanks First National is an ex-con from See-attle."

"No doubt," says Ben, "no doubt."

"*Ja*," I say, "two girl friends of mine in Wrangell wrote that the marshal there is wanted in two states as well as the Canadian territories."

"Don't surprise me none at all," says Ben. "If Soap doesn't have Marshal Taylor here in his back pocket, then the ol' buzzard's just too yellow to wear a star. Hell, Soap's even got some young reporter from the *Skagway News* helpin' him work his con game sweet as you please. This kid's a nice kid, mind ya, thinks the world of Soap and all his book learnin' and high-class East Coast ways. Well, Soap's got him down at the dock every time a steamer comes in, interviewin' all them gold hunters as they come down the plank. Human interest, ol' Soap calls it—his interest bein' in how much cash each of 'em's got in their wallet."

"Are they all so taken in by him here?" asks Nadia. "Even in Sitka we have jokes about his Information Agency—a dollar a consultation, maps, pieces of advice, a free bottle of Skagway brewed beer, and the young cub's wallet lifted from his pants during the transaction."

"Hell," says Ben, "word went round the world about the gold in these parts, but Soapy Smith's the best-kept secret this side of Wrangell— where, if what Ulla over there says is true, they got the same operation. And when any of us more upright citizens calls Soapy's cards on him, you oughta hear the ol' mule squeal. Smoothest talker you'd ever hope to meet. Rambles on about doin' his patriotic duty, keepin' the flow of cash in the U.S. of A., instead of lettin' it float over the Chilkoot Pass into Canada."

"Ah, hell," says Yo. "I hear they got the same problem up at the Beach. A guy come askin', beggin' me, mind ya, for a job at the Sitka mill. Said that if ya go to the Beach, it's best not to take no luggage, cause it'll get stolen even before ya get off the boat. 'Nother guy told me that the coastline was mile-to-mile steamer trunks and rucksacks, all of 'em empty. Who's gunna build an organized dock, he said, with their present operations bein' so profitable?"

While the others chatter, I secretly plan the future of my little ones. For Carl and Stig to go to the college in Washington, like their father. For my pretty Catherine, a finishing school in Seattle so that she can go on Saturdays to the art museums or to hear concert music in the great auditorium built with all this Alaska gold. But not to tell Nadia of my plans, *nej*, she has great misgivings about the terrible prejudice against Indians there and is afraid her dark-complexioned grandchildren will be mistreated, even harmed.

Nadia is all the time rocking Stig back and forth, her eyes closed. "I think I'm going to call them Imperial," she says to me while the men carry on with their talk of gold stampeders and Soapy Smith's newest business, a Revival Meeting and Faro Hall.

"What?" I say.

"The lumber mills," she says. "I think I'll call them the Imperial Lumber Company. Did I ever tell you that my husband once wrote to his father that I was a royal Russian? After he died—we weren't married long, you know—well, I wrote and told him the truth. But I always did think it was sort of funny. When I was just a girl living with a Russian family, they never even considered me altogether human, let alone fit to be called *royal*. And then Noah York—he actually bought me like a box of codfish bait—had the gall to tell his father that he'd married a princess. Imperial Lumber, that's what I'm going to call it," she says, grasping my wrist. "Of course, I guess we'd better not put that brand name on the fish boxes. Who'd want to build a house made out of fish box lumber," she says, lowering her voice, and we both laugh.

Then Nadia is quiet, her eyes looking as if they have fallen back into her head. I see that she has remembered some unhappiness and tell myself, Ulla, don't speak of Nadia's dead husband on this bright and cloudless day.

Tommy returns with a whiskey bottle and a pie tin covered with a white towel. His head is hanging. Nadia pours the whiskey into crystal goblets just imported from San Francisco on the last steamer ship, then uncovers a half-eaten pie. Catherine makes a terrible face. "Tommy ate my piece. Tommy ate my piece," she screams.

Doe-eyed Stig and the baby wake up. My twins begin chanting, "Pie, pie," in their *elvefolk* voices with baby Carl trying to mimic them.

"No," Tommy says, "Joaquin Johnny—Ice Chief, Ankow Glate—he ate it. Share, he tells me, sharing is the great Alaska way."

"Is that old crow back in town?" asks Nadia.

"*Ja*," I say to her. "I saw him on Squaw Hill yesterday sweet-talking *lilla* Mollie Walsh in front of her grub tent." And him with a wife at home waiting for him in California, I think scornfully to myself.

"Ol' nature boy?" interrupts Ben Moore. "He's travelin' with a preacher man and some guide by name of Iowa Dan. The one lookin' for iceburgs to name after hisself and the other lookin' for Indians to convert."

"A workable pair, if I do say so myself," says Nadia, winking at me.

"Came back from up north totin' some drunk Scandia with him," says Ben. "Some Scandia gone *siwash*, married up with a squaw and taken up her ways. Word has it he lives up near Porcupine Creek most of the year, drivin' dogsleds and punchin' Samoyeds. I hear tell them

Scandias've even started takin' over at the Beach. People up there went so far as to organize the Nome Mining District to keep some dumb Swede from running the whole shebang."

Ben pauses and takes a breath, then turns to Yo with a broad smile on his face. "Know how to save a drowning Swede?" he asks.

"N-no," answers Yo.

"Good!" laughs Ben Moore and slaps his knee.

Oh, Jonah, I think to myself. No wonder my poor Gunnar is dead in a soggy grave. The people in the gold country hate Scandinavians as much as they do in San Francisco.

Nadia glances at me, then gives smiling Ben a sour look. "Don't bite the hand that feeds you, Ben," she says. "Our Ulla here's one of those Scandias you're complaining about, and all she's doing is feeding you pie and whiskey. Nothing a body can do about *cheechakoes*," she says. "An old Indian woman once told me that human people migrate just like the geese people, except that men go by some mysterious calendar no one can quite predict."

I hug baby Carl, stroking his dark head. Such thick hair he has for so young a child. I thank *Gud* that they are all healthy, my babies. In my terrible nightmares before their births, I would see Uta's face, over and over, big and flat as a yellow harvest moon. Uta. Nadia and I never speak of her, but there is an understanding between us. Nadia goes to Angoon. Cannery workers, she says. Shathitch is all the time sending word that the tribal communities blame the idiot for witchcraft, for the glaciers blocking their salmon streams. Bad medicine, they say. In this land where the news travels by hordes of miners moving from wood camp to panning creek faster than the spring floods, how Nadia has kept this idiot child hidden in Angoon, with nobody but the Hootznoos and Shathitch to know, is beyond me. Although there is always word that the Indians want to kill Uta, Nadia is more afraid of what the civilized people would do to her. And, oh, Jonah, now it is Nadia who protects me from this man Ben Moore who talks with so much prejudice for Scandias, just as she protects Uta from the outside world.

The men's conversation has turned to the talk of importing the Single "O" Kid from Wrangell to do in Soapy Smith. But the talk of Scandias coming to Alaska makes me think of my folk, of *Mor* and *Far*, whom I haven't seen in five years. Five years. All I have are their letters and the pictures in my photo album, Inga's wedding present to Gunnar and me. Gunnar, oh, Gunnar. If only he could see my three beauties. Is it sinful of me to think that if Gunnar had been their father they would have blond hair and blue eyes instead of dark ones like Yo's? Thank *Gud* they have good eyes and good limbs, these babies who were born from my body like little fishes. But why is it that they don't look more like me or my folk? Gunnar, if only you could see my three beauties.

Tommy is still sulking because of the missing pieces of pie. "No can stop him, no can stop him," he moans.

Nadia tells him not to worry. "We'll get another pie," she says sweetly into his sad face. "This time take a roundabout route so you don't run into that fast-talking Johnny."

"I'll go with him," I say to Nadia, handing baby Carl to Yo.

"Tommy," says Yo with a drunken laugh, "you mind that none of them stampeders put their hands you-know-where on Ulla." I smile back, and Ben Moore pours everyone another drink.

Covering my head from this constant Alaska wind with a black wool scarf, I walk out of the hotel's front door with Tommy. Mud, everywhere mud and ruts. There has not even been enough time to gravel the streets. Tommy escorts me down the plank walkway toward Ma Pullen's grub tent, two blocks away. Men are crowded in the streets, camped even on the walkways, and all getting outfitted to go over the Chilkoot Pass. As we walk I listen to the men standing in the storefronts trading terrible stories of their adventures over the White Horse Rapids: "One ol' geezer—Bear Grease Tom, they called him—well, Bear Grease, he tried four-five times to get over that pass. Every time he'd get to the rapids, his boat'd bust up on the rocks. Even got as far as Lake Bennett once. Then on his fifth try, his raft went aground and sank. And damned if he didn't shoot hisself, yes, sirree." Oh, Jonah, I think to myself, I have heard that one so many times and each time about a different unfortunate.

Tommy is all the time tugging at my arm. "Ulla, Ulla," he says. "Joaquin Johnny, down the street on the corner, Joaquin Johnny." I see the gangly, white-haired man I met on board *Resolute*, still with a small troop of men around him and no doubt spinning some preposterous yarn about his most recent near collision with death and the Holy Maker while exploring a glacier. Tommy is trying to steer me down an alley instead of past the group of men. "It's all right, *liten* one," I tell him.

As we approach, Johnny breaks away from his followers to tip his hat in his gallant fashion. "Hello there, ma'am," he says in his Scotsman's tongue, apparently not recognizing me. "Always ready to welcome a new woman to Skagway. Let me aquaint ye with the lads here," he drawls, even though I have said not a word and Tommy is all the time tugging at my sleeve. "This is Hatless Walt Pritchard, Weinstein, and Joe Sprout, respectively."

My jaw drops open. The nightmare of the red hole in Seattle Charley's back as he lay drowning in that creek near Angoon flashes in front of me. The last of my Gunnar's murderers, I think to myself. The man who brought me to this wild Alaska. "Hello," I say, staring into Joe's thin ratlike face.

Tommy grabs both of my wrists. "Pie," he says, "pie." He pulls me away from Joaquin Johnny and the other men. "Don't kill 'im," whispers Tommy. "Don't kill 'im," he whines.

"*Nej, nej,*" I tell him. But, oh, *Gud,* he remembers everything, this small Eskimo. He remembers that there were two men I was looking for. And he even remembers their names. Never have Nadia or Tommy mentioned the man they buried for me four years ago in Angoon. "*Nej, nej,*" I say to comfort Tommy, and we walk hurriedly toward the grub tent.

So at last I know what he looks like, this Joe Sprout. I know what he looks like and we will meet again, he and I, before my life is over. I will get him. But not to have my husband, Tommy, or Nadia know. Not to cause them unhappiness. From now on, I say to myself, I'll carry Barbro under my apron everywhere. For protection, I'll tell Yo. So many fish wars with other canneries. He'll agree, for protection for me and my three beauties.

There is a long line in front of Ma Pullen's. Men and some women of all ages have themselves a feast before they start over Chilkoot Pass. And all toting their gear with them, those who haven't yet been robbed by Soapy Smith and his gang.

As I stand in line with the others, I look around at the women who have come alone or with their men to pan for gold in Alaska. How will they climb that steep and snowy pass with such long heavy skirts, I wonder? Some of them carry babies on their backs as well as rucksacks. I look into the pale eyes of one thin-faced woman who is all the time trying to quiet her hungry baby by rocking him in her frail arms. The only food in Skagway that's not on the hoof or swimming in the sea is at the few grub tents like Ma Pullen's. Everyone in the muddy street looks hungry. I am wondering how these women with children to feed will keep from perishing on their long and dangerous journey to the Klondike River. Some of the wives who follow two strides behind their men are not even well enough equipped, I think to myself, as I watch a girl in a purple promenade costume and stylish feathered hat become covered with mud as she runs in high-heeled boots behind her husband.

For a long time we wait in line. Tommy is all the time eyeing me. He holds me by the arm with tightly clenched fingers. He is afraid that I will get away from him and kill Joe Sprout. Such a wise thing he is. And such a ribbing he takes from everyone for his thick glasses and his funny talk.

Tommy lets me carry the blueberry pie. He guides me through the boglike streets, careful that I don't get too much mud on my clothes. And careful too that we walk a different route, away from Joaquin Johnny. By Jimminy, I have never seen the likes of this little man.

All up and down the street in back of the hotel are tarpaulin tents. Tent Street, they call it—grub tents and some even calling themselves hotels, but inside are only cots lined end to end.

Beyond Tent Street, workmen are laying out new avenues. Stacks of lumber are everywhere, lumber from Yo's mill at Juneau. Such good business they do, he and Nadia. And this year there is enough money so that Nadia and I do not have to spend late hours, each with a twin in a basket on her back, cutting off the heads of fish and packing them into tins.

In a few years' time, Yo says, we will be able to take the steamer south to San Francisco for the winter, for *Mor* and *Far* to meet Yo and their grandchildren. What joy, I think, to see my folk again, to see Kerstin and Inga. All night I spend sometime with my *Ladies' Home Journal* and Marshall Field catalog, picking out traveling clothes for my little ones and myself—a wool-felt trimmed hat for me, sailor suits for Catherine and Stig, an infant slip for baby Carl. And for Catherine, too, a child-sized ermine muff and coat, because Catherine likes so much to hear the stories that the Russian folk tell her about Princess Maksoutov sitting in the Castle cupola, dressed in white ermine, watching the old Russian fur ships sail out of Sitka bay bound for Canton.

Tommy guides me along, back to the main street and the Golden North Hotel. I pause for a minute as we step down from the plank walk to cross an alley. I look sideways into the narrow space between the new wooden buildings. Joaquin Johnny is leaning up against the wall, talking with Joe Sprout and a broad-shouldered, blond-headed man. The blond man's back is toward me. He is all dressed in Indian blankets and caribou hides. A young Indian woman in a long black dress and mukluks stands beside him. I slip my hands around the pie tin. Johnny waves to Tommy and me. And the blond man, whom I have all the time been staring at, turns around. Red-blond hair grows heavily over his face and his blue eyes dart out at me. The pie slips from my limp hands as my knees give way and the street spins. "Gunnar!" I shriek. Tommy's face appears above me, his mouth filled with a piercing noise.

PART III

1923–28

Mrs. Barnett Zimmerman

(Catherine York)

18. SEATTLE
January 1923

"Mother Delivers Bathtub Gin to Speakeasy in Perambulator. . . ."
Ghastly situation, I thought, as I read the headlines of the evening
Times. Her husband probably left her, and how else is she supposed
to make ends meet? What would I do if Barnett left me, especially
since . . . since I'm part Indian? Of course, no one else in Seattle knows;
all the same, Barnett took his chances marrying me. I can't let him
down. No, I have to learn how to shine in society.

I put the newspaper on my tea tray and stretched my legs across
the blue Georgian couch, then stared out at the view from my upstairs
sitting-room window. The forested shores of Lake Washington drifted
into the horizon, touching the snow-capped cinder cone of Mount
Rainier. But as I smiled at the vista from my Capitol Hill home, the
grotesque shapes of my three stillborn babies started to bob up and
down in the water again. "Go away," I heard myself scream, my hand
gesturing with an involuntary wave.

I moaned, leaning back on my couch and remembering Nana's
Otter-monster Indian-magic stories. "*Nyet, nyet, nyet*," she used to
mimic the Russian priests talking to the Tlingit shamans in Alaska's
colonial days. "*Nyet, nyet*." I'm sure those fetuses are just something
haunting me from my grandmother's stories. What was it that Nana
used to say about shamans? Of course I know from my college anthropology class that Indian medicine men were a little touched in the
head. But what was it that Nana said were the first signs of someone
turning into a witch doctor? Visions. They saw things that no one
else could. Mama had hallucinations most of her life, but that was
because she took a terrible fall and cracked her head in Skagway back
in 'ninety-eight. Poor Mama—living in a dream world all those years.

JANA HARRIS

Then I had a terrible thought. Hadn't Mama's first husband run off and gone to Alaska? It seemed that none of the women I knew whose husbands had left them were quite right in the head. What if Barnett divorced me? If he did, I know I'd be a candidate for the loony bin.

I looked out at Lake Washington again. The three gray fetuslike creatures still bobbed up and down. How could such ugly things have come out of my body? I brooded. They looked more like something that Daddy's rabbit-hound bitch might have dropped on the back steps of our Sitka house than anything related to the Barnett Charles Zimmerman mansion. Outside a column of sun burned through the winter clouds. One of the water babies, spiraled around itself and chewing on its tail, wagged a flipper arm at me.

"Go away," I screamed, an involuntary jerk of my arm knocking the newspaper from my tray. "Goddamn it, go away."

"But I've only just arrived," said a familiar voice. I turned. My handsome husband stood in the sitting-room doorway, wearing a pinstripe double-breasted suit.

"Barnett," I cried, "oh, Barnett, you did startle me." I had to think of an excuse. He'd be so embarrassed if he knew about my little eccentricities. And wasn't insanity grounds for divorce? I couldn't let my prize of a husband suspect that I might be a bit . . . *touched,* like my mother.

"Roaches, darling," I said, giving him a doting smile. "There was a roach in my sitting room, on my writing table. I have all those dinner invitations to do, and you know I'm simply terrified of roaches. I've been sitting here, afraid to go near my desk. Why didn't Amaryllis announce you?"

Barnett yawned and gave his shiny black walking stick a half twirl in his *très élégant* fashion. "What other news on the home front, dearest?" he asked.

"Well," I said, sitting up, turning my back to the lake, and placing my long feet delicately on the floor, "I had the most exhausting morning. I know that Amaryllis is your little pet, but I did have to devote most of my day to teaching her about cleaning the octagonal mirrored bath. She simply doesn't know how to care for modern interiors." I always felt guilty about using my housekeeper as a punching bag, but it seemed that everyone in Seattle society took that attitude to their servants. Secretly I suspected it made them feel better about them-selves—it certainly made me feel better.

"Chin up, old girl," he said, smiling down at me. "And how's the weight-losing campaign?" For a moment his frown lines deepened, and I wondered if the lumber market was on the skids again.

"I've lost three ounces since yesterday," I said proudly. "And Bar-nett—" I folded my large hands into my lap. Oh, dear, if I lost weight, would my hands get smaller and all those lines and rough edges come back? Then everyone would see how ruined my hands were, the hands of a backwoods girl who'd worked in a fish cannery. "Barnett, you really must help me decide on the dining-room chairs for the new Iota Chi sorority house. I have to put in an order at the furniture makers tomorrow, before the sponsors' tea."

"Sounds more like a job for Mater," he said, as he sat down on the couch next to me and rang for Amaryllis. "Why don't you give her a call? I'm not at all sure you're as good as I'd like you to be about famil-ial visiting."

"Yes, of course." Oh dear, my husband's only been home a minute and I've already disappointed him. Then I remembered how formi-dable, white-haired Laetitia Zimmerman had scowled beneath her rimless spectacles at the prospect of her only son marrying an Alaska Territory girl.

"Glass of port after my bath, Amaryllis," Barnett said to the servant who appeared at the doorway.

"Yes, Mista Barnett."

"And have you ironed one of Mr. Zimmerman's dress shirts yet, Amaryllis?" I asked, avoiding her dark, aged face, covered with several even darker moles. "He'll need it for tonight. We're dining out before the mah-jongg party at the country club. Now go into my dressing room and iron it in the doorway there, so I can see you."

"I'll get right to the ironin', ma'am. And does our princess want a cuppa hot milk?" Amaryllis smiled at me as she turned her large body sideways to fit through the entry.

"When Mr. Zimmerman has his port," I answered.

Barnett patted me on the knee, then strolled across the sitting room in the direction of the bath. "Be back in a moment, kiddo," he called over his shoulder, running his fingers through his almost blue-black hair.

Well, what can I do now that I've read the afternoon paper and eaten my last petit four? I glanced at the mail, then picked up the brass telephone. "Olympic two-seven-seven, operator."

"Suzie Q, darling? It's Catherine. *Ia ustja eardha etha ostma candaloussa ewsna.*" Sue always was slow at eggy peggy, even when we were sorority sisters. "Suzie? Sorry, darling, but one has to be careful what one says around the servants. . . . The scandalous news? Well, I heard from a *very* reliable source that Mrs. Clinton James, our new Junior League transfer member from Indianapolis? Don't quote me on this, Suzie, because her husband is in Barnett's athletic club, but I heard that she actually invited a band of jazz musicians into her home for private dancing lessons. And she was even talking about it in public at the Art Museum Guild yesterday. Said they taught her something called—well, it's almost too crude to utter—the *Black Bottom.* I tell you, Suzie—

"What am I wearing to the Iota Chi sponsors' tea? Oh, I'll have to wear some boring black sack of a dress. Although, with my dark hair, Barnett says I look simply stunning in black. . . .

"Why? I'm in mourning for my poor lost baby, of course. . . . But it's really not such a bad stroke of luck. I haven't regained my shape since my miscarriage and couldn't possibly squeeze into one of those new tube-shaped day dresses.

"Oh, you have to go? The nanny's day off, is it? Well, kiss my little godson nap-time for me. I'll see you tomorrow at the sponsors' tea. *Oodga-yeba,* Suzie Q."

I put the receiver down and shut my eyes. Keeping up with society was so tedious. I began to daydream, thinking of how Barnett would look when I presented him with our first infant son. How pleased he would be with me, white teeth smiling into my face, dark pomaded hair parted at the center of his widow's peak.

When we were first introduced at a Pan Hellenic college picnic, he stood next to me, the only man well over my height. "A big woman," he'd said, "I like big women." We'd had a whirlwind wartime romance. And Barnett was ecstatic when he found out that our fathers were both in the lumber business. "Timber in the blood, that's our mutual attraction," he'd said. Barnett didn't give a wig that I was from Indian extraction—Princess Raven Feather, he always used to call me. "You'll be a society *grande dame* in no time if you marry me," he'd promised.

"I'm sure that Daddy's mills and Zimmerman Lumber would work well together," I answered coyly. I remember how he had smiled that broad mischievous grin.

"But let's not tell Mater about our little secret," he'd said. I agreed, though prejudice was hard for me to understand. Half the women in Alaska were part Indian or Eskimo; it was only when they came here to Washington State that it was held against—

What a terrible squeaking. I jerked my head toward the window and saw a nurse in a starched white frock, pushing a pram along the sidewalk edging the green lawns of Prospect Street. Nerve-jarring noise, those wheels make, simply nerve-jarring. Mrs. Clinton James's second baby in two years. The woman seems to have no control over herself. But Catherine, I told myself reproachfully, don't let envy get the best of you. Your children will come into the world soon enough.

"Be sure and use lots of starch on the bib front of that shirt, Amaryllis," I called to my housekeeper as I watched her begin her task. Then, with her as my sounding board, I began to practice my next phone conversation with Sue Querry: "My view from Prospect Street is simply divine, so why the architects put the living-room window seats facing north, I'll never understand. It's just ludicrous, and there's not a thing I can do." Like a schoolgirl, I looked up at my servant, wondering what grade she'd give me for my monologue.

"Yes Ma'am," she said, her cocoa-colored lips smiling as she tested the iron.

I didn't quite know how to talk to Amaryllis. I hadn't any experience in handling servants, but she never appeared to mind when I sounded haughty. Quite the contrary; it was as if she expected me to talk like the Queen of England.

"Then," I continued, "the gardeners planted all the wisteria in the wrong place. I know because I come from a long line of garden-club women; before Mama's illness she had a gift for growing the finest dahlia blooms and the largest cabbages in Alaska. Well, I had a terrible fight with the gardeners over the wisteria and finally had to go outside, dig it up myself, and move it to the other side of the rose garden. When Mr. Zimmerman found out, he was just furious. He doesn't want me to ruin my hands digging in the mud."

"You got lovely hands, ma'am, just like a princess should." She looked up from her iron and smiled at me approvingly, telling me that I was saying just the right thing.

"Now what about all those mirrors in the master bath? Have you cleaned them again this week, Amaryllis? I want you to take a good ammonia and water solution to all that glass and chrome."

Why had my French interior decorators insisted on an octagonal mirrored bath? I was all for culture and good taste, but it seemed that the people with the best credentials often had the most bizarre notions of beauty. I told myself that it must be because of my backwoods Alaska upbringing that my ideas sometimes clashed with the decorators'.

"Amaryllis, have you dusted up on the third floor? And don't forget the new red-lacquered Chinese screens down in the dining room; they're beginning to look dingy. I want you to see to them." I could tell by her unusually subordinate nod that I had conveyed my message with just the note of authority that her former employer, Mater Zimmerman, would have used. But then my spirits sank. Other than my husband, Amaryllis was the only person in Seattle to whom I could really talk. I was sure that Barnett was disappointed in me for not being more popular and having oodles of girl friends to chitchat with.

What's keeping Barnett? I wondered, feeling lonely. Picking up the mail, I sorted through it—haven't had a letter from Daddy in more than a month. I looked at the cover of the latest issue of *Vanity Fair*, then skimmed the table of contents of *True Confessions:* "Diary of an Unwed Mother," "A Debutante's Tragic Love Story," and "My Rendez-vous with Sin—A Nun Tells All." I sighed as my mind wandered into some mental writing of my own.

I was born in the Alaskan wilderness town of Sitka, too late for the excitement of the gold rush, too late for the romance of the Russian colonists who first claimed the northern kingdom for their Czar, building a castle and a gold-domed church. . . .

I stared out at the view of Lake Washington. The grotesque dog fetuses still bobbed up and down through the gray afternoon fog.

"Go away," I motioned to them, "go away."

Then I thought of Mama, sitting up in her room all those years, talking to people no one else could see. "Gunnar, Gunnar," she kept saying. Nana always said he was some cousin of hers who was killed in the 'oh-six Frisco earthquake. Then, of course, with Tommy always making those awful singing noises over her, who wouldn't have gone a little mad?

"My poor, poor mama!" I mumbled, remembering that day when she slipped in the muddy streets of Skagway, cracking her head. And all because I cried about Tommy eating my piece of pie. I had such a good mother. She braved those dirty streets just to get me a treat. I've never been able to forget that terrible day, even though I was only four years old. Everyone said Mama might never come to her senses, might not live through the night, because she whacked her head so hard on the sidewalk. I was terrified that she was going to die and leave me all alone in the world. That's when I made my childish bargain with God; I prayed to Him just like I saw those Russian priests pray. I told God that He could have one of my own babies when I was a mommie, if He'd just let my mama live. Of course, I'm not superstitious, like Nana, but sometimes when I think about my three miscarriages . . .

When Mama finally did die, the winter that Stig was killed in the Great War, some awful bear stole her body from the doctor's back-porch mortuary. It was lucky I was home from my first year at college and could manage the whole affair, because old Doc Spencer was terrified that Daddy'd go off the deep end if he ever found out what had happened. I put rocks in Mama's coffin, and Doc Spencer told Daddy and Nana that Mama'd died of something contagious and under no circumstances were they to open that pine box. When I think of my girlhood days, it gives me the willies sometimes. But that's all behind me now. At least I'll be able to raise my own children with all the advantages of civilized society.

Turning to *Vanity Fair*'s crossword puzzle, I began with number two down. A nine-letter noun, "the nickname of a famous flagpole sitter." I thumbed through the tiny dictionary attached to my gold chain bracelet, the one I'd won as a door prize at Bertha Landis's bridge party, but it was too small for nine-letter words.

Should I give Bertha a telephone call? Better not, I decided. I had this house to run, and Bertha would want me to chair another one of her clubwoman groups. She was always saying that I was a born leader. Let's see, number two down—"Shipwreck!" Shipwreck Kelly, the famous flagpole sitter, of course!

At bridge last week Bertha had asked me to help her edit the *Congregational Ladies' Indian Folklore Book*. I was enchanted. I could rewrite all Nana's wonderful Indian stories, the ones she learned as a girl in Russian Alaska. But even though it would have boosted my spirits, I decided to say no. With my Alaskan heritage and dark complexion I had to keep a low profile. Even though I'd married into the Zimmerman family, my place in Seattle society wasn't secure. What if word got out about my Indian heritage? What would my sorority sisters think? And Barnett's mother? Laetitia Zimmerman was such a stickler for good family breeding, she might try and have my marriage annulled, considering that there weren't any children yet. I shuddered. I really must put my mind to producing. Concentrate on having children, Catherine. Sue Querry says that they'll make life so much more joyous. Besides, as my sweet husband pointed out, it's unladylike for women to write books.

Putting down my crossword-puzzle pencil, I turned to the *Vanity Fair* fashion section. What would I look like with hennaed hair? Striking, simply striking, I wanted Barnett to say, taking notice with the same praise he'd lavished on me during our courtship days. But what could I do about wearing these new boyish-looking suits—get a chest-flattener down at Fredericks' corset salon? All those dresses were ridiculously childlike and Barnett had always fancied me as the full-figured, statuesque Edwardian type.

Out of the corner of my eye I saw the lake water splash. A gray beak-faced water baby blinked at me. "Just avoid looking at the lake, Catherine," I whispered to myself. Now what were those Tlingit words that Nana used to chant to Mama, the ones young women sang to keep from developing a shaman's magic powers? An Indian couldn't have the gift of magic if he or she wanted to marry. I really never believed in all that hocus-pocus . . . but what were the chants that Nana used to sing? "*Ay yay yaaaaah.*"

"I didn't know you were a jazz fan," said Barnett, smiling as he entered the sitting room, followed by Amaryllis carrying a tray.

My eyes met his. Like a child caught in an act of naughtiness, I felt the heat of my rapidly reddening face. But as he sat down next to me, Barnett's face remained jovial. I gave him a playful hug. Thank God my husband still had no idea I had visions.

"Our princess gotta beautiful voice, yes Ma'am," said Amaryllis as she handed Barnett a wedding crystal glass of port.

"Not a word to Mater." Barnett winked at me. "You know all her temperance-league work. She'd die of shame if she saw her son with a drink. . . . Ah," he said, unbuttoning his topcoat. "A man ought to be able to enjoy an afternoon beverage in the privacy of his own wife's sitting room. He sipped his port. "I was talking to Professor Landis today. Now there's a smart man. Got a prescription for whiskey from his family doctor. For medical purposes, of course."

I nodded. "Now, tell me all about your day."

"Well," he said, as Amaryllis put a china cup of steaming milk in front of me. "The market's up and down. Not very interesting conversation material, my dear. Quite frankly the lumber business bores the living daylights out of me. Pater was obsessed with timber. When the market was off, he didn't give a fig about Mater and me."

Barnett's lips turned down, and I noticed that he was beginning to gray around the temples. He looked so burdened. I wondered why.

"But," he continued, "I did hear from the professor that Bertha's running for city council. Wants to clean up Seattle's vice. At my Rotary luncheon today, one chap told me there's a speakeasy on every corner down in the wharf district. He heard that they'd even discovered a load of squirrel whiskey from Alaska, transported in chicken eggs, of all things. Dead giveaway, I told Bertha and Mater when I stopped in at the campaign headquarters on my way home. Hardly a chicken in Alaska, let alone an extra steamer-load of eggs to export to the Outside."

"You're a wizard at these things, Barnett," I said, thinking that he really hadn't spent much time at the lumber office today.

"Yes, the market's up and down," he said again. "Damn union people are always rumbling. You ought to get your father down here, Catherine, to go out into the bush and talk to those men."

"But . . . I'll write to him after I call Mater tomorrow," I said, sounding a bit more nervous than I'd like to. What if Daddy came here to Seattle and brought Nana? I could see the two of them sitting in my living room and talking to Barnett's mother, telling her about how we lived in a log house with a dirt floor when I was born. What if Nana started rambling about the winter of 'seventy-one, when the snowdrifts turned to ice, the food-supply cache fell over, attracting packs of hungry wolves, and she kept herself and Daddy alive by pulling the hair out of her head and weaving it into rabbit snares? Mater'd faint dead away.

"You know, Catherine," said Barnett, sipping his port, "your father has a way with his workers. He's a man of the land. We Zimmermans just don't have the touch with labor that he has. I want you to try and get him down here to talk to the men out at the Snohomish planing and pulp mill."

"Good idea," I replied, trying to be a supportive wife. Yes, Daddy did have a way with labor, and he'd always been able to help Barnett out when the market went into a slide. But, I assured myself, Nana'd never come to Seattle. She was convinced that they still burned and drowned Indians here. No, she'd never . . . An ache shot through my right temple. I always felt so guilty about not wanting my family to visit me. Then I contemplated the prospect of Nana and Daddy in their best catalog-ordered clothes, sitting in my living room, reminiscing about Mama back when she was a fishwife with baby Stig and me asleep in a basket on her back. Daddy would start moaning about Stig getting killed in the war, and how my sweet little brother Carl was just never going to be the fisherman that Stig had been, or raving about pirates robbing the cannery's fish traps. Nana would bring out one of those old letters that Mama wrote to her girl friends after they'd been killed in the earthquake and no one had had the heart to tell her they'd died. Why, when I think of how I would have ended up if I hadn't gone to college and married Barnett. . . . Silently I composed another story for *True Confessions*:

A TALE OF PRIMITIVE PASSION FROM THE FROZEN NORTH
If She Could Have Willed It,
Her Heart Would Have Turned to Stone.

I was wealthy and beautiful, but my dark loveliness was my curse. I was part Indian, a woman of color.

In my Alaska frontier home of Sitka no one cared about my heritage, but I longed for a life of refinement in a far-off cosmopolitan city. I longed, too, for the companionship of cultured young men, but I knew that my heritage might prevent me from marrying well. So might my family. My grandmother was an Indian who'd never converted to the Christian faith, and my mother had suffered strange undiagnosed hallucinations since my early childhood. I knew that if my background were found out in the circles of polite society, I'd be considered unmarriageable.

Then one Alaska June eve, while I was walking home from picking huckleberries, accompanied by my grandmother's adopted Eskimo, a strange broad-shouldered blond man crossed the trail in front of me. From his manner I judged that he was a man of Alaska as well as a man of the world. Although he was old enough to be my father, he was still handsome and spoke a few words of greeting to me with a nordic accent, the same accent my dear sick mother spoke with. Instantly I was infatuated. Sensing my emotions, the blond man's eyes looked at me caressingly. As we stared at each other, not speaking, I felt a new and primitive passion run through my veins. The gold and red rays of Alaska's late-night sun glowed on his light hair and beard. I knew that this man would never hold my heritage against me. His lips turned up in a smile and I suddenly felt radiant. I breathed the fragrance of summer honeysuckle, and my heart raged with a passion that I'd never known before. He reached out to touch my chin, and that was when I saw the wedding ring on his finger. If I could have willed it, my heart would have turned to stone. But . . . I could not.

"Yes, Catherine," said my husband, putting his arm around my shoulder and jolting me from my thoughts, "a man like your father carries a lot of clout with the working man. He knows their ways, speaks their language. Just yesterday one of my foremen said he found a still out back of my Snohomish logging camp. Of course I had them dispose of it before Mater or Bertha Landis's campaigners got wind of it, but the way the foreman described it—kerosene cans and copper tubing—it sounded just like your father and Carl's private still up in Sitka. Yo York's got common ground with the working man, dear. Business has been pretty slow this year, what with labor screaming strike and wage hike. I think your father's just the man who could talk them out of it."

"I'll do my best," I said as I wound the Victrola and put on a Harlem Cotton Club jazz record, hoping to change the course of the conversation. I didn't really want to know how badly Barnett was faring in the lumber business.

"Yes, much better if you made the arrangements with the old man, dear. I think he's still a bit miffed over that last load of Sitka-spruce logs. But, damn it, Catherine, there wasn't a one of them that I could have given him more than a few cents a board foot for. Rankest lumber I ever saw. I'm sure the man thinks I cheated him out of the money he lent me to buy that new mill machinery. But business is business, and he should have gotten it in writing that I was bound and tied to pay him a good price for those logs. Oh, well, my dear, your father'll learn the ways of big city commerce eventually; don't you worry, I'll see to it." He gazed at me with his large watery brown eyes, then sighed and rang for Amaryllis to take the tray. "Poor bastard cut all those trees and then the market took a dive, what with all these railroad land sales and new lumbermen migrating in from the Midwest."

"But, Barnett," I reminded him, "we always have Pater's inheritance money invested in those Baker electric cars and Kelvinator generators. You have a gift for commerce, I know you do. Don't worry about Daddy and the lumber market."

Barnett took a deep breath and looked out at the view of Mount Rainier. "Timber," he said with disgust. "Sometimes, princess, I wish I'd given it up instead of the concert piano." He began to move his fingers across an imaginary keyboard to the rhythm of the jazz record, and I couldn't help but notice how young he suddenly looked.

"Now, we mustn't be late at the club. Mah-jongg's just the thing to revive you after a busy business day."

"Ah, a relaxing evening at Waverly," he said, glancing at his gold Elgin vest watch and then offering me his arm. "Had my life-insurance checkup today," he added.

I felt my face tighten. No wonder the market's down. Barnett hadn't even spent half the day at the lumber office.

My husband guided me through the sitting-room doorway and out onto the stairwell balcony. "Dr. Mott said I was healthy as an ox. Took off my shirt and found some cysts on my back, though. Strangest thing, the man went wild over them. Took a needle and extracted them on the spot. Seems he has a fetish for watching the little white 'worm' pop out. Pleasant enough chap, nonetheless. Reminded me of Carl."

"My baby brother?" I asked, remembering him fondly.

"Yes, Carl," said Barnett. "I want you to invite him down here for a visit along with your father. Maybe he could combine fishing business with pleasure. Yes, that's how we could put it to him. I've got some jolly good plans for Alaska Fish Company and your brother's boats. Some of the boys down at the Athletic Club think it'd be the bee's knees to take a fishing holiday to Ketchikan. Your brother once told me there were more stills than houses there. Might be some big money in it for Carl if he's game."

"Barnett!" I said, keeping my back to the lake and trying not to sound distraught. "Why," I joked, "if I didn't know you better, I'd think you were talking about bootlegging."

There was a distressed look in his brown eyes. "Well, dear," he said slowly, "I'm in a bit of a bind for cash. I invested all of Mater's money as well in those electric Bakers. Now, even a fool can see that the electric is the car of the future, and of course a Kelvinator generator is a must, but the market hasn't been so good lately, what with new gasoline cars having electric starters instead of cranks, and . . . as I said, I'm in a bit of a bind." He put his face in his hands, his shoulders hunched.

Barnett, my strong husband, was he really on the verge of tears? "Darling," I said, trying to control the fear in my voice, "what's this all about?" Was he trying to tell me that we were temporarily out of funds?

What about all the money we'd borrowed from Daddy's war contract profits, the money to build this house? Memories of my childhood among panned-out gold-mining towns and broken old sourdoughs came down on my head like an auctioneer's gavel. What if we couldn't pay our mortgage? I remembered how hard Daddy and Nana worked to keep their businesses together after the stampeders left, causing Alaska's economy to go to ruin. When Daddy took my brothers and me on the fishing boats to the cannery in Ketchikan, I lay under the wool blanket, holding little Carl as we slept in a single berth, and gently explained to him why children couldn't run in the streets of Ketchikan at night, burrowing my hands into his warm stomach and watching the red lights of the wharf buildings dance in the water beneath my porthole.

"I'm sure to recapture Mater's funds and Pater's inheritance in the long run," said Barnett, trying to compose himself. "Electric cars are a sound investment. It's just that—well, to bankrupt one's own mother is almost worse than treason. And I thought that—ah, in order to get a little quick capital . . . and your brother said he's willing."

The back of my neck went cold.

"It would be very low-profile, dear," Barnett whispered. "Just for a year, until I recapture poor Mater's funds. Then it'd be the straight and narrow all the way, you can count on me for that. Just a little funding to make some sound investments on the market and keep the mills going through all these labor disputes."

Amaryllis was moving slowly up the stairs, carrying my black Hudson seal coatee.

"But what if you're caught—" The word stuck in my throat. "Sent to jail? What would happen to me?"

"Think of Mater," he retorted. "It might kill her to find herself without funds. She's so sensitive. Women get to a certain age and—well, they're more fragile than one might imagine."

Frantically I tried to think of something soothing to say to my husband, but I just couldn't find the words.

"Catherine," he said, narrowing his eyes and raising his voice so that it was almost loud enough for Amaryllis to hear, "I thought I could count on you to be more understanding. When are you going to stop being so childish and think about the people who depend on you?"

"But," I protested weakly, "Mater's helping Bertha Landis campaign for city council on a vice clean-up platform. What if—"

"Oh, good Christ," Barnett's face began to redden, "the woman hasn't got a ghost of a chance." He cleared his throat. "But I think it'd be a capital idea, old girl, if you went and campaigned for Bertha right alongside Mater."

"What?" I stammered.

"Campaigning for Bertha'd be a marvelous decoy." He raised one eyebrow and cocked his head at me as if he were joking with one of his fraternity brothers. "Who'd ever suspect a highbrow family like the Zimmermans of bootlegging, eh, kiddo? Besides," he said, caressing my shoulder, "it's no more than a schoolboy lark. Just a little camaraderie with your brother Carl."

"But what if you're caught?" I asked again, my voice turning into a whine. "What'll become of me?"

"What'll happen to you if we're broke? Look," he said firmly, "the only way anyone of Indian origin can hope to gain respectability is to be wealthier than anyone else."

There was a long silence as Barnett's stern eyes looked into mine, just as if he were one of my college professors who was about to say, Miss York, you could do so much better in your studies if you'd only apply yourself.

"All right," I whispered. I gripped the oak banister and began to feel faint.

"That's the old Zimmerman spirit, dear," he said, his straight white teeth shining in a wide grin as he nodded at me in approval. "Quite frankly, the whole business gives me the heebie-jeebies, but we'll give it the old college try for a year, eh, what, Princess Raven Feather?" My husband hadn't called me by my pet name in ages.

Amaryllis handed me my wrap and then turned slowly back to her sweeping. Barnett began moving his feet to the steps of the fast fox-trot, grabbing Amaryllis's thigh in his playful fashion.

"Ah, adventure and big women," he said, putting his arm around my waist and kissing me on the neck. "Nothing like the thrill of a young man about to embark on a new business."

He spanked my thighs to the beat of the record which was playing on the sitting-room Victrola, "I Wish I Could Shimmy Like My Sister Kate," and began singing its words as he guided me in the steps of one of the new dances. His eyes gleamed. I couldn't remember him being more tender or attentive in years.

"Yes," I said, suddenly feeling light-headed, "some excitement." I kicked my heels up and moved my hips almost as shamelessly as a speakeasy flapper might do. I hadn't felt such a thrill since I dated Barnett during my happy sorority days.

"Let's do the Black Bottom," said Barnett.

"Darling! I'm shocked. Where on earth did you learn it?" I giggled as I slid across the balcony floor toward the stairway.

"Oh, it's all over town." He grinned. "Hmm." He raised one eyebrow. "It's a good thing Mater isn't here. She abhors modern music."

With all this gaiety, I'd almost forgotten about Laetitia Zimmerman. Then Barnett grabbed me tenderly around the waist and began a verse of our courtship song, "For Me and My Gal."

Bootlegging, I thought. Hadn't Nana once told me that she'd had to sell contraband hooch to the American fur farmers one winter to keep herself and Daddy alive when her salmon catch had been eaten by raccoons? Barnett jarred me from my thoughts by spinning me across the floor. I couldn't remember my limbs feeling so limber since I was a child dancing to the bells of the Church of Saint Michael, pretending to be Princess Maksoutov at a royal ball. Yes, it was almost as if I could taste the thrill of destiny in the air as Barnett smiled, his eyes shining like the water of Puget Sound in the setting sun.

"I've always hated the timber business," he confessed. "It's been like a damned ball and chain around my leg. But now . . ." He kissed me. "New business, new man."

19. SEATTLE
Autumn 1923

"Well, sister," said my dark-eyed brother, Carl, "Nana always said that it weren't just fate you was born the day that old Russian castle in Sitka burned down, no sir. Just look at this palace you and Barnett got for yourselves. Almost as much red and gold finery as the Church of Saint Michael back home."

It was such a joy to hear Carl's high-pitched voice ring through the walls of my home. His English wasn't quite up to snuff, but I was sure that with our good influences, Barnett and I could have him mixing with the best elements of Seattle society in no time.

"Why, thank you, Carl," I said, sighing with maternal pride. Barnett and my thin-boned younger brother sat in front of our living-room fireplace, sipping an after-dinner *apéritif* and discussing "business." Above the intimate family gathering, Mater's white hair and heavy jowls loomed down from her gold-framed portrait above the mantelpiece. Oh, my, I thought with a twinge of schoolgirl naughtiness, the old walrus would perish if she knew about our "product."

Carl brushed his straight black-red hair from his face and smiled, staring at my protruding stomach.

"Yes," I said, "just a few more months, Dr. Mott tells me, and we'll have a little Barnett Junior to fill our halls with cheerful noise."

Carl reached over and kissed me solicitously on the side of the cheek. "Yeah, sister, ya always told me ya was gonna grow up and live in a house like the Castle," he said, thoughtfully scratching his wind-burned chin.

I blushed, recalling that indeed I had kept some of Nana's Russian royalty stories in mind when I'd called in the decorators. The red-flocked *fleur-de-lis* wallpaper in the marble-floored entry hall and, of course, the crystal chandelier above us in the living room were each inspired by Nana's Russian heritage.

"Yes," said Barnett, pulling at his waxed mustache, "we'll get the cash flow up to peak production beginning in May and run it all the way into the fall, along with the other maritime traffic to and from Alaska." As he crossed his legs in a regal fashion, the high polish on his black patent leather slippers shone in the glow of the fire. Oh, dear, I sighed, looking at Carl's wrinkled suit and four-o'clock shadow. Perhaps after another week of my husband's example, Carl would start imitating Barnett's dressing habits and posture. Why, my baby brother looked just like an old fisherman when he sat all slumped over like that.

"Well," said Carl, "to be quite honest, I got some stills goin' in back of the Ketchikan cannery that Pa don't even know about. Ol' war buddy of mine sent me the copper tubin'. Hell, it could produce fifty barrels of squirrel whiskey a day. Too much for Alaska consumption, 'cept when them big-game hunters come up from the Lower Forty-eight on huntin' tours in the fall."

Barnett raised his left eyebrow and smiled.

"Why, that sounds just like Sue Querry's father," I said, trying to put my two cents' worth into the men's conversation. "He's always talking about barrels a day. Oil, I think it is. You know, Carl"—I smiled maternally at my brother's narrow face—"Sue's father actually has some oil leases in Alaska. Yes, way up past Yakutat Bay near Ketalla, I think he said. Sue told me that they pump it out of the ground as easy as pie, then ship it by railroad to Fairbanks. If you wanted to look into oil leases, I could arrange for you to meet Sue's father. He's never been to Alaska, and—well, it would be just wonderful if you could show him the thrill of big-game hunting. Sue told me that he has everything but a polar bear and a wolverine on his—"

"Catherine," said Barnett, lighting up a cigar, "you must have enough on your mind, what with the nursery to decorate. Why don't you let Carl and me handle the business? Of course, I'm always delighted to have your views, but your brother and I have some important decisions to make tonight. Now," he said, turning toward Carl, "oil in Alaska is simply out of the question; it freezes tighter than a drum that far up north. Besides, I'm sure Sue Querry's father just uses it as a personal income-tax write-off. Ah, the sixteenth amendment, Carl; it's going to be the death of us all, don't you agree? But that's part of the beauty of—"

"Bootleggin'," said Carl, almost too loudly. Barnett cringed for a moment, then regained his composure. "But, ya know, sister has a point." Carl had always come to my defense when I was a young girl in a fishing town full of rough men. "Hell, it's true the oil up there's nearly worthless, but after the war, the government con-verted all its coal-powered steamships to diesel, and Jesus H. Christ if they didn't set aside most of Arctic Alaska for a pet-roleum reserve. 'Course, if it's the same gunk that them Injuns been paintin' on their faces and their totem poles, it ain't worth a plug nickel. Stuff won't even burn, there's so many impurities in it."

"Oh, Carl," I said, suddenly overcome with the remembrance of our Sitka childhood, "do you remember how we used to play hide-and-seek up in Lovers' Lane behind those old totem poles? Remember how we used to count red hummingbirds?"

"Sure do," said Carl, smiling that implike smile of his. "Remember the day the Sitka shopkeepers moved all them totems outa the Injun village so the big-game-huntin' tour people wouldn't have to be bothered by beggar Tlingits when they wanted to see the poles? Put 'em all along Lovers' Lane. 'Course, there'd always been a coupla totems in that there park, but after them shopkeepers got through, the trail gardens was just crowded with wooden spooks."

"Lovers' Lane, dear, that's where the Russian princess used to have tea in the afternoon," I told Barnett.

"And Nana found out her favorite pole was missin'," continued Carl. "God, she was madder than a *hootz* in matin' season when she found out that some minister had the witch-doctor-woman pole sent to a hotsy-totsy university museum back east."

"Carl," I said, seeing Barnett's lips turn down and knowing I needed to involve my husband in the conversation. I was so accustomed to our family give-and-take, I sometimes forgot that Barnett had never had any brothers or sisters and might feel the need for extra attention. "Barnett and I have done something wonderful for Seattle. I hope you won't think I'm, bragging if I tell you so. You know how I miss Lovers' Lane and the old Tlingit totem poles. Well, Barnett and I helped with a similar project here, isn't that so, Barnett?" I asked, trying to shake the faraway look in my husband's eye. "I chaired a series of fund-raising teas and raised enough pledge money to have seven Tlingit totem poles imported from southeast Alaska to Seattle. And we had the opening of Pioneer Square just last month. Oh, Carl, it's a charming little place, right down in the middle of the financial district near the wharf and Alaskan Way. A real tribute to all the wonderful things that Alaska has given us citizens of Seattle."

"Of course, darling," my husband said, absentmindedly gazing into the fire. "Of course."

Now what could Barnett be distraught over, I wondered? It felt as if he and I were fighting over Carl. Hoping that tensions would ease, I said nothing and gazed around the living room, my eyes resting on the far wall where I'd discreetly hung a Tlingit raven mask used at Indian potlatch dances. "Aboriginal sculpture was highly evolved," I told all my dinner guests. I wasn't sure that they took my lecturing seriously, but after I'd sent my Indian drums and Chilkat blankets to the university's Catherine Zimmerman Collection, my raven mask had taken on a definite air of credibility.

"Hell," said Carl, "didja know the government's thinkin' of grantin' them Injun totem worshipers their citizenship? Most of 'em can't even read or write. Got Reverend Hitch's Sheldon Jackson Injun Trainin' School out by Castle Rock, but them Tlingits is real slow learners. If the government goes and gives 'em their citizenship, then they're gonna want legal title to their land, sure as shootin'. Hell, Pa even had to get timber rights to that forest near Sitka a few years back before the government would let him get close to it with a saw. I tell ya, Barnett," he said, in such a familiar voice that it sounded as if the two men might become fast friends, just as I'd hoped, "Washington D.C.'s up there dickerin' with us again. Seems like Alaska's public property. They got federal forests and federal petroleum reserves, and now them Injuns wants the same. Hell, there ain't gonna be nothin' left for a decent person to build a huntin' lodge on, no sir. Lucky I got me a cabin on one of them Sitka islands before the government goes and takes them away too."

"Hmm." Barnett's face was serious. "As millowners, you and your father should pay attention to the legalities of the situation. As you know, Carl, if the government labels a land parcel a National Forest, it's permissible to log it, clear-cut it down the nub. But if they label it a National Park, you can't touch a tree."

"But it's against Daddy's principles to clear-cut a forest," I said. "It causes terrible mud slides."

"Of course, dear." Barnett narrowed his eyes. "But we'd better get back to the subject at hand. As I see it," he said, blowing a stream of cigar smoke and looking straight at Carl, "put all those stills up in Sitka and Ketchikan where no FBI men are going to look for them, and we've got half the old school team almost to the ten-yard line. The problem," said Barnett in the low, controlled voice of a man with years of experience in commerce, "the problem is transportation."

"I got a fleet of boats," said Carl, grinning perhaps a little too widely. The space where he had lost those teeth in the Allied Galipoli campaign made him look almost like a ruffian. Oh, I did want to get him a little more refined before Barnett's mother returned from her South African steamer cruise next month. I wanted so much for her to approve of Carl. After all, Laetitia Zimmerman was the key to a proper social introduction here in Seattle. My, I sighed as my back began to ache and I propped my swollen feet up on Barnett's ottoman. Sometimes I felt that with Daddy and Nana always trying to keep their business above water since those war timber and fish contracts ended, Carl's personal social future was up to me to worry about.

"Wonderful," said Barnett. "Fishing boats, just the thing. But I'm a little hesitant about your father. I'm not at all sure that he'd approve."

"What he don't know won't hurt him," said Carl, sounding almost too eager. "I've already talked with my two buddies down in Ketchikan, Halibut Pete and Paddy the Pig. Boatbuilders, both of 'em, and they're right there ready if any storm should disable one of our craft at the south end of the Narrows. If a boat breaks down, it can pull into Paddy's Ketchikan dock easy as you please. Paddy or ol' Halibut'll have it shipshape in no time—right back out on the tide bound for Seeattle, with no one the wiser."

"Ah," said Barnett, the shine returning to his seductive Rudolph Valentino eyes. "Then the problem is, what are we going to transport our 'product' in? Not old kerosene cans or eggshells, that's been tried and failed. No, it'll have to be something a little more novel, and darn clever. Already have my wife and mother working for the anti-vice woman candidate for city council. We Zimmermans are a respected family. Best decoy possible, don't you think, Carl?" A cat grin was on his face. "We just can't be too careful. Those FBI men don't care who you are . . . of course, I have heard that they accept—ah, gifts."

"Ya don't say." My brother seemed enthralled by Barnett's suave personality. It was wonderful to have a surrogate big brother for Carl, someone to set a sophisticated example. All the pieces of my life were about to fit into place: I was going to give birth in two months, Barnett and I were recapturing Mater's funds and Pater's inheritance, and with Carl and Barnett together it would be a family business just like old times. I thought of Nana and how she had pioneered the lumber and fishing businesses in Alaska. It was wonderful to think that I, Catherine York Zimmerman, might also have a hand in family history.

The baby kicked and I propped my back up with another couch cushion, keeping my line of vision away from the lake. I hadn't seen those little water beasties since my fifth month, but there was no sense taking a risk. Barnett had even caught me chanting at them one morning, just like I remembered Nana chanting at Mama to make her insanity go away. Barnett thought I'd taken leave of my senses, but I quickly passed it off as a symptom of pregnancy.

"Carl," said Barnett, as Amaryllis brought in the after-dinner coffee tray and laid it on the mahogany sideboard at my elbow, "we're going to get ourselves a little capital to invest on the market. I'd be glad to give you some excellent tips, anytime at all."

I poured each of my men a Dresden china cup of Maxwell House coffee, adding three lumps of sugar on Barnett's saucer.

"Good to the last drop, as Teddy Roosevelt says," chimed Barnett. Carl's face clouded. Oh dear, I guess my baby brother had been in the backwoods too long; he didn't know that our former President once wrote jingles.

"Containers," said Barnett again as Carl slurped his coffee. "What sort of containers are we going to ship our 'product' in?"

Carl rolled his eyes and looked thoughtful. "Paddy the Pig told me that he once helped out a Russian whaler who run aground in a storm. He couldn't understand how the clipper drifted as far south as Ketchikan, 'cause there sure ain't no whaling stations in Southeast. Ol' bow-legged Paddy was patchin' the hull and saw that sure enough the captain had a whale in tow, but the critter looked like it'd been dead for a month, half eaten by scavenger fish 'n damaged by rocks. Paddy got his suspicions up and come to find out that the Moby Dick was pickled with vodka. The captain knew a little English and Paddy guessed the rest: The crew traded their potato whiskey for gold bricks somewhere off the coast in international waters." Carl cleared his throat and lowered his voice to a whisper. "Ol' Paddy says the sailors keep the bricks hidden in the ceilin' of the cooks' cabin."

Barnett raised one eyebrow and nodded his head.

I hadn't felt melancholy about Alaska in a long time, but as I listened to Carl I was suddenly overcome by a wave of nostalgia for Daddy's stories of fish pirates and fish wars. For a moment I missed Sitka so much that I could almost smell the damp sea air and see the wooded mountains jut out of the sea.

"The night after Paddy got the clipper seaworthy again," my brother continued, "a big gale come up. The whale broke loose and was beached on some rocks south of Paddy's cabin—it ain't really a cabin, just an abandoned fox farm coop, think that's how Paddy the Pig got his name. Well, I never heard tell of Paddy workin' so hard before. With the help of an Injun canoe, he unloaded that critter before daybreak, and hid them barrels in the tree trunks near his house. Keep shotgun watch over 'em day and night. Now, Paddy's payin' his bills to the Ketchikan shopkeepers with the best imported Russian vodka you'd ever want to taste."

I gasped. The baby had kicked violently at my side, causing me to spill my coffee all over my maternity smock. How embarrassing these natural processes can be sometimes. I dabbed at the stain with my Irish linen napkin. Oh, well, Catherine, it'll all be over within three months. However did Mama manage, carrying twins?

"Got me three trophy moose just last week with my old army rifle," said Carl. "How 'bout that? Sixty Krauts, twenty Turks, and three moose." Somehow the conversation had drifted to big-game hunting in Alaska.

"And one big blond Scandia," I said, recalling a girlhood joke.

"Hell, yes," said Carl, "and one big blond Scandia. That was back durin' the summer of Sitka's biggest scandal," he said, smiling happily at me but directing his story to Barnett. "Some members of the Benevolent Order of Elks came up on a tour steamer and discovered that them Injun women who sell their baskets an' jewelry wares on the parade-ground lawn in fronta the dock there had been sellin' BOE members moose teeth insteada elk teeth. God, what a ruckus; there ain't been another Elks member come to Sitka for big-game huntin' since. Anyway, that night the Elks tourist group had a terrible row with the Injuns and the Sitka shopkeepers. Tried to burn the little Injun village down, one Elks member did, as I recall. I got up real early the next mornin' to fish with Stig. Went down to the dock with my gun—we always takes our guns in case of fish-trap pirates, and with all them immigrant Japanese fishermen that's come to Alaska, ya can't be too careful. Well, there on the dock was this Scandia layin' face down, shot clear through, stomach to back, and dead as a doornail. When the town marshal saw me with my gun, I almost got arrested on the spot. Seems some prankster had told the marshal that the Scandia'd been up at our house the night before, arguin' with my grandmother. 'Course the lawman let me go, but with all them BOE members after them Injun women for sellin' 'em moose teeth insteada elk teeth, they never did find out who killed that Scandia, no sir."

"We could ship the 'product' down here in tin-lined fish boxes," said Barnett, steering the conversation back to its original subject. Those stories about my Alaska youth must bore him horribly, poor man, but I hadn't seen my brother in more than a year, and I just couldn't help recalling old times with him, even if some of my fond memories turned sour on me, as the recollection of the blond Scandia just had. I recalled another *True Confessions* story I'd once composed in my head:

PRIMITIVE PASSION FROM THE FROZEN NORTH
PART II
She Planned to Flee from Her Backwoods Town Forever
in a Mad Elopement, but . . .

I knew I was playing with fire, but I continued to wait on the dark wharf for my mysterious blond suitor whose name I did not even know. When we'd first met on the wooded trail near my family's Alaska home I'd seen the wedding ring on his finger, but when he visited my father's house the following day, he'd not worn his wedding band. I'd watched the episode from behind the kitchen door. My mother, stricken by a mad delirium, raved from her upstairs bedroom as my Indian grandmother demanded that the handsome blond stranger leave the premises and never return. Had he come to ask for my hand in what would have been a polygamous marriage?

Tonight I would meet him on the wharf in hopes that he would proclaim his love for me. And if he did so, I secretly planned to elope with him. With a palpitating heart I recalled his strong arms, wise blue eyes, benevolent smile, and nordic accent. Married or not, he was the man of my dreams. What chance did I have with polite society? I was a girl of color, a girl with a history of insanity in the family. I knew that it would be the handsome blond stranger or no man at all. For hours I waited on the dark wharf, but providence was with me. The stranger never appeared. Next morning I learned the awful truth: He'd been murdered. But by whom? Who was it who knew of my secret plan?

"Won't work, tin-lined fish boxes for carryin' liquor." Carl's voice jarred me back into the present. "Them fish boxes gotta have ice comin' outa them, else they don't look real."

"Hmm," said Barnett with just the slightest note of defeat in his voice. His face clouded, and he looked almost middle-aged.

"Fish tins." I almost yelled it because the baby jumped and kicked my side again. Carl and Barnett both jerked their heads in my direction. "Salmon tins," I said, "forty-two-ounce tins. We could say they were being shipped here to Seattle for labels . . . yes, that's it. Labels made at Barnett's paper pulp mill out in Snohomish. Fish tins full of our 'product' instead of salmon," I said, remembering to use my husband's terminology.

Barnett frowned and sat back in his overstuffed red velvet chair. Why wasn't he excited at my idea? It sounded foolproof to me.

"Well," he said slowly, "it's worth a try—until something better pops into my head. . . ." He stared at the ceiling.

"Oh, Carl," I said, overcome with the excitement of having a share in the family business, "isn't this wonderful?" My brother grinned and reached over to nuzzle his long nose into my cheek, just like he did when we were children. "Of course Barnett and I've agreed that we'll only boot—ah, be in the salmon-labeling business for a year. Then it's back to the straight and narrow with some sound stock-market invest-ments for our new funds. Isn't that right, Barnett?"

My husband slumped down into his chair. "Labeling salmon tins," he muttered. "Hmm. It just might be silly enough to get by the FBI and the revenue men." He extended his china coffee cup in a toast, and so did Carl. "Catherine's idea is harebrained enough to outwit the law." And then, much to my surprise, my husband smashed his coffee cup into the stone fireplace. "Isn't that what the Russians used to do when they made a pact, break their glasses?" He grinned, but his smile looked cold, as if I'd done something terribly wrong.

"If ya say so," said Carl, amiably smashing my Dresden heirloom wedding china onto the hearth. Both men turned and looked at me, still holding my cup.

"Well, how 'bout it, sister," said Carl, waving his narrow wrist in the direction of the fireplace, "gonna bust it?"

Looking up at Mater's portrait above the mantel, I thought of how horribly she would scold when she found out that her heirloom wed-ding gift to Barnett and me had been broken.

"Can't seal this pact without ya," said Carl.

Reluctantly I tossed my empty cup at the stone fireplace but missed, and only the tiny handle broke off as it hit the oak parquet floor.

"Just like a woman." Barnett laughed as he slapped Carl's thigh. "Couldn't hit the broad side of a barn."

20. SEATTLE
November 1926

"Mater, you really must listen to Charles. Your grandson has been practicing the Rudy Vallee Fleishmann's Yeast jingle just for you." The family had gathered in the fernery for after-dinner tea, but Mater immediately began pontificating about politics and child-rearing in front of poor, tired Barnett.

"Catherine," she said reproachfully, her large body sprawled over the new white art deco couch and her bosom protruding like a veranda from her low-waisted black evening frock, "don't you know that radio rots the mind? A good mother should instinctively know these things. Now, where's his nanny? I want to make sure she's taping his mouth shut at night. No mouth breathing for my grandchildren. It ruins their teeth, overdevelops the adenoids."

Mater's guttural voice always filled my house with gloom. And it's only because she needs a new fall fur and a new La Salle that Barnett's decided to delve into another dangerous year of our "fish-labeling business," I thought angrily.

"Of course I'll see to the mouth taping, Mater," I said, trying to quell the sarcasm in my voice. I held Charles's tiny pink hand. My firstborn, the spitting image of his handsome father and so adorable in his little navy blue sailor suit.

He approached Mater cautiously on his chubby legs, singing:

"Oh, you skinny!
reach for a Lucky
instead of a sweet."

"So verbal for an almost three-year-old," I said to Barnett, hoping for some words of praise for my child-rearing efforts. Charles repeated his song. Even his young eyes could see that Mrs. Z had the profile of a walrus.

"Where's my baby girl?" Barnett called to the new French nanny as she passed the doorway going to the kitchen for a bottle.

"Bring Debra Sue in to see her family, Patrice," I said, as the red-haired woman brought my last born into the fernery all wrapped in the pink crocheted receiving blanket that Bertha Landis had given me.

Barnett narrowed his eyes at Patrice. It seemed that he didn't approve of my choice in servants, but now that I had the lives of two children to supervise, I didn't have time to interview new help.

"Here, Patrice, give her to Mummy," I said, reaching out for my blond, blue-eyed, six-month-old daughter. She reminded me of old daguerreotypes I'd seen of Mama as a baby.

"You're the talk of all the bridge clubs in town, Catherine," said Mater, smiling over at Debra's little peach of a face. "Everyone is marveling at how you two brunets produced such a fair-haired child."

"She takes after my mother," I said coolly, then pinched the baby's cheeks to make them pink. "Mama's relatives were cousins of Sweden's Queen Christina, you know." Laetitia Zimmerman smiled a denture-perfect smile. My fib about Queen Christina should put an end to Mater's perpetual doubts about me. I was sure she suspected me of social climbing, marrying her son for a good family name.

Barnett, looking like a sheik in his silk smoking jacket, gave his daughter a doting smile. I waited to see if he'd look up at me or at his mother.

But, I thought, what if Debra has inherited Mama's mental weaknesses along with her features? At least she hadn't taken after Nana's Indian mother, Woman-Always-Wondering. Yes, thank heavens neither of my children was born tomahawk in hand, betraying my family secret.

"She looks just like Mama," I said, "yes, she does." Barnett smiled at me with approval.

"That's what I say to everybody," said Mrs. Z, the edges of her thin lips turning down. "Anybody who's rude enough to ask, that is. Mostly those parvenus over here on Capitol Hill. Them and their Alaska gold. Trouble is they're totally uneducated, most of them, and think that women of Swedish extraction all look like Greta Garbo. I tell you, the movie palaces and radio soap operas have warped everyone's sense of morality. But I'm counting on Bertha. She's going to rid this town of the undesirables and their vices."

I glanced nervously at Barnett, then felt my cheeks flush with anger. Mater was taunting me about my background again.

"She's doing a fine job on the city council, if I do say so," Barnett said casually, lighting a Havana cigar. "Women could do so many things if they'd only put their minds to it, just like Negroes and Indians."

I cringed, putting my finger to my lips, signaling my husband to shush. He gave me a puzzled look, then smiled knowingly.

"It's the immigrant problem again," said Mater. Charles danced in front of her, imitating the banjo-playing Clicquot Eskimos, singing their ginger-ale jingle, but she took little notice of her long-awaited grandson. "Those European countries are ridding themselves of their paupers, throwing open the floodgates of their sewers and shipping us thousands of their lowest elements. Everyone complains about the Chinese. Now, I never did like Chinamen—personally I prefer the emancipated Africans as house servants—but the Chinese are far better than those Irish Catholics, always wrecking railroads, stopping the U.S. mail, or butchering defenseless women in the name of some general strike. Worse than Bolsheviks, those Irish Catholics."

"You're such a little charmer," I said, reassuring Charles of his importance when he finished his banjo-playing improvisation and bowed in front of his grandmother, who waved him away with her lace handkerchief. She certainly didn't take the interest I'd expected her to in the grandchildren. On my first visit home to Alaska with Charles, my family was enchanted with him. I'd even had to nurse him an extra month in order to keep Nana from taking him down to the cannery in a back basket, just as she'd done with Stig and me when we were babies. I didn't want my baby exposed to the tubercular Indians down at the fish cannery.

"Clap for him, Barnett," I said. "It's never too soon for Charles to get a feeling for public address." Charles began another verse of the ginger-ale jingle.

"Bravo, bravo," said Barnett, giving Mater a smile.

Patrice entered from the foyer. Her doe eyes avoided my glance as she took the baby for her evening bottle. "You let me know right away, Patrice, if she starts with any bad habits," I said, worrying about Mama's going into a trance and taking to her bed for years, just from a bump on the head. "Can't be too careful with a future debutante," I added to Mrs. Z. I imagined Debra's coming-out party: She would glide down our circular stairway under the stained-glass dome with Barnett on one arm and a bouquet of white roses on the other to be received by a summer gathering of just the right people. Everyone would gaze approvingly at Debra, then whisper, "Catherine's done a marvelous job, hasn't she?"

Amaryllis knocked at the door and entered, dragging her swollen feet across the new oriental carpet. "A telephone call for Mista Zimmerman."

"*Très gauche*," said Mater, looking despondent. "What kind of people would call during the dinner hour?"

"Yes, yes," said Barnett, trying to humor his mother. "Amaryllis, I do hate to be interrupted in the middle of a familial chat." He walked gallantly from the room but came dashing back a moment later. "It's about Bertha," he said. "Seems she's been appointed acting mayor while Doc Brown's away at the Democratic convention. She's just fired the police chief!" His face was drained of its color.

"That's my girl," said Mater, pointing a decisive finger upward.

"There's rioting down on Seneca Street," Barnett said nervously. "Bertha's got her men trying to stop a truck of beer headed for a speakeasy. I've got to dash." He anxiously pulled his arm through his coat.

I sat motionless on the couch, not daring to think what would happen next.

"The rumor is that there's about to be a police strike," he continued. "The old girl's going to need every able-bodied man she can get to quell this disturbance. Don't worry now, we'll keep everything down to a dull roar."

"Of course you will, dear." I tried to put a note of calm into the situation, but I knew my voice sounded unsteady.

"A strike!" shrieked Mater. "Take care now, Barney. You stay away from those drunken anarchist immigrants."

As Barnett ran from the room, Charles went over to his father's chair and pulled himself up in it, taking his place among us ladies.

"That Bertha. By golly, I'm going to get her elected mayor. Mark my words, Catherine, Bertha could go down in history if she weren't a woman," said Mater, as if she were practicing her elocution.

"Barnett's been talking about running for office himself," I countered, hoping to steer her away from the subject of vice. I turned to watch Charles fancy himself in the mirror. What a handsome son I had!

"Leadership's in the blood." She spread her ample thighs and rose up on her cane. "If those immigrants hadn't brought the influenza here, Pater Zimmerman would have curbed this alcohol situation long ago. I'm not sure who's brought on these flappers and loose living"—Mrs. Z screwed up her mouth—"whether it's the immigrants or the Alaska gold people. All that wealth falling to the lower elements. Hah! Seattle's parvenucracy, new-monied people who haven't the slightest idea of what to do with it other than to revert to their former vices."

I couldn't help but think that if Barnett were still here his mother wouldn't taunt me so. Was that the second or third time tonight she'd taken a potshot at my home territory? Then I remembered that Bertha was out in the streets stopping temperance violators. What if someone had become suspicious of our latest boatload of salmon tins? It was well past the canning season, and anyone who knew the fish business might have tipped off the authorities.

Mater poured each of us a second cup of tea from my wedding silver tea service. "And those marble-hearted matrons who're trading their daughters like cattle, thinking they can buy a good family name. Imagine marrying your own flesh and blood off to a titled European pauper, actually thinking that one can buy a cultured background like a set of dinner china. Good heavens," she said, adding several spoons of sugar to her tea, then vigorously whirling the mother-of-pearl inlaid spoon around and around in her cup. "All those new-monied people are simply ruining the flavor of the Friday Night Cotillion Club. And I'm certain that a large percentage of those parvenus are of Indian or Eskimo extraction."

My God, if she ever found out about my relatives, my marriage would perish. Not only Nana's Indian mother but her convict father. And didn't Nana tell me that her parents were never married, that she doesn't even remember her father, Ilya Ovechkin? If my grandmother was born out of wedlock, does that make me illegitimate as well? My being an illegitimate daughter-in-law would be the last straw, as far as my hopes for Mater accepting me into Seattle society. And what about my own daughter? Barnett took such a chance marrying me. I'm sure that he sometimes regrets it, even if I have produced two heirs. I don't seem to have the wherewithal to run this house or make a splash in Seattle society. A burden to my husband, that's what I feel like. Sometimes I think I should come out and tell Laetitia Zimmerman that I'm part Indian, that my dark features aren't from royal Russian descent.

Well, I sighed, at least I seem to be conquering my heritage from Mama's side of the family. None of my children looked Indian in the slightest, and I was sure now, after Debra's birth, that I wouldn't have those frightful visions of water babies whenever I looked out at Lake Washington. I'd had the windows facing the lake heavily curtained to keep in the heat, I'd told Barnett. Just ignore those demonic little creatures and they'll go away, I kept telling myself. Yet sometimes I was seized with the terror that I'd inherited Nana's Indian superstitions or that Mama's visions weren't only from a bump on the head but from some weak inheritable trait as well.

"The Alaska problem," said Mater, as little Charles watched her enormous breasts billow in and out. "At least old Harding took an interest in the territory before he died. Messy business, that Teapot Dome scandal, wouldn't blame his wife if she had poisoned him. Well, as Mr. Harding said, 'If the Finns owned Alaska, in three generations it would be one of the foremost states in modern times.' A hoard of lazy bumpkins up there, if you want my opinion. Burdens on the taxpayer." She punctuated her sentences by beating her cane into the rug. "Don't pay taxes and couldn't grow a cash crop to save their souls. Now they want statehood and to elect their own governor. Preposterous. It's putting the cart before the horse. Although," she said, giving me a side glance, "I'm sure it was different for your people, Catherine; people of Swedish, or was it Russian, extraction know how to prosper in frozen outposts of progress."

"Oh, yes," I said, smiling through her probing remarks about my relatives. "And mark my words, Mater, Alaska's going to do right by herself someday. Just before he died, President Harding went to Alaska to see for himself that there was oil in Ketalla—maybe even more oil than there is in Texas. Sue Querry's father told me so. He owns stock in those wells, you know. It was very hush hush, but that's why Mr. President planned an election campaign out west."

The French nanny appeared at the door.

"Charles's bedtime," I announced, hoping that once the children were in bed Mrs. Z would leave, and I wouldn't have to be on guard all evening. "None of those fairy tales, Patrice," I instructed the red-headed nanny. "They give him nightmares." Strange, I thought, as I kissed him good night, how my little man didn't resemble my side of the family, even slightly.

"Speaking of fathers, Catherine," said Mater, not showing the slightest sign of calling the chauffeur, "your father should thank his lucky stars that you married into such a good family. Barney tells me that the old fellow's getting quite tiresome about Carl's new fish cannery business. Now that Alaska's got a chance to forge ahead in commerce, your father's dead set against it. And what's this about him taking counsel with an Eskimo?"

I bit into the end of my fingernail. Thank heavens she hadn't an inkling of the true nature of our new "fish cannery business." Then, thinking of Barnett, I wondered what was going on down on Seneca Street. Had Bertha decided to search the wharf for contraband liquor?

"Oh, Tommy." I laughed, trying to make light of the situation. "Tommy's just Daddy's little pet. He was homeless and starving, and Nana adopted him way back when. Nana's full of little charities, you know." Tommy was such a queer little man, I thought to myself. His teeth were so crooked that one could hardly understand what he was saying. I was sure he was at least a little retarded. Daddy flatly refused to send him off to a government institution, where he could get the proper care. But at least no one had to worry about Tommy producing. The Shaker church, even if they did have strange services—what with Daddy's Indian housekeeper, Mrs. Stephan, always talking in tongues and dancing herself into a trance—preached celibacy.

"So tell me, dear—" Barnett's mother took what was hopefully her last sip of tea from her Dresden china cup—"why is your father so opposed to shipping his tinned fish to Seattle for labeling? We have our paper mills right here waiting. It's the most excellent merger that I can think of, Barney's gift for commerce and your father's raw materials. Doesn't your father understand progress and the importance of departmentalization? Why with labor in the state it's in and the government not lifting a finger to curb the unions, departmentalization is free enterprise's only chance for survival against the Bolsheviks. Yes," she boasted, "I always knew Barney was going to be an economic wizard. He showed signs of it at a very early age. My baby's made a fortune overnight, almost. Of course, Catherine, we Zimmermans have always been wealthy in land. My mother was a little girl in a covered wagon when my family came here to homestead. Back then, Seattle was called West New York. My late husband was a financial wizard, never lost track of a penny back in the depression of 'ninety-three. Pater knew exactly how to handle those mobs of rioting laborers down at the Skid Road mill. Takes after my late husband, Barnett does. Count your lucky stars, Catherine, that you have a good man like I did to guard and maintain your funds. It's the Lord's blessing."

If she ever found out the truth about her funds and the dangerous lengths to which Barnett had gone to regain them, she'd the of shame— but not before she'd blamed her son's departures from the law on my bad influence, on my coarse and uncultured background. It seemed that the harder I tried to please Mater, the less she approved of me.

"'Ninety-three," she said, settling back into the overstuffed couch, seeming to forget she'd asked why Daddy was so opposed to the fish-labeling enterprise. "I do believe that's when those parvenus with their new money started rearing their ugly heads in Seattle. Alaska gold panners from God only knows what kind of people moving in here and trying to crash the Friday Night Cotillion Club." She reached for a glass of Bethesda water from the sideboard. "They didn't know the first rule of social conduct, those stampeders, didn't know that a gentleman never plays for money, just with it. A coarse, vulgar herd of people, the nouveau riche element of this city, that's why there's so much vice here; they brought it with them."

How could this woman who'd never worked a day in her life preach to me about money? And where would Mrs. Z and her civic projects like the metropolitan auditorium be if it weren't for Alaska's gold? For a moment I reflected on my own cultural charity, an effort to make my home territory more respectable, the Catherine York Zimmerman Collection of Alaskan Artifacts. I must remember to talk to Professor Landis tomorrow about the latest Indian basket acquisitions.

"Daddy's a bit set in his ways, but Carl's all for Barnett's cannery labeling business." I was trying to change the conversation from vice to commerce but realized I had inadvertently touched on the very same subject. "Carl says he's sending twice as many boats of tinned fish down here after the summer salmon canning season next year. And he just loves the Alaska Fish Company labels that Barnett had printed. Carl doesn't think it's a bit foolish that some of the tinned fish will have to be shipped back for the people in the Alaskan bush. The boats have to go back to Sitka anyway. That was Daddy's only objection all along, you know, sending the catch eight hundred miles for the labels to be put on."

I had tried to blot out the terrible row that Daddy and Carl had had during my last visit to Sitka, before Debra was born. When Daddy'd found out that Carl was transporting hooch in those salmon tins, his tongue got so vile. . . . He called Carl a yellow-bellied coward for not earning an honest wage fishing and for putting the Alaska Fish Company's business license in danger. And even though Mama'd been dead for years, Daddy harped on and on about it being a good thing she didn't know what Carl was up to, because he wasn't a fit son to her. Of course, Nana didn't know a thing about this little business venture either. And then Daddy blamed everything on me, said that fast money and high living would be the death of me. But now it seemed we were all back on an even keel. Barnett had recaptured all our funds and was even able to help Daddy financially—Imperial Lumber and Alaska Fish hadn't had a profitable government contract since the war. A very conciliatory gesture, Barnett offering to lend Daddy money at half the going interest rate, but of course my husband always thought two steps ahead of anyone in my family.

"You know, Mater," I said, beginning to worry about why Barnett hadn't returned. I picked up my embroidery and nervously began chain-stitching the border of a red oriental paisley. "We all have to learn to move with the times. There's an important tea tomorrow at the Iota Chi. Bertha Landis is being sponsored as an honorary member. And the university has changed the dress codes: The girls are no longer required to wear hats. We'll have to discuss what Iota Chi sisters should do. Yes, we're meeting tomorrow to draw up the smoking rules. We've decided to take the big step. If the girls are going to smoke cigarettes, then rather than have them sneaking around in the bushes—well, Iota Chi's decided to permit it. Only under their own roof, of course."

"Catherine!" said Barnett's mother, her heavy jaw dropping. "I'm surprised at you. Don't you know that smoking is a vulgar, filthy vice? A girl who is allowed to smoke won't stop there." Her voice trailed off into a whisper.

"Oh, but Mater," I said, hoping that I'd provoked her into leaving. I had to find out what was going on down on Seneca Street. Were the police really going to riot? Or was my husband being arrested? Oh, why didn't the old walrus leave so that I could have Amaryllis help me find Barnett? "They're going to be very strict rules," I continued, and the girls are only going to be allowed supervised smoking." I watched Mater's eyes bulge behind her rimless spectacles.

"Smoking, indeed!" Mrs. Z put her hand to her chest and fanned herself with her lace handkerchief. "They should be learning what all girls need to know if they're going to entertain polite society. Now what if they went abroad, would they know how to address an English earl? You don't know how many mistakes are made in addressing titled people. You should be drawing up guidelines for these girls, making sure none of them leave school without knowing the modes of addressing peers and peeresses. Mistakes on titled people are so common; I see them constantly in the newspapers. For example," she said, raising her index finger, "suppose you had a Mr. Sidney Cooper and a Miss Lydia Cooper. You might call them Mr. Cooper or Miss Cooper were there no occasion to distinguish them from others of that surname. But, Catherine," she said, taking a sip of Bethesda water, "what might be right in one case is wrong in another. This is where so many of our parvenus show their true colors. In the case of a duchess's marrying a 'courtesy lord,' the title goes partly by rule and partly by custom. . . ."

I tried to control my temper. My husband and I had been planning a business and cultural steamer trip to France as soon as the children were old enough to travel and assimilate the finer arts. I always dreaded making a fool of myself in front of my offspring, but even though I'd read the etiquette books over and over, I never could keep all those rules straight. Now let me see, the daughter of a duke or an earl was called Lady . . .

"Bother," said Mater, who had somehow finished her lecture on titles and moved on to a discussion of the corn on her foot. "And another thing, Catherine, I've seen you make errors along these lines on your dinner invitations but I wanted to point them out to you in private. I can't tell you how much it would upset Barney if he knew you were so ill versed in such matters."

"Oh, thank you, Mater," I said, almost too cynically, I was so worn from her constant criticism. And Barnett never takes my side, defending me against her. It was exasperating, all the etiquette I was never taught as a child. If only I'd had the opportunity to learn these things gradually, so that they could stick to my ribs. But, even if there had been an etiquette book in my girlhood home, I wouldn't have had time to read it, what with taking care of my brothers, cooking and mending their clothes, and nursing poor sick Mama.

I took another chain stitch with the red embroidery thread and listened to Mater chatter about social etiquette. What was keeping Barnett? Should I make some excuse to her about going out looking for him? For a moment I closed my eyes and envisioned Bertha heading a band of socially prominent women as they discovered our latest shipment of squirrel whiskey made in the Indian stills at Angoon. Thank God Barnett had promised me that this was the last year for our "adventure on the high seas," as he put it.

"You were a twin, weren't you, Catherine?" asked Mater, interrupting my thoughts.

"Yes. Yes, I was," I said, keeping my eyes on my embroidery. "But my twin, Stig, was killed in the Great War, helping the Allied Forces. He got a Medal of Honor for going down with his ship. Some foreign head of state even sent Daddy a handwritten letter about how brave Stig had been." Now who had really sent that letter? I wondered. I couldn't for the life of me remember. I'd told Mater so many little white lies to impress her with my family that I couldn't keep them all straight. But somehow, no matter what I said, they just weren't right.

"Twins beget twins," said Mater in an authoritative manner. "It would be nice if there were another male heir in the Zimmerman household. Being an only child was a terrible burden on little Barney. Yes, Catherine, I think that next time you should set your mind on twins. Twin boys, dear, better going through three confinements instead of four. You're from sturdy stock, one of your most valuable assets. One debutante daughter will be a social advantage, of course, but another daughter would just bring too much frivolity into your house. Sons are what keeps this family going. Remember that when you contemplate your next confinement."

"Yes, Mater," I said dutifully, feeling my face redden as I buried myself in my embroidery. Good God, I thought, if this woman didn't stop nagging at me, I was sure to start screaming uncontrollably.

"Mustn't blush," she said, putting down her empty glass. "These are family matters. It's only healthy to discuss them out in the open. I'm not prying in the least. What you and Barney do in the privacy of your marriage bed is none of my business, but when it comes to children, we must all have a hand in the matter. None of this go-as-you-please fashion for the Zimmerman family, no, dear."

Mater stared blankly for a minute at one of the Jamaica potted palms in front of the window seats.

"Sturdy stock," she went on, suppressing a yawn, "that's how Barney described your brother Carl to me. Said he was a good chap, trustworthy and all; that's always important in starting a new business venture. I'm quite pleased at the way the Zimmerman lumber mills and the York mills have been consolidating; Pater always had his eyes on those Alaskan spruce. You should thank your lucky stars, Catherine, that Barnett has made enough on the stock market to invest in your family's fish cannery as well. He'll catapult them to top production in no time, you mark my words."

"Carl's very bright," I said. "He was an extremely clever child." I was thinking that perhaps Carl hadn't been quite as perceptive as my own son, Charles, at that age. "He and Daddy sometimes have their little differences, but that's just how men play, you know. Carl's not married yet, and Barnett and I are hoping to introduce him to the right kind of girl when he comes down with the boats next summer."

I wondered if Mater would approve of the young ladies I had chosen to introduce to Carl. They might be from the wrong sort of family; one never knew all the facts about a girl's background simply from a casual introduction. No, one always had to consult Mater about such things, she was such a stickler for family history.

"Oh, I hope Barnett's all right," I said, no longer able to contain my anxiety. "He's been gone more than an hour. Such a civic-minded man, I live in terror that one of those awful chaps from the billiard or poker parlors will sneak up on him in a dark alley—"

"My son doesn't frequent dark alleys, my dear," said Mrs. Z indignantly. "I brought him up with every advantage. He moves with the best element of Seattle society!"

Oh, my Lord. . . .

The back kitchen door slammed and Barnett appeared in the doorway of the fernery, his overcoat and shoes soaking from a sudden northwestern rain shower.

"You'll catch your death, Barnett!" I cried, rising to help him remove his wet clothes. "Amaryllis, Amaryllis." I had momentarily forgotten how Mater abhorred shouting. "Amaryllis, get Mr. Zimmerman a blanket and a hot pan of water!"

Mater and I helped Barnett to his favorite overstuffed chair in the living room next to the evening fire while Amaryllis went to fetch a dish pan of steaming water.

"Hurry now, Amaryllis," I said, "there are times that you just can't be so slow." The air of authority in my voice surprised me. My spine straightened, and I felt as if, for the first time during all my years in Seattle, I was taking charge.

"Ah." Barnett sank into his chair. "Well, the boat is safe and that's all that matters," he said to no one in particular.

"Boat, what boat?" demanded Mater, feeling Barnett's pulse.

"Just a load of tinned salmon from the Alaska Fish Company that Carl sent down for the labels to be put on," I answered, dismissing Mater's questions as if she were a tiresome child.

"Yes, yes," said Barnett nervously. "Just wanted to make sure Carl's boat was moored safely. Big row down at an Alaskan Way wharfside speakeasy, though. It seems that Bertha got some of the younger officers on the police force to dress up like football players in University of Washington Husky jerseys, even taught them the fight songs. They crashed a wharfside gin mill saying that they'd just won their first game of the season. Begged the proprietor to sell them a drink, even asked where they might buy a barrel of hooch. They pretended to be so high on their celebration that the proprietor never suspected a thing, passed around drinks to everyone, and quicker than you can say *The Sheik of Araby*, the 'team' pulled out their guns and badges and arrested everyone on the premises."

"Land to Goshen, the boy's delirious," said Mater in a high-pitched, frantic voice as she felt his forehead. "What do you mean, a boat of salmon tins, dear? The fish run in summer; the season's been over for months."

"Did the police find where the speakeasy got its hooch, Barnett?" I asked, ignoring Mater's hysteria.

"No, dear," said Barnett, as I took off his shoes and wet socks, putting his cold feet into the warm water. "No, the proprietor never divulged his source. Too bad, it would have been a massive clean-up, a big feather in her cap for Bertha."

I sighed, feeling a weight lifted from my shoulders.

"What boat?" Mater demanded again, calling to Amaryllis to bring a thermometer. "There's no salmon canned this late in the year."

Barnett pulled me into the chair with him. "What a darling wife I have," he said. "Catherine," he whispered, "if Mater finds out, it could kill her and I'll have you to blame, you stupid little half-breed."

"The thermometer, Amaryllis," screamed Mater, departing from her usual proper behavior. "Don't you know that delirium is the first sign of paralysis?"

I stood speechless and shaken by my husband's harsh words. "I'll be myself in just a bit," said Barnett, leaning back, narrowing his eyes at me, then shutting them as if to take a nap. "Just a bit too much excitement," he said softly. "It went to my head."

What could I say? I'd blurted it out about the boat of tinned fish, forgetting that Mater knew all about such things. It was my fault that she was in a snit. Barnett would never forgive me if his mother found out the truth. My shoulders slumped forward. I'd failed my husband again. Barnett was right, I was a stupid little Indian. Why else did I always say the wrong thing, why me? And just when I was feeling so sure of myself.

"He's out of breath from helping the police round up some boot-leggers," I said. "It's just a boat of last year's catch, Mater. Tins Daddy's saved to sell without labels to people in the Alaskan bush. Isn't it wonderful? Daddy's finally seen things Barnett's way. Yes, shipped his entire winter supply down here to get their labels put on. My, Barnett, you're such a diplomat. I'm so proud of you."

Mater calmed a bit, the thermometer hanging limply from her fingers. I took Barnett's hand and beamed over the accomplishments I'd just invented for him, waiting for his response.

My husband fluttered his eyelashes, pretending to be exhausted after chasing temperance violators. "Good girl," he whispered.

But Barnett's praise didn't fill me with the warmth that it usually did. *Stupid little half-breed!* The words turned to an ache that throbbed through my temples. Why did I have to try twice as hard as anyone else? I closed my eyes. What if I said the wrong thing again someday, spilling the beans about our liquor business, and caused all of us to be arrested? My head pulsed in a migraine. Next time my badly chosen words might not be redeemable.

21. SEATTLE
1928

"Debra, you sit still while Mummy helps Charles with his thank-you-for-the-nice-vacation note to Grandpa. Here, dear, draw a picture with your Crayolas for Mater."

The late-summer-afternoon sun sparkled on the ruffled white crepe-de-Chine curtains of the upstairs nursery. I looked at the bright walls, wondering if I'd chosen the right wallpaper for my two formative minds: little bouquets of blue and yellow pansy faces.

"Now, Charles." I took a firm hold of his first-grader's hand. "Remember what Mummy told you about using dots instead of circles over your *i*'s. Circles show holes in your character, dear; that's what Sue Querry says. So always dot your *i*'s; do it just for Mummy."

"Don't," screamed Charles, throwing down his pen in a fit of impatience.

"Don't what, dear?"

"*Don't* touch me, bitch!" Charles cried, shredding the paper in front of me.

"Charles! What if Mater heard you say that? Patrice!" I called to the nanny. "Come wash Charles's mouth out. I'll teach you, young man. That's what dirty people say in alleys; you don't talk like that in this house." Patrice appeared in her black-and-white uniform and led Charles into the bathroom.

"*Mon pauvre petit,*" I heard her say. "Must we, *madame?*" she called to me.

"Just give him a taste of it," I instructed. How could my cuddly baby boy not want me to touch him? And why did he push me away like that?

I never should have let Barnett talk me into taking the children with us on our vacation to Sitka. My babies exposed to the coarse, vulgar summer cannery workers. Or perhaps it was Tommy who'd taught Charles filthy words.

And what about Mater? There'd be no end to her lectures if she ever heard Charles talk back to me like that. She'd know for sure I wasn't a fit mother for her grandchildren. That woman was beginning to do more than grate on my nerves, but maybe she was right. Maybe I wasn't a good mother.

It's times like these that I wish Nana lived just around the corner. How had she managed as a young mother in the wilds, or later, with Mama so sick in the head and Mama's three babies to look after as well? Right now I could use a good dose of Nana's elderberry wine, as well as some advice. The trouble was I wasn't sure I knew how to bring up children. When I was a little girl, I did a full day's work right alongside Nana, sorting fish at the cannery. She'd talked to me just like she talked to the grown-ups. But things were so different when one brought up children in the city.

I looked down at two-and-a-half-year-old Debra's cherub face as she drew a fairy princess, the Crayola tightly knotted in her fist. Gently I showed her how to position the crayon, noticing again how crooked her little fingers were.

Her blue eyes looked up at me. "Mummy," she said, "gimme my hand back."

Crooked, every one of them crooked, I thought, as I let her return to her drawing. Mater always told me that crooked fingers indicated personality flaws; there weren't any crooked fingers on her side of the family, she said. My mama had had crooked fingers. I was just terrified that Debra was going to end up like Mama, raving at people no one could see.

The red gingham hair bow hung demurely on one side of her blond head. My daughter's lips were a little thin, but that could always be corrected later on with a little lip rouge. Modern women were so fortunate these days to have the advantages of cosmetology.

"Oh, what a sweet princess, darling. Just look at those freckles on her nose." Perhaps Debra was even more perceptive than Charles at her age.

"No, that's bugs," she said in her singsong voice, holding up the Crayola and posing with it next to her cheek as if she were about to have her picture taken.

"Bugs, dear? Like the summer mosquitoes up where Grandpa lives in Sitka?"

"Not 'squitoes," she said, cocking her head and smiling, her blond ringlets hanging down to the ruffle of her blue pinafore. "The bugs inside her nose. I drew 'em on top, so everyone can see."

"Debra!" I folded the piece of paper discreetly. "Please never say that to Mater." I was exasperated from my day of helping the children with their thank-you notes. What was I doing wrong? I had two beautiful children, but somehow things weren't going the way they were supposed to. Debra looked up at me, sensing my frustration.

"Mummy," she said, "Uncle Carl has bugs. He said I could have his—"

"Don't you say things like that about your Uncle Carl," I told her, rapping her across the arm with an orange Crayola.

"Mummy," she whimpered, cringing like one of Mater's pug dogs after it pee-peed where it shouldn't have.

"Pull down your dress, sweetheart. A lady never sits like that, not even in her own home." I thought it best to prepare her for the realities of the world outside her home early and a little at a time.

"Poop," she said, screwing up her picture-perfect little-girl face. "Poopie on you, Mummy."

Damnation, I thought, giving Debra's cheek a swift slap. What terrible language the children had picked up in Sitka. "Don't you ever talk like that, Debra Sue Zimmerman!" I said. My God, I hadn't meant to strike her so hard. "Poop is something that old men do in toilets. I never want to hear you use that word in this house again." I took a deep breath, trying to regain my composure.

"Poopie," she said in a little voice.

"You're asking for it, young lady," I screamed. "Don't you egg me on like that."

I pulled down her panties and slapped her bottom until my hand stung. Debra wailed, gasping for breath. Horrified at myself, I burst into tears.

"Patrice, Patrice," I yelled, realizing that I could very well beat Debra black and blue. "It's time for our little girl's nap, she's exhausted."

Amaryllis brought me a tea tray of petit fours as I flopped down on my sitting-room couch and stared blankly at the red velvet curtains that hid the view of Lake Washington. There must be more to life than this, I thought. What was I doing wrong? It wasn't fair. Why wasn't I happy with my two lovely children, handsome husband, and the most enviable house on Capitol Hill? It was the life I'd dreamed of as a girl working in Nana's fish cannery. What was wrong with me? The children simply exhausted me. I was much too tired to go to the club and play a round of golf with the ladies this afternoon. And what about tonight? Barnett had tickets for *No! No! Nanette*. Then there were my recipes for the Ladies Auxiliary cookbook that I had to write, and I had to buy a new frock for tomorrow's tea at the Olympic Hotel. It was all so tedious.

I picked up my ivory hand mirror which lay on the sideboard next to Mama's family album, the one Nana'd given me on our recent visit. There were so many lines under my eyes, and my face was starting to look tight around the mouth, so worn out. Perhaps I should consider a face lift, like Mrs. Clinton James down the block. But hadn't a friend of Mater's gotten her face scarred from a face lift? Hadn't they peeled away the skin and tried to reshape her contours with hot wax? I always thought that if I escaped Sitka and all that hard cannery work, I'd retain my youthful glow far into my thirties. But here I am, looking older than Mama ever did, I thought, as I thumbed through the album.

Barnett said my idea of having family portraits painted from these old photographs was simply brilliant. I looked through the photos. There was Mama as a young woman, Nana, Daddy when he took Mama to a doctor in Dawson just after she fell and bumped her head in Skagway—my, he was young-looking then. Where was that daguerreotype of Nana as a young woman? Wouldn't that make a handsome cameo portrait? I'd go down to Fredericks' furniture department next week and order the frames. But where was that tin print of Nana? I looked through the album's black pages. The glue marks from the tintype showed where it had come unattached. Oh, dear, it had been one trial after another today. The family portraits wouldn't be complete without Nana's wedding day cameo.

Then the back of my neck turned cold. The daguerreotype had fallen out of the album once before, when I was a little girl looking through the photos with Mama as she lay in bed, gazing out into space, mumbling "Gunnar, Gunnar." I remembered the writing on the back of the tin print, queer scratches into the metal. Small-Lake-Underneath, it said—Nana's Indian name. Oh, God, what if Barnett's prying mother finds Nana's picture? Damn it, where was that tin print? If anyone found out about my Indian grandmother I wouldn't be able to hold up my head in Seattle society. Mayor Landis would never ask me to pour at her official teas again—oh, my, I really must put my mind to fund-raising for Bertha's next election. Getting a woman elected mayor once was difficult enough, but twice, as Mrs. Z said, was another matter. Now, where was Nana's picture? . . .

The floor outside the sitting-room door creaked. "Amaryllis?"

"Thought you were out shopping for a new fall frock, kiddo," my husband said in a gay voice as he appeared in the sitting-room doorway, decked out in his golf knickers and matching plaid cap and tie.

"I'm still resting up from our Sitka holiday." I put a cheery note into my voice, not wanting him to see that I was on the verge of tears after my trying day. "I seem to have lost a photo from the family album. Have you seen it, dear?"

"No," he said, considering the question, "not since Patrice let Debra look at them last night." He took an imaginary golf stroke, then stopped in mid-swing. "Oh, by the way, I've got business to attend to tonight. Maybe you and Mater could go to the Metropolitan and take in the musical without me, eh, what? I'm not at all sure that Mater gets out enough."

The thought of listening to Mater lecture me on the effects of maltoilet training made me feel nauseous. And it was rare that Barnett was home or available for an evening's entertainment any more. With the added responsibility of our two children and Mater's expenses, he was having to run the fish-labeling business on a much grander scale. It seemed that the management of our little family business was consuming his every hour.

"No, dear," I said, trying to hide my disappointment, "no, I think I'd better stay off my feet."

"Well, at least give Mater a call." His lips were turned down in disappointment. "Hear from your father or Carl?" he asked, sitting down at his piano, which I'd moved to my sitting room while the decorators repainted the downstairs. Why hadn't Barnett complimented me on my choice of contrasting colors? And he hadn't even noticed that I'd gotten a stylish bobbed haircut.

"We've only been home from Alaska a few days," I reminded him. "I just had the children write their thank-you letters, never too soon to start them out on the right forms of etiquette, you know. Especially a future debutante." I thought of Debra's disturbing fairy-princess drawing. "You never told me. Did you and Carl get a chance to talk business with Daddy?"

"Ah," said Barnett, taking a deep breath and glancing toward the curtained windows. "You know the old boy, all wrapped up in small-town politics. Doesn't really know how to direct his energies. Why, I could hardly get a word in edgewise, with him rambling on with his cronies and your grandmother about the southeast Alaska cessation campaign. Seems most of the local merchants think they could go it alone, get themselves into statehood much faster without having to support the Arctic and the Eskimos. Well, your father's dead set against it, of course, wants all the Alaskans to stick together. Says the merchants are a bunch of Johnny-come-latelies."

Barnett began fingering the chords of a romantic Chopin sonata. He looked so young when he played the piano.

"After I retire, I want to dabble at the keyboard all day," he said, grinning at me boyishly. "I might have taken it up professionally, if the noise hadn't given Mater dyspepsia."

I felt distraught. The few hours that my husband spent at home were devoted to playing his piano. "What about you and Carl talking business with Daddy?" I asked again.

Barnett went to the secret panel in the bookshelf, opened the Encylopedia Britannica liquor cabinet, and poured himself a glass of scotch and soda. Taking a swig, he sat down on the couch, putting his arm around my shoulders.

"I was cordial to the old man, of course," he began. "Our business arrangement is precarious enough as it is. He still won't have any part of our labeling venture. Keeps harping at Carl to stick to fishing and make an honest living."

The thought of my brother and my husband breaking the law all these years was chilling. Risking everyone's finances and good reputation. I was tired of living in mortal dread of Barnett and Carl's being arrested. Well, it would all end soon, I told myself, and then life would be what it was supposed to be, serene and respectable.

"Too bad," said Barnett, "that your father's lumber business hasn't picked up since the war. I didn't mention a word to him about all the money he'd borrowed from Northwest Savings to renovate his mills."

"Why not, dear?" I asked, as Barnett took hold of my hand, playing link-chain with my little finger.

"Well, in the first place, he's convinced that our savings and loan company's just a euphemism for bootlegging money. He doesn't understand my qualifications, of course; thinks I bought my way onto the board of trustees. In the second place, I think I misjudged your father; he just doesn't have the right idea about labor after all. Pays all those Indian and Japanese immigrant laborers an enormous wage. If I've told the old boy once, I've told him a thousand times, those immortal words of Calvin Coolidge, 'The man who builds a factory builds a temple . . . the man who works there worships there.' Yo could have his mills whipped into shape in no time. But no, he and your grandmother fritter away their time preoccupied with fishing regulations, fish-trap pirates, problems with this government hatchery and that government bureau. I told him he should hand the fish business over to Carl. Carl's got the right attitude. Your father almost turned on me. I didn't say anything to you at the time, Catherine; I didn't want to spoil your visit. Yes, one day when you were at Dr. Goddard's Sitka Hot Springs taking the diet cure, Yo nearly lost control of himself. He told me he wouldn't have his company running liquor instead of fish. Didn't have many good words to say about your brother, either. He probably thinks I've led Carl down the garden path." Barnett lowered his eyes and brooded over his drink.

"Oh, of course not, darling." I stroked his dark slick hair, hoping to bolster his spirits. "Daddy and Carl never got on. Stig was Daddy's favorite, you know. And then when Daddy makes a slip of the tongue, calling Carl, Stig, there's a terrible row. I'm just thankful that you have a wonderful relationship with your own son. Charles is such a charmer, just like you."

"Yes, Catherine, I think your father blames me for everything," said Barnett, as if he hadn't heard me. "Not willing to open his eyes and see all the good I've done him amid his terrible economic slide." A look of defeat extinguished the usual gleam in his eyes.

"Now, darling, we do owe Daddy a lot. He helped us out when we were first married, built this house just to make me happy." I told myself it must be my exhaustion that had put me in such an ill temper. But I couldn't help thinking, how dare Barnett complain about my father, when I'd been saddled with Mater all these years?

"I'll write Daddy tomorrow," I said, hiding my anger—I did want to send my husband off to the golf course in a good mood for his game with those other businessmen.

"Ah, but the 'fish-labeling' business has been such a boon, such a boon," he said, his face brightening.

"You will begin to wind our little venture down, won't you, Barnett?" I asked pleadingly. "I'd really like to work on Bertha's re-election with a good conscience. She has been a good mayor, you know. And think of Carl. He's engaged to that nice Betsy what's-her-name— Brown, I think it is—sweet, even if she is a fishtown girl who never graduated from high school."

"Bertha," said Barnett, with a knowing smirk. "It doesn't look good for that old girl, not one bit. She's getting a reputation for being a socialist. They even used the word at the club yesterday. Public utilities, what an idea! You can't put the power of an important city in the hands of the public. Mater's even considering switching her financial support to the more conservative platform of the Ku Klux Klan, what with all the low moral conduct sweeping our colleges. Yesterday she was complaining that she'd read an exposé the Tau Delta literary society published on the difficulties of making love in a Ford as opposed to seduction in a buggy."

My husband and I exchanged glances, then giggled.

"Yes," he said, "Mater's convinced that the KKK's going to set everything straight, curtail all this fast living."

"Barnett, you are going to stop the still works, aren't you?" I asked. "You remember our pact, only a year of our little business, and that was five years ago."

"Well, my dear," he said, putting down his glass and patting me on the knee. "If your father's going to be so irresponsible about his financial affairs, you have to consider your family. We're quite well fixed now, of course, but think of Carl, who's put all his money into his boats. He could eke out a moderate living, fishing and towing logs, but he's your only hope for carrying on the York name. When Carl and little what's-her-name have a son, you'll want them to be provided for, won't you?"

"Yes, but don't we have enough funds to help him out?"

Barnett sighed. "Well, you want Carl to be able to stand on his own two feet, have his own resources other than us, don't you?"

"Can't he make more money fishing now that he's bought more boats?" There must be way for Carl to earn good money other than bootlegging.

"Princess," said Barnett endearingly, "just imagine Charles and Carl's son sharing a seat on the board of trustees at Northwest Savings and Loan. Isn't that the kind of life you'd like your side of the family to have? Fishing is so—so dangerous. Your father told me that four Sitka fishermen drowned last season alone."

I turned toward the curtained window and bit my lip.

"Morally, you're perfectly right," continued Barnett. "I've always trusted you with that. But what if we run the boats for just one more year, old girl? For Carl and the Yorks' namesake."

I said nothing.

"It's up to you, dear. I'll stop the whole operation, close down tomorrow, if you insist. It's just that . . . think of all the good the money would do. You've done an incredible job on your museum collection of Alaskan art. When we stop the boats, we'll have to tighten up a little and—"

"Oh," I said, feeling the heavy weight of decision on my shoulders. "Well, all right. Just—please, be careful. Daddy was telling me about all the murder that goes on in the Ketchikan speakeasy and bordello district. He's sure that Carl has something to do with all that riffraff there. . . ."

"Hush, now," Barnett said, burying my teary face on his shoulder. "Carl's a big boy. He can take care of himself. Sometimes, dear, I feel as if you devote all your energies to your father and Carl. What with the children, I can hardly get a minute of understanding."

I felt my face blush before I burst into sobs. I wasn't doing anything right. I was so pressured. Charles had told me not to touch him, my brother and Barnett were going to continue bootlegging, and now my husband thought I was ignoring him.

Barnett caressed my shoulder, biting me tenderly on the neck. "Princess Raven Feather," he said in a soft voice, "the fish-labeling business isn't going to last forever, it can't. No matter what Mater says, prohibition is a terribly unjust law—keeps the church in charge of the state—to say nothing of the ten boys on the University of Washington campus who went blind from bad liquor last year. I'm always careful to test our product, but some people aren't as scrupulous. We've only got a little while longer to cash in on this business, and then the Yorks and the Zimmermans will be fixed for life, I promise."

My husband went off to his golf engagement and I sprawled over the sitting-room couch. Was it really up to me to maintain the York legacy? What if I made Carl and Barnett give up selling liquor and my brother drowned in a storm while he was out fishing? I would feel horribly guilty. Daddy did seem to be losing touch with the future of his business . . . and Nana—her mind had started to drift a little. Sometimes she forgot what year it was and thought that the new people in town were something she called Boomers. Then there was Tommy. This last time I'd gone home he'd sat on the porch all day talking to a bird, and his teeth had become so decayed that he could hardly chew his food. I guess it *was* up to me to look after the financial welfare of my family, just like Nana had. Oh, my grandmother had so much spunk as a young woman, why didn't I have some of that energy?

Then I remembered the daguerreotype of Nana on her wedding day.

Tiptoeing into Debra's pink-wallpaper and canopy-bed sleeping room, I found her playing with her gollywog doll, singing like a little elf:

"Eeny, meeny, miney, mo,
catch a nigger by the toe . . ."

"Debra dear," I said in a gentle but firm tone, "it's not nice to make fun of Negroes. Don't sing that in front of Amaryllis. She can't help the way she was born. Try this poem; it's one that Nana used to sing me to sleep with when I was little, all about the seasons in the Arctic where the Eskimos live:

New sunshine
Icicle time
Skin bleaching
White hawks coming
Geese coming
Ice breaking time
Raising time
Molting time
Birds fly, leaves fall
Caribou courting
Ice time
Sunset time
No sunshine."

Debra's large blue eyes shone up at me, then gazed out into space.

"Sweetheart, have you seen one of Mummy's album pictures? Tell Mummy where you put the little tin picture of Nana, and Mummy'll give you a nice surprise, yes, she will."

"Rin-tin-tin?" asked Debra, dropping her gollywog doll and putting her hand under her dress, scratching her bottom.

"No, tin print, dear, and don't do that, you'll get your hands dirty."

"Itches," she said. "Itches where I go poopie."

"What did you do with Mummy's picture of Nana? Remember, the one Patrice was showing you in the album last night?"

Charles romped into Debra's sleeping room. "Are you sure of yourself?" he sang, imitating the radio jingles. "Listerine ends halitosis." And then, in a Loretta Young voice and a chorus-girl pose, "Be like me, kind to your complexion, use Lux soap."

Such a little entertainer he was. My son always had a way of lifting my spirits. "Little boys aren't supposed to act like girls," I told him. "Come on, you two, Mummy's got a surprise for you."

We paraded into my mirrored dressing room, Debra reaching up for the exercise bar like a miniature ballerina. I pulled a tissue-covered object from my lingerie bureau and uncovered it.

"A stuffed lion!" said Charles, his dark eyes widening.

"With real lion fur," I told him. "Mr. Matsusaka, one of your father's lumber clients, sent it to you children all the way from Tokyo. Now, which one of my two little darlings am I going to give it to? Which one of you has been extra specially good this week?"

They lined up in front of me. Debra pulled her dress up and down in back like a can-can girl and Charles looked at me with puppy-dog eyes.

"Stop showing off your bottom, young lady, All right, Charles, I think I'll give you the lion," I said, thinking that if Debra saw her behavior go unrewarded, her actions would improve.

The children ran from the room, Debra chasing after Charles, trying to yank the lion out of his hands. "Stop acting like a ruffian," I called out after her, then walked over to my dressing table to stare at all my toiletries.

Did I dare go out alone tonight? I thought back to my happy golden years at the Iota Chi house. How I missed all my sorority sisters and their idle chatter, the companionship, the parties! I had had so much energy back then. Suddenly I felt as if I hadn't enjoyed myself in years.

I studied the makeup on my dressing table, the pots of powder and rouge and vanishing cream. Did I dare go out by myself? I had that new nose veil and a monkey-trimmed black sheath I'd never worn. Ever since I'd come back from our Sitka holiday, the house and children seemed too much to bear.

I switched on the *Philco Radio Hour,* then turned the dial to the Johnson and Johnson musical melodrama. Sue Querry told me just yesterday that Mrs. Clinton James had been seen a number of times at a speakeasy alone. I turned the dial to the Lux Laundryland Lyrics. Oh, bother, it was all so boring.

Turning off the radio, I picked up a copy of *True Confessions.* But realizing that I'd already read the issue cover to cover three times, I put it down and mentally composed a confession of my own:

A MOTHER'S SECRET TORMENT

I Had an Expensive Home, a Handsome and Socially Prominent Husband, Two Beautiful Children. . . . Beautiful to Everyone but Me!

Charles was the spitting image of my husband, but Debra Sue was blond and blue-eyed like my mother. And like my sick mother, my young daughter's eyes showed those same seeds of insanity. Each time Debra gazed vacantly into space, I was overcome with terror that my little girl would grow up to be a burden on society, incapable of fulfilling her duties as a wife and mother.

"It's all my fault," I sobbed. "It was I who passed this tragic familial sickness on to my beautiful offspring. "And since I could confide in no one for fear of my husband's losing his good business reputation and social prominence, I cried alone, telling myself that perhaps Debra's vacant moments were only a childhood condition, that she'd outgrow them in time. Then one day when I peeked into her bedroom, my worst fears were realized. I found her playing, touching that part of her only her husband should touch! My blood ran hot and cold when I realized that perhaps

Debra wasn't destined to be insane. Perhaps someone had taught her this dreadful deed. But who would have done such a thing? Who?

Suddenly I felt that motherhood had become too much for me. Perhaps, Catherine, I told myself, an outing in the night air will lift your spirits. I began dabbing my cheeks with rouge and my lids with kohl and lavender liner. Even though I'd taken several makeup courses down at Fredericks', Mrs. Z still didn't approve of my use of cosmetics. What was it about me that, even though I wore the most stylish Vogue patterns, Barnett's mother could still see that I was an Alaska territory girl who'd grown up in a house with a dirt floor?

Putting on my ermine coat, I walked out of the house toward the garage. Barnett had taken the La Salle, and Martin, our gardener-chauffeur, had the evening off. I sat behind the wheel of the family touring car, driving west along the narrow streets away from the view of Lake Washington. It had been months since I'd seen one of those ugly water babies, but I didn't want to chance my good record—yes, it did seem that I was overcoming my Indian heritage. At one of Bertha's official teas, I'd even had an exhilarating conversation with Professor Landis about Pleistocene Age water creatures that were said to still inhabit the dark corners of the earth. He'd never heard of any of the animals I described to him—under the guise of *Koosta-kah*, Nana's Ottermonster story, of course. But it was such a good feeling when one got things out in the open and discussed them among friends.

The touring car seemed to slide, self-propelled along the brick and cobbled streets, down the evergreen-covered slopes toward Seattle's wharf speakeasy district. Why was I going to the docks? I asked myself. I'd always hated cargo boats and all those rough-looking men—they reminded me of my unhappy childhood. But now, the smell of the damp sea air misting on the car window recalled the joyful parts of my youth, and all the unpleasant memories of unshaven cannery men, glaring and yelling unspeakable things at me when I delivered Daddy's lunch to him down at the fishing boats or helped Nana supervise the stevedores loading a steamer with fish boxes, vanished as if these things had happened to someone else.

The car bumped across Seneca Street and past the Indian totem poles in Pioneer Square. I turned onto Alaskan Way, driving slowly beside the trolley line next to the dock. As the sky darkened into evening, the old pier buildings seemed unfriendly, almost menacing, their huge arched doorways looking like the open mouths of whales. Maybe I should go home.

Catherine, just pretend you're going out on a lark with your sorority sisters, I told myself, remembering my carefree days at the Iota Chi house. For the first time in my life I had had lots of girls my own age to talk to. Why, we didn't have an unattractive girl in our whole sorority, except maybe for Sue Querry, who was really quite striking underneath her kinky hair and glasses. But Sue made up for her appearance by turning out for every extracurricular activity: tennis, dramatics, Shakespeare, glee club. She was the first one of us to marry—the governor's son, no less—and had the first baby. Of course those girls across the street in the Delta Gamma house were jealous. Some of them even let their envy get the best of them, saying that Sue had five babies right away, just because she was plain and had to prove she was a woman. "Before she got married you had to look at her feet to know which way she was going. Now it's her stomach." That's what those catty Delta Gamma girls used to whisper. I giggled. It was true what they'd said about Sue.

Maybe I should go home, I thought again, looking out the windshield into the darkening street. What if Charles had a fever? What if he caught infantile paralysis while his mother was out driving the streets alone? I'd never forgive myself. I had turned up Pike Street toward home when I spotted a familiar car—Barnett's maroon La Salle—parked in front of what looked like a dock worker's transient home, the Donald Hotel.

I stopped the touring car and stared up at the old brick building. Some of the windows were broken and stuffed with dirty rags. What on earth could Barnett be doing in there? My pulse quickened. Was he in some sort of trouble? What business could he have down here on the docks? None of Carl's boats were due to arrive.

Parking the car, I opened the heavy door and stepped out on the sidewalk. Even under the dim streetlights, I could see garbage strewn in the gutters. Somewhere down the street, raucous laughter mingled with "Yes We Have No Bananas." Probably a speakeasy behind that produce store. Even so, it's obviously not a neighborhood for a woman to be alone in.

As I walked toward the sagging steps of the hotel, the nauseating smell of rot and creosote reminded me of an Alaskan fish cannery. A childhood memory of Ketchikan passed in front of me. There was a red light in an upstairs window of the Donald Hotel. I remembered the red lights in Ketchikan's brothel district. My hands shook.

I stepped inside the smoke-filled lobby, my stomach turning as I looked at the matted and stained carpet. Just like a deserted gold-rush hotel, I thought. Perhaps my husband wasn't really here but had only parked his car out front and then gone across the street to check on some storage space in the pier buildings.

The man at the manager's desk eyed me suspiciously, glancing up from in front of his rows of brass-colored keys and pigeonhole mailboxes. "Can I help ya, ma'am?" he asked in a nasal twang. His upper front teeth were missing.

"Ah," I stammered, "I'm looking for a tall dark man, well dressed, about in his mid-thirties with a little balding patch on the back of his head." I reached my gloved hand up to my bobbed hair, nervously describing Barnett's bald spot, praying that the toothless manager had never seen such a man.

"Probably the guy up in Frenchy's room," he said offhandedly. "Number Four-B." He motioned to the stairs. "The elevator's broken."

I stared at the carpet, the pile either worn to the weave or matted with grime. But then, I reassured myself, it might all be some terrible misunderstanding. Barnett might not be upstairs at all. I walked toward the narrow, dimly lit stairway. Did I really want to go up there?

By the time I'd reached the third floor, I'd nearly choked from the dust. That's why the tears, I told myself, from all the stairwell dust.

Four-B. I listened at the door, feeling like a prying parent. But Barnett was my husband. I had every right to know the truth, to know why he was in there—if he was in there—and with whom. Oh, I'd been so selfish with my time, I told myself; lately I'd spent hours on end pouting because I'd felt picked on by Mater. Instead I should have been attending to my husband's need to be cheered after a hectic business day. No, I told myself remorsefully, I hadn't been performing my wifely duties.

I couldn't make out the voices inside the room. Pushing my ear closer to the door, I clumsily banged my foot on the threshold. Inside the room there was a rustling noise, then footsteps. A white-cuffed, blue-suited arm opened the door.

"Catherine!" gasped Barnett, his body flinching from the surprise.

I caught my breath. Behind him was a redheaded woman whom I recognized immediately: Patrice.

Barnett's face flushed, not in shame but in anger. "Catherine!" Why was he yelling at me as if I were a naughty child? Why wasn't he begging for my forgiveness, telling me everything would be all right? What had I done?

"Catherine," he said again, so scornfully this time that my hands felt as if they had come unattached from my wrists and were unable to move under their own power.

"What?" I meant to voice the indignation I felt. Instead, my voice trailed off into a lonesome whisper.

"She knows. She knows about—"

"Quiet out there!" yelled a gruff voice, followed by a loud noise in the street. My mind raced forward. Patrice! She'd shown Debra Mama's family album last night. Patrice had found Nana's picture with the Indian engraving on the back. She knew about me.

"She's threatened to tell Mater about our *business* if I don't give her—"

"Oh, hang Mater," I started to say, unable to control myself, but a shrill whistle blasted up the stairway, followed by the vibrations of footsteps. I jerked my head toward the rumbling at the end of the hall.

"*Les gendarmes!*" shrieked Patrice.

Barnett pulled me inside the room and slammed the door. He ran to a dresser covered with stacks of currency, reminding me of the bricks of five-dollar bills that Daddy and Nana kept hidden away to pay the cannery workers. Barnett quickly put the money—almost tenderly, I thought—into a valise that I recognized as Patrice's. She stared at me, her doe eyes as large and bright as the dahlia blooms in Nana's garden.

Footsteps hammered along the hall of the floor below us. Patrice snatched the valise and ran for the fire escape. Barnett grabbed me by the wrist.

"That bitch blackmailed me," he said sternly. "It's going to cost us almost a whole season's profits. Now I'll have to take the risk of running twice as many boats next year to recapture our losses."

"But how could *she* have?" There were footsteps directly outside the door.

"It's a raid," he whispered, his voice almost hysterical. "It won't go well for us if we're caught here. We've got to make a break for it." He glanced down at my high-heeled pumps. "They'll never find you under here." Frantically he pushed me down under the filthy bed. All I could see were his feet as he dashed to the window.

As the door of Four-B flew open I began to cough violently, almost retching from the dust. A firm male hand pulled me by the leg, dragging me from under the bed.

"Let's go, girlie." A pug-nosed policeman ushered me out into the hall. For a minute I stood speechless in a group of half-naked women, all of them obviously tarts, with their bleached hair and painted faces looking like grotesque Halloween masks.

"But," I protested to the blue suit, "I'm not one of *them*." I coughed.

"Sure," he said in a heavy Irish brogue, "that's what they all say."

"But my husband . . ." I didn't finish my sentence. Barnett was nowhere to be seen.

22.

The square cement-block room had one barred window and smelled of Pine Sol and urine. My eyes watered from the disinfectant fumes as I crouched on the cold floor with twenty other women arrested at the Donald Hotel. A holding cell, Yolanda, the girl next to me, called it, pushing the words out between the spaces in her brown teeth. We'd be processed in the morning when the judge got out of bed, the woman across from me explained; her stomach bulged out from under her blouse at the waist in white scoops of fat like mashed potatoes.

I shuddered, wondering if, by "the judge," they meant Mrs. Clinton James's husband, who'd just been appointed to the bench. Where was Barnett? Why hadn't he come to rescue me? Had he leaped down the fire escape and injured himself? And Patrice. I had always thought of her as a confidant, a less-fortunate younger sister.

The woman with the mashed-potato bulges got up, walked to the corner of the small room, and urinated through a floor hole. Ghastly, I murmured to myself. We're being treated like a band of Skid Row mill-workers.

Undoubtedly, my arrest would get into the papers. I was so wasted from my misadventure that I couldn't help giggling like a schoolgirl as I envisioned Mater's face when she picked up the *Post Intelligencer,* reading about her incarcerate daughter-in-law as she sipped her tepid morning tea. Gracious, the old woman would probably faint dead away. How had I put up with her constant criticism for all these years? Well, now that I'd done something totally unforgivable, perhaps she'd give me up as a lost cause.

My leg muscles began to cramp from the cold concrete floor, and the smell of Pine Sol had become unbearable. The incident at the hotel wasn't my fault. Why did I feel I had to take responsibility for the situation? It was Barnett who . . . all that extortion money. Patrice, my soft-spoken nanny, blackmailing my strong, sure-footed husband. I wondered—but no, I didn't really want to know if they were. . . . Had the bed been mussed? The spread was rumpled a bit, but not enough to—no, they couldn't have. Barnett was only attracted to statuesque Edwardian women.

To be hauled out of a house of prostitution and into jail just like a common woman, how could this be happening to me? Couldn't the bluecoats see I was respectable? Why was I so ill-fated? It seemed as if I were born under an unlucky star—things never turned out right for me. And what about my children? What if they ever found out their mother had been arrested? If word got around, they might lose their little playmates because of me.

The cagelike barred door opened. An officer stepped in, pushing Yolanda's blue- and spider-veined legs out of his path with his large black lace-up boots.

"Catherine Zimmerman?" he called out, reading my name off a white sheet of paper in his hand.

I nodded my head. It was the first time since my marriage that anyone whom I didn't know addressed me by my Christian name instead of my husband's name. "Yes," I said, "I'm Mrs. Zimmerman."

"Come with me," he said, not offering a hand to help me up. "Come on, I ain't got all day."

It was Barnett, come to post bail, I thought, my hopes reviving. To get me discreetly out of jail before the morning newsmen arrived. I followed the officer out of the holding cell and down a narrow barred hallway.

At the booking desk a bluecoat took a small stack of bills out of a brown Imperial Lumber employee payroll envelope, counted the currency, then handed me some forms to sign. I looked across the room for Barnett. Probably outside waiting, I thought, keeping the situation down to a dull roar in his usual jovial manner.

"Did ya have any accessories?" the officer asked.

"Accessories?"

"Yeah, lady's accessories," he said, his aged face wrinkling like old table linen. "Purses, hats, children." He laughed.

"A clutch bag," I said, wishing that Barnett had come inside the station and handled the situation for me.

The bluecoat returned my purse. "Ya can go," he said, still laughing at his own joke.

I walked through the swinging doors, out into the street and early dawn light. No maroon La Salle, no Barnett to greet me with a "Chin up, kiddo, sorry about the scuffle." He must be parked around the corner, I assured myself, turning with the sidewalk, my head down, watching the cracks in the curb. A black aged hand caught my arm.

"Amaryllis." I nearly shouted, taken aback.

"The gardener's got him a car up the next block," she said. Her dark eyes looked at me as if she were announcing an afternoon caller and nothing at all out of the ordinary.

"But—" I stammered, "where's Barnett, where's my husband?"

"Don't know, ma'am," she said, pulling my sleeve. "Come on now, 'fore the newspapermen comes. Pat-rice got me outa bed, tellin' me y'all was down here. Come on now, Miss Lady, come on."

She sat with me in the back seat of the car as Martin drove up the slope toward Capitol Hill. My husband hadn't even come to get me out of jail. I sobbed. Amaryllis stroked my head as if I were a small child.

"Things jes' fine, Princess, things jes' fine," she kept saying in a soothing voice.

"How long has it been going on?" I asked, finally composing myself as the car turned onto Prospect Street. "Between Barnett and Patrice?"

"Eh," slurred Amaryllis, "she foun' out about Mista Zimmerman's whiskey business last summer jes' before you all went on your Alaska holiday. I shoulda seen it comin'. Never did trust a house servant with a lotta book learnin'."

The car crested the hill, and I covered my eyes with my hands as the view of Lake Washington spread out before us. No, God, no, not those grotesque little dog fetuses, not now, not today. Amaryllis cradled my head against her large bosom, seeming to understand.

"Then my husband and Patrice weren't . . .?" I asked, collecting myself as the car entered the circular driveway and pulled up in front of the main entrance. "Whiskey business," I said, turning Amaryllis's words over in my mind as she helped me inside the house and upstairs to my sitting room. Then she knew about the bootlegging. Patrice knew, Amaryllis knew; had they been eavesdropping, or had I somehow let it slip out when I wasn't on my guard? "Stupid little Indian, this whole awful incident is all your fault," I said out loud to myself.

"Mista Zimmerman, he should be a little more tight-lipped 'round the new help, especially when they's foreigners," whispered Amaryllis. "But don' tell him where ya got that bitta advice." She shook her head and put her fingers to her lips. "Ain't heard tell of no Indians 'round these parts in years," she continued, smiling down at me, fluffing the couch pillow under my head. "Chief See-attle, he died 'fore I was even born. Ain't no Indian ever looked like you, Princess, uh-uh, no sirree bob." She removed my shoes and propped my feet up under a cushion.

Barnett. He'd told the servants? The truth came down on my shoulders like two lead weights on the scales of blind justice. All along I'd let myself think that Barnett's timber markets were in a perpetual dive because of the postwar economy or because the poor man was bored with the business he'd been saddled with by his father. But my husband had bungled our "adventure on the high seas" as well. Now, even I could see that Barnett wasn't the businessman he should be.

"Patrice don't like America none," said Amaryllis, fussing over me like the good mother I never had, patting my hand and covering me with an Amish quilt. "Guess she saw herself a quick way to get bank-rolled back to gay Par-ee. She always liked you, Miss Lady, she was always tellin' me that, yessum. Jes' lay back now, an' Amaryllis'll get ya some petit fours."

Barnett, where was he? Why hadn't he come home? Didn't he know I needed him?

The clock on the bookshelf ticked off the hours. Six o'clock, seven, seven thirty. No Barnett. At eight fifteen Amaryllis knocked.

"Telephone, Ma'am."

"Oh, thank you," I said, mustering every bit of sincerity I could.

"Catherine!" Mater's stern voice blared through the brass receiver. Oh, God, I thought, she's read the morning *Post*. "Catherine, what is the meaning of this? Barney's beside himself. Says he's going to move in with me, bag and baggage. Woke me up at the crack of dawn raving about your betraying his trust, spying on him through keyholes. Catherine, what have you done to upset our boy? You can't just think of yourself. Think of what this ill temper is doing to his business—"

"Hogwash!" I screamed. Suddenly my body was filled with wrath like the *saanah* wind sweeping over Sitka Bay. I slammed the phone back on the hook like a wave crashing into Castle Rock. "Damnation!" I shrieked at the walls, Barnett Zimmerman and his bootlegging business was going to be the death of us all. It had to stop immediately, I told myself, remembering that I had a powerful say-so in this family. Hadn't my father built the house that Barnett and I lived in? Weren't they my brother's boats that transported the liquor? It was *York* family money that was being risked as well as the Zimmermans and their blasted good name.

"If Barnett Zimmerman wants to live with his mother, let him!" I proclaimed to the bookshelf, waiting for the waves of regret. But if he was going to come back into this house, we were going to run our family business together, just like my father and mother and grandmother had. "Damnation!" I shrieked again, throwing the brass telephone on the floor.

With a surge of new energy, I jumped up from the couch, put on my shoes, and walked to the window, tearing the curtains away from the glass. I stared directly into the blue, early morning water of Lake Washington.

"I dare you, you little beasts, I dare you to taunt me," I yelled. But nothing appeared. The water lay placid in front of my window, flat and mirrorlike as one of my wedding-silver tea service trays.

PART IV

1934–42

Eskimo Tommy

(Tumukitit)

23. SITKA
1934

Noon. Raven sittin' in the front-stoop spruce, flappin' his wings. One, two, three—four times. Changin' feathers too. I take off my glasses and everythin' goes underwater. Yeah. Put 'em back on and the colors out there in them trees don't swim together no more.

Nadia got her cane caught in the wicker rocker. Last night I heard her through the walls, bangin' her cane on the furniture, dustin' up Ulla's sickbed room. Now she got her cane caught in the rockin' chair and that box of letters done spilled all over the stoop. Raven gonna watch me pick 'em up just right, put 'em back in the decorated box. Got her cane caught in the rocker and she moanin' like a loon over Ulla's old letters.

Catherine and that husband of hers comin' up for a visit next week. We all gonna try to save Catherine from Barnett's witchery again. Me, I've been thinkin' of them magic words used back in Old Times. In Old Times, human people had to be real careful of what they said, 'cause some words was magic. You say somethin' in Old Times and it could happen. Words were magic then, but not now—'cept sometimes. Back in Old Times the human people and the animal people had the same language, so I been askin' Raven all mornin' to sing me a song that'll chase away the terrible bedevilment that Barnett put on Catherine.

Aa, there goes Nadia again. Catherine catch her moanin' over them letters and she gonna put Nadia in the Ol' Pioneers' Home, no matter what Yo says. Catherine and Barnett comin', sure are. The animal people done took to the tall grass and holes in the ground. Bad magic, they can smell it in the wind, those squirrels and rabbits can.

I hand Nadia her decorated box and the ribbons she bundles them letters up in. She got her silent face on, ain't gonna say much for a while. You gotta be careful what words you say when bad magic's comin'. I watch Nadia strokin' the ribbons, her little sea-otter face all wrinkled and squinched, tryin' to think how to drive the witchery out of Catherine. Nadia got her silent face on, but Raven gonna cheer her up, sure will. Send her a mosquito or a no-see-'em fly to hum her a song all afternoon.

Yo pushes open the screen door with his bum leg. I hear him mutterin' about Catherine. He got that look in his eye, like when Stig run off and joined the war, like when the mailman come runnin' with a piece of paper sayin' Stig was dead.

Raven knows this house just fulla pieces of paper. Nadia doin' and undoin' them ribbons again. Letters been read so many times, she don't have to follow the writin'. She just rockin' on the front stoop, lookin' down at the river: down on the roof of the ol' house Noah York built, and on the piers of the trapper shack she lived in before that. Downriver to the bay. More fishin' boats down there than trees on this hillside. Too many boats. They gonna fish all the grandmothers' souls outa the sea. Raven, them boats some fool trick of yours?

Back in Old Times, Raven done made a sea pod, and a human person popped out. Made a fish and a *tuttu,* a caribou; then taught the human people how to hunt. But Raven got scared, real scared, that the human people was gonna kill everythin', so Raven made a big brown bear. Said to the human people, "Watch out."

Raven-in-the-front-stoop-spruce, them boats down in Sitka Bay is gonna fish all the grandmothers' souls outa the sea. Better get to makin' more of them big Ottermonsters quick. Yeah, I seen him just once or twice in my whole life—long, black like a whale, like a boat swimmin' underwater. *Koosta-kah,* Nadia calls Ottermonsters, but my grandmother called him *Tiritchik.* Catherine once told me that the English word was "dinosaur," told me they didn't exist no more. Raven-in-the-front-stoop-spruce, how am I gonna chase the bad magic outa Catherine when she don't believe the spirit of them who lived in Old Times is still here among us?

I watch Yo ease himself into a front-stoop chair. "Ma," he says, "don't go gettin' your dander up about Catherine an' Barnett again. They're too busy with their socializin' and fancy dressin' down in Seattle to be thinkin' about movin' ya into an ol' folks home. I'm gonna beat their butts with that there cane if they upsets ya again this time." Yo lets out a long breath of air, like he was a whale spoutin' water.

"Don't allow women in the Ol' Pioneers' Home," says Nadia in her little sea-otter voice. "Don't take Eskimos or Indians neither," she mutters, lookin' at me. Eskimo, she don't often call me that. People-who-wear-the-tails-of-dogs, that's the name she usually got for my people.

"Don't wanna hear another word about it," says Yo, rubbin' the gray whiskers on his red fisherman's face. "Ain't Catherine or none of them grandkiddies goin' to mess up Ulla's room neither. Catherine's goin' to be so tickled over your new kitchen she ain't gonna have time to be concerned about nothin' else. Got you a fine kitchen, Ma, when ya feels up to cookin' again. Got you colored decorator tiles and a porcelain sink. Catherine an' Barnett always so smart-alecky about their new house in Seattle. Seems they forgot who built it for 'em."

Aa, Yo York, he never stops noisin' for long. Got his voice goin' round inside my head even when I sleep at night. Even when I dream. Don't like havin' Yo's voice in my vision world, uh-uh. Gets my magic goin' every which way.

"I'm tellin' ya, Ma," says Yo, who don't even notice that Nadia ain't listenin', "when this economy takes a turn for the better, I'm gonna see about dissolvin' this partnership with that daughter an' son-in-law of mine. Don't like the way Barnett's family runs them mills down there in Washington State. That Barnett's slicker'n a greased pig an' about as trustworthy. Equal partners, huh. They don't listen to nothin' I say. It's 'Barnett's family this' and 'Barnett's family that.' Catherine comes up here and acts like she's too good for her own kin. Hell, I bet now that the government re-pealed the Prohibition, them kiddies are real short on cash, just like everybody else."

Nadia starts to say somethin' but don't. Just waves Yo's mouth shut with her hand. *Aa,* Yo's noisin's got her magic all confused just like mine. But Yo York's a big man, more than six feet tall, ain't no one gonna tell him to shut his mouth.

"Don't go frettin' yourself none, Ma," he says, and I can tell by her face that some magic word that Nadia almost got hold of just went back into the air. "I'm gonna tell Mrs. Stephan not to be messin' up your kitchen with the makin's of no rose conserve," he says, chatterin' on like a sea gull, "cause I know how ya hate your house lookin' like a bird losin' its feathers when company's comin'. I'll tell Mrs. Stephan that ya got Ulla's room all dusted up too." But Nadia don't say nothin'; got her silent face on. Same here. Raven flapped his wings four times this noon. Gonna be a silent-face day, sure is.

I look down at them boats again. Yo's voice is gettin' louder and louder. Raven-in-the-front-stoop-spruce, Yo York squawks almost as loud as you do. Yeah.

"Tommy," says Yo, as I shut my eyes and try to find the door of the vision world. "Tommy, what's that ya got in your back pocket? Them's bloodstains. Tommy, what ya got in there? Come here. What'd ya do, boy, go rescue another ducklin' from the millpond? Ya done got it squashed in your pants again. Shit."

Inside my head, I'm lookin' real fast for the door to the vision world. In winter, you can always look at the northern lights and get into the vision world, but it's summer now and there ain't hardly a dark hour. So I think back to this morning when me an' Raven went lookin' for eggs up at Swan Lake. Them kids were shootin' ducks up there again. Shootin' the duck people's children too. "Souls, go back to the sea," I mutter, singin' the spirits of those dead ducks down under the bay with the rest of the dead. "Souls, go back to the sea."

"Stop that moanin', Tommy," Yo says, standin' in front of me with a long face on. I look up at him. I'm always lookin' up. Home in Bethel, where my grandmother lived, people not so tall, uh-uh. Nadia and the seal people about the only thing my size round here. And Raven remembers when that preacher man first brought me here to Sitka: I thought Ottermonster'd stolen me in the night, took me to the land-of-giants.

"Souls, go back to the sea," I mumble, "souls, go—"

"Stop it now," yells Yo. "Don't like to hear that moanin'. Shit. Come on, boy, ya can ride shotgun for me goin' over to the mill."

Raven-in-the-front-stoop-spruce, where'd ya hide the door to the vision world? Gotta find me a magic word that'll chase the bedevil-ment outa Catherine. Raven—

"I tell ya, Tommy," says Yo, screamin' in my ear, 'cause whenever

I'm looking for the vision world he thinks I've turned deaf, "the whole world's goin' to hell and that ducklin's probably a lot better off squashed outa its misery. Re-cession, huh. Them fast-talkin' politicians just need themselves an excuse for botchin' up the works. Whole world's goin' to hell and my own kids with it. Maybe it woulda been different, iffen Stig was around to ride herd on things. . . ."

Aa, there goes Yo again, talkin' about that boy who's been dead since the front-stoop spruce was small enough to be eaten by a deer. In Old Times, if you talked about the dead people as if they was livin', it'd come true. But not now, uh-uh. Ain't no talk magic enough to bring the dead back to life.

I follow Yo down the front steps and across the yard to the truck. I don't hear no more of him goin' on about Stig, just listenin' to the mosquito people hummin' their song. Just lettin' my mind sing to the bladders of them BB-gunned ducks, singin' their souls down under the bay.

Mrs. Stephan comes out on the stoop, draggin' her black Indian-woman dress and rubbin' her brow under her scarf. "Ya help Ma move her rocker round the stoop with the sun," Yo yells to her from over by the garage. Indians, they all scared of my magic, sure are. Mrs. Stephan don't come outa the house till she sees I'm gone. *Aa,* she more scared of me than that Bureau of Indian Affairs man who come round, flashin' his fancy silver amulet in her face. Tells Mrs. Stephan it's against the law to speak Tlingit to her kiddies; gotta learn 'em their English. She speak Tlingit to her kiddies and he gonna put Mrs. Stephan in jail, he says. Yeah.

"Got any ducklin's in your back pocket?"

Yo laughs as he gives me an arm up into the open-top front seat of the truck. Nadia waves from her wicker rocker. Raven-in-the-front-stoop-spruce still sittin' on his noontime branch.

"This road gets more holes in it every day," says Yo, steerin' the Ford truck across town to the Imperial Lumber Mill. "Price of gasoline goes up again, Tommy," he says to me, even though I'm tryin' not to hear him, "I'm goin' to con-vert to kerosene. Since that refinery up at Ketalla burned down, they's importin' all Alaska's oil in from the Out-side. A kerosene-powered car, Tommy, just think of that." He laughs,

laughs hard. Long time since he laugh so much, maybe since before he told me I couldn't comb Ulla's hair no more.

Yo parks the truck in front of the planin' mill office. All the men come walkin' real slow outa the lumberyard. They all got long faces on, 'cause Yo's been talkin' layoffs. Ain't no market for lumber these days, he says. Nobody can afford to build nothin'. Five white-faced men wearin' black trousers and suspenders to keep em up; the mill foreman, Fat Moses Black, standin' in the middle.

Fat Moses. Me'n Raven don't like that man. Always tellin' jokes on the Eskimo. Gets me alone in the lumberyard when Yo ain't there and tries to scare me by takin' his false teeth outa his mouth; chases me through them woodpiles with his teeth hooked onto the end of his arm. Comes from that railroad tent town called Anchorage, Fat Moses does. Says he foremanned railroad buildin' across the mountains all the way north to Fairbanks back in 'twenty-two. Those white humans sure got strange ways sometimes: buildin' a road all the way to the green and blue door of the northern lights, probably tryin' to get into the vision world. Guess they don't know that ain't how it's done. Door to the vision world's inside your dreams, can't build no road to it. But white humans like Fat Moses, they don't know nothin' about Old Times and old ways, uh-uh. Just talk all day about railroad buildin' back in 'twenty-two and how much fun it was to scare a herd of a thousand caribou by explodin' dynamite. *Aa*, Fat Moses, he don't know that a leaf fallin' a hundred miles away would scare a *tuttu*.

Them other whisker-faced millworkers look at me now while they's talkin' to Yo. Maybe they afraid I'm gonna put my evil eye on 'em, get 'em laid off. Ain't no wood contracts from the Lower Forty-eight, ain't no more railroad contracts for cuttin' wood into railroad ties. Even so, Fat Moses's got that mill saw goin' faster'n the *saanah* wind blowin' from the southeast. Yeah, that saw eatin' them trees faster'n a fox swallowin' fish without chewin', noise worse'n an avalanche. Raven, white humans like Fat Moses is gonna kill up everything. Better get to makin' a big Ottermonster quick. Tell these white humans, "Watch out."

"Catherine an' Barnett comin' up next week," Yo says to Fat Moses. I watch Fat's eyes move back and forth, and them four other millworkers start to move their feet, which is all covered up in their muddy boots. "Barnett got some fancy ideas for con-sol-i-datin' with his mills in Seattle," says Yo. "Hell if my little girl didn't marry herself a man with sassy ideas."

Fat and them other millworkers walk back toward the saw as Yo gives me an arm up into the Ford truck, revs the engine; but I can't hear it over the noise of that mill saw. Yo steers the truck outa the lumberyard, down the road to Castle Rock, then parks by the wild rose.

"Shit," I hear Yo say as he puts them field glasses up to his eyes and looks out into the harbor. "If Japonski Island weren't in the way, I betcha I could see the *Ulla III* out there. Well . . . ain't no sign yet of that son of mine. Christ, is them motor boats cuttin' up the water in fronta my cannery!"

I got my silent face on. Boats out there gonna fish all the souls of my brothers and sisters outa the sea. *Aa*, four grandmothers ago there weren't none of this. Plenty of bearded seals, plenty of walrus. Four grandmothers ago, just islands and animal people in that bay.

Maybe I'll see Ottermonster out there today, yes sir. Long skinny otter, bigger'n a whale, stays underwater most of the time. . . . Huh, ain't nothin' out there now but Tosha Kamura's fishin' boat. Town folks say them Japs done fished out their own sea and now they's startin' on ours. I watch Tosh nose his boat over toward Yo's cannery; probably goin' to see his wife and the rest of them Jap women that's workin' over there cannin' fish. Couple more hours and all them cannery workers'll come out on the beach, eat their supper sittin' on the Wishin' Stone. Ulla, Nadia, an' me, we used to sit down there waitin' for the mail boats to come in, yeah. But after Ulla fell and bumped her head she got the bad-magic-sickness, so I'd sneak her put of her room and walk her down to the Wishin' Stone, tell her stories I heard when I went through the door of the vision world. . . .

"Don't believe it," I hear Yo yellin' in my ear. "Maybe that yellow-bellied son of mine's gonna stay out for another week runnin'. Hell, now they re-pealed the Prohibition, maybe he'll put his mind to bein' the fisherman he coulda been, if he never got connected up with Barnett Zimmerman."

I got my parka hood over my head, tryin' not to hear, pretendin' Yo's voice is some unhappy wind that's lost its way. But it ain't no use.

Yo, he talks too loud. So I look out into Sitka Sound where them furry red-fox faces used to be, where all them gone-bankrupt island fox farms is all grown over with salal berries.

"Never could figure that boy out," he says. "Scared of water, scared of anything that moves—skittish as one of them caribou. Well, he got himself that nice Betsy now, maybe she gonna straighten him out. Jesus H. Christ, it sure took him long enough to take a wife. But that baby Ivan of theirs, he's the cutest grandkid of 'em all, even if he did inherit Carl's bad temper—squawks and hollers all the time. Don't let on to Carl," Yo says, lookin' down into my face, makin' sure I'm listenin' to him, "but that baby surprised the pants offa me. Didn't know Carl had it in him." Yo puts away his field glasses. "Come on, Tommy," he says. "Maybe we'll have a stop-by at the cemetery before we go home."

Yo revs the motor. I look back at Castle Rock where that old buildin' bigger'n the cannery used to be before it burned down. When the Russians used to be here, they lived in it, Nadia says, along with the head of their tribe. Now every year we have a big celebration called Alaska Day, in the fall after the salmon's canned. All them Sitka shopkeepers dress up like the Russians used to look, pretendin' to sell Alaska to the Lower Forty-eight—Transfer Ceremony, they call it. Back when Catherine was a little girl, they always used to let her play Princess Maksoutov. But then Catherine went away to college and Barnett put his evil eye on her, sure did. Catherine, she ain't been the same person ever since. It's like somebody stole the spirit outa her body when Raven's back was turned; *aa,* neither me nor Nadia's been able to find it ever since.

About six years back, though, I thought maybe Yo was gonna be able to talk some sense into Catherine's head. She showed up on the front stoop one day as unexpected as snow geese in summer. Barnett wasn't with her that time, uh-uh. He was off somewhere else, Catherine said; for once she didn't say nothin' about Barnett. Just spent most of her time down at Dr. Goddard's Hot Springs takin' mud baths. Couldn't get Catherine near a sulfur spring back when Nadia and them other Indians used to go there before the War. But now that this white doctor built somethin' called a sanitarium and put the hot mud into white porcelain tubs, Catherine goes there all the time, sure does.

About a week after Catherine arrived, Barnett come up on a steamer ship with an Old One named Mater-Woman—white-haired, big as a polar bear, with the same personality. Mater-Woman kept talkin' about some kinda papers, divorce papers, and Catherine just shook her head. Brought some powerful magic with her, Mater-Woman did; every time Barnett'd go to talkin', she'd stop his mouth by screamin' for some amulet of hers called "smellin' salts."

Must have been from that polar-bear woman that Barnett learned whatever devilments he knows, yeah. But Catherine, she had some magic words in her mouth on that visit. Told Mater-Woman a story that put a spell on her stronger than any spell Raven's seen since Old Times, sure did. "And your furs, and your La Salle, and your South African cruises, money from my brother's boat business paid for all that. You really haven't got a dime." Them words of Catherine's blew a gale so strong it stole the polar-bear spirit right outa Mater-Woman's body. She called for her smellin' salt amulet and then her eyes rolled up an' she turned white as a crane. Town doctor called it a stroke, said her brain'd gone numb forever. A stroke of luck for Catherine, that's what Raven called it. But soon as they took Mater-Woman to Seattle on a stretcher, Catherine's magic got all mixed up and goin' every which way. Got herself bewitched by Barnett again. Me an' Nadia, we're all the time tryin' to save her, but nothin' seems to work. Catherine, I know she's got some powerful magic words of her own somewhere, sure does. But they don't seem to help her get rid of Barnett's evil eye, uh-uh.

Yo steers the truck along the road to the cemetery; gets the wind goin' hard in my face—just like the *sila* weather spirit in a storm. Yo probably tryin' to make me feel like I'm home in Bethel ridin' in a dogsled again. Yo, he means well; just so long as he don't go on no more about Carl, about Carl bein' the way he is 'cause of how I minded him as a youngun. Carl, he got a special look in his eye; got an angry streak like a badger, too. Once, before Carl was taller than my elbow, I told him about huntin' elk, about singin' to the elk's bladder and sendin' its soul into the sea. Gotta do that, I told Carl. 'Cause the *sila*'s always watchin'. Raven only made so many souls when he made up the animal people, so the *sila* don't like to see no elk dead in the forest with no one to sing its spirit underwater with the rest of the dead. Raven'll fish it out again someday, I told Carl. Then Raven'll put that elk spirit in another one of the animal people. But in the meantime, them dead souls can hear the thoughts of the livin', yeah, know all about what we're doin'. The *sila* gets mad when you don't take care with an elk's soul, I told Carl. Then the *sila*'ll bring you bum weather when you're out in a boat. Your boat'll ice up, get top-heavy, an' fall over, sink into the water.

Sila knows, I think inside, lookin' up to the sky. The *sila* always knows.

Yo pulls up in front of the cemetery, and I walk in back of him to the stone. Wild roses in a vase still got their faces on from when we was up here yesterday. I watch him run his hand over the letters chiseled into the rock: ULLA YORK. His big finger stops a minute between the two ll's of her name. "Ya know, Tommy," Yo says, even though I'm tryin' not to listen, "she still mighta got well if no one'd let on about Stig dyin' in the War." Yo steps over the grass next to where Ulla's in her box underground. "Come up here after I'm gone and keep me an' Ulla company, hear, Tommy?" he says.

I go down by the bog so's I don't have to hear him blubberin' on that stone again. I go to pickin' up pieces of sod and throwin' 'em up-crick and down. Spreadin' the grasses, spreadin' the beetle people. Then I look up to the sky. *Aa*, movin' the sod just like the *sila* weather spirit moves the clouds, singin' just like the wind do in winter:

> Ptarmigan fly round and round,
> ptarmigan fly up-crick and down,
> ptarmigan hungry, so-o-o hungry,
> ptarmigan thirsty, so-o-o thirsty.

Finally I hear Yo start the truck motor. Gives me an arm up, his eyes red like from hooch. "Tommy," he says to me, "don't ya ever worry none. Ya been provided for, I seen to that. I never had no brothers or sisters, but you been one to me, sure enough. Hell, I might even leave ya the whole shebang." He turns into the driveway. "Wouldn't that be some joke on them." He laughs, laughs hard.

Mrs. Stephan in the livin' room, rubbin' Ulla's portrait with a rag. She always rubbin' it, gonna rub the paint off someday. She goes to dustin' the glass-eyed duck and the mantel when she sees me comin'. I keep a special watch on that Indian woman when she's near the fireplace; don't want her chasin' away the spirit-of-the-smoke-hole, uh-uh, spirit-of-the-smoke-hole leave your house, ain't no fire'll ever burn to cook your food no more.

"Mr. York," says Mrs. Stephan, "Betsy an' the baby was up here. Says to tell ya she got a letter from Carl sayin' he was goin' to be crabbin' up near Kodiak for more'n a week. Left her letters here, too," she says, lookin' at me, scared I'm gonna give her the evil eye. "Maybe ya better run 'em back down to her, Mr. York, you and Tommy." Mrs. Stephan is hopin' to get my magic out the door and not afixin' on her. "I keep all my Walt's letters to this day, I do. Fishermen's wives, they got to have their letters to trade round with each other. You run 'em down to her real quick now, won't ya, sir?"

"Sure, sure, after supper," Yo says, glancin' at the envelopes next to Nadia's arm where she's sittin' at the table, gettin' ready to eat.

Mrs. Stephan goes to the kitchen and brings out the venison roast. Gonna all of us have to be eatin' everythin' with a knife and a fork and those little white blankets under our chins when Catherine an' Barnett come up next week, 'cause Catherine likes that. And Nadia ain't gonna be wearin' her mother's wolf-fang and salmon-bone necklace neither. Indian things, they upsets Catherine somethin' terrible unless they're hung up on the wall. Nadia's got a new face on now. Maybe she's gonna talk some, maybe she's not gonna save it all up to blow a blizzard of magic words on Catherine.

Mrs. Stephan brings out the bowl of Russian potatoes and runs like a scared coot back into the kitchen, keepin' her eyes where my magic can't get at 'em. Nadia still got the decorated box next to her, got her spectacles on too. Ain't no Raven at the window neither. Raven knows Nadia's gonna read those letters to us again. I look at the wall. Look at it long enough and, iffen the magic's heavy in the air, I can put my mind straight through that wall and down under the sea. Swim around with the souls of my grandmothers.

"Now, Ma," I hear Yo say, "don't let Catherine catch ya all mushied up over Ulla's letters. Hell, fool daughter'll probably throw 'em away." I stare hard at the wall, at the pebble shapes in the dune-colored paint. Next Yo gonna tell Nadia again that she did the right thing, lettin' Ulla go on for years writin' to her dead girl friends. And that pebble mark is growin', growin' right through the wall.

Now Yo gonna tell Nadia there ain't no one so cruel as to tell a shut-in like Ulla that all her kin down in Frisco died in the quake. "Mark my words," he gonna say, "to this day I still think she woulda gotten up an' about, if Carl hadn't blabbed the news about Stig to her the way he did."

The pebble hole's gettin' smaller. Not enough magic, no sir. Shoulda known. Raven flapped his wings four times at noon. Not gonna be able to go under the sea this time. Ain't no Raven at the window neither. *Aa*, Raven's heard this talk more often'n I have.

"Been years since Ulla left us," says Yo, "but it just seems like last week to me. Concussion compounded with melancholia, huh. Fool doctors, they get stuck to a name and a sickness they ain't got no cure for, and there's no puttin' another idea on earth into their heads."

"Ulla weren't no spineless woman," he gonna say next. Raven knows. "Can't for the life of me to this day," he gonna say, "figure what it was about a bump on the head that set her off so." Got my magic tryin' to see through the wall again, but I know Nadia's lookin' at me. She ain't never gonna say it. She ain't gonna tell Yo about that dead man at Angoon, or about that Scandia Ulla run into in Skagway. Nadia lookin' hard at me. I can feel her eyes on the side of my face, burnin' my magic away. She ain't never gonna tell on Ulla. Ain't gonna ever tell Yo about how we got rid of that Scandia who came round askin' after Ulla, sayin' she was his wife. Nadia musta built the whole town of Osloburg with the money she gave that Scandia to hush his mouth. Osloburg: Little Norway, Yo calls it. And that Scandia sayin' he's Ulla's legal husband livin' there right across the water from here. Nadia, she ain't never gonna tell on me an' Ulla's gun and how I bang-banged that Scandia. Didn't even sing his bladder down under the sea neither. Nadia ain't never gonna tell, she gonna just let Yo go on talkin' his talk. Huh, maybe tomorrow I'll put my mind under the sea; talk to the soul of my dead grandmother and look for the door to the vision world.

Nadia got her spectacles on. She gonna read those letters again. Letters Ulla wrote to dead people. *Aa,* Catherine'll up an' throw those letters away some day. She do that an' Nadia'll blow a blizzard on her colder than the *sila* ever done. Sometimes me an' Raven wonder if there's any magic words left in the world that could save Catherine from Barnett's evil eye.

Nadia picks up one of them letters that Betsy left behind. Picks it up just like it was one of Ulla's letters in the decorated box. Yo ain't even seen what she done, too busy helpin' himself to a piece of blueberry pie.

Raven outside on the front stoop cawin' up a rage over some sea gull. Oughta be listenin' to Nadia, fool bird. Oughta be conjurin' up Ottermonster to scare away all them fishin' boats insteada doin' that angry dance out on the front-stoop railin'.

"Dear Betsy," Nadia says. The words is different tonight, but Yo, he just sits there chewin' his pie crust.

> *"We left at midnight, heavy weather. The Ulla III started icing up, big danger. Remember that new shrimper, the John and Olaf, that went down last December, all lost over here by Kodiak?*
>
> *"Can't let the crew know I'm scared. Started fishing before light. Pulled pots all day. Them crab pots are big as two outhouses, iron, six hundred pounds. Tanner crabs got a look of pain on their crab faces. We rip them out fast. Breaking legs here and there. They look like they're in terrible pain, like they got their legs caught in a hootz trap, but their pinchers keep doing the motions of thrusting food to their mouths."*

"Ain't nice to read other people's mail, Ma," Yo finally says. "I reckon I oughta run them letters back down to Betsy after I have me another piece of pie."

"It's my grandson's mail," says Nadia. "There's nothing wrong with telling one of my kin's stories."

I look through the window. Raven still dancin' and noisin' at the sea gull. Fool bird, ain't never listenin' at the sill when he oughta be. Betsy and those other white human women, they're always readin' letters from their fisherman husbands. Read 'em just like an Indian tellin' a story 'bout her ancestors durin' some long winter night.

> "I'm scared of fishing in heavy seas. The crew don't know it, but I just manage to keep my footing as it is.
> "We ran all night, fished for an hour—three A.M. Slept awhile, then fished again at six, slept, ate breakfast, fished till dark. We pulled twenty pots today, but no crab. Don't look good.
> "The wind—the williwaw, them Aleuts call it—the wind's the spooky thing here. You can see it. The williwaw rips and shreds, lifts the water as it blows across the sea, making it look like there was a huge broom sweeping the water."

Nadia's voice fades into the noise of Raven cawin' on the stoop. She puts the letter back into its envelope and pulls out another.

> "Yesterday we started pulling pots at eight A.M. We got a call from the Chief, a fellow crabber, saying that her skipper and first mate had gone to the beach exploring the day before and not returned. The Chief was just off of Cape Pankov where a stampede steamer ship was beached. The rest of the Chief's crew didn't know how to operate the boat. It took them till morning to figure out the radio. When we arrived we saw a man ashore, high on the hull of that old steamer ship, frantically waving. I called through the megaphone, saying that we were coming to the rescue. I ordered two of my crew, John and Steve, to get out the big skiff. The wind was blowing strong out of the northwest, but Cape Pankov looked protected. I knew the wind was breaking on the beach, but I didn't know how bad.
> "John and Steve paddled to shore, taking about a half hour. Finally they were just beyond the breakers and with them and the skiff for scale, I could see those breakers were huge, maybe ten feet high. I watched John pause, cast out more line, and then make a

mad paddle over a giant breaker toward the beach. Neither one had a life jacket.

"I saw them upright once after they went into the first breaker. Then a second wave swept over them. I didn't see anything in the surf. Then I saw the skiff, bottom up and John clinging to the top. I got a terrible knot in my stomach. I was scared my insides were going to come out of my mouth right there in front of my crew. Steve was gone. Finally, John started struggling through the waves. He kept disappearing; it was like he couldn't get out. I didn't understand why he couldn't get to shore. I was terrified. It seemed like forever that he struggled chest deep in the surf. Then I realized that there was no beach, only giant rocks that the waves crashed through. I saw John dragging something yellow, the color of Steve's rain gear. He pulled Steve across a boulder. The men on the wrecked ship ran to help. They worked on Steve, beating his chest and back. Worked on him for maybe a quarter hour. After a while they walked away."

Yo gets up outa his chair. Goes to the window, mutterin' and shakin' his head to himself. Nadia don't look in his direction at all, just keeps on with another one of Carl's letters. Her eyes ain't even followin' the words. She musta been readin' them all day, 'cause she's just talkin' like she was tellin' us one of them stories she owns—like her story about not killin' an otter or a squirrel, 'cause the animal spirit'll find its way into the body of a woman who'll kill you the same way you done to it.

Nadia finishes all of Carl's *I love you, Betsy*'s and puts the letter back into its envelope. Picks up her fork for a piece of blueberry pie. Got her silent face on again. Yo, he's standin' over by the window, his mouth probably numbed shut from the blizzard of words that Nadia just blew over him. Ain't no tellin' if any of them words was magic or not. Gotta wait and see what happens. Betcha Nadia gettin' ready for her soul to pass over. *Aa*, betcha she's gonna blow a blizzard all over Catherine when she comes up from Seattle next week. And if that don't drive the evil eye away from Catherine, Nadia'll probably start gettin' ready to blow herself out.

24.

Standin' on the back step, makin' sure my belt's done up tight and I ain't got no bloodstains on my back pockets. Catherine, she fussed all mornin' about havin' me at the dinner table for Nadia's birthday party, sure did. Ain't no one, even Nadia, knows when her birthday is, so we always celebrate it when the salmon fish start to run. Eighty-five, she is, or thereabouts, that's what Catherine says.

Catherine always lookin' at me with a long face on. Ever since she an' Barnett started tryin' to run the show at Yo's lumber mills, she ain't been too partial to me, uh-uh. Got my silent face on. Ain't gonna do no talkin', 'cause Catherine gets herself all upset over my English, tellin' me how to speak right and makin' me say it over till I got it like "educated people." *Aa*, I don't say nothin' in front of Catherine no more. To speak like Catherine wants me to might kill the magic words in my mouth.

Last night she told Yo I was gettin' to be a danger to myself. Tellin' him how they got a federal home for Eskimos up in Fairbanks. I'd be better taken care of there, she said. I gotta look right for Catherine, sure do. She an' Barnett ain't scared of my magic—ain't scared of nothin', far as I know.

I go inside the house to the cedar-paneled dining room and sit down at the long table. Catherine got the grandkiddies sittin' near my elbow. And Nadia, she sittin' at the far end, head of the table, with Yo next to her. Huh, ever since Catherine an' Barnett bailed Yo outa that bank trouble a few years back with all the money they got from selling Carl's squirrel whiskey, Catherine's been sayin' that she an' Barnett's family own everythin'. Don't see why Catherine got Nadia and Yo at the head of the long table, uh-uh. Oughta put herself there.

Catherine got Carl and Betsy sittin' across from Yo on Nadia's other side, and then herself and Barnett sittin' in the middle. Ulla's children don't look nothin' like her, don't act like her neither. Look just like their daddy, and only Raven knows what souls he done fished outa the sea to put in their bodies. But Catherine's little Debby Sue—she's just about up to my elbow now—she got Ulla's hair, got her blue eyes too. Debby looks just like Raven carved up an ivory copy of Ulla the day them cranes circled round her bed and flew her away. *Aa*, Raven made a carvin' of Ulla, called it Debby Sue.

I follow brown-headed Betsy with my eyes as her little face watches Catherine call out orders to Mrs. Stephan. Quiet and cheerful as a marmot and works twice as fast, that Betsy. She's holdin' little Ivan in her lap, even though he's old enough to sit up in a chair by himself. Ivan fumblin' at her blouse, and I know he stopped that suckin' years ago. Goin' to school in a couple years' time, little dark Ivan. Don't know what to make of that boy. Always screamin' and tearin' at his mother's blouse or pullin' the wings off insect people.

I sit up real straight at Nadia's birthday dinner, just like Catherine likes. Got my little white blanket under my chin. Watchin' Debby Sue roll her blue eyes over at me. Watchin' her brother Charles carry on just like his daddy, playin' like he got a long cigar in his mouth, tellin' Debby Sue which vegetable she gotta eat first.

Yo cuts the barbecued salmon and everyone starts to eat. I got my fork in my left hand and my knife in my right. Don't want Catherine gettin' no ideas about sendin' me to that Eskimo home, thinkin' I'm half-wit. Gotta be eatin' and talkin' just right all the time Catherine visits. Got my silent face on; don't want Catherine tellin' me she don't like my talk. "It's not 'where's Yo at?' It's 'where is Yo?'" she gonna say. "You simply must watch your grammar in front of the children. Now, if you ask me properly, Tommy, I'll be glad to answer you." No, don't want no lesson from Catherine today.

Barnett, he never say nothin' to me, just shakes his head. Or when he do talk in my direction, it's some story that starts out like, "Hey, you ever hear the one about the naked lady and the Eskimo . . .?" Don't know how he ever got enough magic to bewitch Catherine. Leastwise, I never heard no magic in any of his fool words.

It weren't Nadia's idea, this birthday dinner. Nadia got a strange face on tonight, ain't seen so much fire in her eyes since that fish war down in Ketchikan back in 'oh-eight. Catherine got a white blanket on the table and flowers she spent all mornin' stickin' in a jar. Barnett, he oughta be chewin' his food insteada chatterin' on about some magic spell the U.S. President is trying to put on the country.

Mrs. Stephan servin' Debby Sue an' Charles their children's plates.

I see Mrs. Stephan always lookin' at Catherine outa the corner of her eye. Mrs. Stephan ain't had no time to be avoidin' my magic ever since Catherine got here last week. Catherine always tryin' to learn Mrs. Stephan about which dinner guest to serve first and where the maid gotta stand to pepper your potatoes once ya got 'em on your plate. Me, I don't want no Indian woman pepperin' my potatoes for me. Eskimos can pepper potatoes just fine by themselves. Catherine always tellin' Mrs. Stephan to hold the servin' tray in the other hand and stand on the other side of Nadia's chair. Catherine, she got more superstitions than any Indian I ever met.

I look out at the front stoop and see four ravens on the railin', lookin' in. Reminds me of those four eagle birds that used to roost in them wind-topped spruces round the ol' house. Eagle Tree, Nadia calls this place, 'cause of them eagle birds. They was always watchin' everythin' ya did and never made a sound. But ever since people in these parts took to shootin' eagles like they shoot bears, them birds haven't been around. Ain't been no eagles at Eagle Tree since before Ulla passed over. Raven told me them eagles flew south to the islands down in British Columbia. Raven says them birds ain't never comin' back, no sir.

Four ravens sittin' out on the front stoop lookin' in, lookin' down the long table at Nadia, watchin' the fire in her two black eye holes, in her little sea-otter face.

"What the hell would a Jap or an Indian worker do with a buck-an-hour wage?" I hear Barnett say. "Now, I don't know what those Japs do with their money, but those Indians'll just go down to the Dock Shack and drink it up. Raising an Indian's wages—well, that's just like giving money away to children. And raising a Jap's wages is defeating the principles of imported labor. It's simple economics, Yo, simple economics. No, can't let you do it. I've got to put my foot down and save you from yourself again."

Yo starts noisin' like a whale cuttin' a boat in half with his tail flipper.

"Daddy," I hear Catherine say, like a peacemaker at a potlatch feast, "you should just see all Barnett's civic awards. Why, the Seattle Chamber of Commerce voted him their Man of Progress Award last year.

I was so proud," she says, her moon face too big for her skinny neck. "Sue Querry, my sorority sister in the Iota Chi house—you remember Sue—she and her husband even drove up from Olympia for the presentation dinner. Fifty dollars a plate, it cost, Daddy, and we had our picture in the Sunday *Post Intelligencer*. Remember that new ermine coat that Barnett bought for me last Christmas? Those Chamber wives just couldn't keep their eyes off it. I was afraid they might even drool on it and ruin the fur." She giggles and then looks at Yo with large deerlike eyes. "You know, Daddy, people have even suggested that Barnett run for governor."

I watch Barnett sit there with his gander face on, proud as can be under his shiny black hair—black an' slick as Raven's, 'cept Raven's color don't come off all over everythin'. *Aa*, that Barnett, he's got me an' Nadia's magic all stirred up, got it goin' every which way. Put his evil eye on Catherine a long time ago, he did. Ever since, Catherine ain't had nothin' but fool ideas in her head, except for that one time Catherine came up here alone and sat all day in the Indian hot springs. Why, the last time she was up here, she brang a trunk of dresses on the steamer boat, wore each one once, and then left 'em all behind in the garbage like pieces of paper that'd been written on and used up. Raven, I ain't even sure if all of Nadia's an' my magic put together can save Catherine from Barnett's witchery, uh-uh.

I take off my glasses and the birthday party goes underwater. Try to take my ears off too. Start to listen to the voices inside my head, lookin' for the door to the vision world. Then I start hearin' the voice of the spirit doctor of my grandmother's village.

Long time ago, in the land-of-long-night, there weren't no women, only men. These men, they was polar-bear huntin' one day, when they heard the voice of a woman from the Southland. All the men went lookin' for this woman. Had a big fight. One hunter pulled the woman's feet and another pulled on her head. Pulled her apart, they did. One hunter carried off the woman's lower half and the other carried off her upper half. Then them hunters got out their carvin' chisels and whittled up each woman-half the rest of her parts outa wood. Now, the woman that had wooden feet, she couldn't hardly dance at all, but she sure sewed fine stitches in that polar-bear fur. And the woman with wooden hands, she couldn't hardly sew a stitch all day, but whenever someone went to poundin' on the drums, she danced, danced like an *ilisiilah, a spirit doctor, castin' a spell.*

When Catherine was a little girl, I thought she was gonna be a woman with wooden feet, 'cause Ulla taught her to sew real fine. Then after Ulla took to her bed, after she bumped her head and the magic of that fool Scandia got inside of her, Catherine didn't like to sew no more. Squawked like a duck when anyone'd even ask her to make one of them pictures outa colored thread. Aa, she grew up past my elbow, Catherine did, had to look up to see into her face, just like I do with all the others. Went off to college down in Seattle and ain't stopped talkin' about that sorority house of hers since. I remember when she sent home a picture of herself dancin' with Barnett. Them letters of hers that Nadia read to me, all she wrote about was her sorority sisters an' Barnett an' party dancin'. Got so tall, Catherine did, that now I nearly have to take my head off and put it on a stick to see into that big moon face of hers. She ain't never been light on her feet, Raven knows that. Once me and Raven sat on a log all day wonderin' what kind of a woman Catherine was, a woman with wooden feet or wooden hands. The spirit doctors say that since both kinds of women all came from the same body in the beginning, sometimes a woman don't have to have no wooden parts. But since Catherine got Barnett's evil eye put on her, I think she got wooden everywhere.

I hear Charles start to howl his head off at somethin', his noise hurtin' my ears. Then he beats his fists on Debby's chest. Catherine outa her chair and got her long fingernails into Debby Sue's arm quick as a gull smells garbage. "You stop taunting Charles, young lady," I hear her say. "He's your older brother. You mind him when he says to."

I put my glasses back on and see that Debby's got tears in her eyes and is lookin' down at her plate.

"You spoil your grandmother's birthday party, and I'll paddle you good. Do you hear me?" says Catherine.

"He goosed me first," says Debby.

"Don't contradict me," says Catherine. "And don't use that word, that's what dirty people do in alleys." Catherine gives me a quick look. She's wearing a long face. "You lead him to it, Debra Sue Zimmerman," she says. "Now sit up at the table like a lady. If you don't learn how to eat right, those seniors'll make mincemeat out of you when you pledge at the Iota Chi house."

Ain't no one else at the table says a word, no sir. I watch Debby pick up her fork as Charles jabs her with his elbow, makin' her hand crash down on her plate. Them ravens at the window watch Catherine get up from her chair quicker'n a loon duckin' underwater.

"I warned you!" Catherine screams. "You ruined your grand-mother's dinner. I spent all week planning this party, Debra Sue. Now you go upstairs until you can be civilized."

"Let the child be, sister," says Carl, lookin' down his crow-beak nose. But Catherine don't hear him. My stomach rolls like a boat when the *Sila* blows a heavy storm, and Nadia's shrunken breasts move in and out like a nestin' duck when a dog comes too close to her eggs. Nadia, she better blow a blizzard of magic words on Catherine, 'fore Catherine do somethin' awful.

Them ravens is still sittin' quiet on the stoop rail, lookin' in. Wish I coulda put my mind through the wall and down under the sea tonight, but Barnett, he's got the magic in this place scattered up-crick and down. Yeah.

Carl sits there next to me watchin' Catherine, starin' outa his tiny black-pebble eyes. Yo just stares at Debby's empty chair, used to be Ulla's chair, uh-huh. I watch Yo put his sad face on, but he don't say nothin' to Catherine about how she run Debby round the chicken yard. Betsy's busy huggin' little Ivan, spoonin' bits of food into his mouth instead of lettin' him have a plate of his own. I take my glasses off again. Don't wanna see no more of this birthday party.

"Betsy," says Catherine in her fancy lady's voice, "why don't you start a Junior League chapter going up here in Sitka? You married into one of Sitka's oldest families, and you've got fourteen good years of Junior League service; I wouldn't waste a one of them. It's no secret that I have my big four-0 birthday coming up this year and I'll have to quit the League. The girls say they don't know what they're going to do without me. Barnett and I have been planning a trip abroad, when all that rumbling over there settles down. We want the children to see Paris and Rome while they're still young enough to assimilate the languages easily. Children seem to be able to communicate so well in foreign languages, don't you think?

"Yes," I hear Betsy's little marmot voice sayin'.

"And Barnett's company—Daddy, you'll be pleased as punch to hear this—they've started a fund for the Seattle Symphony and Ballet. Barnett's got it all figured out. It's a marvelous tax shelter for the Imperial Lumber profits. Instead of paying out our earnings in taxes, we pay them to culture. And there isn't a thing that F.D.R. can do about it. Barnett says that he just hands out our tax money to freeloaders. We're going to call our fund the Laetitia Zimmerman Memorial Foundation."

"I suppose I should get interested in community work," says Betsy, talkin' real slow. "I'm so lonely when Carl's out on the boats. But Ivan, he just has one cold and sore throat after another. I'm so scared he's going to get infantile paralysis, like my friend Eva Mae's boy died of last year. And with all the TB and germs that those Indian children carry around, I'm grateful the government's got the sense to keep the Indians in separate schools."

"When he gets old enough," says Catherine, "we'll help you find a good prep school for Ivan. Barnett and I researched them, narrowed them down to two fine boarding schools that would suit Charles's personality to a 't.' It's never too early to start planning your children's future."

"I'd sure like to start a Junior League," says Betsy, "but I've been so tired. Ever since I lost the baby out on the boat when Carl and I got caught in that storm. Dr. Reese said if I'd bled any more, I might have died. . . ."

Don't have to put my glasses back on to make everybody's face come outa the water, uh-uh. I hear a hush come over this table like in the forest just after a gunshot rings out. Everybody knows ya ain't supposed to talk about blood from lost babies in front of Catherine at the dinner table. No, don't have to put my glasses on to see how red Betsy's little face must be. Yeah. I listen to Betsy's spoon scrape up another bite of barbecued salmon, hear it scrape real loud across her plate and imagine her puttin' it gentle-like into little Ivan's mouth.

I put my glasses back on and we all follow Catherine into the livin' room to eat the birthday cake. She calls to Debby, tellin' her to come outa her room. I watch Debby slink down the stairs like a dog that don't know if it's gonna get kicked or not. "Stand up straight and pretty, now, Debby," Catherine says. Debby walks over to Yo and climbs up on his knee. Carl gives Nadia a steady hand as she sits herself down in her rocker, restin' both hands on her cane. Nadia ain't said much all evenin', but she ain't got her silent face on, no. She still got that fire in her eyes, maybe burnin' even brighter now. And those four ravens, just look what they done. They moved clear round the stoop rail so's they could see into the livin'-room window.

I watch little Debby. She tellin' her grandpa Yo that she's eight years old last month. Got long blond hair, just like Ulla, Debby does. And Yo's strokin' it, combin' it with his fingers, pettin' Debby like he used to pet his wife at night after we'd been workin' on the boats all day. Debby smiles, lookin' happy as a white crane that just found a blueberry bush. "Goin' to marry me when you grow up?" asks Yo, squeezin' Debby's waist. Charles is sittin' on the floor, beatin' his hand like a hammer on Yo's bum leg. Yo don't even notice. He just pettin' his little Debby girl.

She quicker than a bear cub, that little girl is. I seen her bear-claw her brother to the ground this mornin' when they was playin' on the front lawn and he tried to pull her underpants down. Now she just sittin' quiet and straight-backed as a swan preenin' its feathers while Yo strokes her hair.

Little Ivan got birthday cake frostin' all over his face, tryin' to get inside Betsy's blouse. Carl pulls him away from his mother, tellin' him to play with his big boy cousin Charles. I see Carl tryin' to sneak his fingers into Betsy's blouse without no one else noticin'. He got fingers like a Dungeness crab, that Carl. Always sneakin' his fingers into Betsy's blouse, pinchin' her so hard that tears come to her eyes, 'cause she can't cry out, leastwise not with Catherine here.

"I don't expect to have many more of these birthdays," says Nadia. I hear her otter voice muffle as she rests her chin on the crook of her cane. "Don't expect it at all."

"None of that kind of talk now, Ma," says Yo. "Couldn't run things round here without ya."

"Mother York," says Barnett, "have you thought about memorial bequeathments, something to help enrich Alaska's culture? This territory's going to be a state someday," he says, "and it'd be nice if this family had a history of guiding her through to the finer arts."

"When you're as old as I am," says Nadia, "guiding other people's affairs is the last thing on your mind."

"But your money could bring a lot of refinement to Alaska, Nana," says Catherine. "A memorial gift to build a good hospital. Oh, when I think of my mother without a good hospital, just wasting away her life in bed all those years. . . ."

"I doubt if any hospital could have cured your mother," says Nadia.

I watch her two coal-dark eyes blaze brighter than I seen 'em do for a long time. *Aa*, I can feel the fire leapin' outa Nadia's face almost as if spirit-of-the-smoke-hole'd gone to live inside her eyes to help her with some magic words, uh-huh. Then just look at them ravens outside, they done moved from the stoop railin' right up to the sill. Sure know they're supposed to be listenin' at the window this time.

"Yes," says Nadia, "I've done my share of 'guiding.' I helped build this town. That's my cannery down there and my land all around, if it's anyone's. As long as Alaska belongs to America, then the laws are going to say that Noah York stole it fair and square. Stole it from his wife's own people and not a word to me about it," she says, liftin' up her chin. "Most people have forgotten that I'm half Indian."

"But you're also half a full-blooded Russian," says Catherine.

"Russian convict," says Nadia.

"Besides," says Catherine, "it's not as if you lived like an Indian. And, Nana, I think it would be a real enrichment for them if you'd extend an invitation to Madame Tulinseff and those other white Russians over in Juneau. Why, they must have had a terrible ordeal having their homes taken away from them by those awful Bolsheviks. You could be a real comfort to them, and I'm sure they'd be pleased as punch to meet you. I once looked up Noah York in one of those East Coast social directories. He was from fine stock, fine Anglo-Saxon stock and filthy rich, isn't that so, Barnett? My grandfather was a son of one of the most prominent families in New England."

"Noah York wasn't your grandfather," I hear Nadia say. This just might be a story with enough magic in it to save Catherine from her bedevilment. "It didn't happen like you think it did, Catherine," says Nadia. "Noah York couldn't have fathered much of anything." Nadia sits back in her rocking chair, and everybody but Yo and Debby start to fidget like birds waitin' for the weather to change. Yo, he never much cared who his daddy was. Nadia, she gonna blow fire tonight, gonna melt the ice cap offa Mount Edgecumbe, she is. Catherine don't like this story, no sir, I can see that. I'm thinkin' that Nadia's found the door to Old Times, back when words were magic and could make things happen. Yeah. I look at Catherine's hair real close, seein' that some of it's turned white. She's startin' to look just like the Mater-Woman. Raven, is that some fool trick of yours? Puttin' that polar-bear woman's spirit into Catherine?

Yo pulls Debby close to his stomach, puttin' his arms round her real tight till she squeals, "Grandpa Yo!" Yo, he ain't even heard a word of what Nadia's saying. He don't believe there's anythin' can save Catherine from Barnett's evil eye. He just goes on playin' with Debby like she was a little Ulla doll.

I watch Carl and Catherine look at each other, Catherine pullin' at her dress. Carl turns to watch his father playin' with little Debby.

"Catherine," says Nadia, with a bull seal's voice in her throat, "your real grandfather killed more white pioneers in these parts than any *hootz* or winter storm ever did. Your real grandfather was an Indian chief, a Tlingit, just like Mrs. Stephan out there in the kitchen. That makes you a lot more of an Indian than you think. Maybe more Indian than I am."

"Nana, where do you get these stories?" says Catherine, forcin' herself to laugh and then lightin' up a cigarette, holdin' it between her fingers like a wand to ward off Nadia's magic.

"I've been turning things over in my mind for years," says Nadia. "If Kat-lee-an had married me instead of Shathitch's sister, maybe Seattle Charley wouldn't have strung him up to the burning tree. The most terrible sight I ever . . ." I hear Nadia's voice disappear into the air, and her two coal eyes dim.

Catherine, yeah, she's got her feathers ruffled from Nadia talkin' on about that Indian chief.

"A hospital," says Nadia. "A home for bedeviled creatures. . . . Now that'd be a fine thing, if the government didn't make it into a hellhole like those other government homes."

Her eye holes start to brighten up again, and I know Nadia's thinkin' about Uta. Probably she's wonderin' if a white human's hospital would have poisoned Uta the same way them Indians finally did when the salmon didn't run up their tribal crick for two years straight.

"Memorial bequeathment," Nadia says, real slow like she was pronouncin' words in a foreign language, "memorial bequeathment. All my money's gone into this land, paying off the bank after I mortgaged it to renovate the Sitka mill and cannery. Don't you think I'd have given my money to Yo if I'd had any after the banks closed? Catherine," she says in a clear voice, "do you think your Indian granny's got her money buried in a tree outside? But I'll tell you where I do have it buried," she says, as Catherine fingers her cigarette. I watch Barnett and Carl each put a new face on. "Tell you where I have it hidden," she says again and stops when she sees that Carl's got his crow neck twisted clear round into his grandmother's face.

"I have it all in that town of Osloburg across the water. Everybody says those Norwegians keep things clean and shiny. Well, that's my money shining over there. I must have paid a czar's ransom to keep that man's mouth shut. No, there's no hospital that could have made your mother get well, Catherine, honey. But Ulla sure would have felt better if that Norwegian hadn't hung around all those years, knocking at our door. 'Take your Athabascan woman back to Porcupine Creek, why don't you?' I used to tell him. 'Just a hundred more dollars'll get me there,' he'd say, promising not to come around and upset Ulla any more. I must have paid a czar's ransom to that blond devil," says Nadia. "Ah," she says, leanin' back in her rocker and givin' me a knowin' look, "he went away, finally." Sure did, I think to myself. Took me a whole week to talk Ulla into lettin' me play with her little gun. Bang-bang, and that Scandia went away, uh-huh.

"Where does she get these stories?" I hear Catherine whisper to

Barnett while she makes what them grandkids call the cuckoo sign with her finger next to her head.

"Which Scandia you talkin' about, Nana?" asks Carl.

"Ulla's husband," says Nadia, with the fire of magic words comin' outa her eye holes. "Her lawful husband, he said. Promised me he wouldn't breathe a word of it to the town people or the marshal. Said he wouldn't say anything about her being a bigamist and her babies born in sin, if I'd just pay him a hundred dollars so he could get back to the Yukon." Nadia settles back into her rocking chair, pretendin' to put her silent face on. But me an' Raven, we know Nadia's just wantin' Catherine to think she's gone off to sleep. Nadia, she's just watchin' to see what Catherine'll say about this story. *Aa,* maybe this story's got enough magic to chase away Barnett's evil eye.

Catherine stops makin' the cuckoo sign. I watch her an' Carl look at each other while Catherine fidgets with her dress. For once she's quiet as a squirrel. "Nana's tired, it's time for her nap," says Catherine. "The birthday party has simply worn her to a frazzle, poor dear. . . . Maybe we should all go down to the Sitka Hotel for a nightcap."

Yo's still strokin' little Debby. Didn't even listen to Nadia's story. He heard it before, long time ago. Back then, he didn't care about Ulla's other husband, 'cause he knew Ulla weren't gonna run off with him, not in her state of bedevilment. Yeah, he knew all that Scandia wanted was money and not our Ulla.

The ravens outside on the sill start to shift their weight. First time I seen any of 'em move since just after we ate the birthday cake. Them birds is doin' like me, wonderin' if Nadia's gonna say anythin' more.

"I'd love to go with you to the Sitka Hotel," says Betsy, "but I should get little Ivan to bed or he'll be a fussbudget tomorrow. Carl," she says, "you go on with Catherine for a drink. You all can drop me off at home on your way."

Carl rolls his eyes down that crow-beak nose of his. "What are ya gonna do with your children while you're drinkin' up the still, sister?" he says jokingly to Catherine. But I know that anytime Carl opens his mouth to joke, it's 'cause he wants somethin'.

Catherine, she still don't have much to say. Still ponderin' over this new story of Nadia's. Yeah, maybe there was some magic in Nadia's words, maybe so. I can see Catherine freezin' up like a tree in winter over what she just heard. "You an' Barnett and Dad go on down to the hotel and get yourself drunk, sister," Carl says. "Drop Betsy an' Ivan off on the way. I'll stay here and mind your kids."

Nadia dozes in her rocker, and Yo pats little Debby on her blond head, puttin' her down off his lap. "I could use a drink," says Yo, standin' up. "But I reckon that me an' Tommy'll head for the Dock Shack insteada that hotel. Hotel's probably fulla them fancy summer tourboat people by now. Them's your type, Catherine. You go on and have yourself some fun."

Yo brings the Ford truck round to the front door. All the way down to the Dock Shack I think about Carl an' Catherine. Every so often, Carl he gets real nice to his sister, offerin' to baby-sit her younguns and all. Lately, he don't have nothin' to do with Barnett. Carl don't like the way he's been tryin' to run the mill an' cannery any more than Yo does. And Carl, he ain't never been one to be bossed around for long, uh-uh.

All the way down Lincoln Street to the Dock Shack, I'm wonderin' what Catherine's gonna make of Nadia's story about Ulla havin' another husband and never been rightfully married to Yo. Usually Nadia just rambles on about her convict father and her Indian mother. But tonight she really stirred the magic up, talkin' about Kat-lee-an and Ulla's legal husband.

Nadia, the one thing she ain't gonna talk about is when she used to go lookin' for her lost ma. Don't blame her, neither. Nadia once told me how her ma was stolen from her tribe, just like them white missionaries stole me from my village up near Bethel. They come with their black hats on to my grandmother's house one day, tellin' me I can't be no spirit doctor. Witchery, they called it. Tried to teach me the Good News book. And when I didn't take to it, they called me half-wit.

Nadia, she told me a lotta other things about her ma, Woman-Always-Wondering. Gets goin' like a wolf cryin' over her dead mate when she talks about it. Probably never tell Catherine that story. *Aa,* that story's got too much strong magic in it, so strong even Nadia don't tell it no more. Besides, Catherine don't like it when Nadia wears Woman-Always-Won-dering's wolf-tooth necklace. Says it makes

Nadia look like a wild savage, like she never got no schoolin' or cul- turin' or nothin'.

Me'n Yo walk into the Dock Shack. Ol' Fat Moses Black's sittin' at the sawyers' table, and there's some Indians sittin' at the cannery- man's booth on the other side of the room. Me an' Yo sit at our table, the one closest to the bar, the one where I carved my name in the tabletop the first week this here bar opened. Carved the name my grandmother gave to me, *Tumukitit*. People round here got their names all over their houses, got 'em on letters they mail at the post, some even got 'em on their P.O. boxes. But me, I ain't got nowhere to put my name, so I wrote it right here on the Dock Shack center table. Now everybody knows this is where me an' Yo's supposed to sit.

Yo goes through two-three bottles of Olympia beer, broodin' the whole time over Catherine an' Barnett and their citified ways. "Carl," Yo says. "He don't even take sides, just sits and watches that Barnett Zimmerman takin' over the whole shebang as if it didn't matter none to him. I tell ya, Tommy," he says, even though I'm tryin' not to hear, "it was a bad day that my little girl met that man, no matter how fancy his family is.

"Carl," Yo says again. "Carl don't even care which way the wind blows. Hell, Tommy, things woulda been different if little Stig was alive and kickin'. . . ."

Outa the side of my glasses I see them Indians at the cannery- man's table are lookin' at Yo real cautious-like. Everybody afraid they gonna get laid off, everybody blamin' Yo York. But they all's afraid to pick a fight with a man his size, so I know I'd better keep myself outa the streets of Sitka for a while. Yeah. Maybe take to the woods with the animal people. Them Tlingits over there point their faces at me. "Dumb Eskimo," they sayin' with their eyes. "Dumb Eskimo." Them Tlingits, most arrogant human people I ever met, 'cept for Barnett and the Mater-Woman, uh-huh.

Yo drives the Ford truck back up the hill and into the Eagle Tree driveway. We turn into the garage and I see the back of Carl's head sittin' in the big livin'-room easy chair just like he was at the birthday party, 'cept he only got the hall light on like when everyone's asleep.

When he hears us walkin' up the front stoop, he's gonna turn round and show that funny crow face of his, sure will.

Me an' Yo come up the front stoop. Them ravens are noisin' worse than the williwaw howlin' over the Bering Sea, so Carl don't hear us. We go past the window in front of where Carl's sittin' and see little Debby in her underwear standin' in front of Carl. Catherine gonna do a wolf dance iffen she finds Debby outa bed so late at night, uh-huh. Yo and I stop for a second, glancin' in. Debby's face is all red and she's coughin' somethin' fierce. Then I sees that Carl's sittin' in the big easy chair with his pants down round his knees and his pecker stickin' straight up. He got his hands one on each side of little Debby's head, pushin' her face down into his lap. He holdin' her head like some sour-doughs I once seen in a bar doin' a salmon fish.

Yo sees too, and he picks up Nadia's wicker front-stoop rocker and throws it through the glass window on top of Carl. Little Debby jumps up, lookin' at us, her blue eyes bright as northern lights shinin' on ice in winter. "Don't spank me, don't spank me," she screams as Yo picks up an icicle-shaped piece of window glass and goes after Carl. Then, quick as a scared caribou, Debby runs outa the house, across the lawn to the old pear orchard.

Yo and Carl scream at each other louder than a boat breakin' up on a sea rock as me an' Raven go after little Debby Sue. Find her hangin' onto the trunk of Ulla's favorite pear tree, cryin' on its shoulder limb. I put my arms round her, her an' the trunk of that old pear tree. Then me an' Raven start singin' loud enough to put Yo an' Carl's screamin' outa our ears. "*Ya, ya, ya, alaaaa. . . .*"

25. SITKA
1942

Rainin', rainin' hard. The whole York tribe's standin' on the beach under them tarps, not sayin' much. Yo got that box under his arm. Now maybe he don't wanna part with them ashes, I don't know. Don't know why white humans would put people's ashes in a gold Christmas-papered box—looks like a bottle of fancy hooch mighta come in that thing. *Aa,* maybe Yo don't wanna take off the lid and look in at his ma's ashes. Don't blame him none, no.

Ain't all the York tribe been together in one place like they is now since before Raven made them new Ottermonsters run thick and fast as salmon in these here waters. These new Ottermonsters got white humans jittery as the northern ice in summer. And all them new-comin' *cheechakoes* got guns bigger than five men can carry hidden in the hills. Got soldiers marchin' up and down the streets of Sitka, 'cept there ain't no roads outa here, so I don't know where they's gonna march to. Got the sky noisin' so much that even Raven got his big black head cocked, just marvelin' at what he done this time. Fool Raven, how was he supposed to know them Ottermonster submarines would drive these human people to doin' a wolf dance and jumpin' off cliffs crazy as a bunch of lemmings? Raven, he gonna stop a minute to mourn Nadia's passin', uh-huh. Rest of the time, he just laughin' his fool head off at how fast he got all them human people scurryin' round. Wouldn't surprise me none if Raven hadn't sat on the stoop railin' next to Nadia in her wicker rocker, tellin' her years ago all about them giant Ottermonsters and this here war he had planned. Yeah.

Yo got the Christmas-papered box clenched tight under his arm as I watch him lookin' outa the corner of one eye, studyin' Carl and Debby Sue. Yo ain't hardly talked to Carl since that night we come home and caught him doin' little Debby like a fish. That night when Yo went after Carl with a piece of glass, it made the magic so bad in this place that the salmon stopped runnin' up Indian River for two years straight, and Yo told Carl he'd better move himself and all his fishin' boats down to the cannery in Ketchikan.

Catherine, she's standin' over on the other side of the tarp, got tears comin' outa her eyes. Got herself some new hair on, looks just like she got an eagle nest on her head, sure does. The points on the back of Catherine's shoes is sinkin' into the sand, 'cause the tide's comin' in. Yo, he better do somethin' with them ashes quick or else the tide gonna come in all over us.

Yo ain't sayin' much, ain't had nothin' to say to Barnett in years. This week's the first time in a crane's life that Yo and I didn't go to each of them little eight-sided forts he built up in these hills. Built 'em after he an' Carl had that fight on the night of Nadia's birthday party. Yo, he goes up to his forts and watches for Carl's fishin' boats every day. Don't want that boy near this place, he says. Makes me come up in those hills with him, totin' supplies.

Raven never saw a birthday party like Nadia had that year. After Yo busted the front-stoop window all over Carl, Raven an' me went down to the pear orchard with little Debby, stood behind them trees watchin' Yo go after Carl up on the front stoop. Debby, she only had her summer underwear on, so I was holdin' her under my parka, keepin' her warm like ducks do with their eggs. Keepin' her from seein' Yo go after her Uncle Carl.

I remember how the blood covered Yo's arm as he held that piece of glass like a *ulu* fish knife, tryin' to stab Carl down where his pants oughta be. Carl was shriekin' like a crow, tryin' to duck Yo's arm and pull his pants up at the same time. "Pre-vert!" Yo screamed. "Vile pre-vert, oughta geld ya like they do a horse. Ya ain't no son of mine," he kept sayin' as he lunged forward at Carl's pecker. Carl jumped away fast, but not fast enough that Yo couldn't stab his face, rippin' open Carl's cheek.

Then, as Raven an' me remember it, a car turned into the driveway: Catherine an' Barnett comin' home from drinkin' down at the Sitka Hotel. Debby was sobbin' and moanin' for me not to tell her ma what she'd done. Had her hair all tangled in the zipper of my parka. I remember that I had a strand of it in my mouth, tasted just like Ulla's hair used to taste, just like the water grass my grandmother used to give me to suck on.

Barnett ran and pulled Yo off of Carl, and Catherine spied me holdin' on to little Debby down in the orchard. Catherine pulled Debby away from me, tearin' her hair right outa my mouth. "Let go of my daughter, you filthy Eskimo!" she screamed.

Raven remembers how Yo started hollerin' from up on the front stoop. "Ya ain't no son of mine," he kept sayin' while Carl was pullin' up his pants. Barnett held Yo up against the railin' with a grip on his cut-up hand. "Just hold on now, Yo," Barnett said. "You wouldn't want to do anything you'd regret."

"Is Debby—ah, all right?" Barnett yelled to Catherine.

Catherine looked round inside of Debby's underpants, feelin' in there with her hand. "Yes," called Catherine. "I think she's learned her lesson this time. See what happens when you go walking around the house in your underwear, young lady?" I remember Catherine sayin' to Debby, givin' her a spank.

Yo pulled free of Barnett and started at him with another piece of glass. "You get your butt outa here, sonny, and keep it out. I don't care if ya are married to my daughter, ya ain't a fit father to your little girl."

Then Charles walked sleepy-eyed outa the front door. "Mummy," I think he said, "all your yelling woke me up." I recall lookin' up into Nadia's window and seein' her silent face lookin' down outa the glass. Never forget how she looked down at us all, uh-uh. Her face spoke louder than any words ever could: Ain't no magic can undo this witchery, that's what her face was sayin'.

Yeah, Raven never saw a birthday party like Nadia had that year. Yo tried to cut up one of his own kiddies. Stopped talkin' to all his younguns and near everyone else too, 'cept Nadia, me, and his mill foreman, Fat Moses Black. *Aa,* after that night, Yo went to buildin' those little eight-sided forts up on the hillside—look just like them old tumbled-down Russian blockhouses, they do. Keepin' a lookout for his children, Yo says. Just makin' sure they don't try to sneak up on him and take over at his mill an' cannery again. "They ain't no kin of mine no more," he'd tell me. "Goin' to leave ya the whole shebang, Tommy, yes sir."

Nowadays people think Yo's up in them hills lookin' for Jap boats an' planes. He even got a commendation from Major General Simon Bolivar Buckner for Jap-watchin'. But Raven knows that's not what Yo's been up to, no. *Aa,* ever since that birthday party, Yo's been crazier'n a rabid fox. Gets on me now worse than he ever did before, stirs up my magic. Don't like that. Yeah, now that Nadia's passed over, think I'll go live with the animal people.

Standin' on the beach, Yo's got the Christmas-papered box clenched tight under his arm, watchin' the waves move in and out. First time he ain't been noisin' like an angry bird.

The wind an' the *Sila* weather spirit got Debby's hair bobbin' like that gold-colored kelp floatin' offshore. "Stand up straight, Debra Sue.

You'll get rounded shoulders if you stand like that," I hear Catherine say. "Oh, Daddy," she goes on, turnin' to Yo, "you'd be as proud of Charles in his Army Air Corps uniform as we were when Barnett and I went to Seattle's Boeing Field last week to see him off overseas."

I don't hear Yo say nothin'. He's just standin' next to me on the beach sand, holdin' that Christmas-papered box under his arm.

Barnett starts to slick his hair back with the ends of his fingers, shiftin' his weight from one foot to the other like them ganders always do. Got his shiny black shoes on too. If Yo don't hurry and throw them ashes out into the sea, the tide's gonna come in all over Barnett's feet.

I watch Carl standin' next to Betsy, lookin' over at Debby, watchin' her blond hair rise, up and down with the wind. Then Carl looks at Ivan playin' soldier in the sand. Ivan taller than my elbow now. "Kapow, kapow," says Ivan, with his fingers like a gun, shootin' his father down. "*Jappy* New Year," he says, talkin' like them soldiers at the Sitka Base. "Only seventy-two more bombing days till Christmas." And I'm wondering what kind of soul Raven put into Ivan.

The tarp we're all standing under flaps in the wind, makin' noise. "Shouldn't we have the Russian priest from the Church of Saint Michael come down and give the eulogy?" says Barnett, talkin' like a voice that comes outa the radio.

I don't hear Yo say nothin', just keeps his eyes fixed on them islands out in the bay. "Waitin' for the Indian women," he says finally.

Catherine puts a new face on, ain't no tears on her face now. "I thought it was going to be just family," she says. "Just family, Daddy. Nana would have wanted it that way." Yo, he don't say nothin'.

Then I hear the noise of Indian women's chatter and see Mrs. Stephan and four others walkin' down the path to the beach. They's all walkin' under one large camouflage tarp, wearing them long black dresses with black bandannas tied over their heads. They stop a ways from us and commence to moanin' their Indian Shaker church song:

"Jesus, Savior, help me.
Jesus, Savior, help me.
Ay yay yaaaaah."

Catherine puts her hand on her chest and gets tears comin' outa her eye holes again. Barnett holds her by the shoulders. "They just don't have the ability to completely readjust themselves to a modern culture," he says. "Now, Catherine, darling, pull yourself together."

Catherine gives him a long face and turns her mouth to Debby. "Stand up straight, Debra Sue," she says. "I'm not going to tell you again. Next year when you pledge Iota Chi, you'll thank me for all this needling that I've had to go through with you."

I watch Yo look over at Debby, look at her with a sad face on. Yo and I ain't seen much of Debby since that night all them years back. Now, he looks at her just like he was lookin' at Ulla. Debby, she sure looks like her grandmother. Grew up tall and sturdy as an Alaska yellow cedar. And me, I know that what little talkin' Yo done with Catherine an' Barnett these past years was only 'cause of Debby. "Tell Debby to write her Granddaddy Yo," he'd say.

The five Indian women are all huddled together under their tarp, watchin' us stare into the water, watchin' Betsy tryin' to get Ivan outa the sand. That kid busier than a sea gull in a garbage can and noises twice as bad. Yo just stares out into the water like he was tryin' to put his mind under the sea. I look out into the bay and at the mess them soldier boys and powder monkeys made of Japonski and all them other little islands where the fox farms used to be.

Raven, that some fool trick of yours? Them soldier boys done moved five bay islands together. Pulled down every one of them trees, trees fatter than a caribou in calf, trees I couldn't reach my arms halfway round the trunk of. Pulled 'em down, they said, to make a place for them planes to land. Built barrack houses for the soldier boys. Got the Sitka Bay tidewaters goin' every which way. Sea tide don't know if it's comin' in or goin' out, just lookin' for the spaces between those five islands where it used to flow. Raven, look at what your giant Otter-monsters got those white humans to do. *Aa*, they even changed the streets in town, puttin' in a new marina. Don't call the woods in back of town Lovers' Lane no more. Call it "National Park." Don't know what they done with most of them Indian totem poles, neither. I don't blame Nadia for blowin' herself out. There ain't no end to the fool ideas these white humans got inside their head. And ain't no magic words I know that can stop 'em, neither.

Yeah, me'n Yo look out into the bay where the seal people used to live. All gone up north now to live under the ice at Yakutat Bay. Spirit doctor of my grandmother's village used to say them seals was once the fingers of a woman drowned from starvation madness. Back home in Bethel, my grandmother used to sit all day on the sea ice, listenin' for them seal people to come scratchin' their noses at their ice-crack breathin' holes. Scratchin' like the fingers of a woman. Ya can learn a lot from listenin' to seals scratch an' talk, my grandmother used to tell me. Yeah. Them soldier boys should listen to what the seal people have to say, but they don't wanna talk to no seal. Don't wanna listen to nobody born in these parts, uh-uh.

Catherine been lookin' at me with a long face on all afternoon. Heard her last night, sayin' I was a danger to other people. "No one in his right mind," she said, "would have let Nana go wading in Sitka Bay. A ninety-three-year-old woman wading!" she said to Yo, angry as a walrus. Well, it was right here on this beach where I took Nadia into the water, right here where the Wishin' Stone used to be before them soldier boys dug up the bay, here where we's gonna throw her ashes into the water. Nadia told me to take her wadin'. Wanted to go out into the water, lookin' for a piece of the Wishin' Stone. Yeah. But I got my silent face on for a couple years now, so I don't tell Catherine nothin'. Gotta be careful with words like in Old Times. If you spoke in Old Times, what you said might happen. And with all the bad magic that's come to live in this place, I figure I better not speak at all.

Didn't tell Catherine about takin' Nadia for a walk on the beach. Didn't tell about walkin' out into the tide with her, helpin' Nadia to keep her footin'. Mid-July and that water was almost warm. Comes all the way from Japan, that water—same as them giant Ottermonsters. Me an' Nadia walked out into the tide with all our clothes on and then sat down in the water. "I want to see what it's like to be out here," she told me. "I want to listen to the noise in the water." We sat there and the tide went out without us. Went out just like it always does and left us sittin' there like them other pebbles and shells on the beach. Didn't find the Wishin' Stone, though. Don't know what them soldier boys did with it.

Nadia, she had her silent face on two, maybe three years before she died. Didn't talk much that day we went wadin' neither. Just told me she hoped the soul of her mother took her down under that water when the time came. Made me proud as Raven, Nadia sayin' that, 'cause Indians like her don't believe their dead go to live in the sea. She musta converted to the Eskimo Old Way 'cause of all my magic. Yeah. That day we went wadin', that was when Nadia gave me her mother's strung-together wolf-teeth and fish-bone necklace. Told me that sometimes them amulets work magic and sometimes they didn't. I always carry it with me in my parka pouch, just like she said for me to do.

"A danger to other people," that's what Catherine says about me now. Yo don't listen to her none, though.

Couple of days after I took Nadia wadin', they flew her to the Territorial Capital Hospital in Juneau. Said she had pneumonia. A month later they flew her ashes back in this here gold Christmas-papered box. *This contains the remains of Nadia Karimoff York,* is what that writin' says on the lid. Remains, huh. Sure ain't all of her in there, no.

Yo rips the lid from the box, and him an' me look inside. The rest of 'em pretend to watch the waves comin' up to the tips of Barnett's shiny black shoes. Don't look like the remains of no human person in there. Don't even look like ashes. Stuff in that box is fine dust with colored pieces here and there. Looks like the dust an' rock that comes outa them volcano islands up in the Aleutians where we used to go crabbin' and shrimpin'—them islands that everybody's fightin' over now.

Me an' Yo sift through the pieces of bone and ash. Found me one that looks like a shark's tooth. Yo got himself a pair of tiny black sticks. He pours some of the ashes into his palm and we sift through them lookin' for her teeth, lookin' for all them pieces of gold an' silver the new dentist from Chicago put in Nadia's mouth. Don't see one speck of it, uh-uh. And I starts wonderin' what they done with all her parts to get her ashes to look like this.

Yo mumbles somethin'. "Didn't want her sent to that hospital nohow," he says. "Betcha, Tommy, that they just put all the bodies from one day's take into a furnace and let their ashes run together, like milk in a dairy. No tellin' whose ashes is whose. Don't see nothin' in here that could make me think this box of dust an' sticks was my ma."

Got me a handful of small salmon-colored chunks that clank together in my palm. Musta been one terrible fire they put Nadia into. *Aa,* ain't nothin' in this box even looks like part of a bladder. How am I gonna sing Nadia's bladder back to the souls of her people when there ain't one left of her?

Huh, for eight years now everybody been sayin' what a great thing it is that the Indian and Eskimo have an opportunity to be American citizens just like all the white humans in Alaska. Citizen. What do that mean? Don't mean you can bury your dead like they're supposed to be, uh-uh. Gotta bury them like the white humans do.

Catherine an' Barnett walk up to Yo. "Don't think of this as terrible, Daddy," Catherine says. "Why don't we all take a handful of Nana and throw it into the tide, just like she said she wanted us to do?"

"Tide's coming in real fast, Yo," says Barnett, like a porcupine who don't wanna get his feet wet.

"Yes," says Catherine, "and I know Betsy's just as worried as I am about Debby and Ivan catching cold out in this rain. Let's just do it, and then we'll all go back to the house for a little memorial service."

"Jesus, Savior, help me.
Jesus, Savior, help me.
Ay yay yaaaaah."

"Them's the memorial service," says Yo, pointin' to the Indian women singin' under their camouflage-colored tarp.

Catherine's mouth twists like an angry dog's and she's about to say somethin' when the sky people start noisin' worse than any thunderbird I ever heard.

"Bombers," screams Ivan, "bombers!" Everyone leans outa the tarp, lookin' up into the rain-mist-fog. Can't see nothin' of what's rumblin' round in the sky up there.

"What if it's the Nazis, Barnett?" screams Catherine. "What if they've taken Russia right while we were standing on this beach? We shouldn't have been away from a radio this long."

"It's the Japs!" screams Ivan. Betsy and Carl both hold him by his shoulders. Everyone's still lookin' up into the rain. I don't see nothin': no stars an' stripes, no risin' sun picture. I don't know what magic symbol them Nazis draw on the sides of their planes.

"It's probably just one of our B-twenty-sixes flyin' out of Anchorage," says Yo. "They fly over here every other day 'bout this time."

"Yo," says Barnett, "I know we've had our differences, but I hope you don't talk about these things to anyone else."

"Daddy," says Catherine, "you know what we've been told over and over. You're not supposed to talk about the bombers. You say things like that to the wrong person, to one of those Jap fishermen, why, we might lose the war."

"Ain't no more Japs in these parts," says Yo.

"Pa's right," says Carl. Carl ain't had much to say to his pa in years, uh-uh. Even Raven stops his cawin', ain't heard Carl's voice in a crane's life. "Them Jap fishermen an' cannery workers is scarce as women up here now," Carl says. "Since they evacuated the single women down to the Lower Forty-eight, the men here have to get themselves wives through a matrimonial agency. It's about the only way you're goin' to get a woman these days"—he laughs nervous-like—"and even then it's risky. Hell, my first mate on the *Blue Pacific* got himself somethin' that looks more like a two-hundred-and-fifty-pound heifer than a mail-order bride from Peoria."

"How was your fish take this year, boy?" asks Yo. I'm wonderin' if Carl knows his dad's been broodin' all summer about the cannery business. Navy made Yo shut down, sayin' his fishin' boats was a menace to defense. "Don't know what the military expects us to eat, if they don't let us fish," says Yo.

"My catch was real bad this year, Pa," says Carl with a seal-pup face on. "Almost went belly up."

"Sorry to hear that, boy," says Yo. "Them Japs sure was good fishermen," he says. I watch him lookin' out into the fog-covered islands, the open box of ash under his arm. "The army done took most of my Jap families to some camp up near Bristol Bay. Hell, one day them Japs was here fishin', and the next day there was boards over their house windows. Signs tacked up on the doors sayin' their property'd been sold, boats and all. Don't recall hearin' 'em talk about movin'," he says. "Not one word."

"Mayor Don way told me that you might be knowin' who bought up their land, Barnett," Yo goes on, still starin' into the tide and out at the mess the soldier boys made of Japonski Island.

"I gave them top dollar," Barnett says, quick as a porcupine about to turn tail. "I gave them top dollar."

"I wonder what them Japs are doin' up in Bristol Bay," says Yo. "I hear tell they got all them fish canneries closed up there too."

Aa, those white humans are herdin' people round like they was caribou. Got the Japs in detention camps, got the Indians and the Eskimos on reservations, got everybody cornered just like *tuttu* they was plannin' for us to eat.

"Daddy," I hear Catherine say as she stares at the Christmaspapered box, "those camps are something none of us are supposed to know or talk about. They had to put the Jap families in camps to protect them. Why, who knows what some drunken powder monkey might do to a Japanese woman thinking it was patriotic duty."

"No one round here heard tell of that land bein' for sale," says Yo, "so it beats the tar outa me how you folks could hear about it way down in Seattle. 'Sides, how am I goin' to operate my cannery again, if there's no Japs to help me fish and can it up?"

"Daddy," says Catherine, "I heard that some of the Japanese cannery workers have been doing espionage for years. One of those Jap spies lived right here in Sitka. They found detailed topographical maps in his possession. Daddy, maybe you've had spies working for *you* at the cannery."

"Get a grip on yourself, girl," I hear Yo say, just like he was givin' orders to those men up at the mill. "This here's your grandmother's funeral. You're supposed to be thinkin' about her—throwin' her ashes out into the water, just like she wanted, and thinkin' about her. . . . Of course those Japs had maps, they was fishermen. Ask your brother there if ya think my mind's rickety. All fishermen gotta have detailed maps. Hell, them Navy boys could do with a few of them maps, and

Jap or Indian sailin' advice too. Some of them soldiers don't act like they ever heard tell of fog or tides. They run them big ships aground 'fore the Japs ever get a chance to take a whang at 'em."

I ain't never heard Yo talk that way to Catherine. Ain't never heard him tell her to listen to her brother Carl neither. Maybe Yo was listenin' to the *saanah* wind last night, just like I was. Wind come into my room with Catherine's voice on—Catherine tellin' Debby she gotta change her clothes before she goes downstairs. Her clothes too tight at the waist, Catherine's wind voice said. "Debra Sue, you remember what happened to you the last time you walked around in skimpy clothing. Lord knows there's enough bad feelings in this family. I don't want you provoking anything by flaunting yourself in front of the relatives, do you hear?" That *saanah* wind had Catherine's voice on most of the night. Yeah. Betcha Yo heard it too.

"By the way." Barnett turns to Yo. "How're things at the mill? General Buckner was hoping to have a load of Sitka spruce from Imperial Lumber for Boeing to build his new fleet of trainer planes. Now I know we all haven't been on the best of terms. But I still feel obliged to see that that lumber gets delivered on time. It would be awfully embarrassing for the family if Alaska was taken by the Japanese."

Yo turns round, puttin' the box of Nadia's ashes in my hands. I watch him go for Barnett's throat, knockin' down one of the poles our tarp is hangin' on. Them Indian women start in again real loud: "Jesus, Savior, help me. *Ay yay yaaaaah.*" Yo backs away, his face redder than the salmon meat up in Bristol Bay. "How the shit do you smart-ass bastards expect me to run a mill when you put all the labor in prison camps? Now, just what the fuck do you want from me, Barnett, you and that *family* of yours?"

Betsy runs over and puts her palms over little Ivan's ears. "Grandpa said the "F" word, Mommy," he says. "I heard it. I heard it." I watch Betsy fidget with her dress. Debby bends down to fix the tarp poles and moves round them poles till she's standing next to her Uncle Carl.

The sky people come thunderin' over again, but I still can't see nothin' up through the rain. "It's the Nazis," screams Catherine. I look at her. If she's so worried about them tribes comin' across the water to get her, why didn't she bring her bundle down here to the beach?

Them soldiers told us we all gotta have bundles, two weeks' clothes and food. If them Nazis or Japs come over the ice from Russia, we's all supposed to take to the hills with our bundles. Always supposed to have your bundle with ya, them soldiers say. Don't know why Catherine didn't bring hers down here to the beach, no sir.

"It's all right, Catherine," says Barnett. "Get a hold on yourself. General Buckner assured me, when I bought up that Jap land, that everything here was safe. 'Well on the road to being an arsenal of democracy,' those were his very words."

I roll Barnett's words round inside my mouth: "Arsenal of democracy, arsenal of democracy." Ain't no magic in those words, uh-uh.

Debby walks over to me with that Ulla face of hers and takes a handful of ashes outa the box. She throws the ashes into the tide. Then I take a handful and throw 'em in too. But the wind blows the ash dust back into our faces. "Sometimes I think you're the sanest one of them all, Tommy," she says to me, hunching her shoulders down so's I don't have to look so far up into her face.

The Indian women are singin' softer now, and I reckon the sky people ain't gonna drop no fire outa the clouds, no, not this time. Yo takes the box of ashes and passes it along to the others. They each throw handfuls into the tide, but only the bits of bone sink into the water. That *saanab* wind blows the ash dust into our clothes and hair. I got Nadia ash all over me. Yeah.

"Nana used to tell me stories when I was a little girl," Debby says to me, and I see that she's got tears on her face. I fumble with the pieces of bone in my hand while she's talkin'. Talks just like Ulla talked. And her hair's all wet from the mist rain and lookin' like water grass. These here pieces of Nadia, some of 'em feel just like them bits of bone and wolf teeth on her mother's necklace. Always feelin' that necklace, uh-huh, always makin' sure it's safe in my parka pouch.

"I remember this one story," Debby says, "about the star that came down out of the sky. The star made a big noise, Nana told me, a big noise and a fire—just like these bombers do now. The stars and the star people used to come down out of the sky all the time, Nana said. Stars came down, stars went up, she used to say. But now the stars don't come any more," says Debby, takin' a heavy breath, "just the bombers...."

"I'll always remember Nana's stories," says Debby. "Don't tell my mother, Tommy, but someday I want to write them all down in a book." I look at the wet ash on Debby's face and fumble with the ash bones that clank like metal in my hand. "What do you have there, Tommy?" she says, brushing the black dust away from her eyes. I show her the pieces of Nadia bone. "What are you going to do with them?" she asks, her eyes as big as them two blue lakes up in the mountains in back of Sitka.

Had my silent face on for a couple of years now, only talk to the animal people. But I don't reckon that Raven'll be upset if I break it for little Debby. "A magic stick," I says. "Gonna make a magic stick. Gotta send Nadia's bladder back to the sea spirit, but they burned her up. Can't tell where in them ashes it's at. Gonna make a magic stick outa these here bones and pray her soul back under the sea."

Debby sifts through a handful of ashes and puts some bits of bone that look like shark's teeth into her coat pocket. "Me too, Tommy," she says, "me too."

I hear Raven start to noise worse than the sky people.

"Look at those big birds, Tommy," Debby whispers to me, pointin' to a dead branch at the top of a spruce tree. *Aa*, ain't been seen in these parts since before Ulla passed over, those birds. And now there they is, four eagles watchin' all our doings, quiet as deer. Raven, he's squawkin' about it louder than he done when that stars-an'-stripes bomber crashed into the bay last week. Just look at them birds, even bigger than I remember.

I look at the eagles and know that this strange-lookin' dust gotta be Nadia's ashes. Them birds wouldn't come back here for no one else. Ain't no other human person besides Nadia that they'd risk bein' shot outa the sky for, no sir. Nadia sure was partial to them birds. Roosted up in her spruce trees, she said, ever since her husband died way back when.

I turn and look at Debby Sue. Slowly, so that no one notices, I take Nadia's mother's necklace outa my parka pouch and put it into her hand, just like it was some Nadia ash. Debby looks down, her eyes glowin' like spirit-of-the-smoke-hole's favorite coals when she recognizes it. "Tommy," she whispers in that Ulla voice of hers. "Thank you, oh, thank you." I watch her run her finger over the curve of one of the wolf fangs. . . .

"Kapow, kapow," says Ivan, shootin' the eagle birds with his pretend finger gun.

Debby moves over next to her Uncle Carl, and they both go to throwin' handfuls of ash into the tide. I see their arms touch each time they throw out the dust, Debby givin' Carl quick shy glances. Carl touches her shoulder. Ain't nobody notices, 'cept me.

Yo shakes the last handful of dust outa the box, heavin' the ash into the water like a bad catch of fish. "Throw 'em all back," he says, and hands me the gold paper. It shines like Sitka Bay in the summer sun, sure does. Carl and Debby standin' in back of me, their faces shinin' in the gold box, like in a mirror. Carl standin' with his arm touchin' Debby's shoulder. Raven knows that ain't no one ever really loved little Debby Sue, ain't no one ever looked at her and seen that she got her own face on. It's bad magic when people do that, *aa*, and I don't know no words, no thoughts that can set it straight. Carl smiles that crow-face grin of his at Debby. She thinks he sees her, but he don't. Don't wanna look no more. Don't wanna see. I heave the empty gold-papered box of Nadia out into the tide. *Throw 'em all back.*

PART V

1959–74

Donna Lee Douglas

SITKA
1959

"Joey Redfish, you gi'me and Kooska a turn on the stickhorse," I yell as he rides the broken broom handle toward Gramma Raven's mobile home. *The loose sole of his shoe flaps thunka thunka in the mud like the noise of horse hooves in a cowboy movie.* "Come on, Kooska, let's get him." I twist a switch from the pear tree, tearin' it like celery, then peel off the leaves.

"Rocks," Kooska says, runnin' toward the graveled driveway. "Let's stone him, Donna Lee." *Her black hair is the same color as Snow White's in my fifth-grade fairy-tale book.*

I watch Joey's two eyes blink off and on beneath the trailer where he's hidden near the car hitch. "Come outa there, Redfish, an' give me and your sister a turn on the stickhorse."

"You throw that rock at me, Kooska, and I'll tell Gramma Raven on ya," he calls from the black murk under the mobile home.

Kooska looks at me, brushin' the rain mist outa her dark face. "We gotta go in after him."

I ain't goin' under there. *That's where bums sleep at night. That's where Mr. York found my Christmas-present kitten, dead with its hair comin' off. Things die under there in the dark, 'cause that's where Gramma says the Ottermonster lives.*

Kooska throws a rock, hittin' the side of the trailer next door. *The clank echoes between the metal houses.*

"Indian, you get outa here," calls Urna McLaren's big brother from inside the screen door. He appears on the porch, carryin' the rifle he's been cleanin'. "You break one of my pop's windows and zap, right between the eyeballs." He shoulders his gun and points it at us.

"She didn't mean nothin'," I tell him.

"Donna Lee?" he calls to me, then shifts his weight from one foot to the other. *His jeans is hung so low on his hips that I wonder if they might fall down. "Don't you got better things to do than play with a dumb Tlingit?"*

"I'll do what I wanna." He gives me an angry look and leans forward. If Urna's brother comes after me, I'll hide under Gramma Raven's trailer with Joey. Ain't as scared of the Ottermonster as I am of Mac McLaren.

He parks his rifle by the door, vaults the porch railin', and picks up a piece of gravel. "Donna Lee, you little hatchet face, you're so ugly that your Ma musta screwed a Indian to get you." The first rock whistles past my ear and hits Kooska's arm.

"What's going on down there?" says a man's voice from up on the highway. I look through the scrub alder and the trailer-park houses to a Stetson hat on top of a sheepskin jacket. I.Y.—Mr. York, our landlord.

"Mac McLaren threw a rock at Kooska," I tell him. His cowboy boots squish through the mud as he walks down the driveway towards me. Kooska stands straight-faced and still, but I can see that her eyes is gettin' red. "Mac threw a rock at Kooska, and Joey won't come out from under the trailer and give us our turn on the stickhorse."

Urna's big brother turns and walks back inside the trailer, slammin' the door.

"Your mother know where you are, Donna Lee?" I.Y. picks me up under his arm, the same way Mac carried his gun. He's as strong as Pop, and while he balances me in the saddle between his ribs and hip, I pretend that I'm a bird flyin' away from Sitka. I.Y. waves at my mom, who's standin' in the kitchen window.

"Has she been playin' with those Indian kids again, Ivan?" The trailer door locks shut behind us. Mom don't usually talk that fast, even when she's mad. I take a deep breath of the boiled-potato air, then move closer to the landlord's leg. He takes told of my hand. As long as I.Y.'s here she won't hit me. "Donna Lee!" Mom scolds. "I've told her, Ivan, I just keep on tellin' her, not to play over at Gramma Raven's. Last year I couldn't get rid of the head lice she caught from them kids to save my life."

I listen to I.Y.'s breathin'. For a while nobody says nothin', probably cause the baby's sick again and Mom's listenin' to see if our voices woke her up.

"Davy's not here," she finally says. I watch Mom's eyes move back and forth faster than her hands fidgetin' with her dress.

"*Thanks for bringin' her home,*" *she says, takin' the potato pot off the stove.* "*Davy should be here any minute now, if ya wanna check back in an hour.*" *She opens the door for I.Y. He tips his hat at us, then slicks down his shiny black hair. Mom holds onto my shoulder, diggin' her red fingernails through my jacket. The screen door bangs shut.*

"*I told you not to play with them kids any more, Donna Lee.*" *She runs to the door.* "*Thanks for gettin' Davy back on at the pulp mill,*" *she calls, wavin' her hand.*

"*Come over here, Donna Lee, and put your head in the sink.*" *She opens the cupboard, reaches for the Wesson Oil.* "*Get your hair into the sink as far as you can, hon. I got enough messes to clean up around here.*" *Her voice whines like the engine of Pop's car when it won't start in the morning, and I know that I could get away from her if I tried. But I don't wanna make her cry again. Last night, even though I did all the dishes, she sat at the kitchen table and bawled till Pop got home from workin' swing shift.* "*Keep still now, Donna Lee.*"

I shut my eyes and wait. How come she's gotta do this? It'll take a week of washin' my hair before my head stops lookin' like a ball of old yarn. And all the kids at school'll tease me:

"*Mop top, mop top,*
Sleep with an Indian
and you'll catch the golly aw-fuls. . . ."

"*If you got any lice from them kids, this'll nip 'em in the bud,*" *she says, as I feel the cold, syrup-thick oil fall over my head. And even though I got my eyes shut real tight, tears fall out of 'em. Mr. York, how come he went away so fast? If he'd stayed I just know Mom wouldn't be doin' this to me.*

26. SITKA
January 1966

I wonder if I could the from bleedin' so much? Can't they hurry up and do the Sitka High basketball fight song, so I can scream without

Bonnie Ostahowski knowin' how crazy I feel? "Hurry up," I moan as I sit on the top row of bleachers, waitin' for my school pep club to burst into a chorus of:

"Turnaround, fadeaway, back shot, in.
Turnaround, fadeaway, back shot, in.
Go-o-o Czars!"

"Hey, Douglas," says Bonnie, jabbin' me in the ribs, then turnin' a pink rose-petal cheek towards me. "Did ya see Joey Redfish's free shot?"

She didn't hear me. Oh, thank you, Lord, thank you. I've just gotta tell Mom about the abortion. I gotta make myself tell her when I get home from school today so that we can figure out a way to pay back Mr. York.

"Holy moly, Douglas, did ya see the Animal make that basket?" asks Bonnie. "He's such a hunk I can't even look at him without turnin' on like a leaky faucet. What if he asks me out for the Anchorage Winter Carnival? I'll pee my pants. Do ya think he noticed my new bubble cut? How 'bout the blond streak, what'd ya think of my blond streak?"

Please Bonnie, I say under my breath, *just shut up for five seconds. Just sit next to me and don't talk about nothin'. I've got to think this through again.*

You can't thread a movin' needle, that's what everybody says about sex. I didn't really believe you could get pregnant from just doin' that! And Bob told me he always used Trojans, that nothin' could happen. Well, it did. And I didn't wanna end up an unwed welfare mother like Urna McLaren. Or like Mom, married when she was sixteen, livin' in a mobile home for the rest of her life. No, I wanted to win that college scholarship, so I could get off the Rock and outa Sitka. That's why I told I.Y. I knew that if there was anyone in this world who could help me, it'd be him. I still have all the over-sized dolls he gave me for Christmas on my bed at home. Besides, I'd been prayin' all summer that I'd get chosen to play Princess Maksoutov in the October Transfer Ceremonies up on Castle Rock, 'cause then I.Y. would notice I was a grown-up woman. And when he offered me a ride home after the pageant I told him . . . that I thought I was p.g.

"The last time I talked to you, Doni D., you told me all you and Bob Knutsen did on your dates was kiss," he said after we drove his pickup to the top of Harbor Mountain Road and parked in front of one of the eight-sided sheds that his Grandfather Yo built durin' the war. I watched the dimple line in his cheek deepen as he reached for the radio knob and switched off Roy Orbison's "Mean Woman Blues."

"Bob doesn't even know yet," I said weakly, "because he left last week, on that crew that's pilotin' your Louisiana shrimper up here to Southeast."

Ivan's face turned red. He twisted his weddin' ring and stared over my head, down at all the wooded islands in Sitka Sound.

"Does Davy know about this?" he asked, and I noticed that his broad fisherman's shoulders were hunched forward.

"N-no, I ain't told Mom and Pop nothin'." I avoided his eyes, and looked down at the bay, thinkin' that Gramma Raven once told me those islands was whales who got beached in a storm.

"I ought to have Officer Ostahowski lock up that Knutsen bastard the minute he pulls into port." Ivan gritted his teeth. "Or have someone take him out back, butt-fuck him and show him where it's at."

I cringed at the anger in Ivan's voice. "No," I protested, "then Bonnie's father would find out. Everyone in Sitka'd know."

I remember how I.Y. put his arm around my shoulder. That must have been when I started cryin'. He pulled me across the gear box, huggin' me close. I moved to pull my skirt down over my thigh, and my elbow accidentally knocked open the glove compartment. I.Y.'s Colt forty-five fell on the floor, bruisin' my toe, and I bawled like a little kid.

"You look just like your mother did when she was your age," he said, tryin' to take my mind off cryin'. "I've known your family a long time, Doni D. Hell, I was the one who introduced your mom to Davy. He and I were hunting buddies before . . . before I went off to school in Seattle."

I smelled the aroma of his Jade East, thinkin' that if I ever got married, I'd want someone just like Ivan York—head of a big corporation, but strong and rugged as well. Not a man like those sissy junior executives who are always visitin' Sitka from Seattle, wearin' ties, white shirts, and three-piece suits.

"If I help you, Donna," he said in a stern voice, "you have to give me your word you won't see that Knutsen boy any more."

I nodded my head. He took out his handkerchief and wiped my eyes.

I'd never heard the word abortion before, and I sure didn't know it was goin' to hurt so much. I'd told I.Y. that I'd pay him back some day, after I got outa college and had a job, other than workin' in his fish cannery, but he'd just shook his head. "It's not the money," he'd said, kissin' me on the cheek. "You'll be able to do something for me some day."

Bonnie jostles my shoulder, yelling as Joey Redfish aims the ball at the orange hoop and scores again.

"We're the fighting Bears of Kodiak,
We stand when others fall."

"Big Bert's wavin' to ya, Douglas," says Bonnie with a smile so wholesome lookin' that she could pose for a toothpaste ad. "God, he must be six-three if he's an inch. Douglas, whatsamatter with you? How come ya didn't try out for basketball rally again insteada workin' for Mrs. Taggart on that stupid yearbook?"

DONNA LEE DOUGLAS: Activities: Varsity Basketball Rally; Yearbook Staff; Honor Roll. Favorite Pastime: writing all the sports news to Private "Butcher" Bob Knutsen. Future Plans: College at the University of Washington. Honors: The Catherine Zimmerman Young Alaskan Women's Scholarship.

DONNA LEE DOUGLAS: Activities: thinking about suicide. Favorite Pastime: screwing around with one man while being in love with another. Ambition: husband-stealing and general whoring around. Honors: going to Seattle for an abortion.

"Douglas!"

Oh, God, Bonnie, I wanna say, please don't make me talk. I just gotta tell Mom about my "operation" tonight. I have to make myself do it.

"You gettin' your period or somethin? Ya got cramps? Come on, ya want me to go with ya to the can?"

"No, Bonnie, honest, I'm okay," I say, tryin' to smile. Maybe she knows. Maybe they all know, maybe they can see it. Bob Knutsen always said that girls look different afterwards. "I'm okay, Bonnie, honest."

God, how come Gramma Raven had to the last winter? She'd help me get rid of this awful feelin'. Didn't I once hear her say that eatin' yew berries was how Indian women got rid of babies they didn't want to have? Or was that what they ate to keep from gettin' pregnant? I.Y. even flew up here from Seattle for Gramma Raven's funeral, 'cause she'd been his grandfather's housekeeper till he died. Mrs. Stephan, that's what I.Y. always called her. For a wealthy Anglo, he sure has a lot of respect for Indians.

"Douglas," says Bonnie, "you look like a cold turd on a paper plate. Whatsamatter, Butcher Bob hasn't written to ya? What if he finds another girl? So what? You got that scholarship. All those college men, makes me drool. I wish I was as smart as you, Douglas—gettin' straight A's in advanced math. But if I was you, I'd go to modelin' school. You're real photogenic with that dark-red hair and high cheekbones, real high-fashion, and that's what they like."

"I got a letter from Bob yesterday." For a minute Bonnie's praise makes me feel like I'm sittin' near a fireplace on a cold day. Then I wonder if I.Y. would be mad if he knew I was writin' to Bob.

"Oh, yeah, Douglas? Where's he now, huh?"

"Some place called Vietnam."

"Veet what? Crud, where's that? You keepin' line scores like Coach Shyves asked ya to?"

Lemme alone. Please everybody, just lemme alone. "Yeah, what *was* that, a field goal?" I ask, tryin' to sound interested.

"An attempt, Douglas, an attempt. Ya need glasses or somethin'? Attempts, rebounds, assists, fouls. Ya oughta know by now. . . . Crud, look at that Kodiak guard block Joey Redfish. Looks like a refrigerator on roller skates. Douglas, look at that dude. What a hunk. That was a foul on number seven. Ya got that marked down? Douglas, where ya goin'?"

"I've gotta go to the can. See ya at the Dock Shack after the game, okay?" I climb down the bleachers, not waitin' for her to answer.

"Douglas, what about the line scores?"

Cram the line scores.

Walkin' along Front Street's rain-wet sidewalk, I open the storm door of the Dock Shack. The pilings that hold up the narrow, weathered building have sunk unevenly into the bay, so like most of the businesses along the marina, the Dock Shack looks like a stubby one-story version of the Leanin' Tower of Pizza.

"A double cheeseburger and some bloody fingers on the side, Kooska." I smile at the short-order cook, takin' a breath of the warm grease-thick air. What am I doin' in here, anyway? Oh God, there's Bonnie and the Animal sittin' at the Dock Shack's *seniors only* table. I wish Ivan was here. He hasn't called me since. . . .

"Douglas," Bonnie yells to me, "we won seventy-six to seventy!"

Come on, Donna Lee, socialize—force yourself. It's the only way you're goin' to stop feelin' so terrible. "Mom wants me home early tonight, Bon. She's got a T.O.P.S. installation dinner, and Pop's workin' night shift at the mill, so I gotta stay with Sicky Vicky." Besides, I think to myself, Ivan might call me. Just to see if I'm okay. I've been bleedin' for a month now, but I think I finally stopped. I don't wanna be here, I wanna be at home listenin' for the telephone to ring.

"Crud, Douglas, when we graduate we're gettin' outa this hole. I don't wanna end up married to some pulp-mill worker, tryin' to diet off my turkey wattles at some ol' Take Off Pounds Sensibly club for the rest of my life. I'm goin' to Anchorage Business College and then get me a legal secretary's job Outside, down in Seattle. Maybe marry a lawyer. Ma says that legal secretaries get paid the best. Just think, Douglas, we can have our own apartment together."

Sure, Bonnie, I say to myself, if I live till next week. . . . Oh, God, here comes hog-jowl Bert Dysokar, starin' right at my tits. I'm goin' to get sick. His lips look just like raw liver. How come I always get stuck with the creeps?

"Hi, Bert," I say, tryin' to sound cheerful. "Nice game."

"Hi, Douglas," he says still starin' at my chest, "whatcha hear from the Butcher? Christ, Donna, did ya see that last play? I got this break, see, and the Animal got a rebound." The Animal grunts, knocks over his chair gettin' up from the table, and heads for the men's room.

"That's real good, Bert." 'Course I didn't see you, I was busy tryin' to get up the nerve to tell my mother about my abortion, so we can figure out how to pay Ivan York back. God, what if Bert asks me out? What if he tries to touch me? "Got a letter from Bob yesterday. Said to say *hello* to ya, Bert."

"Yeah, Bert," says Bonnie, combin' her blond streak with her Pink Heaven polished nails. Maybe she'll lend me her nail polish for the Winter Carnival. Betcha Ivan would fall in love with me then. If he shows up, that is. "Yeah, Bert," says Bonnie again, glancin' over at the boys' bathroom, lookin' for the Animal. "Bob's over in Veet Weet, or somewheres. I think Donna's feelin' bad about him bein' so far from home. So you all be nice to her, hear?"

"Vietnam," I say.

"Shit," says Bert, movin' his eyes back and forth from my tits to Bonnie's bigger ones. "Douglas, did Bob say what he was totin'? An M-sixteen automatic? Oh, would I like to get my hands on one of those babies. *Bam-bam-bam.* Those mothers take the whole sport outa things, make it too easy. What'd he say about the women over there, Douglas? Ha, ha, just jokin'."

"Come on, Bert," says Bonnie in her little girl's voice. "Don't joke about Bob. Donna hasn't seen him since last fall."

"Jesus," says Bert, pointin' his liver lips at me, "no sex for four months. No wonder you've been in such a piss-poor mood lately."

Oh, God, he knows. They all know. They can see it in my face. Bonnie, how come I can't tell you about my real feelin's? I don't give a shit about Butcher Bob, I want I.Y. And how am I goin' to tell Mom tonight? Which words should I start out with? Mrs. Taggart says that I'm real good at explanations in my journalism writin', so there must be some way to break it to her. Like, "I don't wanna upset you, Mom, but I had to have an emergency operation. . . ."

"Bert," asks Bonnie, "what happened to the Animal? I thought he went to take a leak."

"Probably out back changin' his oil," he answers. "Douglas, you on the rag or somethin'? Let me tell ya, Donna," Bert says, admirin' the big red *S* on his letterman's jacket. "This Kodiak guard was breathin' down my neck. I jumped, backed off, and flipped up the shot. *That* was one hell of a turnaround fadeaway."

Shut up, Bert. God, I can't stand this any longer. I gotta get outa here. Maybe I should tell 'em that Mrs. Taggart wants me to work on the yearbook.

"Douglas," says Bert, givin' me a hurt look, "you listenin'? You followin' all this? Where ya goin'?"

"Be nice to her, she don't feel so good," says Bonnie in a motherly tone.

"Whatsamatter with her, ain't had it in four months?" asks Bert, loud enough so that everyone in the Dock Shack can hear. I put my arm through my raincoat sleeve. God, they're all lookin' at me. There must be a thousand eyes in here burnin' holes through my back.

I step out into Front Street and the constant rain. Rain. Can't it stop for just a day? I look up through the fog towards the center of town and the gold onion dome on the Church of Saint Michael. Jeez, sometimes the chimin' of those bells is the best part of my day. Five o'clock. Listen, Donna Lee, the bell tower's ringin' off another hour that you've managed to stay alive. Hard to believe—I'm sixteen, may not make it to my birthday next month, and that tiny gray and white church is more than a hundred years old.

I take a deep breath and my nose fills with the damp smell of seaweed, creosote, and diesel fumes from the fishin' boats. As the bells of the Russian church chime the melody of some Slovakian song, they almost drown the chainsaw and bulldozer noise of the loggers and construction workers in back of town. Maybe if I could just see the sky for once this winter, then I wouldn't feel so bad. Maybe if it didn't get dark at three o'clock. If I.Y.'d call me, then I'd feel better again, I just know I would.

Crossin' Lincoln Street, I walk up Kat-lee-an Lane. I.Y. was so good to me after I told him about my *problem*. "This doctor down in Seattle'll fix you up," he said. "Don't worry. It might hurt a little, sure, everything good hurts a little. You've never been to Seattle? Well, maybe I could get you into college down there next year. That way I can keep an eye on you, you pretty little thing. You stay away from the boys now, understand? It's just a little operation, be over in nothing flat. Sure, I'll call you before I fly up to Anchorage for the Winter Carnival Fur Rendezvous. Don't worry, it's nothing."

As I walk up the hill through the rain-mist, the seiners out in the bay blow their lonesome foghorns, soundin' like a Billie Holiday blues record. But how am I goin' to pay I.Y. back, I wonder? He said not to worry about the money.

The muddy street steepens and narrows as Kat-lee-an Lane rises above town, windin' through the white clapboard houses, their eaves drippin' with rain, their front-yard spruce trees the same dark cough-syrup green as Three Sisters Peaks. Somewhere a raven calls out the comin' of high tide, and sea gulls chatter in their naggin' voices, sendin' sharp pains through my temples. Huh, you'd think that after swallowin' all those aspirin last night that my headache would at least go away.

Davy & Emma Douglas
#5 Old York Homestead Mobile Home Court

No mail. Well, I.Y.'d never write to me anyway.

I walk down the graveled driveway and stop for a moment in front of Gramma Raven's deserted trailer. Pieces of peelin' pink paint have blown like dogwood flowers over her cluttered yard, and someone's used the Shaker crucifix above her doorway as a target for rifle practice. I never understood why Indians put all their furniture in the front yard, summer and winter. The rain-soaked couch smells like mildew, and the raven pole guardin' the walkway to her front stoop looks sad, like it misses the aroma of Gramma smokin' salmon in the converted outhouse in back of her trailer.

I stoop down and break off a piece of horsetail grass, pullin' its segments apart and suckin' out the water. Gramma Raven always said that horsetail grass was good for your blood. God, I hope I've finally stopped bleedin'. . . .

Jeez, is that bulldozer noise loud. "Looks like Bert Dysokar's bald-headed father at the wheel," I think out loud as I watch the yellow dozer flatten another piece of the old York homestead for a new trailer berth. What a mess, rain and mud. Just think, Donna Lee, I fantasize, if you married Ivan York then this trailer park would all belong to you. I smile to myself, rememberin' that next year when I'm at college, I'll be workin' for I.Y. at the Imperial Lumber office in Seattle.

Ah, Mom, do ya gotta sit in the kitchen window with your hair in rollers all day? Hmm, the Chevy's here, she must have already taken Pop to work at the mill. We'll be alone, so I can tell her . . . if I could just think of the right words to start off with. Crud, is that her Bible that she's lookin' at, or is she countin' her green-stamp books again?

"Hi," I say, slammin' the metal door of the trailer.

"Hello, dear." She rests her elbow on the chrome and Formica table of the tiny kitchen. As usual Mom's wearin' her old blue-chenille bathrobe, and her overweight face is greasy with moisturizin' cream. "Quiet now, Vicky Lynn's resting. How was the basketball game? Must not be so much fun now that Bob's in the service. . . . Donna Lee? The girls' dean called me today, said you missed classes all week. Asked me if there was some kind of emergency at home. You been talkin' to someone about your daddy's drinkin'? You goin' to school and tellin' family secrets, hon? If word gets 'round, he could get laid off again, and not even Mr. York'll be able to get him his job back."

"No, Mom, I never say nothin'," I answer. Mom, I wanna say, will you just shut up for a second and listen to me? Will you just stop talkin' about Pop and Sicky Vicky and put down your Bible and listen? Mom, I wanna kill myself. I did somethin' awful, you'll never forgive me. I wanna die. Mom, can't you hear me, please?

"Where you been insteada in class?" she says as her frown lines deepen. "You can't get to college skippin' classes, hon."

I've been thinkin' about swallowin' a bottle of aspirin. I blew it, Mom. I'm a slut, a damaged woman, and if I tell you, you'll hate me. . . . "I've been workin' real hard on the yearbook," I say out loud. "Helpin' Mrs. Taggart plan the layout for pictures of the big game at the Anchorage Fur Rendezvous. I'll get those cut classes excused, Mom. Honest. Want me to unroll your hair and comb it out? It's not good to leave it rolled up for more than two days in a row."

"No, hon, just sit down here and I'll get ya a piece of diet crumb cake. Kept it frozen from my T.O.P.S. meetin' last week especially for after-school snacks for you and Vicky Lynn."

"No thanks. I ain't hungry, my stomach feels kinda upset." I avoid her glance by starin' at the news clippings taped to the refrigerator door. Next to the *Saturday Evening Post* cover of two hands prayin' are almost every *Sitka Times* article ever printed about the York family. A black and white picture of Nadia and the codger who started the whole clan, Noah. The article attached to it tells all about Mrs. Nadia York's royal Russian heritage, and sayin' that Noah was one of the first American pioneers in Russian Alaska. I stare at the most recent news-clip, a picture of me acceptin' the Catherine York Zimmerman scholarship at the high school awards banquet, and an article about Mrs. Zimmerman's Alaska Anthropological collection at the University of Washington. I can feel Mom watchin' me. I blink and my eyes focus on a year-old editorial, speculatin' that if Ivan York moved his permanent residence from Seattle to Alaska, he'd make a crackerjack senator. "A man who has zoomed this state to top production in the construction business is the economic tonic we need in Washington, D.C.," the editor wrote.

I remember how Gramma Raven always talked about Nadia, just as if she was still livin' and Gramma was keepin' house for her. Sometimes Mrs. Stephan heard Nadia's voice in the wind, and she'd leave a bowl of bear-paw stew with *oogruk* seal oil on the kitchen table for Nadia's spirit. "Was her favorite dinner," Gramma always said, as she took hold of one of the old woven baskets which filled her trailer's livin' room. "Mother-of-Stories made this for Nadia long time ago," Gramma said, strokin' the blue and green glass beads that hung from a sphere-shaped basket. "And the old canoe," Gramma would say, pointin' to a decayed cedar log in her front yard near the raven pole, "that's what she paddled down Indian River every day to sort fish at the cannery. Same cannery where you and Urna work in the summer. . . ."

"Now you keep your attendance up, Donna Lee," Mom says, closin' her Bible and beginnin' to count her green-stamp books. "I don't want you gettin' your father worried and takin' it out in the bottle again. It was real God-lovin' of that foreman of the Jap pulp mill to let your daddy come back on the line. There's not much work available, and we just gotta start catchin' up on Vicky Lynn's asthma bills."

How come you can't look at me and tell that I'm sick, Mom? I wanna ask her. Ever had an abortion? It hurts like hell. Probably hurts more than when Pop gets drunk and starts swingin' his wine bottle at you, hurts more than any black eye you ever had. And nobody bought me any ice cream like they always do for Vicky Lynn when she's sick.

How could I have let Butcher Bob touch me when all the time I was thinkin' of Ivan? And I remember the way he looked at me, the way he put his arm around me after we left that abortionist in Seattle. I'm no little girl to him any more.

"Look here, Donna Lee," Mom says, holdin' up a newspaper clippin'. "I cut this out from the 'Points from Paula' column for you. Know how you've been complainin' about that new bra that's so tight? Well, a new bra's always hard to break in. But see here, this lady wrote to Paula, tellin' her that if you save your old powder puffs and slide one of 'em under your bra hooks, it'll stop it from pinchin' and you've got that new bra broken in in no time. I'm goin' to dig around in the bathroom an' find one for you, soon as Vicky Lynn wakes up. . . . What's the matter, hon? Don't you turn your nose up at Paula's column now. Someday when you're a wife and mother she'll be a comfort to you, too."

"Thanks, Mom," I say, tryin' not to sound too sarcastic. Mom, it's a padded bra. You'd the if you knew that I had a padded bra. I stole it from the Mode-O-Day dress shop, broke the seventh commandment. I don't even need to wear a bra, Mom. I stole it to wear to the Alaska Day transfer pageant, 'cause I thought it would make I.Y. notice me more than usual. I *had* to talk to him, Mom. And, if you'd just listen, I have to talk to you too. I have to tell you. There's gotta be some way I can pay Mr. York back. He said it wasn't the money, but that I could do somethin' for him someday. He's never touched me *that* way, so I know he doesn't want sex. What does he want from me? I'm in love with him, Mom. I'm in love with a married man.

"You gettin' the flu, babe? Your cheeks don't have the color they should," she says, lickin' a sheet of green stamps. "We can get ya a flu shot free over at your daddy's pulp mill. Want me to drive you over there tomorrow when I take him to work?"

"No, Mom, them pulp fumes smell so terrible. Yesterday I had to leave French class, 'cause they was comin' through the furnace vent and makin' me sick." I watch Bert Dysokar's bald-headed father shift gears and maneuver the bulldozer up an incline outside the kitchen window.

"Donna Lee, you got more excuses than a fish got scales," she says, cuttin' herself a slice of diet crumb cake. "Them fumes don't hurt nobody. And that mill's two miles from here, now how's the smell goin' to float into your French-class furnace vent? The mill foreman just wants us to drive through the car wash 'cause them fumes has a bad effect on metal, not people. Besides, hon, if them Japs hadn't built that mill here, your daddy'd be out of a job again. Not havin' a job makes Davy feel like he's not a man. Almost as bad for him as losin' his religion. And what with all of Vicky Lynn's doctor bills . . ."

That whimperin' brat. Little Miss Never-Do-Wrong. Mom just likes her best, 'cause she's blond and looked like Shirley Temple when she was little.

"The Lord works in mysterious ways, Donna Lee," she says, takin' the last bite of cake and scrapin' her fork across the plate. "Yes, He does. The Lord gave your daddy and me little Vicky Lynn 'cause He chose us to take care of one of His more fragile creatures. We're all born wrong, Donna Lee. Some of us show it and some of us don't. We're all born wicked. That's why we gotta pray to Him and read His word. We all got that sin born in us."

I love you, but prayin's not goin' to make me better, Mom. I got somethin' to tell you. I had to do it. I didn't wanna end up like you, livin' in a metal trailer and sleepin' on an ol' mattress, the holes where the stuffin's come out all filled up with Kotex. . . . Jeez, that bulldozer noise is so loud that I can hardly think. . . . Or like Urna McLaren, with a baby, on welfare when she's not workin' summers at the fish cannery.

I look out the window at the raven totem pole next door in front of Mrs. Stephan's deserted trailer. If I stay around this crummy town, I won't have a chance in hell of makin' somethin' outa my life. The only woman who ever did anythin' here other than have babies and be married to a fisherman or millworker was Nadia York. I glance back at the newspaper picture of Nadia taped on the refrigerator door. I'd sure be pretty if I had them Russian eyes, I think, slantin' my lids with my two forefingers. "Donna look like Nadia a little," Gramma used to say. "And wise woman like her too." For a moment I recall my childhood, playin' grown-ups with Joey Redfish and Kooska. I always got to be Nadia, boss of the cannery and lumber mill. We'd collect pieces of cordwood, pretendin' they was salmon we was sortin' and gradin'. "Throw that one back," I'd yell to Joey. . . .

I take a deep breath and open my mouth, but the words don't come out: I had to do it, Mom. I had to get rid of that baby, so I could go to college and make somethin' outa my life.

"A man from the pulp mill came to school yesterday to talk to the seniors about jobs," I say, hopin' that if I change the conversation subject from Mom's religion to work, I'll get up courage. "I didn't know they made cellophane outa wood pulp. I didn't know that's what Pop does."

"Sometimes that's what he does, hon," she says, turnin' to the Psalms. "That mill down in Ketchikan where your daddy used to work? They made rayon there. Didn't smell near as bad at the Ketchikan Jap mill. But, ya know, I think that's where Vicky Lynn started havin' such bad attacks."

"Anyway, the man from the pulp mill said that there'd be some summer jobs, mainly just for boys unless ya could take shorthand and type and use a Dictaphone. So I guess I'll work in the fish cannery or cook on one of them fishin' boats like Bonnie and Urna and I did last summer."

"See what I mean about takin' a shorthand class before you go to college, Donna Lee? Now, if I'd just finished business school. . . ."

God, I don't wanna work in that fish cannery again. Betcha I've bled more than all them fish I cleaned last summer. I'm so sick of the smell of blood that I'll never be able to go near the cannery again.

"That Ivan York's been awful good about givin' you a job, hon. Awful good," she says, lookin' up from her Bible. "Why, when he called last night, he was so impressed to hear that you'd gone to Seattle with the Sitka High Model UN for the Christmas convention."

"He called, Mom?" I almost shout. "You didn't tell me Ivan called." Oh, thank you, Lord, thank you. He called. God, I wonder how many other times he's called and I wasn't here? Maybe he does love me after all.

"Wanted to make sure you was keepin' up with your studies," she says with a serious look. "Said that Model UN trip must have been one of the reasons you won his aunt's college scholarship. He kept tellin' me over an' over how well you played Princess Maksoutov in the Alaska Day pageant. . . ."

"Mom, how come you didn't tell me Ivan called?" I ask, almost glad that she still believes I went to Seattle for a Model UN meetin' instead of an abortion.

"Well," she says, "I just did, didn't I? And he said that it was a good thing Bob Knutsen wasn't around this year so you could buckle down and study hard." I watch her lips move as she finishes readin' the Sixty-Ninth Psalm, her favorite. "Ivan York's a lonely man," she continues. "That's why he calls your daddy and me all the time. I guess it's his marriage. His Aunt Catherine arranged it for him, you know." Her words fade into the bulldozer roar outside. "And he's always fightin' with his cousin Charles over the family businesses. Ivan oughta move back up here and run for governor," she adds with a new energy in her voice. "Then there'd be lots of jobs for everybody."

"Did Ivan say he was goin' to be up in Anchorage at the Fur Rendezvous?" I ask anxiously.

"Let me see. I was right in the middle of my dessert recipe," she says with a far-off look in her eye. "Diet cherry cola with gelatin and Cool Whip, so rich and hardly ten calories a square. It's T.O.P.S. charm-bracelet night, hon, and I'm gettin' a charm for my diet desserts."

Mom, I whisper under my breath, *I had an abortion. Ivan helped me. That's why I was in Seattle during Christmas vacation.*

"Oh," she says, turnin' to Matthew, "you know who's comin to our T.O.P.S. dinner tonight, hon? Urna McLaren. Guess she wants to take off some weight after the baby. Sure looks part Indian, that baby girl, cute as the devil, though. Wasn't she a year ahead of you in school? Well, I don't know if we'll vote her into our chapter. . . . Guess it wouldn't be God-lovin' not to, poor thing. It's hard for a woman to go through life in her situation. . . ."

Shut up, Mom, I want to scream. Will you and that bulldozer outside just shut up for once and listen to me? It's me and Urna all the way, Mom. We're two of a kind, soiled and ruined. What would you do if you knew that, Mom? What would you do if you knew that a soiled and ruined girl shared the same bed with your precious little Vicky Lynn? What would you do if you knew that the blood for an illegitimate baby that some doctor scraped out of me got on my p.j.'s at night and touched innocent Sicky Vicky? What would you do if you knew that, Mom?

God, that dozer noise is makin' my headache worse. What's it knockin' over this time? Holy—

"Donna Lee," Mom says, lookin' concerned, "why you cryin', hon? You gettin' little Susie this week? I thought you had little Susie last week."

"No, Mom, it's not my period," I say, as Bert Dysokar's father rams Gramma Raven's front-yard totem pole with his dozer and knocks it over. . . .

You can't thread a movin' needle, that's what Mom would say if I told her I got pregnant. She'd tell me that it was all my fault. God, I can't wait to go to college so that I can get outa this town.

I wipe the tears out of my eyes and glance out the kitchen window at Gramma Raven's trailer. That totem pole didn't have a chance in hell.

27. SEATTLE
1968

Glancing up from my journalism book, I look over Rick Howard's mop of curly red hair and stare nervously at the Mickey Mouse hands on the Giant Burger clock. Only another half hour before I go back to the sorority house to get ready for my dinner date with Ivan, and then a visit to his family mansion.

"Hey, man, could I interest you in a monorail ride over to the World's Fair space needle before our Sigma Nu kegger on Friday night?" asks Rick, as he wipes a dab of hamburger grease from his blue monogram cashmere sweater.

"No thanks," I reply, eyeing his broad nose and freckles through the ice in my empty Coca-Cola glass. Jeez, no matter how I look at Rick, I can't pretend he's Ivan. I.Y.'d never use all that hair oil. Besides, Rick doesn't shut up long enough to chew his food. And if I have to look at the mayonnaise inside his mouth much longer, I'm going to puke.

But Rick Howard does have his good points. All he seems to want from me is someone to talk to. He's never even tried to put his arm around me, not like those other frat guys who want to find out right away if you're going to sleep with them. And if you're not, then they want to know who your father is and how much money he makes. . . . Why can't it be Ivan who puts the make on me? I've been working, supplementing my scholarship, at his Imperial Lumber office for almost two years, and until now all he's done is take me out to lunch; asks me about my studies, my boyfriends—my love life, he calls it. I sigh, remembering how I.Y. always hugs me good-bye, then pats me on the fanny as I get out of the car. He's never once mentioned repaying him for my abortion. But when I told him that I was still writing to Bob Knutsen overseas, Ivan got so upset I thought he was going to walk out of the restaurant and leave me there alone.

I watch Rick chew his hamburger, picking out the pieces of pickle and putting them on the side of his plate. It must mean something that Ivan's finally asked me out to dinner and then to his family mansion. The latest rumor at the office is that his marriage is on the rocks again and his wife's divorcing him. Maybe that's why he's finally asked me out, to tell me he's a free man.

"Too bad," says Rick, sitting back in the orange-vinyl Giant Burger booth and glancing out the storefront window at his silver Corvette double-parked on University Avenue. "The Sigma Nu kegger's going to be a blast. If it doesn't rain driving downtown to the monorail, we could take the top off the Vette and wind her little V-eight engine from zero to sixty, just going down the freeway on-ramp! Back home in Jersey, the girls at Pennington Academy would consider it the climax of their weekend if I offered them a ride down the turnpike. Ah, come on, Donna, say *yes*—talk about a treat."

It's *talk* with an *l*, Rick, not *tawk* with a *w*, I think to myself, wondering how this guy gets straight *A*'s in journalism. On my last day of school at Sitka High, Mrs. Taggart gave me a copy of Dale Carnegie's *How to Win Friends and Influence People,* and told me that if I was going to do well in college, I'd have to start talking in standard English, not slang. "Keep your conversations short at first, Donna," Mrs. Taggart told me with a smile. "You wouldn't want to turn anyone against you just because you said something wrong."

"So, Donna," says Rick, "I had a little talk with the Vette last night, and we decided on how to structure my investigative-reporting senior project."

"That's nice." *This guy talks to his car?*

"The Vette and I decided to do my project on cancer." He wipes the french-fry catsup from his hands and raises one bushy carrot-colored eyebrow at me. "This university has one of the largest research facilities this side of Johns Hopkins."

I close my eyes, thinking of what it would be like to make love to Ivan. Rick reaches across the table, touching my hand. I flinch at the thought of kissing Mr. Mayonnaise Mouth.

"I'm going to focus on sensationalism in cancer research," says Rick, scratching the pimple on his chin. "When I was a little kid, my favorite grandmother died of liver cancer. It was god-awful. We used to go visit her once a week at the county hospital, watching her get yellower and yellower. I thought I could get more people interested in supporting cancer research if I wrote an article from a sensationalist point of view. And Donna, this project's got mass-market appeal. I mean, did you know that biochemists use things like fresh baboon carcasses in their work? Let me show you, I've got a copy of an animal biological-supply catalog right here." He fumbles through the books in his attaché case. "Really, man, do you know how much bread a biologist has to pay for a fresh baboon carcass?"

"No idea," I say, as I tally Ivan's handsome face, his wealth, and the fact that he's almost twenty years older and wiser than I am, against Rick, the son of a New Jersey garment worker—Rick who's more interested in humanitarianism and investigative journalism than in making money, and whose sole possession is a silver Corvette Stingray.

"And that's only the beginning," says Rick, drawling his vowels like a street hood in a gangster movie. "Those cancer-research biochemists use snake venom, newt eyes, rat piss, and even freeze-dried fire-fly tails!" he says, swallowing a bite of hamburger whole. "See. Here, Donna," he shoves the catalog in front of my face, "they order it all. And get this—for an ounce of snake venom, a hundred bucks! Christ, I could get the Vette a set of platinum spark plugs for that kind of money."

"Really?" I say, trying to imagine Rick and I living together—probably in a trailer just like Mom and Pop's. Rick would go off to work every day to his job as a newspaper copy editor while I'd sit home, reading *Family Circle* magazine, trying to think up budget dinners so that we could make ends meet. Donna Lee, I tell myself, if you want to make something out of your life, then marriage to a poor student isn't in the stars for you, that's for sure.

"But I can see you sitting there asking yourself, 'All right already, Rick; so a cancer researcher orders strange animal parts out of a catalog, but what does he do with them?' Well, I'll tell you. . . ."

Then I think of Ivan's family's Capitol Hill mansion and his stone lodge on one of the Sitka Sound islands. I'd have a maid and my own car right from the beginning if I married Ivan York. None of this scrimping and saving for ten years, just so we could buy a trailer. And no lonely nights of being a single girl-reporter in some city like Fairbanks, I tell myself, recalling a job-interview schedule I'd seen posted on the journalism-department bulletin board.

"See," says Rick, "scientists grow these cancer tumors in rats, and then they sprinkle the tumors with a little snake venom here and a little rat piss there. *Poof.* Sometimes things happen. That's an extremely watered-down version of the scientific process, you understand, but you get the point. Fascinating, don't you think? I just wonder if I should market it to *Scientific American* or the *New York Times?*"

"I dunno."

"It's a sure *A* for my senior project," says Rick. "In the pocket, ol' Professor Cushman told me. He's really keen on my—"

Rat piss and snake venom? Sounds like the medicine remedies Gramma Raven told me about when I was a little girl.

"And," says Rick, not even noticing me watch the Giant Burger clock, "those biologists use radioactivity. You know, the stuff in uranium. That's how they give the rats cancer in the first place, by zapping some critter with a little radiation." Rick eyes his double-parked car through the window. "Ol' Cushman's so excited about my project that . . . Where're you going, Donna? Listen, this next part's really exciting."

I doubt it. Even though I haven't read Rick's article, I can tell that it doesn't have a life of its own. I like to write the kind of journalism that tells a story, has a plot just like reading a novel.

"I have to leave now," I tell him as politely as possible, "or I'll be late for an appointment."

"Well, gee," he says, looking hurt, "can the Vette and I offer you a lift back to the house?"

"Sure," I answer, lowering my eyes and practicing a coy look for my "big date" with Ivan.

I wave good-bye to Rick as a group of pledges all dressed up in rag costumes slam the giant glass and wrought-iron door of the brick sorority house on their way to a prisoner-of-war theme party.

> "Iota Chi, I love you truly,
> Truly I love Iota Chi. . . ."

Only another hour before Ivan picks me up, I think as I dash up the red-carpeted spiral stairway to my room, making sure my best blouse is pressed and smells laundry clean. I didn't really want to join a sorority, and even though I've been living here two years, I still don't feel like I fit in; but my Catherine York Zimmerman scholarship wouldn't pay my college room and board unless I pledged Iota Chi.

I check my mirror image before I go downstairs to the study room to wait for Ivan. Still the thinnest girl in the house, I smile at myself, rolling my pleated blue skirt up at the waist so that it hangs an inch above my knees.

Sitting at one of the long oak tables next to Martha and Joyce, I take two of my journalism books out of my book bag. I don't believe it, I've finally been invited to Ivan's family mansion. Maybe it's a small get-together, or maybe Ivan has something special to tell me—I.Y. was in such a rush at work yesterday he didn't say.

"I just don't know about this hippie independent movement on campus," says Martha, buttoning the top button of her Lanz Original study robe so that it frames her sculptured curls and Greek-goddess face. She cautiously examines a mangled diamond- and ruby-studded Iota Chi sorority pin, looking at it like it was a dead fish, then hands it to Joyce.

"No lie," says Joyce, her kinky red hair in giant pink rollers to keep it straight and flipped up shoulder length on the ends. "I'd be lost in this blackboard jungle without Iota Chi." She hands the pin back to Martha as if it had cooties on it.

Must have belonged to that girl—I forget her name—who got married last year. The morals committee counted up the months between the time she got married and the time that birth announcement came around, and ruled that she'd have to return her Iota Chi pin. But considering its damaged condition, I'd say she drove over it with a car before complying with their wishes.

"You know, Donna," says Martha, putting the pin down and casually underlining a sentence midpage in her elementary-education book. "If you're thinking of marrying that G.I. you keep pen-palling with, there's a Pan Hellenic preparation-for-marriage chat over at the Delta Gamma house tomorrow. I think it's on postcoital depression or something," she whispers. "Anyway, it's only open to senior women or engaged girls *with* rings. But—who knows—maybe you'll get a surprise from Bob in the mail today. Then we could get your candle-lighting ceremony scheduled," she says, winking at Joyce, "and get you to these preparation-for-marriage chats."

"The last candle-lighting engagement announcement," says Joyce with perfect Iota Chi voice inflection, "I thought it was yours for sure, Donna, honest I did. Sally Bradshaw," she adds, raising one plucked eyebrow, "what a surprise."

"Well, Donna," says Martha, filing her luxurious fingernails, "it would really be nice to get you over to the D.G.'s post-coital chat tomorrow."

"Might work out just dandy," I say, opening my interpretative reporting textbook. God, these girls aren't too subtle about telling me I don't belong here. I wouldn't have Corporal Bob Knutsen on a Ritz cracker, let alone at the altar. But I have to have some excuse for not being interested in dating boys who usually treat me like I was the leftovers from last night's dinner. Besides, I want to be here just in case Ivan calls me.

"What's going on after supper tonight?" I ask, carefully piecing my words together to imitate Martha and Joyce's sorority phrases. Maybe they'll ask me what I'm doing. Just think, Donna Lee, you're going on a date with a real adult man.

Martha and Joyce glance nervously at each other. "It's cocktail-length dresses with heels for dinner, darling," says Joyce, fitting a Winston menthol into her gold cigarette holder. "We're having an after-dinner function with the Sigma Nu boys."

"Sigma Zoos," says Martha, screwing up her mouth and hiding her perfectly straight white teeth. "They're such a bunch of hamburgers, they haven't pledged a face man in the last hundred years."

"Maybe since you're an *almost* engaged girl, Donna," says Joyce, glancing sideways at Martha, "you'd rather come upstairs after dinner with Sally Bradshaw, Martha, and me. We're helping Sally pick out her china pattern. She's got stacks of brochures and, poor thing, her head's just swimming. Might be a good idea for you to look over all of Frederick and Nelson's contemporary patterns. Not that you should change your mind about that Blue Willow pattern—just, you know, broaden your horizons."

"I have a dinner appointment," I answer, feeling that my moment of triumph has been defeated. I glance at the huge flagstone fireplace at the far end of the Iota Chi study room, then turn the pages of my advanced journalism textbook and skim the subtitles. Anything but to have to look Martha straight in the eye. They just want to get me out of the room during the Sigma Nu function. How was I supposed to know that Rick Howard was the Sigma Nu who broke off with Iota Chi President Sally Bradshaw two months before she got engaged to some Sigma Alpha Epsilon? Chalk up another social blunder for Donna Lee Douglas. I gave Miss Priss Bradshaw her two-month period of grace, but Rick still keeps asking me out. Now—four months later—I don't have an excuse for not going on a before-dinner study date with him.

I turn Rick's name over in my mind several times as Martha continues to discuss china patterns with Joyce. Except for Rick, all those fraternity men look alike to me, as if they spent the whole day in the bathtub shaving. Not a speck of dirt or a hair out of place. Maybe that's why I always feel dirty and awkward around them. Rick Howard, on the other hand, talks nonstop, so I don't have a chance to make any *faux pas*.

I glance over at Martha's gold wristwatch. One thing is for sure, when I'm with I.Y. I'm not homesick for Alaska. Tuesday night: I'm missing the family spaghetti feed at Pop's Elks Club. For a moment I shut my eyes and conjure up my father's lean, slightly disheveled image, topped with his green and yellow John Deere baseball hat. After dinner at the Elks, everyone will push the tables and folding chairs back against the wall, while Bonnie's father, potbellied Officer Ostahowski, tunes his fiddle and Pop begins calling out the square-dance maneuvers for the Virginia reel.

"Honestly, Joyce," says Martha, testing the clear lacquer on her fingernails, "you wouldn't believe what I saw on my way to audiovisual-aids class today. These men in pink-pastel pajamas jumping up and down, throwing flowers. One of them gave me a stick of incense and then wanted me to pay him for it. It smelled so bad that I almost upchucked on the spot. Anyway, I threw it on the ground. So what do you think he does? He starts running after me, yelling 'Krishna, Krishna, Hare Krishna.' I was *sooo* embarrassed. I didn't know where to run or what. And he looked like he had head lice, because his head was all shaved. Isn't that what they do for lice, Donna?" asks Martha, turning her clear-skinned baby complexion toward me.

Is she asking me that because I look like the kind of person who's had head lice or because she thinks I'm a nursing major? "The science classes I took last semester were in anthropology, not hygiene," I say sweetly and look back at the chapter on "How to Write Obituaries."

"Oh, that's right," says Martha, "your hobby's Indian artifacts, just like Mrs. Zimmerman's."

I wonder how Ivan's Aunt Catherine got me into this sorority? I remember Sally Bradshaw making excuses to check the pledge list, just to make sure my name wasn't some kind of mistake, then asking me if I was sure that the Iota Chi house was my cup of tea. Mrs. Zimmerman wrote me a long letter, saying that she'd sponsor me because she too had played Princess Maksoutov in the Sitka Alaska Day celebration. She'd even worked in a fish cannery once, she said. Told me that Iota Chi could be the most important thing in my life, a real chance to better myself, to help me move up the ladder of success with a secure future in a good husband. And what a funny old bat she turned out to be when I met her at the sponsors' tea back before I was initiated—all those furs and jewelry. Another pledge told me that she'd had so many face-lifts that she was only allowed to smile three times a day for fear of undoing the results of her most recent operation.

But even though Iota Chi's wealthiest alumna sponsored me, these girls still look down their noses at me, especially Martha and her manners committee. Jeez, sometimes I can even hear her voice in my sleep: "Donna, a lady always eats with her napkin in her lap, not under her chin. Donna, a lady always sips her soup away from her; remember, 'just as ships go out to sea, I push my spoon away from me.'" Ivan, where are you? I wonder who'll be at his family mansion.

"Well, you'll never guess what I saw," says Joyce, balancing her cigarette holder between her thin fingers, her hand posed like a ballet dancer's. "This girl with hair down past her you-know-what, barefoot, and a miniskirt so short that I could almost see her crotch hairs. I mean, I could actually tell that she didn't have any underpants on, let alone a bra. She was just asking for it, walking down the street like that. And in all this rain. She was probably on drugs or something. . . ."

God, what would Joyce and Martha think of Bonnie? What would they say if they knew my best friend quit her job as a legal secretary and went to work as a go-go dancer in Anchorage? In her last letter she said that getting her first G-string was the most exciting moment in her life so far.

I don't blame Bonnie for quitting her job. I've about had it working part-time in the secretarial pool, typing lumber invoices for a dollar-fifty an hour. If it weren't part I.Y.'s company and I didn't need the money for school, I'd have quit long ago. Besides, I made more money working in the fish cannery in Sitka. The only thing good about my job is that I sometimes get to use the telephone to call Bonnie in Alaska.

"When I was on my way to Advanced Newswriting this morning,"

I say, deciding to try to be a part of Martha and Joyce's coffee klatch, "there was this speech going on in the Student Union about Vietnam. They were all shouting 'Out Now,' waving banners with some initials on them—S.D.S. or N.F.L., I've forgotten which. I don't know what they were shouting about, but Bob always writes me that things ain't— ah," I stammer, correcting myself, "*aren't* very pleasant over there. It's just a job that has to be done."

"Oh, agreed," says Martha, opening her *Early Childhood Learning* and squinching her mouth up like she'd just bitten into a sour berry pie.

God, another social blunder, I think, cringing behind my textbooks.

The house intercom pulses a static noise, then sounds two short beeps and two long beeps: my call number. Ivan, Ivan must be here.

"How do you like it here, Doni D?" Ivan winks one brown eye at me, then fishes for a cigarette inside his suede sports jacket.

I *ooh* and *aahh* at the hand-painted mural on the walls of the tiny Russian restaurant atop Capitol Hill while waiting for my dinner plate, which I.Y. sent back to the kitchen because the chicken Kiev was cold. "Oh, it's just divine," I say, remembering one of Martha's Iota Chi expressions. "Am I really going to see the Zimmerman-York mansion?"

"Sure, Doni, it's just up the street a piece. I thought you'd like to meet some more of the family."

Donna Lee, I tell myself, he's actually taking you home to meet "the family"! Let's see, I've met his Aunt Catherine, and I work for Charles. I wonder who else . . . maybe his father? The waiter returns my plate, but I'm almost too nervous to eat.

"The mansion belongs to Auntie," I.Y. says, as he orders another cognac from a waitress in peasant costume. "But since she has arthritis so bad and her husband died of a heart attack, Aunt Catherine lives in Palm Springs most of the time. She gave the house to Charles and his fourth wife, or maybe his fifth, I can't keep them all straight." Ivan's eyes glaze over for a moment. "Charles doesn't have such good luck with wives."

As I.Y. surveys the restaurant patrons, I study his tall frame and strong jaw. Mom says that a good wife always pretends that her husband's face is Jesus Christ. That way whatever he does is wonderful. Of course, I wouldn't have to do much imagining; I.Y.'s eyes look just like those religious paintings in the Church of Saint Michael before it burned down last year.

He reaches across the table, his hand brushing against mine. "This oil strike up in the Arctic at Prudhoe Bay is a biggy," he says in a hushed voice. "Could mean a whole new economic future for Alaska what with motel and housing construction slowing down. This could be the break we've all been waiting for."

I had been going to tell Ivan about my new boyfriend, Rick Howard, but since I.Y.'s taking me to meet his family, well. . . . And he always disapproves of my boyfriends anyway. I try to eat my dinner as delicately as possible. If I married Ivan, Mom and Pop would be so proud of me—more proud than if I got a reporter's job in a newspaper office. Maybe Ivan and his family have something special to talk to me about tonight, a really big favor to ask. Ivan never did tell me how I could repay him for my abortion. Fifteen hundred dollars is a lot of money, even for the Yorks.

"With all that oil," says Ivan, twirling his spoon in his cold beet soup like a little kid playing with his food, "America won't have to worry about the Arab countries nationalizing our oil refineries."

I smile. It must mean something, Donna, if he's talking to you about business.

"I may fly up there next week. Charles is checking into ice-ramming tankers so we can cut through the Arctic freeze year round and haul out the oil." He lowers his voice. "There's even talk about building a pipeline across the tundra clear south to Anchorage. And, can I trust you with a secret?" he asks.

I nod, feeling a warm glow all over.

He leans over and whispers. "The state's going to auction off oil land leases in about ten months. Standard Oil, Humble, Sohio, they'll all be bidding. Big bucks, really big bucks. Charles is trying to fix it up with the governor so the state of Alaska deposits all that lease money in Northwest Savings and Loan, right here in Seattle. Then we can zoom the cash right back up north, invest it in construction, and get a really big piece of the action."

"Why don't you put the money in an Alaska bank?" I ask, amazed and flattered that I.Y. has taken me into his confidence.

He scoots his chair around the table. Our shoulders touch and he whispers in my ear. "We're talking maybe nine hundred million dollars here! You can't put that kind of money in an Alaska teamster-owned bank." He looks at the dinner check, pulls out his wallet, and leaves a large tip.

"Maybe I should go into economics instead of journalism," I say, as I.Y. guides me out of the restaurant and into his new black Coupe de Ville. "I just love listening to you talk business."

"Do you?" His eyes look almost watery as he puts the key in the ignition. "It bores the hell out of my wife. 'Course she's got her hands full with those two little wildcat girls of mine. And by the time I get home at night, well. . . ."

I.Y. floors the Cadillac, spins around Twenty-Third Avenue, and onto the green, hawthorn-lined yards of Prospect Street. "Hell," he says, ignoring the speed limit, just like Pop would, "Charles has already talked the governor into building a trail-road across the Yukon, north to Prudhoe Bay. I have to hand it to that cousin of mine," he adds, as we pass a row of Tudor homes, each larger than a fraternity house, "Charles really has the knack of making people see things his way. Soon as that trail-road's built, oil-rig construction can start faster than you can say 'north to the future.'"

Ivan turns the Cadillac into a circular driveway and stops in front of a white house which looks like Scarlet O'Hara's mansion in *Gone with the Wind*. Holy Mo, it must be four stories high at least, with stained-glass windows just like the old Church of Saint Michael, and a balcony the size of a tennis court.

"The fourth floor's shut off," says Ivan. "It's the old ballroom, too inefficient to heat all year round." He unlocks the huge front door and steps into a marble-floored entry room. Jeez, this place is even gaudier than the Iota Chi house. . . . But why didn't the maid answer the door?

I.Y. guides me past a living room bigger than an olympic-sized swimming pool. The windows are heavily draped and a lonely black grand piano looms in the far corner near the fireplace. There must be an incredible view of Lake Washington on the other side of those curtains, I tell myself, staring at the huge blue and red paisley rug. Down the wide hall, past an octagonal mirrored bath, we enter a room filled with moose-head trophies and gold-framed portraits. Another paisley rug. Gee, for rich people, the Zimmermans sure have bad taste.

"This is the study," Ivan announces proudly. "How about a Scotch, just to get you warmed up?"

I look over at the couch, but there's no one there. Wonder where his father is? All the picture eyes stare down at me as if they were waiting for my answer. "Who are these people?" I ask.

"The family," he says. "I wanted you to meet them. Just a second and I'll make the introductions."

My heart falls into my stomach, and I can feel my eyes turning red. I look back at the portraits. Mom and Pop's whole trailer would fit into this room.

Ivan hands me a drink. "Most of these people are members of the dear departed," he says, appearing not to notice my sullenness. "Some were painted from old pictures and daguerreotypes, and the others were posed for. But this one,"—he guides me toward a family portrait almost as large as the Iota Chi dining-room table, framed in something that looks like a gilded Christmas wreath, and points to a corner of the painting—"this is me when I was just a little pecker with my Pa, Carl, and my Mom, Betsy."

"Where are they now?" I ask, staring at the full-breasted woman holding an infant, then at the ruddy-faced father gazing off into space. Get hold of yourself, Donna Lee, I urge myself silently. I.Y.'s still a married man; you have to take things one step at a time.

His eyes look suddenly downcast. "Mom died of cancer about ten years ago. She had a mastectomy, wore a rubber corset so that no one could see how she caved in on one side." He took hold of my hand. "One night, when I was about fourteen, I snuck into her room and tried it on. I've always felt guilty about that, like it was the worst thing I've ever done, a sort of sacrilege." His voice breaks off, and I give him a gentle pat on the back.

"And Pa," Ivan says, regaining his composure, "he retired from the company back in 'fifty-nine, when Alaska became a state. Staked a lot of family money on Alaska legalizing gambling. To have a secure economic base just like they have in Nevada, as he put it. Pa was so sure that the legislature was going to legalize gambling that he had two casinos built and ready to roll right outside of Ketchikan. A lot of family money went down the tube on that venture." Ivan takes a deep breath. "The way my Pa spends money, probably all I'll inherit from the old man is a big tongue to lick Master Charles' boots with."

Ivan looks at me with sad, puppy-dog eyes. "Pa comes and goes on his yacht these days, mostly to the South Pacific, probably for those Hawaiian women. He has a reputation as a real rake. Even before Mom's operation, everyone said he had a girl in every port."

"And what about the other people in the portrait," I ask, hoping to cheer him up. Talking about his parents seems to have put him in a cloudy mood. "Of course, there's your Aunt Catherine," I motion to the other side of the portrait with my entire hand, because it's not ladylike or polite to point. . . . Wonder what I.Y.'d say if I told him about the day when some pledges and I cut off the legs on all the dining-room chairs, then propped them back up. When the old ladies showed up for an afternoon sponsors' tea, their chairs collapsed on them and Mrs. Zimmerman had to be revived with smelling salts.

"That's the head madam herself," he says with a laugh. "Next to her is my dead Uncle Barnett, holding hands with Charles when he was a little boy. The blond is my cousin Debra. She was Auntie's undoing." He smiles. "Ran away from home a week before the Cotillion ball. Then they shipped her off to art school in Paris where she got the notion to go live in the South Seas with the natives like some famous painter did. Good-looking, but a crackpot if you want my opinion. No discretion. The last time I saw her she talked about all her sex problems out loud in front of everyone. Debra married some minister missionary named Sims, but now that he's dead she and her children live in one of those free-love communes."

I look at the blond girl with hunched shoulders and downcast face. I wonder how I.Y. could be talking about the shy, beaten-looking child in the portrait.

I stare down at the hardwood floor. Ivan must have brought me here for something special, not just to look at his family portraits. Maybe . . . it doesn't sound like his wife is very understanding. She's over thirty, so she must be all bagged out and uninteresting looking . . . probably really let herself go to seed like Mom. Maybe he does care about me. I wonder if we're going to *sleep* here tonight. I feel a wave of anticipation run from my mouth down to my thighs.

With his large but gentle hands I.Y. guides me around the room, telling me about each of the faces inside the cherub-festooned gold-leaf frames: his Grandfather Yo, who tried to leave all the family money to an insane Eskimo. His Grandmother Ulla, who took to her bed one day and never got up. His Uncle Barnett, who had the Eskimo committed to a territory asylum. I notice that Ivan has his father's nose and his Grandmother Ulla's high forehead. Maybe even his Aunt Catherine's dark complexion.

I move away from the huge pictures to a small cameo face in a light wooden frame; *Nadia Karimoff York,* it says on the plaque underneath the girl's picture. I remember the newspaper photo taped to Mom's refrigerator door. "Nadia doesn't have black hair," I say with astonishment, looking at the portrait. "It's dark red, almost like . . . some Haida Indians have." Her eyes stare straight at me, looking either terrified or as if she was about to kill someone.

"That there's my great-grandmother, a royal Russian," says Ivan proudly.

Nadia, the woman that all the Sitka barstool fishermen were always spinning yarns about when Bonnie, the gang, and I used to hang out outside the Mooseloose Saloon, trying to get someone to buy us liquor. I can't take my eyes off her picture. "You grow up like her," I remember Gramma Raven telling me, "a woman who does things."

Suddenly Ivan bends me over and pulls me down on the red and blue carpet. He pushes his face into mine, plunging his tongue into my mouth. Then he flinches and backs away as if he were short of breath.

"You look just like your mother when she was a girl," he whispers, and begins gently stroking my cheek as if I were a little kid.

"But Mom's blond," I say, trying not to sound too nervous. I look up at Nadia; her black eyes glare at me, as if she were trying to say something.

"It's your smile," Ivan says, moving toward me again, putting his hands under my blouse. Unhooking my bra, he pets my breasts, as if they were two small kittens.

I shut my eyes and wonder what *it'll* be like. I can feel the moisture between my legs begin to form tiny rivulets. A whole lot better than making love to Bob Knutsen, I tell myself. I didn't feel anything then, just something sliding in and out of me as if I were eating without tasting the food.

Ivan pulls my skirt down, stroking the pyramid of hair between my legs. "What's this little pink button down here, Doni?" he whispers, then nibbles on the soft part of my ear. "We have to give you a name. Hasn't your mommy ever named you? I know your mommy's name, it's Donna Lee. Hi, I'm Fatso," he says and rubs his erection on the inside of my thigh.

I open my eyes and glance up at the Nadia portrait. Her painted face looks at me imploringly. "Run," she says in Gramma Raven's voice, "run."

Slowly I take Ivan's erection in my hand, moving it back and forth the way Bob Knutsen taught me. I.Y. flinches, pulls away, and jumps to his feet. Even from the floor I can see that his face has drained of its color. He fumbles for his pants, then yanks his arm through one sleeve of his Pendelton shirt.

Slowly I sit up. I begin buttoning my blouse. "What—what's the matter?" I ask in a small voice, staring at the tiny pearl buttons so that Ivan won't see my tears. "What's the mat—"

I look up as Ivan runs from the room. Rising to my feet, I hear the front door slam. "Wait," I call to him, "wait for me!" I hear the engine of his Cadillac turning over.

28.

Alaska Fish Company, Imperial Lumber, Inc., 26th floor . . . I push the elevator button in the lobby of the giant marble skyscraper on downtown Seneca Street. God, please let Ivan be at work today, so I can ask him what happened last night.

Maybe he didn't want to be unfaithful to his wife. But everyone says they're getting a divorce. Maybe he's testing me. I probably shouldn't have been so easy. "Always keep the boys at an arm's distance," that's what Mom used to say.

I open the huge saloon-style swinging doors into the fed-flocked wallpaper and Alaska-gold-rush decor of the Imperial Lumber offices, then walk to my desk against the back wall of the typing pool. Hazel, the gray-haired secretary next to me, nods. Don't see any work in my "In" basket.

Buzz.

"Imperial Lumber," I say, picking up the phone. "Zimmerman-York executive offices."

"Doni D.?" booms a familiar, deep-throated voice.

"I.Y.! Ah, Mr. York. I'm sorry," I try to compose my voice. He called to apologize. Oh, thank you, Lord, thank you.

"You're the sweetest telephone-answerer this side of Sikta. Listen, will you tell Charles that I'll be just five minutes late for our meeting this morning?"

Click.

I stare blankly at the phone receiver, then place it back on the hook. He didn't even say he was sorry. . . . Well, I console myself, at least he's not mad at you, Donna Lee. He'll be in later, you can talk to him then.

A stockbroker whom I recognize from the firm downstairs walks through the swinging saloon doors with Mr. Zimmerman. Charles's dark graying hair looks as if he just left the barber shop, and there's not a wrinkle in his pin-stripe suit.

"Get me a flight tomorrow to Anchorage, Miss, ah—Douglas," he says, dropping his attaché case on my desk. "Then hook me up with a bush pilot who'll fly up to the Arctic come hell or high water, and I don't want any lame excuses about the weather."

"Yes, Mr. Zimmerman. And Mr. York called to say he'd be about five minutes late for your meeting, sir." Charles grimaces, then turns to the stockbroker.

"Donhauser, let me know as soon as you find out who the decision-makers at Standard Oil and British Petroleum are. This Arctic strike is really hot."

"You bet," says the pale-complexioned stockbroker, pulling at his Brooks Brothers button-down collar.

"Listen, Donhauser," says Mr. Zimmerman, leaning on my desk, "this is the game plan: We get a contract for Alaska Fish to barge some oil construction rigs and prefab modules up to Prudhoe, and at the same time we use Imperial Lumber to front a construction firm to build the modules."

Donhauser takes out a pocket scratch pad and nervously begins to scribble notes, as I dial Alaska Airlines.

"Take it easy, old boy," says Charles, patting the stockbroker on the shoulder.

"Yes, sir."

"You should have been at the Rotary meeting yesterday." Mr. Zimmerman rolls his brown eyes as if someone way back when told him he was cute when he did that. "I knocked them dead with this one. See," he begins another one of his unhappy-husband jokes, "there was this executive who wanted his wife done in. So he called up an old war buddy of his named Arty, whom he knew was a hit man, and tells Arty that the best time to catch the missus is in the morning at Thriftway. So Arty says, 'Well, I know I owe you a favor, but I can't do a job for nothing, I have to think of my reputation. But, tell you what I'll do; I'll charge you a dollar.' So the next day Arty goes to the Thriftway and waits for his buddy's wife. He catches her over by the meat counter looking at the pork chops, puts his hands around her neck, and ch-ch-chokes her to death," says Charles, making squeezing motions with his hands. "Then Arty looks around and sees that this old lady over in the produce section saw him and he runs over and ch-ch-chokes the old. . . ."

The two men disappear into Charles Zimmerman's office and I pull out my bookbag, glancing through the Pan Hellenic newsletter before I begin my first job of the day, xeroxing invoices.

"Next morning the headlines read, 'Arty chokes three for a dollar at Thriftway!'" I listen through the open office doorway as the two men laugh jovially. If you're the boss, everyone laughs at your jokes, no matter how dumb they are. Now where's Ivan, why doesn't he come to work, so that I can ask him what happened?

I look through the newsletter calendar: "Marital preparation chat, senior women and engaged girls with rings, Delta Gamma house, one o'clock: Dr. Marilyn Wilyard (Delta Gamma '54), speaker; Mrs. Ivan (Pamela) York (Iota Chi, '57), hostess." Holy Jumping Jesus! I never knew that his wife was in the I.C. house! Yeah, well, I think, trying to calm myself, 'fifty-seven, that was a long time ago. She probably looks like one of those fat, dishwater blonds with thin, straggly hair whom I've seen at the sponsors' teas. Wonder if I should go and get a glimpse of her. Maybe I'll be able to tell by looking at Mrs. York if she's going through a marriage separation. Mom always says that it makes a woman look like she's gone to seed.

I put the newsletter back into my bookbag and walk over to the twenty-sixth-story window, gazing down at the rain-mucked urban-renewal construction site surrounding the old Tlingit totem poles in Pioneer Square. Seattle looks like a giant-sized Sikta, except the high mountains are farther away and there're no ravens or bald eagles perched on the rooftops.

If I took a late, extended lunch, I could just about make it through the premarital chat—Ivan wouldn't care if I was away from work for an extra half hour, not after what happened last night. God, the rain's coming down so hard that I can hardly see past the freeway they built above Alaskan Way, in front of all the pier buildings. . . . A finger taps me on the shoulder.

"Ivan . . . Ah, Mr. York." I feel my face flush.

"Coffee at three, Miss Douglas?" he says in a businesslike voice, winking one brown eye at me. He holds his Stetson in one hand and a briefcase in another. As he smiles the dimple line in his tanned face makes his grin look even wider.

"Yes, sir," I reply in a soft little-girl's voice. He cares, he really cares about me. Just remember, Donna Lee, it's hard for men to show their feelings. You'll have to be understanding, you'll have to help him to talk about last night.

Ivan steps into Charles's office as I begin cleaning the copy machine with a solvent that smells like the lye and vinegar fumes at the Sitka pulp mill. Through the open doorway I listen to Charles run through the meeting agenda.

"This Prudhoe Bay project's going to be the biggest thing since the Great Wall of China." I can just barely hear him. "And it keeps us right behind the eight ball if Boeing goes under and we lose our biggest account."

I open the photocopier and see that someone's left a document inside the machine. *E.M.D. Corporation,* just like Mom's initials, I think to myself, glancing at the letterhead, then skim the page: "This is to confirm the negotiations for the lease of right-of-way . . . between your corporation and the Stevens Village Tribal Community in consideration of eighty-five dollars per year for ninety-nine years, hereinafter called. . . ." Legalese, that's all there is to read around here. I lay the document down on my desk.

"Oil tankers," says Ivan from inside the office. "Ice rammers. There's plenty of them idle, like the *Manhattan*—been hauling grain to India. We could lease her for pennies on the dollar. Now the Arctic Ocean and the Beaufort Sea are real shallow, but listen to this, Donhauser. . . ." I hear Charles shuffle through some papers. "It's called Project Ploughshares. If we use an A-bomb to dredge out the Beaufort Sea, then we could supertanker all that oil out of—"

"The overland project might be simpler," interrupts Charles. I peek in, watching the stockbroker take notes. "But it's got to be very low profile; we don't want any activist lawyers going on the warpath. I'd say we could get right-of-way permits for the whole eight-hundred-mile strip for under a quarter of a million."

"Donhauser," says Ivan, "what's your opinion, the Juneau governor's mansion or a senatorial office in D.C.? Six months to a year residence in Alaska is all I figure I need. We could control this project easier than moving pieces on a chessboard."

"Let's take this matter up later," says Charles in a stern voice, "after I've thought it through."

My heart races. Ivan, he's going to run for office? Governor, I hope, because if he were in D.C., I'd never get to see him. I could be his press secretary! Maybe one of his aides. He'll need someone who's good at hostessing, especially if he hasn't got a wife. I always thought Martha's manners committee was a crock, but I'll pay more attention now; Ivan's going to want someone who's really polished. Oh, I know he'll pick me for some special campaign job. Maybe he'll tell me about it at coffee this afternoon. This could be my big chance to pay him back. And on my next trip home, I can start setting up the Sitka campaign headquarters . . . in the old schoolhouse next to the Pioneers' Home.

The pale-complexioned stockbroker emerges from the office. Charles follows, escorting him to the door.

"Mr. Zimmerman," I call out to him, then answer the phone and press the hold button, "someone left this in the copy machine." I hand him the document; he gives it a puzzled look. I go back to my phone call, something about an inaccurate invoice, six hundred board feet of two-by-two clear-cut spruce delivered to a shopping-center construction site, instead of six thousand feet.

"Listen, Ivan," says Charles, resuming the meeting. "I don't want any more public talk about you running for office. It would be totally unethical, out of the question; you haven't had a legal residence in Alaska for fifteen years."

"I'm one of the few native sons," says Ivan self-assuredly. "And there isn't a soul up there who doesn't know my name. I've employed thousands, Charles, and I didn't just do it out of the goodness of my heart. I've been thinking this through for a long time. If I were in the governor's mansion, we could wind this project into peak production in less than two years, and those fancy-ass oil companies couldn't do diddly without *our* okay."

"Pamela detests Alaska," says Charles. "She doesn't like rain, and she's allergic to mosquitoes."

"Fuck Pamela," says Ivan, his voice turning angry. "She knew about my plans when she married me. Let her go through with the divorce for all I care. Hell, Alaska's full of single men, she's not going to lose me any votes."

"Ivan," I hear Charles taking a deep breath, "why don't you concentrate on cleaning things up in the fish company."

Ivan raises his voice. "Just what's that supposed to mean?"

"You must buy at least two Louisiana shrimpers a year. How big a fleet do you need? If you ask me, you're not managing things very well."

"Shrimping's big business in the Aleutians," Ivan roars. "Just leave

Alaska Fish to me, okay, Charles?" I can hear Ivan pacing the floor. "I grew up in that business, my father had me fishing before I could walk. Just keep your nose out of it. Agreed?"

"Then keep your nose clean," says Charles in the tone of a high-school principal reprimanding a student. "Too many boats outfitted for the tropics just doesn't look right up north."

Buzz.

I reach for the phone, and the inner-office conversation fades into a background of secretaries typing. "You want prefabs, extension two-five-six," I tell the party on the other end of the line.

"Votes, all you talk about is getting votes," Charles is almost yelling now. "The construction worker's vote, the fisherman's vote, the pulp-mill worker's vote. But now you've gone too far, Ivan York, I won't let you go public on *that* information. It's damaging. I won't let you embarrass my mother, she's very sensitive about *that*. High profile has never been the Zimmerman motto."

"I'm not a Zimmerman," says Ivan in a controlled voice.

I hear chairs moving. For a moment no one speaks.

Charles clears his throat. "Go ahead, pretend you're Nelson Rockefeller; run for governor of Alaska, I don't give a damn. Just don't embarrass my mother by spreading that information around, thinking it'll get you a few more votes from another sector."

Ivan says nothing. I wonder what Charles is talking about. What would upset I.Y.'s Aunt Catherine so much?

"But before you dive off the board into an empty swimming pool," Charles's voice is definitive, "just give this whole thing some serious thought. The governorship may sound like power, but you lose a lot of pull being a public person; you have to answer to people. And, my dear cousin," Charles sneers, "I know that's not your favorite pastime."

Hurriedly I walk through the rain, down the brick and sycamore streets of the University of Washington's Fraternity Row. Ten minutes after one. Damn. I'm going to be late for that premarital chat at the Delta Gamma House. I just have to get a glimpse of Pamela York.

I walk into the blue and white wallpapered dining room of the D.G. house and sit in a chair against the back wall. At the podium, Dr.

Wilyard, a petite blond woman, is talking about the book she's writing, *Married Women and Celestial Joy*. What a beautiful blue cashmere sweater she's got on, and those must be real pearls. She looks just like a picture from a Halo Shampoo advertisement in *Seventeen* magazine.

At the hostess table I see a chubby woman with stringy dishwater blond hair, wearing a car coat and holding a child on her lap. That's her, I tell myself, that's Pamela. And that must be one of Ivan's little daughters.

I strain my neck around the girls who're sitting in front of me, so I can see I.Y.'s wife's face. Looks just like one of those good Bible-reading ladies from Mom's Jehovah's Witnesses' Church. She looks awful, poor woman, like the divorcées working up in the Sitka fish cannery—all bedraggled and at loose ends. Well, she certainly seems to be going through a marriage separation. God, I wonder if I'll have the nerve to say *hello* to her when she pours tea after Dr. Wilyard's talk?

The Grace Kelly carbon copy at the podium clears her throat and continues. "The myth of women's sexual passion is perpetuated by prostitutes and other similar types of women. Men who patronize streetwalkers need ego flattery, so these women moan and move their hips in pretended ecstasy, because they know they'll be well paid. Prostitutes always confess all of this to the doctors who attend them when they go to be treated for venereal disease." The blond speaker blushes attractively, takes a small breath, and continues. Jeez, if I could look and talk like that woman, I'd really do right by I.Y.'s gubernatorial campaign. I'd be the best press agent ever.

I wonder what Pamela thinks about all this talk of prostitutes and nasty sex? I'm surprised she doesn't cover her little girl's ears. Urna McLaren once worked in the Yorks' Sitka island summer house as a clean-up girl and she told me that Mrs. York was the coldest fish you'd ever want to meet.

"Doctors know about the myth of women's sexual passion," says the speaker, "but most other men don't, and they carry these misconceptions with them into their marriages when they instruct their new brides in what is commonly known as"—she pauses and lowers her voice—"boudoir cheesecake." At the hostess table Mrs. York blushes redder than cranberries.

I try to giggle quietly like all the other girls, even though I don't agree with what Dr. Wilyard's saying. It's true, I never had much sexual passion for Bob Knutsen, before or after I slept with him. And I sure didn't have any for a long time after my abortion, until. . . . Until last night with Ivan. I glance at the wall clock. I'll get back to work just in time to go to coffee with him.

I move closer to the front and notice that the straight-backed brunet next to me is Sally Bradshaw, and smile at her in my best sorority-girl fashion. Practice smiling now, Donna Lee, I tell myself; you're going to need it for I.Y.'s campaign.

"You must impress upon your husbands-to-be," continues Dr. Wilyard, "that a woman's physical pleasure is largely aroused by romantic overtures like candy and flowers, and not by local prurient excitement. . . ."

I take a long look at the speaker. Maybe Dr. Wilyard has spent so much time writing books that she's never had time to meet the right man. And I thought that Martha said this talk was going to be on postcoital depression. Those newsletters are always getting their facts wrong.

Mrs. York fumbles with the buttons on her car coat. What's that white-bibbed dress she's got on? Looks like a maid's. . . .

"Where's Mrs. York?" I whisper to Sally Bradshaw.

Without moving her head in my direction, Sally extends a well-manicured hand forward, gesturing toward the petite Grace Kelly behind the podium. "The main speaker was ill," she says in a soft voice.

My jaw drops helplessly as I stare at the slender figure of the Halo girl. Sally twiches nervously and gives me a disapproving look.

The door, God, where's the door?

Through the rain on the front porch I focus on a horde of freshmen pledges being led in a hazing stunt by Rick Howard and five of his fraternity brothers on the lawn of the Sigma Nu house across the street. The raspy voice of Janis Joplin singing "Piece of My Heart" blares out of the Tudoresque fraternity-house windows.

I run down the street, ignoring Rick as he calls out a friendly greeting. At the crest of the hill I stop, look out over the city—Lake Washington on one side, the canal and Lake Union on the other. That was Ivan's wife? God, I'm such an ugly duck next to her, what can he see in me? A whore, one of those prostitutes who moan and move their hips in pretended ecstasy? I look back at the U.W. campus, larger than the whole city of Sitka. But we didn't go all the way. What does Ivan want from me?

Walking down the traffic-congested, litter-strewn sidewalk of University Avenue, my feet mechanically move one in front of the other and my numb hands dangle from my coat sleeves.

He'll tell me all about it when I have coffee with him this afternoon. Poor man, maybe his wife makes him feel bad about himself. She's just written a whole book on celestial joy, saying that women don't have sexual passion. How does that make I.Y. feel? Probably incompetent . . . maybe even impotent. Could that be it? Maybe that's why we didn't go all the way at his family mansion, because he's . . . because he *couldn't*.

In the ladies' room of the Imperial Lumber building, I run cold water over my face before going back to my desk at the back of the typing pool. I wave a hello to Hazel, but she doesn't look up from her typing. Opening my desk drawer, I reach for the apple I put there this morning, but it's not there. Then I notice that my vase of strawflowers isn't next to my typewriter either. A pink envelope. I pull it out from the typewriter, ripping open the sides. "You are hereby terminated. . . ." and a check for a week's wages. I look up and see that my belongings are stacked in a box next to the door. What the . . . ?

I was only an hour late getting back from lunch. Surely . . . I reach for the phone and dial I.Y.'s extension. One ring, two rings.

"What is it, Hazel? I thought I told you to hold all calls," says Charles Zimmerman.

"This is Donna Douglas, sir. Would you connect me with Mr. York?" My muscles tighten. I didn't know that I could sound so official.

"Mr. York's indisposed at the moment. Is there something I can help you with?"

"Ah—" My voice cracks, and I feel myself about to burst into sobs. "No."

Even though I've never had the nerve to call him at home, I know Ivan's phone number by heart. I dial and wait for the ring. "Is Mr. York in?" I ask the housekeeper. "Fairbanks? But when did he leave?"

A man's hand engulfs the telephone, breaking the connection. I look up into the narrow brown eyes of Charles Zimmerman and for the first time notice the yellow nicotine stains at the corners of his mouth.

"Don't ever try to contact my cousin again, Miss Douglas," he commands in a stern voice low enough so that Hazel at the next desk can't hear above her typing. "Do you understand?" He takes hold of my wrist, squeezing it, digging his short, well-manicured nails into my skin. "Do you?"

I drop the receiver, and stare at the red marks on my wrist. "Yes, sir," I stammer, trying to remember which hotel Ivan always stays in when he goes to Fairbanks on business.

"But why this?" I hold up the pink termination slip and feel the tears begin to run out of the corners of my eyes.

Charles mumbles something about Boeing. "Without that big aerospace contract, the economy's shot to hell. There's no room here for casual labor, Miss Douglas." He walks to his office and slams the door.

29. FAIRBANKS
Winter 1972

Three years of being a cub reporter, writing obits for the *Chena Times*:

Rafferty, Malcolm (Two Bit)—In Fairbanks, February 21. Beloved brother of Dixie Robertson of Eagle Creek. Dear Uncle of Billie Perkins of Boise, Idaho.

A native of Sabetha, Kansas.

A fifty-year member of the Benevolent Paternal Order of the Elks. . . .

Obit policy won't let me say anything about how Rafferty got drunk and burned up in his bed trying to stay warm. And the fire chief told me that by the time they got to him his mattress had burned through the floor. Well, who needs the *Chena Times* to tell people what happened to Two Bit? Half the town must have shown up at his fire, even if it was thirty-five below outside. Fairbanks, nothing to do here but go to fires and bars in the winter, and watch the bears play out at the dump in the summer.

Three years of writing obits and three years of festering about Ivan York. How could I.Y. have been my fairy goduncle all my life, and then suddenly drop me like a hot potato? What'd I do wrong, and what did he want from me in the first place? Well, as Bonnie always puts it, "just another guy from the 'come-on, come-on, *stay-away*' school of romance."

Taking a deep breath, I pick up a copy of the galley proofs of the front page of tomorrow's *Chena Times*:

INJUNCTION AGAINST TRANS-ALASKA PIPELINE
CONTINUES
Environmental and Native American concerns have caused a
three-year delay . . .

"Lead it out and then send those takes down to the printer," yells the editor, Mr. Dinwiddie, to the new gofer. "I want the headline to read 'Pipe Construction Camps Waiting and Ready to Go.'"

God, I mumble, old Widdie's got a face as gray as the cinder-block walls here in the Polaris Building. And writing for a newspaper sure isn't the creative job it's cracked up to be. There's about as much life in these articles as there is in those acres of snow outside my window.

"How about focusing on the pipeline company name itself," continues Dinwiddie; "*Nuna,* an Eskimo word meaning 'Land.' Come on," Widdie roars, "I need some action around here."

He turns to the gofer. "Bring Miss Douglas a couple of last August's human-interest clips up from the morgue."

Now, where are the galleys of that "Memories of Summer" feature that Widdie had me write up for this Sunday's edition? Leave it to the editor of the *Chena Times* to want to run pix of Mrs. Lindstrom posing with her twenty-pound swan-shaped zucchini in front of her First Avenue Hair Care'n Manicure shop last summer. Jesus H. Christ, it's so cold today that you can't go outside without a ruff parka and a felt face mask, and Dinwiddie's torturing the readership with memories of summer. . . . Now, what'd I do with the pix of the University of Alaska's seventy-two-pound cabbage?

"Hurry it up," calls Dinwiddie from the far end of the room.

Okay, okay, get with it, Donna Lee, I tell myself. Jeez, here's a copy of yesterday's Sitka newspaper. I'm almost scared to read it. Last time I opened up "Social Whirl," Sicky Vicky'd just married Bert Dysokar. The column said that Mom wore a blue dress and Pop had a blue-tinted carnation in his lapel for the ceremonies at the new Cathedral of Saint Michael. . . . I guess that my family never believed my letters about how Ivan York lied about me. Well, someday. I'll show them. I'll get a by-line in a big important newspaper; then they'll want to see me again. But I'll never forget opening that letter from Mom, thinking that she'd sent me my airplane fare home after I'd dropped out of the University of Washington because I got fired from my job and was distraught over Ivan's Houdi-ni-like disappearing act.

Dear Donna,

I would have written you sooner, but I've been to see the minister every day this week. I've been putting on weight and my T. O.P.S. diet doesn't seem to help. I just want you to know that I've been praying for you, but still don't understand how you could have done this to us. We brought you up better than that.

Mr. York called me up last week, just before your letter asking for money arrived. He told me all about how he found you whoring in Seattle and taking drugs. The man actually broke down and cried over the phone about how he tried to rescue you way back when you were in high school. Now there is a story all over town about how you let Bob Knutsen take advantage of you and when he found out that you were in a family way, he got cold feet and ran off to enlist. Poor Bob is a communist prisoner now and I'm afraid that it's all your doing. All because you didn't have faith in Him, and let the sin in you win over.

Mr. York told me how you talked him into helping you kill your unborn baby. The man actually asked for our forgiveness and we are praying for him, hon, just like we are praying for you.

Now I'm pleading with you to take out your Bible and read Matthew, if not for your own sake, then for your little sister's and father's. Matthew will tell you how to pray to Him. We are all born with sin in us, Donna, and I know that my little girl can still be saved. Your father and I are just afraid that Vicky Lynn has your same bad blood. We are doing all we can to save her from a life of sin and drugs, so your father says that if you ever show up at our door, I'm to turn you out. Donna, I want you to take hold of yourself and put yourself in the service of the Lord. He is your only salvation. We'll be praying for you, hon, and Mr. York says he will too.

Love,
Mom

Why did I.Y. tell my mother about my abortion, and why did he try to discredit me with all those lies about drugs, whoring, and Butcher Bob deserting me? He was the one who got Bob to enlist. Ivan's never answered my letters or phone calls, and, much as I hate to admit it, other than being desperate for money the reason I took this newspaper job in Fairbanks was because I knew he'd be here politicking for the pipeline. Someday I'll find a way to make him see me and explain. But so far the only times I've seen him he's been surrounded by the press or pipeline people.

Oh good Christ, Donna Lee, I tell myself to stop dwelling on Ivan York. He's become the infection of my life. But someday I'll meet him at his Waterloo. There's got to be a way. . . .

"Miss Douglas," yells Widdie across the glass-partitioned room, "how many inches of obits today?"

"Ah, about eight, I think." Oh, God, what'd I do with the graph on Rafferty, I just had it. Huh, here's a take on that old lady over on Illinois Avenue. News about the Vietnam War and the Pipe delays may be the front-page headline today, but that old lady's what they'll all be talking about at the Flame Lounge tonight. Had a whole house full of dead animals in shoe boxes. Cats, small dogs, birds. It says here that she couldn't part company with her little friends even when summer came and the ground thawed out enough to bury them.

Oh, Lord, here comes Dinwiddie. "Red," he says, using the nickname I've earned because of my shoulder-length auburn hair. "Here're my notes and three pix on that truck-trailer pileup." He wipes his nose with a wrinkled handkerchief. I find myself wondering how he makes it with the missus with a paunch on him like that. "See if you can make something out of all this."

"Okay, sir." Well, anything's better than writing obits, but I bet I don't even get the by-line.

"And have those 'Cradle Corner' takes on my desk before you go home tonight," he says, calling over his shoulder.

How come everyone around here gets promoted but me? Just wait till I get my college degree this spring. No more night classes at the U. of Alaska. No more obits, "Cradle Corner," or "Mrs. B's Caribou Recipies." And old Mr. Dinwiddie won't have an excuse in the world for not giving me a raise.

I put my pencil down and stare out the window next to my desk, then across the barren, snow-covered Tanana Valley. With my index finger on the pane, I trace the line of the frozen Chena River, marked by a thin row of leafless birch trees as it snakes its way north toward the White Mountains. Christ, I never thought I'd miss the color green. Fairbanks in the winter is a desert as far as the eye can see. I shudder with imagined cold as I gaze at the low rolling hills, so unlike my Sitka home eight hundred miles to the south. With a pang of loneliness I remember the steep, perpetually evergreen Three Sisters Peaks and the smell of the tide coming in under the fish-cannery wharf. Outside my window here at the Polaris Building, the cinder-block houses and mobile homes of the Fairbanks suburbs stretch out mile after blizzard-covered mile with little sign of life—only a few Arctic chickadees and white ptarmigan perched on occasional ice-covered pine trees. After a heavy snow Warner Brothers could use Fairbanks and the interior of Alaska as a film set for an outer-space movie.

Aimlessly I begin pecking at my typewriter, hoping that Mr. Dinwiddie'll think I'm busy at work, instead of staring at the northern horizon and the dim outline of the White Mountains in the distance. Closing my eyes, I envision the vista beyond them: rolling brown and snow-covered tundra, dotted with frozen muskeg bogs, all sloping down to the Yukon River, then rising up again into the Brooks Range. In Stevens Village, the squat, broad-faced Eskimo inhabitants are gathering their packs of Husky and Samoyed sled dogs in front of the sod-roofed houses. And like the other natives of the Interior, they're huddling inside their coyote-ruffed parkas, watching the aqua-blue northern lights fan across the dark sky.

In my mind's eye, I trace the proposed route of the pipeline across the Brooks Range to Prudhoe Bay and the Beaufort Sea. "North to the Future," that's what all the bumper stickers in town say now. . . . And that pipeline's going to get me a better, high-paying job too, that's for sure. Last year Congress paid the Indians in Alaska almost a billion dollars for the use of their land where the Pipe crosses over it. What more can there be to hold up this job? If I have to work at the *Chena Times* through one more Fairbanks winter, I'll either freeze to death or die of boredom.

Ivan York's gubernatorial press secretary, that was the job I'd dreamed of having when I was a student at the U. of W.—expense accounts, penthouse hotel rooms, important people, a secretary, and an office of my own. Wonder what happened to I.Y.'s political ambitions? I haven't seen any mention of him running for office since the oil companies decided definitely to build the pipehne instead of tankering the oil out through the frozen and too-shallow Beaufort Sea. And I still can't sleep some nights wondering why Ivan had me fired from Imperial Lumber. There's just got to be a way I can get to him. . . .

"Miss Douglas," Dinwiddie calls across the room, punctuating his sentences with a deep cough, "I'd like you to cover that Old Alaska exhibit at the university museum tomorrow. And localize your article a little. I've got an important luncheon with those Sierra Club people and their injunction against the Pipe. Hear there's another reporter from the *New York Times* in town again, too."

"Yes, sir." God, seven obits, "Cradle Corner," and now this.

Preoccupied with Ivan, I stare at the keys of my typewriter. I've got to find a way to get to him, I tell myself, planning what my next move might be. God, could I use a drink to help me think this thing through. I glance up at the wall clock; another half hour of writing obits before everyone hits the bars on their way home from work.

ALASKA

* * *

Better be careful, or you'll have an alcohol problem like Pop, I tell
myself as I walk through the swinging doors of the Flame Lounge.
Twenty-five moose-head trophies and three giant taxidermized
Alaska king crabs eye me from above the split-rail bar as I walk across
the sawdust floor to a log table, straddle a tree-stump stool, and look
across the room at the other Flame Lounge regulars: Angoon Arny
Kolosh and two of his Indian friends wave *hello*, Aleut Rena go-go
dances on the table next to me while some *Nuna* pipeline management men, drinking whiskey on the rocks, try to slip twenties into her
G-string. I take my wool face mask off and order an Irish coffee.

"Hey, is that *you*," says a man's voice from across the table, "or do
you just look like my choice for the Sigma Nu Luau Queen?"

I look up from my thoughts and see Rick Howard in a blue Alaska
parka, holding out his hand.

"Donna," he says, "my old Iota Chi girlfriend." He runs his hand
through his red hair, which has been fashionably styled in a bushy
Afro.

"Well, this is a surprise," I say, happy to see someone other than
the crew at work to talk journalism with. "What are you doing in Fairbanks of all places?"

"Got a job as a stringer for the *New York Times*," he says. "I'm covering the Pipe and the whole bit. I figured it was safer than covering
Nam. You married?"

"No," I say. "I'm a reporter for the *Chena Times*." Jesus Christ, I
think to myself with a pang of jealousy, this guy's working for a New
York newspaper? I got the same grades in school as he did, and I'm still
a cub, writing obits.

"Great," he says smiling, his broad teeth going on forever inside
his mouth.

"How's the Vette?" I ask, not knowing what else to say.

"Fine, fine, got her garaged in a heated warehouse out in Jersey."
He nods his head up and down, smiling, no doubt at the thought of
his silver sports car. "Hey, man," he says, slapping me on the back, "we
could work together on this. The Pipe is going to be some story. Right-
of-way permit's been tied up in the courts and Congress for three years

339

already. What can you tell me about it, Donna? What's the local senti-ment?" He pulls out a yellow scratch pad and pencil.

"Everybody's just waiting around for the permit to come through so we can get good paying jobs with *Nuna*," I say as Rick pays for my drink. Then I remember the document I once found in Imperial Lum-ber's copy machine. Ivan and Charles were probably trying to buy up Indian-reservation leases cheap, before anyone got wind of the Pipe. Well, that plan sure backfired in everyone's face.

"You going to work on the line, digging trenches?" he asks, punc-tuating the end of his sentence with a cynical laugh.

"Huh? No," I reply, thinking that this was the first time since I left Seattle that anyone had reminded me, point-blank, that I was a girl, and there're some things that girls can't do. "With my journalism expe-rience," I continue, feeling smug, "I thought I could get a job doing public relations or writing ad copy."

Angoon Arny sits down on the stool next to me as the Flame Lounge Wurlitzer jukebox belts out the first verse of Grace Slick's "Surrealistic Pillow," and Rena moves her hips in time to the music.

Rick turns toward me. "That's kind of why I was sent on assign-ment up here," he says in a low voice. "You know, to make sure all the 'perils of the pipeline' don't get written up for the media in some ter-rifically distorted fashion," he continues excitedly, as I remember his enthusiasm for do-gooder endeavors. "I know that the Pipe is going to run from Prudhoe south to Valdez—I visited the tank-storage farm down there before I came up here. Amazing feat of engineering at Val-dez, Donna, truly amazing."

"Really?" I say, watching Angoon Arny sneak a sip of my Irish cof-fee, then chase it down with a swig of beer.

"Yeah, man," says Rick, "but the tank farm's got some terrifically bad press. I mean, you know, there was some quake there back in 'sixty-four. . . ."

"Uh-huh, we felt that one clear down in Sitka. Whole town of Val-dez got wiped out, most of Anchorage too."

"Well, that's the point," says Rick, impatient because I interrupted him. "The tank farm's built to withstand any quake known to man. But those dumb Friends of the Earth people don't mention that in all their danger-to-fish-and-wildlife propaganda."

Rick Howard working for the *New York Times*. God, I can't wait till I get my degree. Then I'll be able to get a good job, working for the Pipe and *Nuna*—and save a lot of money and start doing something with my life.

"Donna, I'm not sure you have a handle on the seriousness of the issues here," he says as I watch Angoon Arny trying to figure if he can take Rick for a five, a ten, or just another beer. "Look," Rick toys with his new moosehide mittens, "do you remember back at U.W. when I was doing investigative reporting on cancer and radiation?"

"Yeah," I sip my drink.

"Well, I got a grant to go to Japan," he says in a hushed voice, "and the things that radiation do to your body before you die are god-awful, really. I saw the evidence."

"I know. I read *Hiroshima*."

"Donna," he gives me a hurt look, as if I'm not taking the matter seriously enough. "I don't think you understand the urgency of the pipeline issue. The West Coast already uses twice the fuel it can produce. To make matters worse, OPEC's playing games with prices and supply, when they're not threatening to go to war."

"Rick," I drawl, beginning to feel impatient with his superior attitude, "just because I live in the backwoods of Fairbanks, Alaska, doesn't mean I'm uninformed. I know America needs more oil on her own territory. Women need to earn their own money, and America needs to own her own oil," I say, verbalizing my new outlook on life.

"Okay, okay, no offense. The Vette wouldn't like it if I offended you," he says, smiling. "The Vette always did like you best of any of my U.W. girlfriends. . . . But the problem runs a lot deeper." He lowers his voice and returns to the subject of oil. "If the pipeline doesn't go through, the only backup energy is nuclear power. You remember that giant tower near Seattle?"

"Yeah." I recall a tall cement phallus amid the farmland of the Columbia River.

"That's a nuclear-power plant, Donna; it produces nuclear waste—

radioactive fallout, you know—radiation. And believe me, the impact of nuclear energy is a lot worse than just some black goo mucking up a few acres of frozen tundra *à la* your usual pipeline oil spill."

"No shit," I say, remembering that I heard the same spiel at the Earth Mother Festival held on the University of Alaska green last spring.

"So, Donna, maybe you could help me. Is there any way I could get into your paper's morgue?"

"I just write obits and 'Cradle Corner,'" I say, sipping the Cool Whip off my second Irish coffee. "I bet you're the guy from the *New York Times* that my editor was telling me about. He's really impressed. Tell you what," I continue, trying to sound professional, "come by the office tomorrow morning and I'll introduce you. I'm sure he'll give you the key to the whole damn newspaper."

"Great," Rick smiles. "So what have you been up to, Donna? How the hell'd you get stuck working in Fairbanks at the *Chena Times?*"

"I ran out of money and had to take this job," I say without lowering my voice. At least in Alaska it's no sin to be poor.

"Figured that," he says, ordering me another Irish. "What I really want to know is, how's your love life been? You married?"

"You already asked me that." I look straight into Rick's aquamarine eyes. Maybe he likes me. All those study dates I turned down to wait for that bastard Ivan to call me and apologize. Maybe if I'd gone out with Rick, I'd have gotten a good newspaper job too. "I'm not married yet," I explain as Rick watches Rena's glitter-covered nipples ripple up and down while she dances to the Wurlitzer's acid rock. "That G.I. I was tight with?" I say, remembering the excuse I always used when I didn't want to go out on a date. "He's been missing in action for three years now."

"I'm not married either. . . ." Rick's voice trails off as he watches Arny's scarred lower jaw twitch.

"Hey, really seriously, maybe we could work together on this pipeline article. I need a local like you to sort of, well, help me get a feel for this place. Like, what's happening with all the heavy equipment and oil derricks that Arco shipped to Prudhoe Bay in 'sixty-nine—they just waiting around? I want a local's point of view, Donna, come on."

"In the first place, Rick," I say, thinking that I must sound like one of his old Sigma Nu fraternity brothers, "I'm not a local. I'm from Sitka in Southeast. Alaska's a big state, three times the size of Texas. Where I'm from, the scenery's just like Seattle, almost—rains a lot, but nothing like that four feet of snow and ice lying outside the door here. And in the second place, if you don't remember all this, you'll always be an Outsider. And when you leave here, you'll be going 'out' with a capital 0 and—"

"What are you doing tomorrow?" he asks, interrupting me mid-sentence.

"Oh," I say watching Angoon Arny nurse his beer and study Rick's Timex. "I have to cover this exhibit at the University of Alaska Museum. Something on old Alaskan artifacts and pioneers."

"Me gonna be there too," says Arny, slurring his words into his draft Oly. "Gonna be in the Tlingit totem-pole exhibit."

"Oh, yeah," I say jokingly to Arny, recalling all the afternoons I spent listening to Butcher Bob talk basketball while we sat under the totem poles along Sitka's Lover's Lane. "What are you going to be doing?"

"No gonna do nothin'," he says, pulling his army-surplus parka across his open-necked long underwear. "Just sit an' pretend to carve one up, like my ancestors, whatever they did."

"I know about all those totem faces," I tell Arny, wondering what Rick's thinking about a drunken con-artist Indian being hired by a museum. "The whale, the raven, and the Abe Lincoln one with the tall hat." I smile at Arny, thinking that maybe he's my favorite of all the regulars at the Flame Lounge.

"Abe Lincoln?" Arny says, rolling his bloodshot eyes. "Who's that fucker?"

"He was an American President about a hundred years ago," I answer. "He freed the slaves. And since the Indians were slaves, they made totem poles of him, because they were so happy that he set them free."

"Totem of a white man with a beard and tall hat?" Arny asks.
"Yeah."

"White bogeyman totem," Arny says, his words muffled through the beer foam. "Stole Indian's children. Didn't know he's called Abe Lincoln. Shit, I hear that fucker's name all over the place."

Rick pulls out a pad and pencil again and starts to scribble notes. "The local Indian perspective," I hear him mumble, as he glances up at Rena, who's making slow, circular motions to the music of Iron Butterfly. "Hell," Rick says, "I talked to a lady this morning about that exhibit. Said that the captions around some of the pioneer portraits are all wrong. Like the notes on her great-grandmother, for instance."

"Who was she?" I ask inquisitively.

"I don't know. Some lady who's going to speak at the exhibit. She had some long hyphenated name. You know, like those English people who string one family name after the other."

"Was one of them York or Zimmerman?" I ask offhandedly.

"Yeah, that's it," he says, "York-Zimmerman-Sims."

I gulp, almost dropping my Irish coffee on the barroom floor as Rick gently puts his arm around my shoulder.

"The captions say that Mrs. Sims' great-grandmother was a cousin of some Russian princess, but this lady told me that her mother just made it all up. The great-grandmother—York I think her name was . . ." He checks his notes. "She was really the illegitimate child of a Russian convict worker and an Indian slave girl. It seems that Mrs. Sims' mother fabricated the whole story for some screwball society reason. If you're going to that opening tomorrow, Donna, maybe you could look into it. Hell, I'll even share the by-line." The liquor from the Irish coffee rushes to my head. Mrs. Sims must be Debra, I.Y.'s cousin. I remember the hunch-shouldered blond child in the York family portrait. I look over at Angoon Arny, but instead of seeing his scarred dark face, I see the picture of Nadia in the Zimmerman mansion. *She* was an Indian? But it makes sense: Nadia's red Haida hair, Gramma Raven's stories about Nadia's medicine potions. That's why all the local Tlingits liked her, not because she was the boss lady at the cannery, but because . . . she knew witchcraft. "A woman who does things," Mrs. Stephan used to tell me. . . . And that means that Ivan, and Charles, highbrow Charles Zimmerman, and his mother—they're all part Indian!

"Penny for your thoughts?" says Rick, looking hurt because he thinks I'm not listening to his story.

"Sorry, what were you saying about a by-line?" I ask, planning my visit to the museum tomorrow. Wonder if I'll see Ivan and Debra? Well, it doesn't matter. This time he'll *have* to see me.

"I'll share the *New York Times* by-line with you," continues Rick. "It'll be a great local-color feature. Mrs. Sims had some fantastic stories. A necklace of her great-grandmother's is on display there; the gallery just labeled it 'shaman necklace, *circa* eighteen-sixty.' Anyway this lady told me the story behind the story." Rick looks back at his notes. "Seems that Mrs. York used to sail around the southeast Alaska islands, looking for her lost mother. She did this for years and finally heard about an old Indian woman who'd been shot for stealing some winter supplies by a missionary father near Metla, ah—"

"Metlakatla," I say, helping him with the Alaska Indian pronunciation.

"Yeah, well, Mrs. York hadn't seen her mother since she was stolen from her at the age of ten, so it was hard for her to identify the body, which was, you know, probably all crapped out and eaten by worms." Rick rolls his eyes. "But the dead woman was wearing this necklace, this string of shaman amulets, that Mrs. York remembered from her childhood. My notes are a little vague," continues Rick, "but maybe you could do an interview with Mrs. Sims and turn it into something."

I smile. Rick pulls me closer to him and kisses my cheek.

A woman who does things, I think to myself as I run my fingers through the sideburns of Rick's red Afro. But why did Gramma Raven always say that I would grow up like Nadia? What'd she mean by that?

Trudging through the snow-covered sidewalk on my way to the University of Alaska Museum, I watch a copy of yesterday's *Chena Times* blow across the brown salt- and sand-layered street.

Being careful not to slip on the ice, I cautiously climb the steps of the angular cemetery-gray museum building and smile at the red-nosed Pinkerton at the door. Across the slate floor of the museum foyer, I see Rick standing with a group of pressmen near an exhibit of historical paintings entitled, "Alaskan Forefathers." I wonder if he'll ever stop pumping people for information on the Pipe?

Walking through the museum gallery, I stare into the painted eyes of I.Y.'s Aunt Catherine and Uncle Barnett, then at Ivan's father, Carl, and his mother, Betsy, holding I.Y. as a baby in her arms. Debra and Charles Zimmerman stand in the foreground while Ivan's father looks off into space, as if uninterested in the demure domestic scene.

Rick turns toward me, nods, and says, "Hi there." The other poker-faced newsmen don't say anything—probably wondering why a reporter from a New York paper would be talking to the girl who writes obits. I sigh, recalling Rick's warm body in my bed last night. As he'd snuggled his head into my stomach, I'd caressed the downy hair on the back of his neck and stared out my window at the phosphorescent arch of the northern lights. "Gramma Raven said that was the door to the vision world," I told Rick, wishing I had him in my bed every night.

I scan the museum artifacts. No Ivan. And no blond woman who looks like she could be Mrs. Sims. Now where's the oval portrait of Nadia York?

"Imperial Lumber," I hear Rick say to one of the other reporters, "one of the primary contractors on the Pipe, eh? Don't know a thing about them."

I stare through the glass display window at a collection of pioneer diaries—pages of Governor Alexander Baranov's fancy wide-looped script, and a Bible belonging to someone named Reverend Hitch together with a letter written in his tight, controlled hand informing a Mrs. Björklund about the lost remains of her gold-miner husband, found dead in a bruin trap. And, look here, Donna Lee, here's a leather-bound diary of *Noah York:*

July 14. The hemlock trees in Sitka Sound glitter in the rain. Betweentimes the sky is bright. Towering clouds. Four bald eagles nest in the spruce snags, the fiery sunset shining on their heads.

I study an odd drawing labeled "secret encampment" at the bottom of one of the diary pages. "The indomitable pioneer spirit," reads the museum caption below his leather-bound journal. But where is she?

Where's the portrait of Nadia? I walk to an open glass case, a large plaque looming in front of it:

Nadia Karimoff York, wife of Noah York and cousin of Princess Maksoutov, wife of the last Russian governor of Alaska. York, the son of a wealthy northeastern timber magnate, pioneered two of Alaska's most prosperous industries, timber and fishing. Mrs. York's regal background was an indispensable asset to her husband's business establishments.

"So Mrs. Zimmerman made that story up, huh?" I whisper as I stare at the girl with the red Haida hair in the portrait, the same face I'd stared at in the black and white newspaper photo taped for years to Mom's refrigerator. I look at the daguerreotype that the picture was painted from and then at the shaman necklace that Rick told me about last night. So Nadia was the illegitimate daughter of a convict father and an Indian-slave mother.

You sure look unhappy in there, little Nadia face, I whisper to the picture. Then reaching into the glass case, I unhook the small oval painting and slide it out under my coat. Just like old times when I shoplifted that padded bra from the Mode-O-Day dress shop to make Ivan notice me. The eyes in the dim daguerreotype follow my arm as I mentally type my next letter to I.Y. "If you want your Indian grandmother back . . ."

I hear the reporters exchanging a joke with the Pinkerton. "Shot of whiskey's just like a woman's tits," Dinwiddie says. "One's not enough and three's too many." The men all laugh even though that joke's been circulating through all of Fairbanks' Second Avenue bars for two winters running.

The daguerreotype fits into the palm of my hand, as I reach into the display case a second time. I pull it out, turning the back side of the tin print up; the words *Small-Lake-Underneath* are scratched into the metal. I replace the daguerreotype and take out the shaman necklace, putting it in my parka pocket.

"Hey, Donna. Donna," a man's voice calls from the far side of the gallery. For a moment my body freezes. Then, thinking that whoever

347

it is has seen me, I turn slowly around, the portrait under my down coat.

"Arny, Jesus Christ," I almost scream out of relief, "you scared me." I walk toward the totem-pole exhibit where Angoon Arny Kolosh sits amid a pile of wood chips, pretending to sharpen a stone adz.

"Hey, Donna," says Arny, as he motions to the totem of a bearded white man in a tall hat. "This bogeyman, what'd you say his name was? What'd you call him?"

"Abe Lincoln," I reply, starting to walk toward the door, praying that the portrait frame isn't poking out of my parka. "He freed the slaves," I say, calling over my shoulder and then nodding my head to the red-nosed Pinkerton who's reading the headlines of the *Chena Times* late edition:

VENEZUELA THREATENS NATIONALIZATION OF
AMERICAN-OWNED OIL FIELDS
Foreign oil cutbacks and price hikes predicted unless . . .

"Yeah," I hear Arny's voice echo through the museum's Old Alaska exhibit as I walk out the door, "stealing an Indian totem for his own. Just who does that fucker think he is?"

30. TWENTY-FIVE MILES
NORTHWEST OF FAIRBANKS
Late Summer 1973

Nadia's painted eyes look down at me from her place on the wall of Rick's and my sod-roofed cabin as I daydream about Ivan York. Just like playing a goddamn game of chess, Donna Lee, I tell myself. It's been more than a year since you captured his great-grandmother's portrait, and he's yet to answer the questions in your letters: Why did he walk out on me that night at his family's mansion? Why did he fire me from my job? Why does he pretend I don't exist?

Remembering that cold winter day at the University museum gallery, I toy with one of the wolf-fang beads on Nadia's shaman necklace—far-out flower-child jewelry you got, Rick said, the first time he saw me wearing it. Rick, I think to myself, looking around at our neatly kept cabin, why can't I just be happy with you instead of thinking about Ivan all the time?

After my museum caper, something about the awkwardness of the situation, compounded by the level of adrenaline that was pumping through my veins, made me decide it was time to leave the *Chena Times*, pipeline job or no, and strike out on my own as a free-lance journalist. Now, as the Alaska summer sun shines through the pine trees, a Yukon horsefly bangs at the windowsill while I bide my time with Ivan and type my latest article, written on speculation for *RV Travel* magazine: "Campfire Caribou Cooking." Boring as hell, I mumble, then give myself a pep talk: Hang in there, Ms. Douglas. After you've sold a few articles, you'll be able to get a magazine contract for an important interview; something that sits up and shouts, "I'm alive."

The wall above my desk next to Nadia's portrait is covered with rejection letters that suddenly bob up and down as Rick opens the cabin door and slams it behind him.

"Hey, man, mail call," he says, rubbing one hand on his red-flannel shirt. Rick drops two envelopes on my desk. A card from Bonnie in Anchorage, and a letter from *Rod and Reel* magazine. "Hey," he says again, as I look up from the typewriter he gave me last Christmas. He bites into an apple, then, sitting down at the slit-rail table in the center of our one-room house, swallows without chewing. "Guess what?"

His blue eyes shine on me, his red hair reminding me of the sun when it finally peeks through the clouds after a dark Fairbanks winter. For a moment I marvel at my feelings for him; it's as if I was a fishing boat and he was the sheltered harbor I'd tied up in during a storm. But where did all this joy come from? I ask myself.

"Probably another rejection letter," I answer, staring at the white envelope from *Rod and Reel*. Huh, looks like a little two-dimensional coffin. Wonder how I'd survive as a free-lance journalist without my unemployment checks and Rick's *New York Times* stringer salary?

"No, not that," he says, giving me a kiss on the top of my head, then begins to unlace his Chippewa boots. "The Pipe Authorization Act . . ."

I open the card from Bonnie first:

> . . . *bumped into our old boss, Ivan York. He said that he knew you was having a feud with your family, but that you ought to know your father was in a car wreck last week. I.Y. wanted me to make sure and tell you that Davy was going to be o.k. and back at work real soon, but if any unexpected complications came up, I.Y. 'd be in touch.*

"What the . . .?" I say out loud.

"When I finished my interviews down at the union hall today," Rick says, oblivious to the puzzled expression on my face, "I called into New York and the guys at the paper read me the latest AP print-out: After being stuck in the Senate for two years, the Pipe just ended in a tie, forty-nine to forty-nine."

I drop Bonnie's card on the floor. What am I supposed to make of this? With Pop's drinking problem, it's not his first car accident, but Mom could have at least broken her silence to write me.

Then I remember the news about the Pipe. "Oh shit," I rip open the letter from *Rod and Reel*. "If this pipeline doesn't hurry up I could starve to death."

"No, Donna," Rick says, taking a strand of my almost waist-length auburn hair and coiling it around his finger. "Agnew cast his vote and broke the tie. . . ."

Could this be Ivan's round-about way of trying to communicate with me? Sure hope Pop is okay, but if he was drunk when he got in that wreck, he'll lose his license for sure this time.

"It passed!" Rick breaks my thought with a triumphant shout. "All the supplies and prefab modules for the pipeline work camps came out of storage as of eight A.M. this morning!"

I glance up at Nadia, whose eyes look very serious today. "Saved by the bell. Only one more month before my unemployment benefits run out." I give Rick a playful hug and he bites my ear. Back at U.W. I never thought he was handsome; now I imagine that every woman in the world is after him. And when I think of all the emotional energy I wasted on romantic fantasies with Ivan, it makes me. . . . What did I.Y. mean, he'd be in touch if there were any "complications"?

"Yup, this calls for a celebration." Rick walks over to the cold-storage box under the sink and pulls out a six-pack of Olympia beer.

I take the letter from *Rod and Reel* out of its envelope.

"What does it say?" Rick hands me a bottle of beer.

"They rejected my article on salmon fishing in southeast Alaska because they thought by southeast, I meant salmon fishing in Georgia."

Rick senses that I'm distracted and not as overjoyed as I should be about the pipeline news. "Common error among ignorant Outsiders, my dear, common error." He tries to humor me by mimicking a pompous college professor, then bloats his cheeks and pulls his chin down with his thumb and forefinger to further his act.

"You're still from the Outside too, you know. You've only been here a little over a year," I retort. Should I write Bonnie and ask her to call Ivan's Anchorage Pipe construction office and tell him, "thanks for the message"?

"What else does the *Rod and Reel* editor say?" Rick asks, ignoring my mood.

"He was amazed that I knew about his magazine way up here in Fairbanks." I skim the letter for a second time. "And suggests that I write about what it's like to be a lady fisherman way up here with all these men," I add, trying to think of an angle to rewrite from.

"Chauvinist pig," says Rick, rubbing my shoulder affectionately. "You have to keep at it, Donna." He's still trying to humor me. "Hell, it took me a year before the *New Republic* bought my article on cancer and radiation and another year before they published it. Besides, it's better than that letter from *Ammo Monthly,* suggesting you write a feature on what it's like big-game hunting so close to the Iron Curtain."

I look at him, and we both giggle. "Yeah, you're right." I tack the rejection letter up on the wall next to Nadia's portrait. "Well," I say, remembering the good news, "now that the Pipe's coming, I can go to work writing advertising copy for *Nuna.*"

"Sure, sure," says Rick, opening another beer bottle and narrowing his heavy red eyebrows."

"What's the matter?" I smell the change in his attitude like a Sitka fisherman senses the weather by the change in the smell of the sea. "Don't you think I can get a job on the Pipe? I've had more than three years' experience working for an Alaska newspaper, you know."

"No, it's not that," he says, looking downcast. "Well, I mean I'd hate for us to have to break up housekeeping here because you got a high-paying job somewhere else. I mean, I think we've got a real solid relationship. We could be another milestone couple, like Sartre and de Beauvoir, the Brownings, the Curies, who knows? Isn't working on your journalism more important to you than some job, Donna? I mean, why else would I have taken you home to Jersey to meet my parents last Christmas?" His voice trails off as he forgets that he's just opened one beer and opens another, taking a swig.

"Rick," I say, remembering Newark and Trenton with a shudder. God, those places look like they've been bombed. "Rick, are you saying I don't care for you?" I try to take his hand, but he pushes me away.

"No, that's not what I meant." He peels the label off the beer bottle and tacks it up with the other liquor labels on his side of the cabin wall. "It's just that you're getting awfully independent, and well. . . ."

"What are you talking about?" I say as a sudden burst of anger blots out my preoccupation with Ivan's message. "You go away on your newspaper assignments, leave me for weeks at a time. Once last winter when you were gone, it was so cold that our truck didn't start even after I boiled the battery. I was stuck here alone, wearing two sleeping bags, and did I complain?" With mixed emotions I remember how I used to wait hour after hour for Rick to call me during those cold winter nights. Just the sound of his voice over the phone would make me feel warmer. There's something frightening about needing someone so badly, I tell myself.

"It's okay, Donna," Rick says, backing down. "I didn't mean it that way. It's not that I'm in favor of a double standard—"

"Look, Rick, all I want is to make my own way in the world. That's all, and to have a way of making money that doesn't bore the living daylights out of me. I don't want to end up like my mother, with no way of making a living and counting green stamps for the rest of my life."

"It's okay, Donna," he says again, and tries to put his arm around me. I stiffen. "I didn't mean to upset you." He looks at me longingly.

I force my body to resist his affections. No, I tell him with my eyes, I don't want this argument to end with us going to bed together again. If our relationship is so strong, then I want to get everything out in the open. Now.

I take a deep breath, as if about to dive into cold water. "If I get a job working for *Nuna,* the only place they'd send me other than their office at Fort Wainwright here in Fairbanks is Anchorage, or maybe their headquarters in Seattle. I've hung out here with you for the past year, wouldn't you come with me? Shit," I yell, suddenly feeling betrayed by Rick. "It doesn't matter where you live, you can do your Pipe reporting from anywhere in the Northwest."

"Please, Donna," he says, nervously handing me another beer, "it's okay. We'll talk about it later."

"No! I want to talk about it now." Christ, I think to myself, what's wrong with this guy? He's acting like I've turned into a monster just because I got pushy.

"We can't, that's what I'm trying to tell you, if you'd just—please— calm down." Something about the pleading, bewildered tone of his voice makes me give in a little. He extends his hand in a truce, and I take it, sighing. Christ, Rick, what is it that frightens you peacenik city slickers so much about having a little confrontation? For a moment my mind drifts back to Sitka, where barroom fights and loud domestic arguments are as common as the rain.

"I met an old friend of yours when I was interviewing down at the union hiring hall today," he continues, looking at me meekly. "I got to talking to this woman heavy-equipment operator, come to find out she went to high school with you. So I invited her here for dessert tonight."

"What? Who're you talking about?" I ask, my mouth opening in surprise.

"Urna McLaren," he says, smiling. "She'll be here in a couple of hours."

"Urna? Urna's in Fairbanks?" I ask, recalling her empty chair in my civics class after she got pregnant and had to quit high school. We were next-door neighbors in Sitka's Old York Homestead Mobile Home Court, and when we were little, Urna was the only other Anglo kid who used to play at Gramma Raven's. Now, who was it she always wanted to be when we had a game of grown-ups? Kat-lee-an. I smile as I remember how Urna used to "massacre" anyone who called her Tub-of-Lard. And if I wouldn't share my after-school snack with her, Urna'd play "medicine man," saying, "I'm going to put a witch spell on you an' make you fat, then no one'll wanna play with you, ever."

The glass in the cabin window shakes, and the pots and pans hanging from the log ceiling beams rattle together as a loud noise thunders down the road outside the house. Rick and I exchange puzzled looks, then run to the front door.

"Holy Moses," I say, stepping outside onto the front porch. "They've actually started building the Pipe." We both stare at a long stream of Peterbilts and Mack truck-trailer rigs pulling yellow bulldozers, earthmovers, graders, and mobile-home-green prefab housing modules. As we watch, a convoy of supply-carrying Hercules helicopters appears in the distance, making a terrible whirling noise, like a million Yukon horseflies.

"Jeez, all those choppers remind me of a Vietnam photo I saw when I worked at the *Chena Times*," I say, thinking of politics: Now that Ivan's helped lobby the Pipe into actuality, I bet dollars for doughnuts he resumes campaigning for governor.

Rick puts his arm around my shoulder, kissing me on the neck. We turn away from the heavy equipment and go back inside the cabin. As he unzips my Levis, I run my palm across his broad shoulders. How could a man who'd grown up in the city and never worked as a logger have shoulders like these?

With our clothes strewn across the plank floor, Rick pulls me close to him, cradling my naked body in his red-haired chest. I move away, lying down on the couch, and pull him on top of me.

"Such pretty white breasts," he whispers and takes one nipple between his lips, gently sucking it into a hard pink pebble.

Pushing his head back, I bend over myself like a morning glory closing up at night, and take his erection in my mouth. His body flexes.

He pushes himself gently across my teeth, then pulls out. I stroke the tip with my tongue, as if he were an ice-cream cone, remembering once last winter when I poured chocolate sauce over him, and it had taken me an hour to lick him clean.

He pulls me up, putting his tongue into my open mouth. Why is it that I can never get enough of him? My knees unlock, and I open myself to the universe, feeling possessed by something other than my own will.

At first we move gently, a boat rocking on the Sitka tide, back and forth with the infinite motion of the sea's current. Rick never rushes to his own climax without me, as Butcher Bob always did. With Rick I feel engulfed by the motion and warmth of his body.

The sound of him moving in and out of me recalls the cadence of one of Gramma Raven's Tlingit chants, and I am suddenly filled with magic. But as my body lunges forward, then vibrates with a prolonged spasm, tears begin to swell in the corners of my eyes. How long before this secret power evaporates, I wonder?

Five minutes after I'd taken Rick's favorite dessert, a wild-blackberry cobbler, out of the oven, Urna McLaren knocks at the door. Hasn't changed a hair on her head since I last saw her in Sitka back in 'sixty-six, I think to myself, as Rick shows her in.

"Urna!" I hug her large body, resting my chin on her workshirt-clad shoulder. "Long time no see."

"Hi, kid," she says in her husky voice, smiling her old, friendly smile. "The man here tells me that Sitka's little Princess Maksoutov is a college grad-u-ate, writin' newspaper stories." She runs a broad hand through her thin, brown hair and shifts her weight from one work boot to the other.

"Right on," I say, grinning into her wide face. The three of us sit down, and in five minutes Urna and I are talking just as if we were back in the Sitka High School cafeteria.

"Nice oil paintin', kid," she says, motioning to Nadia's portrait. "Got a few oil and velvet picture paintin's myself. The guy who sold 'em to me said they came all the way from Mexico."

"Thanks, it's a relative," I say, glancing sideways at Rick, who never batted an eye when I told him that it was a portrait of my great-great-grandmother. Lucky for me he was so busy pumping people for information about the Pipe that he never had time to see the portrait exhibit at the museum the day I stole it. And because *Nuna,* or the presidential primaries, or the war in Vietnam were always front-page news, the *Chena Times* article on the portrait and necklace theft was on page twenty-eight, with the grocery-store ads.

"Well, Donna," says Urna after a pause, "looks like I'm finally goin' to get me a job through the Operators' Union up here." Urna takes an enormous bite of cobbler, the juice from the blackberries dripping from one side of her mouth. I giggle in my beer, thinking, if only my Iota Chi sister Martha and her manners committee could get a load of Urna McLaren.

"They got a quota on local hire," she says. "Gotta take on Alaska residents first. That's what the Teamsters Union says."

"So what else have you been doing with yourself?" I ask, as Rick and I silently play a game of footsie under the table.

"Hells bells, Douglas, it's been a long time. Went to heavy-equipment school down in Anchorage. The welfare paid my tuition," she says, her fork clanking into her empty bowl. "Should have gone to truck-driver's school, then I coulda gotten into the Teamsters local. Got a whale of a president, all right. You shoulda heard him speak down in Sitka last year, Douglas, just like goin' to a holy roller church, 'cept better, 'cause it's your job that's at stake insteada your soul. People gettin' up behind the podium and testifyin' as to all the benefits the Union's gotten for 'em—twenty bucks an hour wage, plus all-expense-paid in-surance coverin' all your medical, dental, optometric, and pre-scription bills. Yeah, and if someone in the audience calls it a lie, the Union president—looks just like one of them Sitka bald eagles, if ya want my opinion—says he'll jump head first outa ten-story window if it is. Better than goin' to a movie most times, listenin' to them Union teamster guys preach. They really make ya feel like you're important in this world."

"No shit," I say, wondering if I should learn some kind of skill to supplement my free-lancing work. "I'm going to get a job writing ad copy for *Nuna,*" I tell Urna, as Nadia looks down on my little after-dinner dessert party—Urna and I sitting across from each other and Rick at the end of the table, pretending to proofread the copy of his next week's *Times* article, though I know he's really taking notes on Urna. Probably got it under the heading of "Local Sentiment." I smile fondly at him.

"So how's everything in Sitka?" I ask cautiously, wondering if I.Y.'s story about me being on drugs and whoring in Seattle ever made the rounds among the residents. But then I tell myself, why should I worry about morals around Urna? She had an illegitimate baby, went on welfare to keep it, and as I recall, no one was ever sure who the father was, not even Urna.

"The same, kid, the same," she says, grinning, her large, square teeth shining in the late-evening light of Arctic summer. "Mama keeps care of my little girl, Ramona, and they're still livin' in the same trailer court. Oh, maybe there was a few changes the last time I went back to visit." She opens an Oly and takes a swig. "After Bert Dysokar married your sister, he got shipped off to Nam, you know. My brother Mac finished his tour of duty over there, now he's back working at Alaska Fish. And the Animal's still pinin' because he lost Bonnie to show business."

Urna and Rick laugh about something that happened down at the Union Hall this morning. I glance over at my writing desk, where the letters addressed to my mother marked *return to sender* are stacked. Then I recall a fragment from a recent dream about Nadia. Her portrait was talking to me in Gramma Raven's voice: "Long time ago," she whispered, "words were magic, and if you spoke them things would happen. . . ."

"What?" I realize that Urna's asked me a question.

"Is your dad goin' to get a job with the Pipe?" she says again.

"Probably not. He was just in another car wreck, but everybody says he's going to come out of it just fine." I remember Bonnie's "message" from Ivan. What did I.Y. mean, he'd be in touch? How come he's playing good guy again, not only forgiving me for stealing his family's heirlooms, but pretending like it never happened? Maybe he's just too busy mapping out his gubernatorial campaign to be bothered with me.

"Yeah, kid," says Urna, after I explain that I don't have much contact with my family anymore. "Your sister, Vicky, went back home there to your parents' trailer till Bert gets back from Nam. Guess when he's discharged he'll go to work for Alaska Fish again like my brother Mac.

"The last time I called home, my little Ramona answered the phone pretendin' she was Daffy Duck," Urna says with a proud grin as she begins a mother's my-kid-is-so-cute story. Remembering Urna's taste for the Indian boys over at the Bureau of Indian Affairs High School in the old Navy base on Japonski Island, I begin to wonder just which one of them was her kid's father.

"How's Bonnie, ever hear from her?" asks Urna after a brief conversation with Rick, comparing V-eight Corvette engines and D-eight Caterpillar earthmovers.

"She's in Anchorage, go-go dancing," I tell her, thinking that maybe I should tell Urna about my archaeo-journalism project, maybe she'd remember some of Gramma Raven's stories. "Bonnie had some big, important booking during the King Crab Festival, got to be one of the judges in the taxidermized crab contest. Says she makes a hundred dollars a night in tips sometimes." Christ, Donna Lee, once you sold an article for a hundred dollars to *Trip and Tour* magazine, while your old high-school friend Bonnie's getting that kind of money every night, just dancing topless on tables.

"No kiddin'?" says Urna, slapping her knee good-naturedly. "I thought she'd get married right outa high school."

"She's a looker, isn't she?" pipes up Rick, then gives me an embarrassed look, as if I'd already jumped on him, saying, "Stop mouthing off about women and acting like a fraternity man." I say nothing, and Rick and I both giggle. Then he gets up from the table, rolls a joint, lights it, and passes it to Urna.

"Ain't none of this good grass or liquor gonna be allowed in them Pipe camps," says Urna, taking another toke off the reefer.

"Really?" asks Rick, making notes.

"Yeah," says Urna, "*Nuna's* got real strict rules, just like that Sheldon Jackson church school in Sitka—no drugs, no liquor, no whores on campus or off, or ya lose your job." She glances down at the table, following the grain of the wood with her fingernail. "Ya know what this table needs?" says Urna after a pause.

"A tablecloth?" asks Rick in a sincere voice.

"No," she says with her deep laugh. "No, this table reminds me of the Dock Shack in Sitka. You remember, Donna, where we'd go after the games?"

"Yeah," I say, beginning to feel the grass go to my head, "what this table needs is initials!"

Immediately Rick pulls out his red Swiss army knife and starts digging a big *T. V.*—for The Vette—into the table, then passes the knife to Urna just as the pots and pans hanging from the cabin rafters begin to rattle.

"Another convoy of heavy equipment," says Rick, as all three of us run to the door and stare out at the long stream of yellow Caterpillar earth-movers, tractors, and bulldozers.

"Probably all bein' towed to the first Pipe camp north of Fairbanks," says Urna, taking another toke. "Livengood, they call it, used to be an old gold town. Shit, them *Nuna* dudes ain't wastin' a bit of time."

"Let's follow them," says Rick, slipping into his investigative-reporter role.

The three of us pile into Rick's and my GMC pickup and turn north toward the Hickel Highway and Livengood Camp.

"Can't use the Hickel Road," says Urna. "On the other side of the mountains, it sinks into the tundra, looks almost like a river. But hell, that's probably what all them earthmovers is for," she continues. "Afore they lay the Pipe they gotta build an access highway. Everybody down at the Operators' Union calls it Haul Road."

Our truck speeds north behind the convoy, up through the aspen-covered White Mountains toward the Yukon Valley and the river. Along the road blue lupine and orange poppies in the alpine meadows shine like neon lights among the thin-trunked white birches. Our truck passes two red fox pups playing in the dirt of their fox mound. All this sudden highway noise doesn't even phase those little critters, I think to myself, watching the pups roll in the dust. Hum, Pop always used to say that that was how foxes took a bath. Pop . . . How could he have believed I.Y.'s lies about me and told Mom that if I ever came home, she was to turn me out? How could he . . .? But if he's in the hospital, maybe this would be a good time for me to go back to Sitka and set things straight with Mom. 'Course, if she ever finds out I stole the York portrait, she'll be convinced I have "bad blood" for sure.

"Largest privately funded project in the world," says Rick triumphantly as he waves a hand at the long convoy of yellow heavy equipment on the road in front of us.

I remember when I told Rick about Ivan York's Project Ploughshares plan to A-bomb the Beaufort Sea, to make it deep enough to tanker oil out of Prudhoe Bay; the thought of all that radiation sent Rick into hysteria. Now he thinks of the pipeline as our own personal conquest over destruction.

"In just a few more weeks I might be drivin' one of them rigs," says Urna, pulling a pack of Winston menthols from her shirt pocket and lighting up. For a few minutes I stare at Urna's full chest, trying to picture her in the Iota Chi sorority house. Then I remember how we always had to measure an index-and-middle-finger space above our left breast before pinning on our Iota Chi pins, because hanging it any lower would "call attention to the part of a woman's anatomy to which a *lady* never calls attention."

"Yeah, man," says Rick, "this Pipe is really going to be an environmental masterpiece. I've seen some of the plans, Urna," he continues in an excited voice. "When the Pipe's not buried and has to be above ground, they got walkways across it so that the caribou and moose can migrate."

"No shit?" says Urna.

"But that isn't all," says Rick, seeing that Urna isn't fully impressed with all of *Nuna*'s wildlife safeguards. "They even put up a test bridge north of the Yukon River last year, just to make sure it'd work."

"Huh," says Urna. "What happened? A moose eat it?"

I stifle a giggle, and Rick gives me a hurt look.

"Of course not," he says, as I turn from his serious face, looking out across the White Mountains and back toward the view of the Tanana Valley sprawling with one-story houses up and down the muddy banks of the Chena River. God, in just a few months' time all this green will turn to white and be covered with ice. Out of the corner of my eye I watch a ptarmigan whose brown summer feathers are already fading to winter white.

"They found hoofprints going over the Pipe bridge," Rick continues with an emphatic note rising in his voice.

"Well, I'm not surprised," says Urna. "Hell, a moose would go through, over, or under near anythin'. Kid," she slaps Rick on the knee, "I've seen a moose go through an eighteen-wheeler without a scratch—near demolished the machine, though. But a caribou, now a caribou is a critter of a different color. A caribou is scared of his own shadow."

"As I said before," there's a heavy edge to Rick's voice, "they have hoofprints as evidence."

"Hoofprints?" says Urna mockingly. "Hell, most *Eskimos* can't tell the difference between a moose print and a caribou's, let alone some Outsider scientist hired by *Nuna*."

"Donna," says Rick, changing the subject, "did you put some film and the camera bag in back of the truck?"

"Yes," I answer, trying to envision the job I'll get working for the oil companies.

"I'm going to get some shots of the first work done on the Pipe," he says, as he turns the truck up the final grade before we plunge down into the Yukon Valley. "'First Earthmover to Bite into the Tundra'—maybe that's how I'll caption it. Hey, man," he smiles, "this could be my lucky break."

"Mine too," says Urna. "Goin' to get me a job that'll bankroll me right into a piece of prime Alaska real estate, a sort of nest egg for me an' Ramona. Then I won't have to always be waitin' on my kid's father or the welfare to come through with them monthly payments."

"Oh, child support?" I ask, taking note. So, she does know who the baby's father is.

"Kinda," says Urna, as the truck climbs the last quarter mile of the steep grade. The birch and apsen give way to a few scraggly pines dotting the craggy snow-covered mountains above the timberline. "More like money to keep my mouth shut," she says in a cynical tone. "Which I do . . . usually." She smiles.

Wonder which Indian guy it was? Maybe one of those Tlingit missionary teachers at Sheldon Jackson School where they don't even allow you to drink off-campus, let alone have an illegit kid with a high-school girl. My hands fidget in my lap as I restrain myself from asking Urna *who* he is. Probably some high-caste Tlingit who got a whole lot of money out of the Native Claims Act. Bonnie said that the Indians in Sitka are building themselves a chain of hotels with all that money.

The truck crests the hill, and Rick pulls to a stop.

"Holy jumpin' Chinook," says Urna as we stare down at the hundreds of yellow earthmovers, graders, and dozers that dot the Yukon Valley. "Whatta mess."

Rick stares open-mouthed at the vista of overturned tundra and fallen scrub pines. The sky rumbles, and one of the small hills across the valley explodes in a series of dynamite blasts, forming a red cloud of moss and muskeg mud across the low-hanging Arctic sun.

"Jesus Christ," I say, thinking that the landscape is starting to take on the characteristics of Newark, New Jersey. Slowly Rick climbs out of the cab and fishes around in the bed of the truck for his camera bag.

"It looks,"—he stammers—"it looks like those pictures of Hiroshima," he says in disbelief, his voice fading off into the cold late-summer Interior breeze.

"Looks like the landfill site at the old Sitka garbage dump," says Urna.

"Well," says Rick, resolving himself to the dishevelment below us, "at least it doesn't cause cancer."

"Just looks like one," says Urna passively. "'Course, what could you expect with that turd, my kid's father, havin' a hand in things."

"Who was he?" I blurt out, suddenly turning toward Urna.

"I thought you'd guessed," she laughs, unfazed by my question. "Our old boss, I.Y.—Ivan York."

31.

The bargelike green and white ferry, *Rhododendron*, sails around the snowcapped tip of Mount Edgecumbe and heads for the Sitka marina. I forgive him for everything. The evergreen cones of Three Sisters Peaks come into view, then the white beehive-like boxes, the grave markers in the veteran and pioneer cemetery on the hill above town. Wonder if they buried him there?

How come Mom didn't write me, how come I had to read about my own father's death in the library when I was scanning an obit column for old times' sake? "From complications due to injuries incurred in an automobile accident, compounded with cirrhosis of the liver and diabetes. Age 44. Devoted husband of . . ."

The long, slug-slow ferry nears the wharf; the wide lawn of the stucco and pink-tiled Old Pioneers' Home appears, then the bridge to Japonski Island. . . . I study the shore. It's gone, the Dock Shack's gone. They tore it down to build the new suspension bridge.

Davy Douglas. What was I doing the moment he died? Typing one of my articles? One of my Nadia stories?

I disembark the ferry with the other passengers, mostly elk and deer hunters who've come down to Sitka from Juneau for the opening of the season. Their red-orange fluorescent hats and vests shine like neon through the fog and *saanah* rain of the late fall. Guns, gun cases, ammo belts, hunting knives. As I walk down the plank onto the dock, I wonder which of them won't come back.

Pop, what was he thinking of the moment he died? The gray sea fog that's rolled in over my hometown feels like the fog inside my head. Then I wonder what my mother's going to think when I show up at her door. He was my father, she could have at least told me. . . . Wonder how she's going to get by now?

For a moment I smile, thinking of Rick. He said he'd come with me, but I told him I had to make this trip alone. "Going home alone," I laughed—something quite different from going home with your new husband (which I don't have), or going home as the scholarship girl who made good (which I didn't). I was going home to make friends with my mother.

I follow the hunters as they strut like Canadian geese, along the wooden dock lined with seiners and salmon trawlers, their decks cluttered with fishing gear, with radar and radio antennae. I head toward Lincoln Street, then down Kat-lee-an Lane past the Alaska-rose hedge in front of the Pioneer Home, toward the Mooseloose Saloon, Pop's favorite watering hole.

I glance up at the wide verandah of the tile-roofed rest home where Paddy the Pig and Halibut Pete are sitting as usual on deck chairs covered with blankets, chewing the fat with a deer-hunter tourist who wants to hear stories about frontier Alaska. The bronze statue of "The Prospector," carrying his pick and shovel, looms over the sloping lawn.

The cement sidewalk turns to mud and boards as I approach Indian Town and the Mooseloose Saloon. Walking into the wharfside bar, I slip into a back booth, gazing at the familiar surroundings; a pool table at one end, crowded with Tlingit boys, a huge brass ship's bell—free drinks all around if you've got the hundred bucks it costs to ring it—and the walls plastered with eight-by-ten framed pictures of every ship that ever pulled into Sitka harbor. The Saint Lazaria run aground in a storm; the Icy Queen listing badly to one side; the Fa Do, a Chinese junk owned by some summer people. Above all the ship photos, his nose still high in the air, a moose with a stringy beard spreads his huge rack of antlers almost from one cobwebbed corner of the ceiling to the other.

"Whiskey on the rocks," I tell Leona, the fortyish waitress-bartender. Pop's favorite drink. Odd, even when I was a little girl he looked middle-aged to me, his thin, olive-complexioned face furrowed like the potato fields of Idaho he'd abandoned to move here. Davy Douglas, it was almost as if I didn't know him; he hardly ever talked to me, but I think not out of neglect; he was either working two shifts at the pulp mill or asleep: "Quiet now, Daddy's had a long night," I can still hear Mom's voice whisper. "He has to work two jobs so we can get ahead on Vicky Lynn's doctor bills." Vicky. Now why didn't *she* tell me our father died? How come my own sister didn't even tell me about the funeral?

The hunters in the next booth are matching whopper stories with the local fishermen. "Where's that king salmon you promised me, Earl?" asks a black-bearded man in a red-and-black-checked Roomy Richard jacket.

"Outside," says Earl.

"Where?"

"In the sea," retorts Earl's baritone voice. Everyone laughs. "Hey,

Leona, you get a bigger bra size, or have I just been out fishin' too long?"

"We always miss you 'round here, Earl," says Leona in her forty-five-going-on-six-year-old-little-girl voice.

"I'll bet," says the black-bearded out-of-town hunter, "just like she misses the clap."

I rest my chin in the palm of my hand, thinking, this is where Pop spent most of his waking hours when he wasn't at the mill. I look out the window at an Alaska spruce gnarled like the body of an old woman. Behind it the tiled roof of the Pioneer Home. . . .

Leona turns up the radio loudspeaker. "KRAB Sitka, Channel ninety-three point seven A.M. on your dial. Local weather: there's a Southeast gale alert, folks, tie down your rigs and hold in. . . ." The D.J. rambles on for a moment, then plays Tammy Wynette's "Stand by Your Man."

I sip my drink hoping it'll give me the courage I need to face my mother. I close my eyes, trying to recall an early memory of my father:

I am about six years old, dressed in my Sunday-go-to-church dress and rubber boots. Mom and I are in the old Chevy, Pop's driving. Vicky Lynn is asleep in the back seat. Mom holds her Bible on her lap, while Pop talks about elk-hunting season: He's going to bring home a haul, he says, keep Mom busy canning it up. Or maybe, he says, we'll have enough left over at the end of the month to rent a frozen-food locker down at the packing company.

Pop pulls up in front of the Pioneer Home. He's humming his favorite tune, the theme song from Davy Crockett.

I look past my mother's lap into his steel-gray eyes. "How come you didn't give me a name with a TV show? I don't like my name."

My mother's lips turn down, she looks sad. "Doni, Doni Lee, queen of the wild frontier," sings my father. "You gotta pretty name, little girl," he says, "real pretty. And someday you'll grow up and marry a fisher-man who'll name his boat after you."

Pop lets us out his side of the car, because the other door doesn't open and is tied shut with a piece of rope. Mom and I join a group of Jehovah's Witnesses church ladies who are wearing gray rain hats. I wave to Bonnie and Mrs. Ostahowski, then to Pop, who waits for us in the car while we go to read the scriptures to the patients. The church women walk along the rose hedge, up the walk, then past the bronze statue of "The Prospector." "What's his name?" I ask.

"Mr. York told your daddy his name was Seattle Charley," Mom tells me. We sit on the Pioneer Home verandah, and Mom reads Matthew to Mary Richardson. I look down at the car with Pop in the driver's seat, lifting a bottle of beer to his lips.

Mary Richardson is covered in blue blankets the same color as my dress and sitting in a wheelchair. "Behold I send unto you prophets, and wise men, and scribes," Mom begins.

Mary Richardson isn't listening. "Why ain't there no bronzed woman out there with ol' Seattle Charley," she screams, but not at my mother, not at anyone. "Why didn't they bronze her heavy skirts, the baby she carried on her back, and her fifty-pound pack of provisions?" Mary raves, lifting herself up from her wheelchair. I hear a bottle drop on the sidewalk, then roll into the gutter. As I look down across the lawn at Pop, he smiles back at me; even from where I am I can see his two wolf-fang teeth.

"And some of them ye shall kill and crucify; and some of them shall ye scourge in your synagogues, and persecute from city to city," Mom continues.

"Women climbed the Chilkoot Pass and panned for gold just like men did. So how come they didn't bronze a statue of Seattle Charley's wife?" the old woman demands to know.

"All these things shall come upon this generation," Mom finishes.

I look from my mother's placid eyes to Mary's angry toothless mouth, then stare at my father. He waves, shaking his head. . . .

One more Mooseloose Saloon drink, I tell myself, then I'll be ready to walk up to Mom's trailer.

"What ya doin' tonight?" Earl asks me as I go to the bar. I ignore him and look out the open barroom door to the wharf. The charred ruins of a pier building stare back at me. Holy Mo. . . .

"What happened to the Alaska Fish cannery?" I ask Leona.

"It burned down, honey," she says, raising her plucked Tokyo Rose eyebrows and pulling at a bra strap that's fallen across her bare shoulder. "Some California hippie fucker got pissed off at Ivan York for firin' him, so he torched it," pipes up Earl, running his rough calloused hand over my arm.

No shit. I stare at the blackened posts and pilings of the cannery where I used to work. I saw a sea of fish blood in there, I brood, my thoughts returning to Pop. Wonder if it hurts to die. Wonder . . . if his soul is still here, if it hasn't gone off to the hereafter yet, but is still in this bar somewhere, watching me. I scan the hunters walking down the boardwalk outside the bar, thinking I see my father among them—tall, lean, black chinos, blue workshin, hard hat, bent shoulders.

I miss Rick.

The KRAB disk jockey roars, "It's Sha-Na-Na time for all the folks from the Tanana Valley," then plays the flip side of Johnny Cash's "Folsom Prison Blues." Before I came here Rick and I made our plans for working on the Pipe. I tried to get a job writing ad copy for *Nuna,* but it seemed that they'd contracted all that work out to advertising firms in Houston, just like they'd contracted most of the construction work to Imperial Lumber in Seattle. So much for hiring local Alaskans, I told Rick when it became apparent that the only job I could get was as a Pipe work-camp secretary. But what the hell, I told myself, it'd make good material for a feature article, and the pay was out of sight. In just one year working on the line, I'd made more than I'd made during my three years at the *Chena Times.*

I thought my college education would help, but it didn't. According to the gossip at the Flame Lounge, when the pipewelders who'd been imported from east Texas and Oklahoma lit up their torches, they found that their Arctic engineer supervisors wore Arrow collars and Harvard T-shirts under their Yukon parkas. As the Harvard kids pointed to the time clocks and coaxed the welders to give it the old college try, they found out that nobody tells the good ol' boys in the pipewelders-and-fitters local to do anything. And word soon got around that anyone sporting a college degree on his chest was due for a broken nose at least.

"KRAB, ninety-three point seven A.M. on your radio dial," says the too-happy-to-be-believed D.J. "Our time is your time, and it's three thirty-one in Southeast. Gale warnings up. But folks, there's a man in

our studio right now who's not just blowing a gale, no sir. Ivan York—
I.Y. to his friends—and he's got a lot of them hereabouts."

Ivan. Ivan's here in Sitka! Oh Jesus. The shot glass slips out of my
hand, and an ice cube skids across the Formica table. But maybe it's a
tape.

"So the Trans-Alaska Pipeline is really going to happen?" says the
radio D.J. as Earl pulls out a deck of cards.

"The largest privately funded project in the world," says Ivan's
voice, very polished and controlled.

"And I guess this means jobs, jobs, jobs?" The D.J.'s voice sounds
as if he were a V-eight engine winding up for the Indianapolis Five
Hundred.

"Bigger than the Great Wall of China," says Ivan, and I remember
that he borrowed that line from his cousin Charles.

"So when's the Man going to run for governor?" asks the D.J., pop-
ping his fingers into the radio microphone.

"The Pipe's barely under way," Ivan says, sounding almost coy.
"There's a lot of hard work left to be done."

"But surely," says the radio announcer, "a man who's moved something as big as the pyramids of Egypt from the drawing board into
reality could be one king salmon of a governor." God, Ivan's got them
begging him to run; they're eating out of his hand. . . . Well, maybe
he wouldn't be such a bad governor. Then I remember Urna; Urna's
illegitimate daughter. If that story ever got out, I.Y.'s political goose
would be cooked. So Urna was Ivan's lover. I still don't believe it. Wonder why he picked her over me? And she said he was always watching
our trailer out the window when he visited her, watching Mom in the
kitchen. Creepy. I shudder and nurse what's left of my drink. Leona
pulls a hankie out of the depths of her cleavage, dabs at her mascara,
and replaces it.

Earl and the bearded hunter in the red-and-black-checker jacket
strike up a game of gin. "I'll bet ya two of my best thirty-ought-
six deer rifles for that Russian A.K. forty-seven you smuggled outa
Nam . . . with the bayonet," Earl bargains.

"Throw in your Bowie knife."

"You're on," says Earl. Another hunter rings the huge brass ship's bell above the bar, and Leona passes out a free round of whatever drink you've got in front of you.

"No, I couldn't do it in good conscience. Not right now," blares Ivan York's voice over the loudspeaker. "At best, I'm an undeclared nonpartisan candidate." Jeez, that man is smooth, he's got everyone eating out of his hand.

Hey, Ivan, why don't you tell your listening audience about your unclaimed Indian granny? Leona turns down the volume on the radio.

"Goin' to take me a long vacation down on Seattle's Fifth Avenue," says Earl." I wanna bring Leona back one of them black-lace you-know-whats."

I close my eyes and try to block out the noise of the card game, hoping to resurrect the image of my dead father, then with sadness realize that the man I lived with for seventeen years is a stranger to me. I take a sip of my third drink. How many whiskeys do you have to have, Donna Lee, before you're ready to do your *housekeeping?* I make a mental list of my *chores:* visit my father's grave; confront my mother, trying to make friends with her; and now, maybe even finish some old business with Ivan. No wonder Pop drank. After three shots, I'll be ready to take on the whole United States Army.

Then I remember a Sunday when I was about seven or eight. Pop's in his faded blue p.j.'s and a white terrycloth robe; a slipper hangs from one foot. It's autumn, hunting season, like it is now, and Pop's been laid off again at the mill. The wind rattles the screens on the trailer windows as Pop watches a TV football game. Ivan's there; stopped in on his way to the bush for a trophy elk. The two men are laughing and drinking Olympia beer. I climb on Pop's knee and he bounces me, while I pretend I'm the Lone Ranger on a horse. I smile at Ivan; he pats me on the head. "She's going to be a heartbreaker when she grows up. Look at that smile and that hair. Red always was my favorite color."

A player on the TV screen is tackled on the ten-yard line and carried off the field. "Ah, shit," yell Pop and Ivan simultaneously. A commercial flashes across the tube and Pop bounces me harder. Ivan says that Pop's layoff will only last a week at most. Then both men start talking about hard times in the nineteen-thirties.

"I was just a little bugger," I.Y. begins, opening another bottle, "but

I remember all those WPA workers the government sent up here. Frank Roosevelt, now there was a man who knew how to play all the angles. If it weren't for him, we wouldn't have that fancy Pioneer Home building. 'Course, then there were all those artists F.D.R. sent here."

"Artists?" asks Pop.

"Yeah," says Ivan, handing me a silver dollar. "Give this to the widows and orphans, Miss Lone Ranger," he tells me. "Yeah, they painted portraits of the old-timers. Even painted my Grandfather's Eskimo sidekick, my Grandfather Yo's Tonto." I.Y. looks at me and laughs.

"But after those WPA artists got finished painting, the war in Europe broke out. Know what they did with all the canvases? Wrapped artillery in them, and sent them to the Allied Forces."

"No shit?" says my father. His narrow face fills with a wolf-fang grin.

"Can you imagine, Davy, what some British soldier thought when he unwrapped a U.S.-made cannon and found a picture of a senile half-wit Eskimo?"

I open my eyes, and all the boat photographs on the wall of the Mooseloose Saloon blur into one. The radio D.J. has moved from his interview with Ivan York to a cut of "Your Cheatin' Heart." Funny, the only time I remember Pop being happy and playing with me when I was a kid was when I.Y. was around. Now how come Ivan didn't tell me about my father dying? He told Bonnie that if there were any complications. . . . Oh, what the hell.

Slowly I rise to my feet, making my way to the door, my stomach feeling like a swamp full of leapfrogs. Three drinks is too many, Donna Lee. I put on my rain hat and go out into the fall drizzle, walking up the main street of town toward Sawmill Road and the Old York Homestead Mobile Home Court. I smile. The liquor has put an invisible shield between me and the rest of the world.

A bell chimes, followed by the melody of a Slovakian song echoing between the green cinder-cone mountains surrounding Sitka. So they rebuilt the old Russian Church after it burned down the year I went off to college. Looks just the same, except they painted it gray and all the corners are square. Too bad they couldn't have made it sag a little, just for old times' sake. I turn up Monastery Road, past the deserted and decaying House of Bishops; then the trailer court comes into view—pink, green, and blue mobile homes like little Easter eggs planted in the scrub alder.

Number Five Old York Homestead. Staring at the mailbox, I'm overcome with a wave of sadness that crashes down on me like the Sitka tide in a storm. Davy Douglas. I wipe my eyes and move on. Strange thing about the sea of grief, I tell myself: The tides are unchartable. Some minutes I'm okay, and others, God, I feel like I can't stop crying even though I'm in a bank or on a ferry or. . . . Mom's trailer comes in sight. She's in the kitchen window, same as usual. I put my hands to my lips. What am I going to say to her? How do I start? I watch her standing with her back to the window, wearing a blue bathrobe. Her arms are animated. Who's she talking to? Sicky Vicky, probably. My shoulders droop at the thought of having to confront my mother with my sister looking on.

I walk toward the kitchen steps. Voices. Like an argument. Maybe she and Vicky have finally had a falling out. I smile to myself. No, it's a man's voice. I stop at the first step on the kitchen porch. God, these trailer walls are thinner than paper.

I hear the man saying, "laundry," or is it "launder"? Maybe Mom's taking in wash again, like she did when I was little, to earn pin money. I catch my breath.

The man's voice is Ivan York's. In an involuntary motion, I turn to run. Confronting them both at once—I'd need more than three drinks to do that. But as the words pulse out from the trailer walls, my feet stand motionless in the mud.

"I don't care," I hear Mom say, her voice raised. "I won't do it any more."

"Emma, Emma," says Ivan," It's not illegal money, we just used the E.M. Douglas Corporation to launder funds, so we can pump them back into the economy a little faster. It's simple economics, it's . . ."

I remember the letter I saw in the copy machine when I worked for Imperial Lumber.

"What would you have done without it?" asks Ivan. I reach for the doorknob. Is he going to hurt her? "Davy was drunk on his feet half his life and—"

"He was a good man, a good, God-fearin' man," says Mom. There's more energy in her voice than I've ever heard. "You won't talk about him that way in his own house. He did a lot for me. He didn't have to, he wasn't my Christian husband. It was all *your* doing."

"My family had other plans, that's all," says Ivan, his voice retreating a little. "Look, how long do I have to say, 'I'm sorry'? I've helped you with that daughter of yours for years—"

"My daughter! Donna's your daughter too," Mom screams.

My hand falls from the doorknob, my body feeling like I've walked into a high-voltage electric fence. Turning, I run down the gravel road to where Gramma Raven's pink trailer used to be and jump into the tall rhododendron bushes that still grow in her yard.

"Donna's your daughter too," rings from one side of my brain to the other. That's why all Ivan's attention, that's why the abortion, the college scholarship. It wasn't because I earned them, it was because I.Y. felt guilty. No wonder Pop tossed me out, I wasn't . . .

The feel of Fatso between my thighs comes back to me.

"No," I scream, diving under one of the rhododendron bushes, their wide dark leaves all looking at me like those eyes in the portrait room of Ivan's family mansion. "No, God, no." I throw up until the vomit blots them out.

32. FAIRBANKS
1974

"*Who's* getting heavy?" asks Rick. "I know you're going through an identity crisis, so if you can't handle *us,* it's okay, the marriage plan is off."

No, Rick, you don't know what I'm going through. You don't know what it's like to grow up with one set of parents, one family, and then suddenly find out you belong to another—at least half to another. You don't know what it's like to have lusted after your own father.

We walk over Fairbanks' University Bridge, crossing the Chena River. A summer mosquito bites my arm as I look down into the wide, slow-moving water; just a few short months ago it was covered with two feet of ice, which made the noise of cannon shot when it started breaking up in the spring.

"I'm not even trying to talk to you about us," continues Rick. "I'm talking to you about telling the court what you know about Ivan York."

I cover my ears when I hear the man's name. "You have the sensitivity of a horsefly," I retort. Donna Lee, who is this person leading this surreal life? And why do these horrible things keep happening to you? Here you are, twenty-five years old, your life is a mess, and your journalism career is barely off the ground. When I was in high school I thought that by the time I was in my mid twenties I'd have a yellow-brick *Sunset* magazine ranch house, a husband, children, and if I wanted it, a job in a nice office. Instead, I'm temporarily employed as a pipeline secretary at Old Man Work Camp, wondering who I *am*.

"You have to testify for the prosecution as a character witness," Rick insists. "Now, no one's got any solid evidence on York's foul dealings concerning the pipeline, but like I wrote you in my letter, an Alaska Fish boat got busted on a narcotics rap last month. One of York's largest shrimpers was running all kinds of barbiturates and coke, heroin, you name it. The man's guilty, Donna. And with York, the head construction contractor, behind bars, maybe work on the Pipe'll slow down long enough for Congress to take another look at what's really going on up here."

I try to blot out Rick's voice by remembering that warm late-summer day almost a year ago, when Rick and Urna and I were happily contemplating our jobs on the pipeline. But the Plan and the Pipe didn't quite turn out the way we figured. Rick's attitude toward the project as his great triumph over radiation-producing energy and cancer was rapidly turning color. Like the war in Vietnam, the price of the Pipe had escalated—from under one billion dollars to over ten billion. And as the landscape north of Fairbanks began to look like a Warner Brothers set for *World War III*, the energy that powered the heavy equipment in the Arctic nonstop through the winter of 'seventy-three–'seventy-four could have heated the entire city of Seattle for two years running. Somehow Rick felt responsible for the situation, saying—with an air of self-importance that was beginning to annoy me—that all the good press he gave it in the *New*

York Times could have swayed Congress's opinion when they finally granted the pipeline right-of-way permit. But instead of bearing the full blame, Rick held Ivan York personally accountable for his great triumph going amiss.

"Christ, Rick," I say, watching a blue Clorox bottle float down the Chena River, "this is my first R and R from Old Man Work Camp in three months. I'm exhausted. I don't even have the energy to get into a conversation. You promised me that if we saw each other again there wouldn't be any hassles." I should have known better. Ever since my eventful trip to Sitka, I hadn't been able to cope with getting up in the morning, let alone with a potential marriage.

"I walk around most of the time feeling like I've got the flu," I say, trying to stifle the edge in my voice. "I think at this point *any* male-female relationship would make me sick." Did I really say that? Is that really me? Maybe I'm finally getting smart about leaving a love affair before it goes sour. God, I wish Urna were here. I've never been to a shrink, but talking to her must feel just as good as talking to a therapist would—and it's a heck of a lot cheaper.

We turn into the Fairbanks campground where Rick is supposed to be interviewing people who've come north to get work on the line. Jeez, wall-to-wall Winnebagos, Airstreams, anything that can be hooked up to a four-wheeler and moved. The population of this city seems to have doubled overnight. Just look at these license plates—Texas, Arkansas, Texas, Illinois. I turn my head away from the cars to the Chena River. Birch trees on the rocky bank bend in the wind, as ptarmigan in brown summer plumage fly from treetop to treetop.

"All I know about Ivan York," I begin, "is that he'll probably be Alaska's next governor, and he's my illegitimate father. Not exactly solid evidence for a narcotics case."

"He's your father, and he tried to molest you," says Rick, angrily raising his voice.

"How do I know I didn't try to molest him?" I think of Fatso, and my stomach feels sick. "I was really hot on I.Y. when I first met you," I confess in a small voice.

"You're being irrational, Donna," Rick says, his face reddening. "The man knew he was your father. He led *you* on, not vice versa.

Now," he says in his older-brother voice, "I want you to get your head together and start thinking about testifying."

We sit down at a campground picnic table, watching the sludge of the Chena flow by, looking at all the crashers who are sleeping off last night's drunk under the University Bridge.

"How do I know that you're not just mad at I.Y. because you think my newly discovered past fucked up our relationship? And what good's my testimony going to do anyway? Besides, I never want to lay eyes on Ivan York again. I just couldn't handle it."

"Look, Donna," says Rick emphatically, "I've been doing a lot of investigating on this guy. I've got stacks of depositions and affidavits. You're just one witness, but we need all of you to make this case stick. No doubt the defense'll have every top government official in Alaska testifying on his behalf."

God, yesterday I didn't think I'd live through being a camp secretary, and now I don't think I'll live through my R and R. "So one of his boats was carrying drugs, how do I know *he* had anything to do with *that*? And other than scramble my brains, what's Ivan done that's so terrible? You're just using him as a scapegoat."

Rick rolls his eyes with impatience. "York's into illegalities up to his ears. You know that bank you told me he was a trustee of down in Seattle? Well, it and Imperial Lumber and the whole state of Washington would have gone under if the Pipe didn't get built. You have no idea of the lengths that man's gone to to get this insane project moving. And God only knows if the pipeline'll actually work."

"It might not work? The oil companies would put up ten billion for a project that might not work? That's incredible. Besides, only a few months ago you thought this project was going to save the world. Now you're trying to save the world from it."

Rick shrugs. "They won't know for sure until it's built."

Nervously I run my fingers through my hair.

"There's got to be a better way, Donna," he says, gazing up at the high clouds above the White Mountains looming in the distance beyond the sprawl of cinder-block houses and the Fairbanks suburbs. "I've been doing research on energy produced by—"

"Your opinion changes with the weather," I retort, feeling annoyed.

"Every morning I pick up the paper and read about destruction: Nam, Watergate. Then I look outside my camp dormitory window and see piles of gravel where the greeny-brown grass of the tundra used to be—more destruction. What makes you so sure something new won't mean more of the same? At least this pipeline finally got me a high-paying job."

"You're a secretary," he says in a superior tone, rubbing his newly cultivated red beard.

"I get paid twenty-five thousand dollars a year!" I almost shout, suddenly feeling angry and wishing that Rick would just leave Alaska so I wouldn't have to worry about ever seeing him again. "More than I got at the *Chena Times* pursuing my career. I'm doing damn well for someone with a shipwrecked psyche. To say nothing of the fact that I make more than you do as a stringer, so put that in your pipe and smoke it, *Mr. New York Times*."

"Hey, man, come on," he says, putting his arm around my shoulder, "don't get shook. I got you plenty of by-lines, didn't I? I got you into a lot of doors, Donna. Now's your chance to do something for me, okay?" He looks at me as if I were a naughty child.

So what good did those by-lines do? I ask myself. Mom probably never saw my articles, she doesn't read the New York papers; all she reads is the Sitka shopping news. And she still sends my letters back, marked *return to sender*. But I can't really blame her for not being able to deal with me; how do you tell your own daughter that you've been lying to her about her father for twenty-five years?

"Ivan York's done everything from extortion to murder," says Rick, "and you can help put the finger on him."

I narrow my eyes at him. "I don't believe you."

Four heavily made up young women step out of a Winnebago from Illinois, each wearing a pompadour wig and a Frederick's of Hollywood slit-to-the-waist miniskirt. Everyone said that the pipeline would open up the Arctic to development and make Fairbanks an international city, but I don't think fancy call girls were what they had in mind.

"Come off it," says Rick, the soothing patience of an indulgent parent dissolving from his voice. "Ivan York was desperate. The oil companies took him for all he had, they know a good goose when they see one—he's power mad as all get out. They got him to have Northwest Savings and Imperial Lumber put up a whole lot of money on spec, to promote this project. You know, like sending that flotilla of heavy equipment from Seattle to the Arctic, so that Imperial Lumber could be one step ahead of the other construction companies as far as building contracts go. A whole lot of money, way beyond federally insured regulations. The oil companies are too smart to risk their own necks. Hell, *they* haven't done anything illegal. If the Pipe didn't win in Congress, Northwest Savings and Imperial Lumber would have folded, and the whole thing dominoed right down the line. Crash. Worse than in nineteen-twenty-nine, in this part of the nation anyway. And no skin off the oil companies' noses."

"*York Love Child Testifies Against Father Who Helped Finance Jobs for Thousands.* Rick, my testimony would have the credibility of the *National Enquirer.*" I put my head down on the picnic table, feeling like I want to go to bed for a week. "Ivan doesn't even know that I know about him being my birth father." Wonder what he'll do when he finds out? Well, at least I know why I.Y. tried to discredit me, why he told Mom and Pop those lies about me whoring and taking drugs. Ivan didn't want my parents to know that he'd had incestuous ideas about me. He fixed it so that if I ever told Mom and Pop about my "big date" with him, I wouldn't be believed. Mom would have just thought I was on dope and hallucinating.

"Just think about it, Donna, that's all I'm asking you to do." He gives me an annoyed look, then takes a deep breath. "And testifying isn't all you can do," he begins slowly. "You could get things, facts, information out of York. You could—"

"Stop it," I scream. "Don't you *listen* to me? I told you I don't want to see him, let alone *use* him. And why do you hate him so much, anyway? If there's anyone who should hate him, it's me."

"Well, don't you?"

"I don't know. I don't know what to think about him." I turn away from the river and stare at the low, rolling pine-covered hills that look like a green sea surrounding the iceberg-like White Mountains. Then I remember Gramma Raven's story about Koosta-kah, the Ottermonster who kidnaps sleepers and leaves them amid the mountain ice. But since Mrs. Stephan was brought up by missionaries at the Sheldon Jackson School, most of the stories of her Indian people must have been taught to her by Nadia—my great-great-grandmother. My great-great-grandmother, I say over and over to myself, trying her name on like one would a dress. I'm a York, I whisper. But it just doesn't feel right, it's not me, Donna Lee Douglas, whoever that is; a girl the Ottermonster stole away in her sleep, abandoning her on a mountain glacier. Just like the poor unfortunates in Gramma Raven's story, I woke up one day and all my surroundings were different. It was never me I.Y. was in love with, it was Mom—or the person my mother was when she was sixteen. God, I wonder if I'll ever be sure of anything again . . .?

"Just because my psyche feels like it's been abandoned on the tip of an iceberg doesn't mean that Ivan York abandoned me completely," I tell Rick. "He watched over me most of my life. He didn't have to, you know."

"The way Ivan watched you from Urna's bedroom, when you were in high school. The man is totally amoral, totally—"

"Urna takes full responsibility, she told me so. She was hot to trot—those are her words, anyway. She hated high school, she thought that having a baby would make her grown up, and she didn't want to get married—tied down to some millworker like her mother was."

Rick bangs his fist on the picnic table. "I'm tired of you defending Ivan York all the time." The feathery green birch trees next to us bend to and fro in a sudden wind. "What'd the Yorks ever do for you?"

"They did a lot . . . in their own covert way. In the first place, I.Y. helped me get an abortion, so I wouldn't have to get married at sixteen like Mom. . . ." For a moment my voice fades as I remember that my mother had to get married because of me. "They sent me to college. I.Y.'s Aunt Catherine even tried to help me 'climb the ladder of social success' by sponsoring me into her sorority. And Ivan never turned me in to the . . ."I stifle my words in a cough, because I never told Rick the truth about stealing Nadia's portrait and my "flower-child" jewelry.

"Donna," Rick says, as if he hasn't been listening, "your testimony may not seem like much, but with all the others put together, the prosecuting attorney has a good case. Besides, it's not coming up until fall, so you've got a couple of months to think it over." He digs the heel of his Chippewa boot into the dust. "You're not alone. I've got depositions from construction workers York never paid, shopping-center owners who think his construction is slipshod, and a stack of fishing violations for Alaska Fish vessels as long as your arm."

My mind must have wandered. "What's that got to do with the drug trial?" I ask impatiently. Rick pulls a baggie of pemmican out of his down vest and offers me a handful. I shake my head as he chews a pinch as if it were snuff.

"You've got to think of this evidence in the broader scheme of things," he says.

I take a deep breath and swat the two mosquitoes biting my arm.

"Look, Donna," he says, "I know I'm on to something. York's been having me followed, and my phone is bugged. I'm sure of it. Everywhere I go I see these two thugs behind me."

"You've been reading too much about Watergate," I reply. Christ, why can't I.Y. just disappear so I'll never have to hear his name again.

"Everyone'll think I'm testifying to get even with him, or to get his attention. *Illegitimate daughter*—"

"Perfect, Donna, you're the perfect character witness. Just get up there and say anything you can to sway the jury. Expose the guy for what he is."

"But what about *my* character?" I ask angrily. "And what about my mother? She'll be humiliated. Then she'll *never* want to see me again. Besides, the jury may not even believe me. All Ivan has to do is smile at them and they'll forgive him for everything. And then where'll I be?"

Two ptarmigan approach our picnic table, pigeon-like, expecting to be fed.

"Just because I've had personal problems with him doesn't mean he'd make a bad governor. Besides, what if work on the Pipe did stop? You lived in the East, you know they need heating oil there. Bonnie told me that when her agent booked her dancing act on the Chicago bar circuit, it was colder there than when she worked in Fairbanks." I close my eyes and think of Bonnie's last letter: "I've got a marvi new night-club act, Donna Lee. First I come on stage in a gold lame pants suit, just like Diana Ross would wear. Then I do something that looks like I've lit myself on fire! And *whoosh*, I strip down to a rhinestone G-string. My agent can't decide if we should call it 'Bonnie Bonfire' or 'Aurora Bora Erotica.'"

Christ, my high-school girl friend who quit after one year of business college makes a hundred dollars a night and is probably hooked up with a famous country-western nightclub singer, while here I am, the Sitka scholarship girl who became an emotional paraplegic.

"Sure the country needs oil," Rick retorts, as two more dusty pickups drive past us through the campground, looking for a nonexistent camping site. "But I doubt if this oil's going to go to them," he says, waving toward the trucks. "It's sour crude, full of sulfur. Do you know what that means?"

"The refineries are going to smell like rotten eggs."

"No," he says authoritatively. "You can't use sour crude for lubricating oil, it doesn't stick. And you can't burn it for gasoline because of the air-pollution laws. All the oil in Alaska won't do your car a bit of good when it runs low on the dipstick mark. Not only that," he adds, his hands becoming animated, "I've been doing some research, and there isn't an American refinery that can handle this much sour. It's all going to get super-tankered to Japan. When everything is said and done, Alaska oil'll probably cost more than Arab oil. And I'll lay you odds that the oil companies planned it that way all along. They probably had a deal with the Japanese from the beginning. Did you ever wonder, Donna, why there were eight hundred miles of four-foot pipe shipped all the way from Japan to Valdez even before *Nuna* got the permit to build this thing? Christ, I can almost smell the hanky-panky."

"But Rick," I say, listening to the family at the next picnic table as they complain about Fairbanks rents—a one-bedroom for $400 a month and a waiting list as long as your arm. "They passed a law saying this oil couldn't leave the country. Besides," I add, feeling more exhausted than ever, "you ecologists are all alike. You have a terrible bent for intrigue and melodrama."

"A lot of good a law that no one can enforce will do," he says sulkily.

"Then if the law's no good, why do you want me to testify against one of Alaska's most popular personalities?" I counter.

"You're getting irrational again," he says, his face turning red. "You're letting your emotions rule your logic. My investigation is vitally important."

"And Donna Douglas's damaged psyche isn't? Is that what you're telling me?" I feel like I could go for his throat.

"Listen, Donna," he lowers his voice, "it's a conspiracy. You've at least got to help me infiltrate Ivan York's operations."

I breathe heavily, like a bull ready to charge. Now I've heard everything.

"And if you won't do that, you could at least help me get into some sensitive-information files up at Old Man Work Camp."

"Why should I? All I've heard from you is some vague gibberish about illegalities and—"

"Donna," he says with a faraway look in his eyes as he gazes across the Chena River toward downtown Fairbanks, "I don't have an airtight case, but this is how it goes: There's a rumor that the oil companies own most of the stock in America's nuclear-power plants. Now, a consortium of oil companies is building a pipeline that'll produce more sour crude than anyone knows what to do with. Are they building any refineries? No. So they're going to send it to Japan. Okay, but why, I asked myself, do they they want all this oil in such a hurry? Then it came to me—for barter, for oil dollars, to trade to oil-poor underdeveloped countries for the uranium to power their nuclear plants. There's a few holes in my theory, I know, Donna. But one thing's for sure, underdeveloped countries can burn sour crude gas because they don't have any laws about sulfur in the air."

I say nothing, just give him a cold stare.

"This pipeline has to be stopped, Donna," he says, looking at me in earnest, then turning away to avoid my caustic stare. "I can tell you don't understand the magnitude of this problem. There may be volumes of nuclear regulations, but as far as preserving human life goes, none of them are worth diddly. Did you know that a truck carrying enough radioactive waste to cause cancer in everyone within a one-mile radius drives from a research facility down Broadway in Manhattan at least once a day? Do you know what it says on the side of the truck, Donna? *Ken's Trucking* in yellow and purple letters, that's all—

probably some sick joke on the yellow and purple radiation-warning emblem.

"Christ," says Rick, giving me a disparaging look, "I feel responsible. I wrote a lot of good press to get this pipeline going, and now it's up to me to stop it. I've only got one chance in hell, Donna," his voice cracks, "and that's to put Ivan York behind bars and hope work on the line slows up a little. That'll give me time—God," he moans, "time, that's what I'm doing, buying time to get Congress to give this project another serious look."

"So," I say, watching the Arctic chickadees bathe in the dust of a campfire pit, "what you're telling me is that if Donna Lee Douglas doesn't testify against her illegitimate father, the whole country, the whole world," I add for emphasis, "may the of cancer."

"No," says Rick, playing his trump card, "you may the of cancer."

Our eyes lock in a stare. Now *that*, I think to myself, is the first thing he's said today that makes sense. Maybe Rick is onto something, maybe.

Rick sighs and takes a long look at me. "But look, Donna," he says, "if it's all going to be too much for you, well, I don't want you to crack up just because I insisted you do this. There's," he stammers, "there's other ways you could help. You've got what it takes." He leans over the picnic table. "You're pretty enough. You can infiltrate the oil companies, you could . . . you know. We could work together on this. . . ."

"Stop," I scream. "I'm tired of people trying to use me. You can all go to hell." I bang my knee on the picnic table as I get up to leave. "You can just go to hell," I shriek over my shoulder and walk toward the bridge.

33.

Max, the ruddy frown-faced driver shifts his yellow and green *Nuna* Peterbilt into low gear and turns north onto Haul Road. Gazing out the passenger side window, I survey the landscape: Five miles outside of Livengood Work Camp and the Pipe-related destruction has hardly begun to thin. Tractor trailers pulling loads of gravel or forty-foot lengths of four-foot-wide green pipe roar along the dirt highway. The diesel smoke hanging overhead reminds me of Sitka fog, so thick that I can't see the choppers buzzing around upstairs, bringing in camp supplies or just looking for gravel digs, an excuse to give the Caterpillar operators a chance to turn the hillocks and muskeg bogs into so many piles of dirt.

I lean back and close my eyes. After I stomped out of the Fairbanks City Campgrounds, leaving Rick in a cloud of dust behind me, I went back to my room at the Cripple Creek Hotel and slept for two days straight. When I woke up, the receptionist gave me a radio message from Urna McLaren: "Have to talk to you, please come back to work quick." So I caught a ride with Max, a blaster pulling a load of dynamite to Old Man Camp. As we head across the Yukon valley toward the Brooks Range and the Arctic Circle, I study him out of the corner of my eye. Looks a little like Pop, my not-father, I think to myself, watching Max's brown, weather-beaten hands as he steers the eighteen-wheeler across the bridge over the muddy Mississippi-like Yukon River. Funny, Pop's been dead almost a year, and I still think I see him on the street sometimes. Or like with Max, I always find myself looking for Pop in someone else.

Wonder what Urna wants? I ask myself. I only have another half day of vacation before I go back to work—couldn't it have waited?

Then on the north bank, I begin to see ptarmigan feeding on the pale-green lichens and tundra grass, while in the distance across a valley of muskeg bogs, I think I see a herd of brown caribou. The Brooks Range looms in front of the truck—sharp, gray mountains with steep valleys no white person has ever set foot in, and so many rugged treeless peaks that no one's bothered naming them all. As we speed along Haul Road, I watch wind-pruned pine trees bend in the Arctic breeze, and the pink of wild-onion flowers peeks out from behind the tall grasses. But just when I think I've spotted a skittish caribou, the whole vista disappears in a cloud of dust and a passing gravel truck.

Oh God, I moan, trying not to think about my disastrous R and R and my big fight with *Mr. Howard*. But, I rationalize, maybe he's just trying to reach me. Must be hard relating to a woman who's been living in a daze. I have to admit that I still care for Rick, but I don't want to testify against Ivan. What good would it do? And I don't know that I.Y.'s done anything wrong. Christ, maybe I should just give Rick the Old Man Camp confidential files to pacify him.

About two hours south of the Arctic Circle, a red fox darts out from her mound and runs alongside Max's truck, just as if we were one of the wild animals of the tundra. Her fur is as red as Mom's hennaed hair, with a black-tipped tail and face and a pointy black nose. She runs alongside my passenger-seat window the same way that I've always imagined African cheetahs would run: fast, going from zero to twenty miles an hour in seconds. As Max pulls the Peterbilt to a hault, the fox stops too, as if we were in a game together.

"You going to give her part of your sandwich? Feeding animals is against *Nuna* regulations, you know," I say, then wish I hadn't, because I sound like I'm talking to a little kid.

"'Course not," drawls Max, giving me a disdainful look. "Hell, most of them Arctic foxes is rabid. Did I ever tell ya about the time last year when a buddy of mine had his tail-end bit into and the critter's jaws wouldn't unlock?"

"Yeah," I answer, remembering that that story was a lesson in my pipe-camp orientation class out at Fort Wainwright.

"Oh." Max looks disappointed.

The red fox ducks into a hole, and the Peterbilt speeds on toward Old Man Camp.

"Did I ever tell ya the one about me and my partner and this grizzly bear down near Valdez last spring?" asks Max, raising his furrowed brow.

"No," I answer, taking a deep sigh and wondering how many grizzly-bear stories I'll have to listen to before the pipeline is built.

"This old brown mama bear chased us up into a fir tree, woohaha, about twenty feet up. Had us corralled up there till someone sent a whirlybird after us to scare the critter off." He takes a breath and shifts the truck into a higher gear. "I ain't never seen country like that there east of the Port of Valdez," he continues, chewing on an unlit cigar. "Mountains so steep you have to use ropes to climb over 'em, and hell, it snows *sixty feet* in the winter. Ya know what sixty feel of snow'll do to a dynamite blast, honey?"

"No idea," I yawn. "Where'd you work before you got on here at the line?"

"South Africa," he says, sucking his cigar.

"They have lots of oil there?"

"Hell, no, honey," he says, "ain't got a drop. Worked excavatin' mines. Some guy with a fancy-ass British accent'd point the way and I'd let her rip with the old blastin' caps."

"What kind of mines?" I ask, thinking that the blasters, like the pipefitters and welders, have some sort of worldwide circuit that they move through.

Max holds his cigar between two fingers in one hand and steers the truck with the other. "Copper, zinc, uranium."

I catch my breath. Uranium. Just calm down, Donna Lee, I tell myself; file it in the back of your head and tell Rick about it the next time you see him, if you see him. God, how could he have been so insensitive? How could he not understand that I just can't handle seeing Ivan? Rick always makes me feel like I'm caught in the middle between him and my "father." Just give Rick the Old Man Camp confidential files, I tell myself, then he'll feel like you're being loyal to him. But, Christ, why should I let him manipulate me like that?

Max babbles on about his grizzly bear encounters as I slump down in the cab of the Peterbilt, looking out over the yellows and greens of the tundra grasses, remembering the broad, low-hanging heads of the black bears that Rick and I and Angoon Arny used to watch out at the Fairbanks dump. Often a bear would eat too much and just lie down flat on his wide behind to take a snooze in the late-night Arctic sun, amid the mosquitoes and Yukon flies. Rick and I did have some good times together, I remind myself, beginning to feel guilty about walking off and leaving him in the campgrounds.

Max drives through another cloud of dust, talking about laying the Pipe: digging the trench, packing it with spun-glass insulation and meters to measure the heat and cold. Sinking drainpipes into the trenches to siphon off water from the permafrost melting from the oil-hot pipe. Above-ground vents, below-ground vents—eight hundred miles of the most highly specialized trench in the world.

I sigh, wondering when I'll get my energy back, when I'll feel normal again. Then I recall Gramma Raven telling me I would grow up like Nadia, "a woman who does things." Did Gramma know that Ivan was my real father? And what did she mean by "does things"? That I have certain powers? I twist one of my long auburn braids, remembering that the Tlingit shamans got their magic from their hair. Ever since that day I overheard Ivan and Mom talking about me, I've let my hair grow, not just the hair on my head, but on my legs and under my arms. As I realize that I'll probably never feel like my old self, the Donna Lee Douglas I was a year ago, my shoulders fall forward. Then I fill my lungs with air—a woman who does things—and I already feel a lot better.

I gaze over the hilly tundra spotted with blue cornflowers and white puffs of Alaska cotton, thinking that maybe I'd just seen the eerie face of an Arctic wolf behind the last jack pine. Those wolves, they're sure not the comedians the black bears are, nor the fireballs those red foxes can be. No, wolves are like haunted spirits with a strange crazy look in their eyes, strong legs like a horse's, and huge feet. They don't look like dogs at all. I stare out at the tundra where the Pipe hasn't been laid yet, wondering if, after they dig it up, the Arctic will ever be the same.

Back at Old Man Camp, I make a beeline for my dormitory room and flop down on the narrow bed below where I've hung Nadia's picture on the thin fiberboard wall. Next to it hangs her mother's shaman necklace. Just one more day to recover from my R and R, I tell myself, reaching up and running my fingers across the brush strokes of Nadia's black-red painted hair. Nothing else for me to do here but work on my journalism articles, read trashy novels, or lie on my back, looking out the window up at the corrugated aluminum ceiling. And where's Urna? Wonder why she told me to come back early?

I stare at Nadia. I have your hair, I whisper, and your stories. Gramma Raven must have known that I was your great-great-granddaughter. Gramma'd never say, "Let me tell you a story, Donna Lee"; she'd say, "Let me give you a story." Gramma told me that the Alaska Indians owned their stories, that no one else had the right to retell them, and that an Indian would only give her story away to her child, or to someone special. I glance at my desk, at the stack of Nadia "digs": *Raven Stories,* I call them now. They won't get lost, Small-Lake-Underneath, I whisper to the portrait. I promise.

Then I begin to contemplate my other York "relatives": Catherine Zimmerman, I wonder how she regards me? As a secret kindred spirit, a girl who grew up in Sitka, worked in a fish cannery, and was chosen to play Princess Maksoutov in the Alaska Day Transfer Ceremonies Pageant like herself? Or am I just another one of her little charities? I think of her museum collection at the University of Washington, all the Indian art she took away from Alaska. Then I look up at my wall at the long wolf fangs of the shaman necklace; well, at least some of it's found its way home, I laugh to myself. I stroke one of the fangs, wishing that my energy would return, that I would have the mental and emotional power that those teeth once had.

I roll over. Guess I could go over to the "library" and watch the poker game. Why not? Big Urna'll probably be over there, hanging around that handsome new gambler in camp. Hootz Mercer, is that what Urna said his name was? Might be good character material for one of Rick's and my pipeline interviews, if I ever decide to speak to Rick again. But, I think as I stare out my dorm window, wonder if there's anything to this conspiracy theory, or if he's just deep into another one of his eco-journalist melodramas?

God, look at all those D-eight Caterpillars out there today. They've knocked over almost all the pine trees, and there isn't a grassy hill left, just piles of smashed white rock. I don't blame Rick for wanting to stop the Pipe; maybe I should give him those files. But they're mostly a stack of requisitions. Now how does he think those are going to help him?

I watch a Cat move like a Sherman tank across the horizon. Urna says that there's nothing to driving heavy equipment. Always making fun of me because I'm college educated and make only half as much as she does as an operator. Says I could get on easy through Local Hire, just like she did. Only takes a couple of hundred dollars to buy your way into the union. Urna told me that she was just hanging around the Fairbanks Union Hall one day, trying to pick up a date and picking up a job instead. Said that on my next day off she'd give me a driving lesson when the timekeeper goes to the potty or the break tent for doughnuts and coffee.

Well, I'll drop in over at the library and return these overdue paperbacks, *Savage Hunger* and *Destiny in Del Rio*. I walk out of my room and down the long fiberboard hallway. Dormitory Module D looks just like a bigger version of Mom's trailer.

Outside, the sun glares bright enough for me to be wearing dark glasses, even though it's almost midnight. I walk across the mud and gravel courtyard of Mod Six, to the library and poker-pinball room, listening to the noise of bulldozers and dynamite. These hills are beginning to look more like gutted buildings than a wilderness area. I glance over my shoulder toward the Brooks Range. God, the night shift's going hog wild, Cat drivers, drunk on the latest load of contraband vodka, playing touch tag and keep-away with the heavy equipment.

"WELCOME TO THE LARGEST PRIVATELY FUNDED PROJECT IN THE WORLD," says the sign over the entrance to Mod Six. At the far end of the metal room I see Urna watching Max, the blaster, and a couple of ex-Vietnam chopper pilots playing blackjack with Hootz Mercer. She gives me a quick glance, her cigarette hanging from the side of her mouth and burned down almost to the filter. I return the two books to the shelf next to the *Star Trek* pinball machine and pull up a metal folding chair next to Urna's large body.

Fuck you, Urna, how come you can't say *hello*, I think. I'm just back from my two-week R and R, had a royal fight with Rick, and I'm wondering why you left a message for me to come back to work early.

I watch her stare at the cards in Hootz's hand. In the center of the table are at least enough fifties to cash two payroll checks, enough money so that the guys are too preoccupied to greet me with comments about the various parts of my anatomy.

I glare at Urna's stringy brown hair and red face. Looks like she's been partying for a week straight.

"How ya doin', Douglas?" she says in her deep, rapsy voice, hardly moving her eyes off of Hootz. There's something about that man that reminds me of Ivan: handsome, swarthy, the center of attention, a little on the silent side at first. A man who appears to have the situation in his back pocket, but still fits in as just one of the boys.

"Well, I'm here, ain't I?" I retort, thinking that working in this camp isn't helping me improve my English.

Max, the blaster, wrinkles his ruddy, frown-lined forehead and picks up another card. "Look, Dillingham," he says to one of the Yul Brynnerheaded chopper pilots, "lemme give ya a little *ad*-vice. You're goin'' to need protection workin' up here, but don't never buy yourself a registered pistol. Picked this little bit of info up from an officer way back when I was workin' prison guard. Get ya a pistol off the street, see, and don't never register it, but don't never get caught with it neither," says Max, throwing another fifty into the pile. "When ya have an encounter with an *intruder*, or whatever ya be callin' it, make sure ya hit him at almost point-blank range. Then discharge a coupla cartridges into the wall, wipe your prints offa the gun, put it in the intruder's hand, squeeze his hand around the piece real hard, just to make sure there's a good clear thumbprint for the *po-lice*, and then *vamoose*. No way in the world the law can trace it to ya. They'll just be thinkin' the guy slipped and shot himself by accident."

Oh, God, I think, nervously fumbling with the button on my bell-bottom jeans. I remember that Rick told me he thought Ivan was guilty of everything from extortion to murder. But Rick always gets carried away. Then I recall something Gramma Raven once said. "All Indians have stories. The stories of their ancestors, and the story that is their own." And since I'm maybe one-tenth Indian, I must have a story. But what is it? The story of the pipeline, of men sitting around discussing the finer points of murder. . . .

Urna, can't you take your eyes off that man for just a second and tell me what's going on, why you wanted me here?

"Funny," says Hootz, his bloodshot brown eyes slanting into a sneer, "I shoulda taken you for a guard. Your face is ugly enough."

"Done time, I take it?" says Max, as the Bobbsy-twin chopper pilots study their cards.

"Yeah," says Hootz, "done it and done with it."

Hootz cracks a smile and Urna stands up, taking a dollar bill out of her wallet. She scribbles a few words on it with a felt pen and passes it over to me: "Got a favor to ask. I'll come by your bunk in about an hour. Big U."

Urna, are you for real? Can't we talk now? Or do you want me out of the room because you're afraid I'm going to horn in on Hootz?

There're only four of us women in this camp. Lady's choice, the welders from east Texas say. Well, Urna, you can have the guy. What would I do with a professional-gambler flim-flam man anyway? Sit home alone, waiting for his luck to run out? Besides, he reminds me too much of I.Y. I bite my lip, trying not to think of Fatso.

Max starts talking about the latest camp fatality, a runaway Peterbilt mowing down a group of Bechtel engineers.

"A setup," says Dillingham, one of the chopper pilots, in an Oklahoma drawl. "Them welders don't take kindly to fast-talkin' executive types. Always tellin' em, 'do this, do that,' just like they was your mama."

"Old Man Camp is almost more unhealthy than Nam," says the other chopper pilot.

"Who gives a shit about a bunch of smart-ass college boys?" says Max, wrinkling his forehead. "Hell, their faces all look like a baby's behind."

Rick's right, I tell myself, this pipeline has gotten out of hand. No telling how many people get killed around here. Rumor has it that the only deaths that go into the *Nuna* statistics are their own employees, not those who get killed doing work *Nuna* contracted out to some engineering company.

I walk out of Mod Six into the courtyard and the diesel smog. Guess I could go over to the cafeteria and have an early breakfast of bacon, eggs, steak, pancakes—the works. Standing in front of the "slop shop" prefab, I try to decide if I'm going to eat one breakfast or two today, while three guys load an unofficial pickup truck with cartons of frozen turkeys. Huh, probably going to sell them to the Indians over in Stevens Village for a little quick cash.

A loud smashing noise echoes through the hills. Where the land slopes down into Beaver Creek two dozers disengage from each other, the trunk of a birch tree caught in the tanklike treads of one of the Cats. Christ, this outfit is going to have every bump on the land flattened before the Pipe goes through. I watch Angoon Arny, the Operators' Union's one claim to Native Hire, raise his fists at the driver who rammed his dozer, and listen to the two men exchange strings of obscenities. Last week the Hercs flew in two loads of government men just to watch an Indian at work. Too bad they aren't here to see Arn try to beat the shit out of the guy who smashed his heavy-equipment shovel.

I walk back to Mod D, watching the operators ram and butt their dozers like stags in the spring. I wonder what the best way would be of getting Rick those "confidential" camp files. Should I Xerox them, or just mail them to him? Then if anyone notices they're gone, "Well, they must have gotten lost," I'll say.

Shutting the aluminum door, I walk into my room, thinking that maybe I should write to Rick, try to patch things up. But what's the use? He'll never forgive me if I don't testify against Ivan.

I pick up a copy of *Line Camper,* the pipeline newsletter. Reminds me of working at the *Chena Times,* except that this paper's classified, and personal ads are more interesting. Let's see, two perforated applications for the "Need-a-Date-Service"—Specify your female preference: short, fat fanny, medium brunet, or tall and blond. And here's Urna's ad:

> *SINCERE Fairbanks lady, mid-20s, seeking permanent relationship with gentleman 30–40. No long hairs or east Texans. I enjoy cooking, dancing, light drinking, sewing. Write to Happy Bottom c/o Line Camper.*

Huh, nothing in here about Ivan running for governor, and nothing about Imperial Lumber to give me an excuse to write to Rick.

Wonder what kind of favor Big Urna wants? I have to give her credit, though. She really stuck it to I.Y. I still don't believe it: Urna McLaren had his baby way back when we were in high school together and has been blackmailing him, as she calls it, ever since. Just think, one of my best friend's baby is my half-sister. Sounds like a soap opera. I groan, trying to blot Ivan York's visual image out of my brain.

"Well, little Nadia face," I say to the portrait hanging over my bed, "someday I'm going to have a really nice apartment, on the beach near Santa Monica maybe, a nice place to put you on the wall so that you can watch the tide move in and out all day. Then I'm going to polish up all your stories and send them to a New York publisher."

I stroke her slanted eyes, thinking of my "second cousin," Charles Zimmerman. Why was he so ashamed that his mother's grandmother was half Indian, and why didn't he want Ivan to go public on it if he ran for governor? Charles. What did he think of me? Was he just trying to help, letting me work for Ivan at Imperial Lumber, or did he keep me around to remind I.Y. of his fuck-ups, until I got too close, that is. But if Charles kept me around as Ivan's scarlet letter. . . . Ivan wouldn't put up with being treated like that, would he?

The door of my aluminum dormitory room shakes as Urna muscles it open, walks in, and sits down on the bed next to me.

"Hi, kid," she says in her low voice.

"Hi, Urn, what's up?" I ask, trying to sound light.

"Listen, kid," her wide face tightens around the lips, "there might be trouble."

"If you mean Hootz, you can have him," I say, feeling really proud about being so out front.

"Nah," she says, "I don't mean man trouble, I mean real trouble."

"Oh, yeah," I say, expecting her to lay some heavy camp gossip on me.

"I mean, I've seen trouble." Oh, God, she's just like Rick, always building you up for the melodrama. "Like," she says, "when I got preggers with Ramona and never let out a peep 'bout who the father was. Just went through the motions, ya know, like I was any other mother. People don't want ya to do that. People want ya to be down and ashamed, and when ya ain't, they can't adjust," says Urna, always talking as if she were holding court. "Well, that was trouble, but what I'm about to lay on you is the real McCoy." She takes a drag off her half-smoked Winston menthol and coughs from the latest camp virus.

"Ah, Urna, get to the point. It's three A.M."

"Like," she says, "I didn't tell ya 'bout the whole scam I got with I.Y. Yeah, I get four hundred dollars every month for keepin' quiet about who fathered my little girl. And he wanted to take me to Se-attle to get rid of it, just like he did for you. But, uh-uh, not me," says Urna, spreading her legs out over the octagonal-patterned floor carpet, her large thighs bulging the seams of her tight Wrangler jeans. "Then I found out about some of Ivan's other indiscretions and I.Y. floated me an' Ramona real well till I got on here at the line camp." As Urna lights another cigarette, I crawl under the covers of my bed. The I.D. bracelet that I got over at Fort Wainwright with *Corporal Robert Knutsen, POW, 1969*, engraved on it dangles from my wrist, then catches on the blanket, fraying it.

"So yesterday," says Urna, talking to my covered-up head, "Ivan comes through camp, checkin' out the project for some bank investors down in *Se*-attle, and of course, as usual, doing a little politickin' on the way."

I pull the covers tight around my ears. "I.Y. was in camp yesterday?"

"Yeah, and he told me that it'd really be worth my while to have a little talk with you. Said that he's been keepin' tabs on ya, knows you're real friendly with a reporter named Rick Howard who's been makin' life kinda difficult for him. Ya know, if those pantywaist conservationist congressmen ever got wind of some of the things that go on up here at the line camps, the whole Pipe could go belly up. End of I.Y.'s investors, end of my good-payin' job and yours too, Donna Lee."

"You mean," I say through the blankets, "if someone *official* got wind of a few of the numbers I.Y.'s pulled to get this pipeline into operation, that'd be the end of his hopes to be the first Alaska-born governor?"

"He said to tell ya, Donna, that he'd make it plenty worth your while to convince Rick to go write about Brazilian oil. Says he knows you've got what it takes to convince the guy." She pulls an I LIKE I.Y. button out of her pants pocket and shoves it under the covers.

"Very originial," I say sarcastically. "Is that the heavy news?"

"N-no," she stammers. "Then I told him that I wanted a few extra dollars a month, seein' as how I knew about you bein' his daughter."

"What!" I throw the blankets off and sit upon the bed.

"The man turned white as sheet, Donna. Kinda freaked me out." She lowers her voice.

"What'd he say?" I demanded.

"Nothin'. That's what's so odd. I mean, I always figured I.Y. liked me to hassle him for money. And he'd never have paid me child support unless I hadn't threatened to tell all his secrets. It's as if he loves the attention an' gets high off the danger of a scandal. 'Course, after ya get past that, Ivan can be a real nice guy, ya know?"

"Shit, Urna," my voice becomes angry, "why'd you tell him? You promised you'd keep it a secret. Some friend." I narrow my eyes at her.

"Anyway," she says, avoiding my stare, "it kinda knocked the wind outa him. He looked real bummed out."

"Just what other 'indiscretions' do you have on him?" I ask.

Urna runs her hand nervously up and down the side of her face. "Well, ya know how I.Y.'s always buyin' Louisiana shrimpers and bringin' 'em north?"

"Yeah, one of his Aleutian boats just got busted."

"Small wonder," she says, taking a drag off her cigarette. "It's a front. I.Y.'s been runnin' drugs from Central America for years."

God, wait'll I tell Rick.

"Yeah," Urna whispers. "Coke, meth, H, you name it. Take a look around, Donna Lee. Most of this camp is stoned or drunk day and night. 'Cept maybe for those east Texas welders who can get high on just beatin' the shit outa people with pipe wrenches. What'd ya think keeps these guys goin' on a twelve-hour shift? Coffee? I.Y. comes up here with his crew sayin' he's just checkin' out the line camps for some bank. My ass he is. Donna," she whispers, "this could mean big money for both of us." Her voice trails off.

"And that still ain't the whole story," she continues. "'Member back when we was still in high school, how Bob Knutsen went to Guatemala to pilot a shrimper up to Sitka? Then suddenly enlisted and got shipped off to Nam?"

"Yeah," I say, toying with the bracelet on my wrist. "Ivan made me promise not to see Bob anymore. So I wrote him a Dear John letter, and about six weeks later he wrote me back from boot camp."

"Yeah, well," says Urna, "truth is that the Butcher got real pissed off at Ivan 'cause he almost OD'd on some bad south-of-the-border-made LSD and threatened to spill the beans on Ivan's operation. But before Bob could do anything somehow I.Y. got him drafted and sent to Nam."

"No shit!" I put on my shoes, thinking that if I send Rick a radio message, he could be up here in ten to twelve hours. "So," I continue, trying not to appear too eager to get to the camp radio, "what else is Ivan up to these days?"

"I don't know," says Urna, shrugging her shoulders. "He was kinda speechless after I told him I knew about you bein' his daughter. Just mumbled somethin' about uranium stocks and maybe makin' a business trip to South Africa . . . probably a trumped-up excuse for bein' late with my next month's payments. I.Y. really gets off on me hasslin' him for money."

"What?" Holy Christ, maybe Rick's not imagining things. Maybe there is a conspiracy.

"So," continues Urna, annoyed with my questions, "will ya have a little talk with Rick? Huh, Donna Lee? Tell him to take a slow boat to Rio de Janeiro or somewhere."

34. Autumn 1974

I sit alone, huddled in a doorway. My face muscles ache from crying, and as I look up, the Fairbanks Federal Building Courthouse across the street looms like a dark cloud in front of me. A cold Arctic wind blows a yellow MacDonald's hamburger wrapper down the almost-deserted sidewalk, and the ptarmigan flying overhead have turned from brown to winter white.

I take a deep breath, and step by step try to recount what went wrong. But as I stare at the walleyed courthouse windows, the same fog that engulfed my brain after Pop died descends on me again. All I can think of are the prophetic words of Gramma Raven: "Donna Lee, you will own many stories, the ones that I give you, and the one that is the story of your days." Then I recall radioing Rick from Old Man Work Camp, the day my story began unrolling in front of me like a scroll.

I look into my totebag at Nadia's portrait. "What am I going to do, Small-Lake?" I ask, hoping to read an answer painted into the expression on her small face, but tears blur my vision. "Am I going to tell that jury the *whole* story or not?" Then I close my eyes, trying to piece the words and events of the last month together. "What happened?" I whisper. "What went wrong?"

* * *

"I've got something really big," I tell Rick as I meet him at the Here landing pad near the gray-green muskeg bog just outside of Old Man Camp. The helicopter blades whirl overhead as Rick greets me with a questioning twist to his smile.

"Just pretend I happened to come up here with a load of camp supplies," he says as we walk toward Mod Eight, the office module where I've been typing requisition forms, all summer. "Just move at a casual pace." Rick steps into his Clark Kent, reporter-of-crime-and-intrigue, role.

"What's up?" he asks as we sit, hiding in the aluminum office-supply room, him on one side of the mimeograph machine and me sitting next to a filing cabinet on reams of *Nuna* letterhead, the same stationery that I've been swiping to type my *Raven Stories* on. "So what's the big news?" Rick asks again. "Your radio message said that it was urgent."

Outside Mod Eight, the loudspeaker blasts one Muzak version of the Rolling Stones after another. Slowly, in a hushed voice, I outline the details of Urna's story about Ivan's drug dealings. "I.Y. even told Urna to ask me to have a little talk with you, to convince you to go report on Brazilian oil," I add.

"Wait until I tell the prosecuting attorney about this," Rick says, his face widening into a Cheshire-cat grin.

"And that isn't all," I continue. "I may have something on that conspiracy angle you were talking about." I watch Rick's eyes widen. "Yeah," I say, knowing that the cards are stacked in my favor and almost relishing the thought that I know something that Rick doesn't know and wants to.

"And?" he asks like a little kid who's waiting to hear the punchline of a scary joke. "And?"

"Well, it's just hearsay," I continue slowly, "but Urna told me that Ivan was babbling on about uranium stock and a business trip to South Africa. Of course, she just chalked it up to their little extortion game—Urna says I.Y. likes it when she has to hassle him about paying her 'child-support' money."

"What?" gasps Rick in a loud whisper. "Listen, Donna," he gives me a solemn look, "now I know I'm right. It may not be a conspiracy, but it's at least high-echelon deception. Donna," he says, as I slip half a ream of *Nuna* letterhead inside my purse, "now it's vitally important that Ivan York be convicted and sent to prison. We've got to catch him in the act of selling drugs, make the case against him airtight. Is there any way you could arrange it so that—"

"Not on your life," I snap. "Urna told I.Y. that I found out about my true parentage."

Outside Mod Eight, the loudspeaker switches from a Muzak version of "Gimme Shelter" to the voice of Sister MacElroy's Tundra Radio Ministry, "Altar of the Air."

"But the fate of our nation's—the *world's*—health is at stake here. You've got to be cooperative," he says emphatically, running his hand through his curly red Afro. "This oil probably won't be used to heat anything. They're just going to barter it for uranium. If a nuclear-power cooling tower like the one south of Seattle ever exploded, the farmland around it wouldn't be usable for five hundred years! Donna, you're his daughter. He must care about you. He's probably just been waiting for a chance to get together and lay all the cards on the table," pleads Rick. "I'd take care of the rest. You'd just be a plant, sort of a—"

"A narc."

"On the shores of Babylon, there we sat down," blares Sister MacElroy's country-western accent from the loudspeaker outside.

"No," I say definitively. "I don't care what Ivan's done, I won't set him up. And how many times do I have to tell you, I just couldn't handle seeing him." What if he touched me, I ask myself, remembering how he used to always pat me on the fanny when he took me out to lunch back when I was at U.W. I shudder. If he touched me, I'd probably throw up all my guts.

Rick angrily waits for me to reconsider his plan. I try to ignore him and recall the tundra-radio disk jockey reading of today's noon announcements: "Will Helga Mae please call her sister, all is forgiven," he began in his twangy but official radio voice. "Roy B. of Circle City, Roy B. of Circle City. There's a parcel for you at Stevens Village. Rick Howard of Fairbanks, Rick Howard of Fairbanks. You have an urgent message at Old Man Camp." Christ, I think to myself, these are supposed to be the best years of my life, and where am I? In the Yukon, sending messages over the country-service radio.

Rick clears his throat, prompting me for an answer.

"No, I won't testify. I won't see I.Y., and I won't set him up for you, Rick, so stop trying to manipulate me," I say, proud of myself for being so honest. But why do I always feel controlled by other people? Suddenly I'm overcome with the revelation that I've been controlled by the York family all my life. As a little girl I used to live for I.Y.'s visits. And when I played grown-ups, I was Nadia or I didn't play. When I was in high school it seemed that the only way I got my mother's approval was to do well in school, so I might earn the Catherine Zimmerman Scholarship. But don't be too hard on Mom, I tell myself. She just thought that if you were like the Yorks, you'd be happy. I sigh. It's sad that she thought that was the only way I could have a better life.

Rick's freckled lips turn down. "Yeah, man," he says in a tired voice, "you're right. I'm sorry. I really am sorry." He puts one hand gently on my shoulder. "But it's just that I feel so damn powerless. All I ever wanted to do in life was to make the world better for people, and look what happens." His voice cracks as he motions out the supply-room window at the piles of gravel dotting the tundra. "But shit, Donna, do you want Ivan York to become governor?"

"No. I sure don't," I answer, as I watch a hillock explode into a cloud of red mud. More of Max's handy work, I tell myself and look back at Rick.

His downcast eyes begin to water; I take a long hard look at him. One voice inside me says, "Donna, help the poor guy out, he's suffering." Another says, "Who is this person standing here thinking that *his* feelings should be paramount in *your* life?" In the end I compromise, deciding that I won't testify, but I will give Rick's and my relationship another chance. Maybe since he's so tuned into his feelings of powerlessness, he's one of the few people who could understand my position.

"No," I answer, "Ivan knows I know he's my father. If I make a move to see him, the man'll run like hell, believe me. But I'll give you the confidential files. Anything that's in this drawer you can have." I unlock the metal cabinet I've been leaning against and Rick begins pulling out manila envelopes.

The intercom inside my office next door to the supply room buzzes loudly. I go to answer it. Pressing the intercom switch, the bull cook from over in the slop shop yells through the receiver, "Donna Lee, is that you, Honeypots? Order me up two more cases of Crisco, okay?"

Returning to the supply room, I find Rick looking more distraught than ever. "All it is is invoices," he says with disappointment. "I mean, from these it looks like this camp consumes two twenty-pound torn turkeys per person per day, but I'll need more evidence of mismanagement than that." He jams the envelopes back into the file cabinet and slams it shut, then gives me a sour look.

"I'm not going to testify," I tell him with a shake of my head. "There's a new shipment of oil pipe in the welding yard out back," I say. "Why don't you go out for some air and have a look?"

Rick walks out into the quad, and I jam a kitchen-supply requisition form into my IBM Selectric and begin banging on the keys. Shit, first I fall for a guy who talks to his cock, and he turns out to be my father; then I fall in love with a man who talks to his car. The next thing I know, I'm talking to a portrait as if it were alive. . . . Just what did Rick expect to find in those files anyway, the Watergate tapes?

Looking out the office window, across the mounds of gravel and earth dotting the once-green rolling tundra, I watch Rick walk in the direction of the pipe-welding yard. Two men, one in a red letterman's jacket, seemed to be moving in the same direction. Huh, that guy looks like he's wearing a Sitka athletic-awards jacket. Then, jumping from my desk to the window, I see a giant monogrammed S. As the two men turn the corner, I recognize Bert Dysokar and the Animal, even though I haven't seen them since high school. Bert, my old classmate and present brother-in-law; wonder what he's doing here in camp, and with the Animal to boot?

Glancing over toward the dormitories, I see a man in a Stetson hat and a sheepskin jacket walk toward the helicopter landing pad, swinging a briefcase in one hand and a beer can in the other. It's I.Y.! Ivan York, what's he doing in Old Man Camp? Oh, God, I think as I dash out the door of Mod Eight at a dead run toward the pipe-welding yard. Two men, Rick said that two men were following him. The radio message. I.Y. probably heard the radio message that I sent to Rick. Without

Urna knowing it, I.Y. conned her into getting me to radio Rick to come here. God, what have I done?

"Rick," I shout over the noise of a heavy-equipment shovel loading gravel for the Pipe trench into a Mack dump truck. "Rick!"

Sister MacElroy's Tundra Radio Ministry sings out, "Amazing Grace, how sweet the sound," just before the noise of falling pipe echoes through the crisp Arctic air. Ptarmigan nesting in the muskeg grass at the edge of camp rise up in a brown cloud of wings, screeching *come-back, come-back* in frightened bird voices. Over in the welding yard a piece of green, four-foot-wide oil pipe roars like the *saanah* wind as it rolls to a stop against the yard's chain-link fence.

"Rick," I scream imploringly. "*Rick.*"

But I was too late.

I pull my bulky Cowichan Indian sweater tight around my neck, and watch the Fairbanks coroner walk up the cement steps of the Federal Building Courthouse. As the heavy metal and glass revolving door slams behind him, I remember that the last sound that Rick Howard heard on this earth was that of a ton-and-a-half forty-foot pipe rolling down on top of him from the welding-yard stacks.

"Didn't know no unauthorized visitor was on the premises," the east Texan cutting a T-joint told the state trooper who came to investigate Rick's death. The trooper listened to the welder's story, shifting his weight from one black boot to the other. "Another accident," commented the welder. "We'll see what the coroner's inquest has to say about that," the trooper responded, adjusting his beaver-fur hat as he handed the statement to the welder for his signature.

Some accident, I groan as I stare at the Venetian blinds in the Federal Building. Then, putting my hands into my tote to keep them warm from the Fairbanks wind, I run my fingers across Nadia's face. Oh God, why'd they have to ask me to come identify Rick's body? How come he had to die, how come I never told him that I still loved him? Damn, the muscles in my face are so sore they feel like they'll crack off if I start crying again.

I look beyond the courthouse, across the brown water of the Chena—the mountains at the northern end of the Tanana Valley are covered with their first autumn snow. What went wrong, Donna Lee, is that Rick was a dead man the minute he set foot in that work camp—all because you didn't see through Ivan's plan. Angrily I flail my fist against my thigh.

Now what are you going to tell that coroner's jury? I ask myself. You ought to tell them everything, it was Rick's last wish. He didn't live long enough to find out that the prosecuting attorney dropped the narcotics case against Ivan and Alaska Fish. I groan, making a mental list of evidence the mere rumor of which would stop Ivan York's gubernatorial campaign dead in its tracks: *If it please the court, Ivan York is my illegitimate father. He tried to seduce me. He had my high-school boyfriend shipped off to Vietnam. No, your honor, I'm not talking about the deceased in question. Not yet. I'm talking about my boyfriend, Bob Knutsen, whom I.Y. hired to pilot his drug-loaded shrimpers from the Gulf of Mexico to the Aleutians. . . . The facts concerning the death of Rick Howard? Before he died Mr. Howard told me that he believed Ivan York was having him followed and had his telephone tapped. Yes, your honor, Mr. Howard did say why. It was because of the uranium-oil-dollars conspiracy. . . .* My back slumps. The jury'll just think I'm some stoned hippie if I ramble on like that. And if this coroner's inquest ever hits the newspapers my mother'll be humiliated, she'll become a shut-in, she'll never see me again. "You're being irrational, Donna, you're letting your emotions rule your logic," I hear Rick's voice in the Arctic wind.

Two figures appear, walking slowly down the sidewalk from the direction of the Flame Lounge. As the couple approach, Urna McLaren and Max, the blaster, wave, calling out a greeting. Huh, seems that the coroner wants to question everyone who was at Old Man Camp on the day of Rick's death. I wave back, imagining Urna's testimony: *No, your honor, I weren't nowhere near the pipe yard when this incident occurred. No sir, I didn't notice nothin' out of the ordinary goin' on in camp that day.* I glance at my watch. Only a half hour before the inquest begins. I cringe, wondering when Ivan'll show up.

Gazing across the Chena River toward the Fairbanks suburbs, I try to put the hearing out of my mind. I rub my hands together inside my tote, and stare at the rows of gardenless, cinder-block houses with pickup trucks parked in their front yards where lawns ought to be. Inside my purse I stroke Nadia's painted cheeks again, then close my eyes, trying to remember one of the stories Gramma Raven told me about her. . . .

It was the afternoon of my fifth-grade Christmas party. I watched Mrs. Stephan through the open door of her trailer as she swayed back and forth, talking in tongues, dressed in a black Shaker-lady skirt and bandanna. Then I recall how her language turned into the broken English that Tlingits often spoke. "Small-Lake," mumbled Gramma Raven, "there is terrible noise under ground. Be watchful. When warrior-enemy comes, take the blue flame of winter fire, put this around you." Gramma's eyes opened for a moment, and she looked a hundred light years away. "Put this fire around you like long hair of bear. Put piece of cedar bark over your stomach, and when you see warrior-enemy, look them in the eyes before they look at you. If you do this, Small-Lake, no one will come through your fire hair, no one will steal your soul from your body."

I open my eyes and reach into my purse, pulling out Nadia's mother's shaman necklace. Fastening it around my neck, I arrange the fangs and fish spines under my sweater. A little good luck charm never hurt, I tell myself, as a yellow Tundra Taxie pulls up in front of the Federal Building steps.

A tall, dark, graying man wearing a pin-striped suit gets out of the back seat, along with a statuesque blond woman. Charles Zimmerman! What's he doing here? As he leans forward to pay the driver, Charles glances across the street in my direction, waves to me, then whispers something to the woman. She looks directly at me. Debra. Debra Zimmerman Sims. I recognize her from the family portraits, not from the painting of her as a child but from my memory of her grandmother Ulla's face. God, what's she doing here? I huddle into a ball, trying to be inconspicuous. As I glance back at her, Debra's deep tan and golden hair seem to glow against the gray courthouse steps. And despite her hippie-like Greenwich Village fur coat, she looks as if she belongs in the receiving line of some head of state.

Are they scared I'm going to talk? Is that why they're here, because I might ruin Ivan's chances to be governor, because I might let it slip about their Indian grandmother?

Ivan York's long black Cadillac pulls up in front of the Federal Building. I.Y., wearing his sheepskin jacket, two men with briefcases, and a middle-aged woman in a dowdy cloth coat get out. "Charles," I.Y. calls to his cousin, but Debra and her brother walk up the steps and slam the front door behind them. *Yes sir,* I imagine myself telling the coroner, *I saw Ivan York near the pipe-camp welding yard on the day and at the time of Mr. Howard's death.* I think of how my stomach will turn as I look across the courtroom at my *father.*

Ivan rushes up the Federal Building steps after Charles, followed by the two men with briefcases. The woman catches her heel in the cracked cement and bends back to free it, her hennaed hair blowing away from her face. Oh, my God. It's Mom! That bastard brought my mother to the inquest. He knows that if she's in that courtroom, I won't say shit about him being my illegitimate parent. God, now what do I do?

Suddenly my brain feels like it's on fire. As Ivan walks through the courthouse door, I dart across the street and up the cement steps. "Mom! Mom!" I grab onto her coat sleeve just like I did when I was a little girl. She turns, almost falling backward.

"Donna Lee!" she gasps, her face filled with the *O* of her surprised lips. She pulls me tight against her, and I feel her bony chest. Jeez, she's lost so much weight. I brush a tear from my cheek into my hair and look at her. Her face is younger than I remember, less burdened somehow.

"Donna, honey," she stammers. "Mr. York told me all about your boyfriend gettin' killed. He said that you might need me. . . ." She bites her lips and looks downcast. "I know we've got some fences to mend, but . . . you're still my baby girl and. . . ."

My face tightens, and I can't hold the sobs back. "Mom," I hold onto her hand, noticing that she's still wearing the wedding band Pop gave her. "Mom, Ivan killed Rick. He set him up." My mother pulls her hand away from me and covers her mouth. "What's that you've got around your neck, Donna Lee?"

"A necklace, just an old necklace. Mom didn't you hear me?" I gasp. "Ivan killed—"

"I've been prayin' for ya, hon," she says, looking at me as one might look at a retarded child. "Mr. York said you were beside yourself with grief, he even—"

"Oh, God. Stop it," I yell, looking at her imploringly, and lowering my voice I tell her, "I know I.Y.'s my father."

Her hands fall to the sides of her worn brown coat, and the blood runs from her cheeks. She sighs and looks away from me, her shoulders drooping. She shakes her head. "It's the only time in my whole life I've ever sinned, Donna Lee."

I grab her. "Please, Mom, don't cry. I don't give a damn, really."

"I think I'd better wait out here in the car," she says, moving slowly away from me and down the steps.

Sadly I look back at her, then up at the courthouse windows. Debra and Charles have been watching from a second-story window. Debra smiles down at me. What the . . .? As I climb the steps I realize why they're here; they *want* me to testify, they want me to stop Ivan. I stare back at them, remembering how Charles Zimmerman once dug his fingernails into my wrist. I don't smile.

Recalling Gramma Raven's warrior story, I take the portrait out of my tote and push the oval frame under my sweater, securing it over my stomach into the waistband of my Levis. Then I remember the ring of blue flame on Mom's propane trailer stove and imagine that I'm inside the circle of blue fire, wearing it like a hoop skirt, the gas jets shooting flames hot enough to melt the tires of I.Y.'s Cadillac.

"Donna Lee," my mother calls to me. I turn and watch her running up the stairs behind me, carrying a black book. "Take this," she says, handing me her tattered Bible. "It'll give ya somethin' to hold on to." She looks at me with her gray-blue eyes that water just like Rick's did when he was unhappy. I take hold of the book, feeling where over the years her fingers have pressed themselves into its once-hard cover. "Hon . . . I'll be out here if you need me."

I smile and nod, then turn away, walking through the courthouse door. As it slams behind me I feel the power of the Sitka Bay tide surge through my fists. Like Gramma Raven said, be quick. Tell the jury everything you know. And get Ivan York in the eyes before he has a chance to get you.

404